# Mayhem at the Mill

(Book I of The Osten Chronicles)

Author: Daniel Thorman



ISBN: 978-1-963913-34-7

Imprint: Native Publishers, The

# The Osten Chronicles

Dedicated in loving memory of

Bernard H. Thorman, Jr.

# CHAPTER ONE

# The Miller

"How far that little candle throws its beams! So shines a good deed in a naughty world."

*~ William Shakespeare ~*

"Take it back," Gregor said.

His insistent demand met with my mulish mindset and could have been more simply ignored had he not punctuated it with yet another shove to the back of my head. The weight of his knee ground painfully into the crook of my back as my nose dove once again into the dirt of the field. I squirmed and writhed, but the pressure only increased on my arms which were pinned neatly behind my back in his firm grip.

Now as the miller's son, I was no weakling, but I had nowhere near the strength of the older boy.

"Very well," I said through the grit in my teeth, "I take it back."

He flipped me onto my back, leaned in close, and squinted at me through those piggy eyes to assess my contrition. Finally, he hawked and spat into the grass nearby and lumbered back to his feet. It occurred to me that I may have gotten off easy as I slowly lifted myself up to a sitting position and began to wipe the soil from my face and tunic. Didn't my father say just last night that the Cains weren't a family to cross lightly? Although he had been referring to Otis Cain at the time, I suppose this lesson in humility suggested that it should include his son, Gregor.

The Cains worked a tenant farm for Lord Westarbor near the outskirts of the barony. They were very insular, coming to town only once every few months. The whole clan was rumored to be short-tempered and standoffish, taking no part in the life of our small hamlet of Meadowfork. Despite the many enticements of our village, the Cains seemed to shun social gatherings of our good folk, instead maintaining a haughty self-reliance.

Otis and Gregor were here only to pick up supplies needed for the winter. It was a mystery to my father why they had chosen this late in the season to insist on having their grain milled. But when Uncle Robert rode into town last week, he had borne a message from the Cain stead. We were to expect two wagon loads: one of wheat and one of corn. This had put father in a foul temper. Everyone else had made their appointments far earlier in the harvest season, and he could plan to set the mill to one type of grinding at a time. Moreover, the millstones were showing signs of wear and badly needed to be re-cut, a task that should have begun two days ago. The stone dresser was due to come back through town soon, and now we would have to work night and day to have the millstones disengaged and ready for his ministrations.

"You'll be speaking more respectfully of Pa from now on," said Gregor, "unless you're wanting more of the same."

His hands balled into fists and his shoulders hunched as he issued the statement. It seemed that I should say something more. Wanting to head off his ire, I clamped down firmly on my first instinct to defy the threat and instead sighed deeply.

"Gregor," I said, "I agree that family is very important, and it was wrong of me to give insult to your father. I was just angry over what you said about Royland."

"The dummy?"

Wincing, I started again. "Let's agree that Royland is odd. Still, he's a nice person, and he has a name. I love my cousin, and calling him 'dummy' is hurtful to him when he hears it."

Gregor pondered this for a moment then nodded once. "Hey, I know a good way to wash off," he said.

***

Cautiously, I tested the water with a finger. Being as it was late autumn, it was fairly cold. The sun setting on the horizon reminded me that I had gotten permission to stay out late tonight to 'show Gregor around and keep from underfoot.' Tomorrow's grind would be a busy time. The Cains had arrived too late in the day to begin it. After we had readied the mill, my father had broken out a clay jug of spirits to drink with Gregor's father while they shared war stories.

"Take this," demanded Gregor, thrusting a pole toward me.

Looking it over, I guessed it to be about five feet long. It had three sharpened tines on its smaller end. Gregor had made two such from some low branches of a nearby river birch and sharpened them with his overly large belt knife. He'd also quickly stripped off their bark. From the way he had worked, I could tell that knife was as sharp as his skill with it.

"There aren't ever any big fish in the mill pond, Gregor," I informed, "Just little blue-gills."

"Listen," he said.

I did so. I didn't hear anything, apart from the splashes and raucous squawks of a nearby family of ducks doing a little fishing of their own.

"There's bullfrogs," Gregor said. "These here are prime gigging sticks. My pa and I go out all the time. I'll show you how."

"What's the point?" I asked, accepting the proffered pole.

"Frog legs are delicious," Gregor declared with a sincere glint in his squinted eyes.

I shrugged and said, "Okay. What do we do?"

Gregor produced a small burlap sack from his shoulder pack and also what appeared to be a large tin tankard with a funny cap. On the side opposite the handle was a bulging piece of glass. He then lit a small candle from our campfire and set it inside the strange device. Oh! . . . . A lantern, I realized, but

3

instead of brightening our general surroundings, a broad cone of light shone forth from its circular glass window.

Gregor explained that it was called a bull's-eye lantern and showed me how to open and close a shutter on the light using a thumb trigger atop its handle. As the sky had begun to darken, this resulted in a long swath of light one could play across the waters of the pond or along its edge. More interestingly, Gregor showed me how the bullfrogs' eyes reflected the light and could be spotted at a pretty fair distance without disturbing them much. The size of these reflections allowed us to estimate the worthiness of the frog for 'gigging.' He described how one of us would flank the prey, approaching quietly to a short distance from it. At this point, his partner would suddenly unshutter the light, and the flanker could then creep forward while the animal was blinded and 'gig' it.

It turned out to be a lot more fun and exciting than I had expected. The frogs were quick and cunning foes. This led to some frustrating but hilarious escapades. It took us a while before we were able to properly coordinate our attack, but then our campaign began in earnest. We circled the entire mill pond, crossing over the stream that was its source and working our way back toward the race that fed the mill. A few hours later saw us tromping back to the campfire in mud-splattered boots. Gregor's sack bulged with trophies of our kills. He had kept the muscled legs but cut away the other parts. Throwing them out to the ducks, he declared: "They aren't so particular. Might as well help fatten them up for the table later!"

Gregor spitted the frog legs on some slender sticks he had sharpened for the purpose after he had skinned and battered them. This explained why he had begged a cup of flour at the mill. Cleaning and putting away his other gear, he produced a small can of spices from his shoulder bag.

"Pan fried is better," he said, "but this'll have to do. Here. Hold this," he said. Handing me one of the slender spits, he sprinkled a pinch of powder onto the skewered limb.

I nearly jumped out of my skin as the amputated member kicked vigorously, and I promptly dropped it on the stones ringing our fire. Gregor chuckled heartily, pointing at me and hugging the can to his chest. I bent down and warily retrieved the now-still stick while eyeing Gregor suspiciously.

"Was that magic?" I asked.

"No," he guffawed, his lips still twitching with only half-suppressed mirth. "They sometimes do that if they're fresh when you put on salt. I just wanted to see what you'd do."

I smiled. It *was* kind of funny.

"So that's just salt you've got there?" I inquired.

He shook his head, laughter forgotten, and said with a solemn face, "Secret family blend."

The fire had mostly burned down. We set on a fresh log and leaned the prepared skewers against it, turning them occasionally. As we squatted there, the radiance from the orange coals banished the night's chill. The soft grease pops from our dinner punctuated the low murmuring of the night insects and the frogs that had escaped our wrath.

"I wish it *was* magic powder in your can," I said wistfully.

"Oh, it's magic alright," said Gregor. "Wait until you taste some."

Then his face became more serious. "Pa says," he continued, "our family's only 'magic' is in being prepared for the unexpected. We don't rely on that other kind."

Growing up, I had been told my grandmother, Abigail Wagge, was a notorious witch of some renown. She was greatly disappointed that her children showed no sign of sharing her gifts. When her daughter defied her to marry a young soldier, they had a falling out. Of course, I never knew mother. She died giving birth to me, and father, now an old millwright, rarely spoke of her. If it weren't for uncle Robert and his stories, I wouldn't know anything about the Wagges. I'd heard it said that magic often runs in families, so I always wondered whether I might have some.

"Some of my ancestors were mages," I said quietly.

"Does your pa have the gift?" asked Gregor, surprised.

"Not unless you count 'the miller's thumb,'" I replied. "Father has a sharp mind and loves to build things. That's why lord

Westarbor let him set up the mill here at the keep. Father used to be a soldier back during the goblin wars. That's where he hurt his knee."

"My pa fought the goblins too," said Gregor, straightening up from his usual slouch. "They say those were tough times. A lot of good folk were lost. My older kin all share tales about it at the Remembering."

"Anyway," he drawled, "I judge these frog legs fit for eating."

And with that, he withdrew several of the skewers we had been turning over the coals and handed me one.

Dubious, I nibbled at a piece.

Gregor was right. Frog legs *are* delicious.

***

The next morning saw us all breaking our fast with my father's griddle cakes and some bacon we had set aside for when we had guests.

Father and I obtained the precious meat in a three-way trade. When in operation, the mill produced a great deal of dust. This could be dangerous, which was why we couldn't bring open flames anywhere near. As an apprentice, one of my many tasks was to dust the place down from the rafters to the mill floor and sweep it out regularly. These sweepings consisted of fine flour, regular dust, grit, chaff, dead bugs, cobwebs and dirt; however, it was mostly flour. Since there was no easy way to separate out the nasty stuff, I would bag this all up and give it to the baker's apprentices. They, in turn, would use this grit-flour to learn their craft, baking it into various practice loaves, cakes and pastries. Finally, this foul, gritty bread was delivered to Master Verney who was Meadowfork's main butcher and swineherd. His hogs would eat anything, but he claimed that supplementing their main diet of acorns and other slops with grit-bread fattened them up for the slaughter the best. In payment, father and the bakers received some of the older cuts from his smokehouse. 'Waste not; want not' my father would say.

The sun was barely up when I got the order to open the sluice gates. Gregor decided to accompany me, and we hustled up to the head race. Gone were the overcast skies of the past week. As brilliant sunlight burned away the morning fog where it pooled in the low weeds and hollows, a light breeze from the northwest carried the scent of freshly mown hay from farmsteads nearby. The keep was awakening, and we could hear the distant clatter of the knights performing their early morning drills. It was a gorgeous start to the day, belying the hardships that were to come.

I showed Gregor how to divert the stream into the race. Since we were fairly far into the season, and it had not rained of late, the level of the mill pond was a little lower than was usual. I took my time turning open the sluice gates until a steady stream began to fill then flow through the race. With a low groan you could almost feel in your bones, the great water wheel began its majestic turning.

We made our way back down to the mill and climbed up to the sack floor at its top. The area was already brimming with bags of grain we had hoisted up the previous afternoon. We would start with the wheat. The hopper was primed and ready. Powered by the wheel, the main shaft slowly turned. All that remained was for father to engage the stone nut to the spindle, and the grind would be fully underway.

As the spindle engaged, the runner stone began to spin up. If stood upon its edge, this massive disc of limestone would be as tall as a grown man. When fully engaged, it completed several full rotations every second. It spun above the bed stone, which was of similar size but lay unmoving. My father began making adjustments to the tentering gear, lowering the runner stone to within a hair's width of its counterpart. Here is where the miller's art really took shape; the distance between the two stones, their sharpness, the speed of rotation, and the qualities of the grain itself, all combined to determine the flour that would be produced.

"Give us what's in the hopper then, Lucas!" my father shouted up over the whirring and clacking sounds of the millworks.

I turned the hopper release and shook the damsel rod to guide the first wheat grains through the shoe and into the open center of the mill. As they pattered down the shoe, a rhythmic 'shushing' began to sing above the low thrum of the spinning stone. Dust spread in a thin white cloud, painted golden where sun's rays slanted in from the door and windows. The smell of wheat wafted about as the milky-tan flour began to emerge through the grooves of the stones and made its way into the chute. I waited while my father tested this first small run.

"Too fine," he decreed, rubbing a pinch between his thumb and forefinger.

"Again!" he commanded after making some adjustments.

After the third try, I received the 'thumbs up' signal to continue, and the grind began in earnest. I poured bag after bag of the golden grain into the hopper insuring that a smooth, continuous trickle was fed in, while my father filled the bin at the bottom of the chute below. Periodically, he would sample and make slight adjustments. A competent miller could detect variations in the grist by its temperature, its feel, and even by its smell. He could then compensate to produce a nicely consistent flour. My father was a perfectionist. Never was it said that Elliot Harper didn't keep his nose to the grindstone.

Working continuously, our mill could grind about three bushels per hour when producing fine quality flour. The Cain's wagon-load of wheat came to about fifty bushels. Provided there were no problems, the wheat grind alone would take us into late evening. From time to time, I had to open the sluice gates a little further as the level of the mill pond drained its way on down.

We usually left it to the bakers to bolt and sift the grist into pure flour. We just weighed and bagged the normal run of the mill. My father occupied his time scooping the freshly ground flour from the bins and weighing it into small peck bags of precisely fourteen pounds apiece. Each was stamped with the seal of the lord's mill. By the end of the long day's grind, we had 187 such. As was custom, 156 of these belonged to the Cains, and 31 were now the property of Lord Westarbor. My father stood proudly reviewing the product of our effort. He was caked in a film of fine white powder from head to toe.

Otis Cain entered the counting room. He looked like a larger, thicker version of Gregor minus the curly hair. He wore a straw hat, overalls, and a frown of suspicion. At least now I could see where Gregor got that piggy squint. He performed his own count and then looked around the mill to make sure none of his flour had been set aside. He even examined and tested the scales my father had used. My father took no offense at this behavior. He had always reminded me that the farmers worked very hard to grow and harvest their wheat over the long summer season. They deserved the utmost respect and fairness when the mill's services took one in six as a banality. Finally satisfied, Otis called Gregor over, and they re-loaded their first wagon.

***

The trouble began when my father went back to clean and ready the mill for the next day's grind. A general clean-up could wait until after we ground the corn tomorrow. The millstones, however, had to be serviced and picked clean. By this late hour, the sun had all but set, and since we couldn't risk a lantern for all the dust, we had the front door and windows wedged wide open. Unwilling to leave it until tomorrow, my father hastened about his tasks in the last glow of twilight. Exhausted by my own day's labors, I nonetheless began to straighten up and roughly sweep the main room.

Father had used the tentering gear to raise the runner stone to its greatest height and then disengaged the stone nut from the spindle. Although the main shaft still spun lazily above, it no longer connected to anything. Its low creaking and grinding served only as a backdrop to the ring of father's light hammer taps and my own shuffling about. Then tragedy struck.

I didn't see exactly what happened. The only warning was a loud creaking and rending sound. I turned in surprise and saw father scrambling back as that *beast* of a runner stone first sagged to one side and then dropped. It landed askew with a noise like a deep, echoing thunderclap, raising great clouds of dust and bringing down a hail of debris from up above. Suddenly blind and choking in the thickened air, I had but one thought: *please don't let my father die*. I must have cried out, because next I heard my father's voice through the gloom.

"Lucas!" he shouted frantically, "you need to get out of here. Run!"

But running wasn't even an option for me. Disoriented, I tried to find my bearings in the unlit room by waving my arms about through the thick clouds of dust obscuring my sight. Stepping forward, I promptly barked my shin against the hard edge of some protruding piece of equipment. My breath came in ragged gulps, and I managed to croak out, "I'm okay, are you hurt, father?"

There was a short stretch of silence, broken only by the continued soft creaking of the main shaft above us, its rhythmic sound as reassuring as a steady heartbeat. Then alarm bells began to toll from the keep. Doubtless, the night watchmen were responding to the calamity.

"I'm trapped but mostly unharmed," my father finally replied in a weak voice. "Get yourself clear, Lucas."

The dust was beginning to settle somewhat. Instead of a solid wall of white, I could now make out little whorls and eddies where it was stirred by the evening breeze. I could see a bit of light from the direction I presumed the door and windows must lie.

"I'll go get help," I promised, as I staggered toward the opening.

It was now verging on full darkness. Emerging into the fresh night air was like awakening from a dream. Across the field, I spied the Cains stepping out of our barn where they had been sleeping with their wagons. Otis was rolling up his sleeves and Gregor, a stumbling step behind, was rubbing the sleep from his eyes. In the other direction, the beacon fires atop the keep's gatehouse were brightly lit, bathing the outer courtyard in a flickering pool of light. As the alarm continued its clangor, men of the night watch were already hustling toward the mill.

Needlessly, I waved my arms to attract their attention as I crossed over the small wooden bridge across the mill's race and out onto the main thoroughfare. As they approached, I recognized Trenton Arenson at the head of the detachment. Trenton was the son of our liege, Vincent Arenson Lord Westarbor, and currently the squire to our local knight commander, Sir Declan Highcastle. I had never gotten on well with Trenton. About three years my senior, the young lord tended to look down upon the lowborn, which he reckoned to be just about everyone except the high knights and their squires.

Apparently, even highly skilled tradesmen such as my father didn't measure up.

"Over here, quickly!" I hollered.

"What is this *racket* disturbing the peace of the keep?" demanded Trenton, shining a bright light into my face. As I began a stuttering reply, he stepped in closer and spoke over me. "And what is that on your face, *jester makeup*?"

Agitated, I blurted out, "The millstone fell and father is trapped. We must hurry, Trenton."

He straightened and began striding toward the mill. "We shall see," he said, "And you will address the son of your proper lord as 'Sir' Trenton. Come, men," he commanded.

"You *cannot* bring a lantern in there!" I cried out in horror, realizing his intent.

But he was not listening. "Do not tell your betters what they can and cannot do, you discourteous whelp . . . "

That was as far as he got in his diatribe. My father was in there, and I'd sooner be *hanged* than see him burned to death. As *Sir* Trenton strode onto the small wooden bridge, I threw myself forward and struck him hard in the back with my shoulder, pitching him over the side and into the shallow waters of the mill race below. I heard a mighty splash and was immediately enveloped by darkness when his lantern was doused. By the time my eyes adjusted to the dim moonlight, I saw Trenton looking up at me in red-faced fury.

"Restrain him! Lucas Harper must pay for this insult!" he bellowed, pointing at me.

The guardsmen behind me looked confused, but several bared steel and appeared ready to comply. This was wasting time. I would happily receive whatever punishment Trenton cared to hand down to restore his honor. But only *after* we had rescued father. I did the only thing I could think of and ran back into the dusty mill.

The air had cleared somewhat, but the shroud of night had claimed the interior of the building. Being very familiar with the space, I crept over toward the millstones while keeping my hesitant pursuers groping about back-lit by the windows.

Shouted arguments could be heard from out front, but I couldn't make out what was said. Then I spied my father slumped over the demolished collecting bins.

Suddenly, a bright light flared into existence, illuminating the area and casting long shadows upon the far wall. For a moment, I was terrified that the guardsmen had brought another flame nearby, but then I recognized the effect from Gregor's bulls-eye lantern and realized that it was drawing no closer. Bless him.

Moving over to my father, I could see his shoulders heave as he drew in ragged breaths, but perhaps mercifully, he no longer appeared to be awake. His face was a rictus of agony. The runner stone rested off-center from its bed, and my father's left hand and forearm lay pinned beneath it. There was surprisingly little blood, but surely his arm was *crushed*.

The other men in the room rushed forward, their pursuit of me forgotten, and began trying to free my father. I could see that it would do no good. With proper leverage and the right equipment, we might eventually hoist the errant slab. But it wouldn't happen any time soon.

I cast my gaze heavenward in silent prayer. *Moon and stars wheeling above*, I thought, *please don't let me lose my father!* I wished that the stone would be lifted up as I had witnessed so many times before – even just for a moment. Then a strange feeling calmed my panicked thoughts and suffused my being. My eyes were drawn to the far wall where shadows of the great water wheel's paddles played their way slowly up one after another. All sound became oddly muted, and a deep feeling of peace and possibility blossomed within me.

One of the men prying at my father's still form lurched backwards with father in tow. The runner stone slowly began to rise upward and right itself. It hovered there, gently turning in the eerie light for several heartbeats while a dozen men stared agape from the doorway and windows of the mill. Then it gently settled back down to rest. My memories after that are muddled. I recall dizziness; then the floor rushing up to meet me; then silence.

CHAPTER TWO

# The Baron

"The people are the most important element in a
nation; the spirits of the land and grain are the
next; the sovereign is the least."

*~ Mencius ~*


I awoke in a strange place. The bedding was clean if a bit
lumpy. I hesitated to emerge from the warm downy quilt into the
bracing air of the unfamiliar chamber; however, the strong urge
to relieve myself provided the needed impetus. I found myself to
be clean and dressed in an overly large, linen nightshirt that
draped to my knees. Looking about in bewilderment, I noted that
one wall was made of stone and had a small barred window set
way up high. From the angle of the sun, it was either
approaching or just past midday. On the opposite wall, stood a
stout door of wooden planks. In the far corner, to my soon-to-be
great relief, rested a chamber pot. As I sleepily performed my
first morning task, I decided I must be in Westarbor Keep
because, apart from the mill, not many other buildings were
made of large, fitted stones.

*The mill!* In an instant, I relived the past evening's events in
vivid detail. My father had been hurt badly. I needed to find him.
I ran to the door wondering where my clothes had gotten. I
turned the handle and pulled the door inward to be immediately

confronted by the incongruous presence of my cousin, Royland. He was seated on a low bench just across the hallway.

"Royland, where's my father?" I asked sharply.

I shouldn't have shouted. He rose unsteadily to his feet, staring off to the left. His shoulders were stooped forward, and his mouth worked soundlessly. It was this behavior that caused others to assume he was a half-wit. I knew that Royland was actually very clever indeed, but he was somehow lost within himself. He was at his best and most focused when others around him were calm; however, this was not often enough the case. His dislike of making eye contact or being touched marked him as odd, and he reacted badly to mockery or shouting. Royland was a good head taller than I and four years my senior, but even I had to keep reminding myself that the lanky young man was not a child. He was neither deaf nor dim, and talking louder or more slowly would only further distress him, for he could tell when you were being patronizing.

"Royland, do you know where your uncle Elliot is?" I tried again in a calmer tone of voice.

Still not fully meeting my gaze, he adopted a saddened demeanor and nodded.

"Please take me there," I coaxed.

Shaking his head in negation, my cousin pointed a slender digit at the bench from which he had arisen. There lay an outfit of my clothing.

"Oh. Thanks, Roy," I said as I retrieved it and slipped back into the room.

Once I had dressed, Royland led the way down the hall to the room where they had my father. Uncle Robert met me at the door.

I remember when I was very young that uncle Robert would come from his farmstead to stay with us at the mill two weeks each spring. Father had explained that uncle Robert needed to fulfill military obligations as part of being the baron's tenant. I liked uncle Robert. He was a cheerful man who would always hold out his hand to shake but then pull it back and muss my hair instead. This was usually followed by some laughing remark like: 'Young Lucas here is growin' like he slops from the king's own table.' During his stays, he kept his spear and shield and an old, battered leather helmet on the mantle above our hearth fire and reported every morning to the keep's central courtyard. I would sometimes watch the men drilling in spear formations or marching out the gates and into the countryside to train. When uncle Robert returned in the evenings, he was tired, but after a good meal, he always found the energy to wag his tongue around.

"He's sleeping now, lad," said my uncle in a hushed voice. "You can see him for a minute, but try not to waken him. The apothecary has taken away his pain."

"How bad is it, uncle Robert?" I asked.

"I won't lie to you; it's bad," he replied. "He was lucid for a bit but in a lot of hurt. Elliot said it was the hammer that saved his arm. When that big old rock fell, the steel hammer head kept it from being crushed completely. It did bite his hand pretty hard though. The chiurgeon says he'll lose a couple of the smaller fingers. It could have been a lot worse, so thank the stars, say I."

Grimacing, I entered. My father was asleep in a bed not so different from the one in which I had awoken. Instead of a quilt, he was covered only by thin sheets. This room was windowless and thus warmer than mine had been. There were linen bandages wound all about his left arm up to the elbow and one across his forehead. His peaceful countenance, however, so at odds with the way I had last seen him, set my mind at ease and gave me hope.

***

When I returned to the hallway, my uncle steered me aside.

"Lucas," he said, "we couldn't rouse you. I know you must be hungry, but I told the baron I'd let him know the moment you awakened. They have questions, and . . . there have been some accusations made. I told the lord's men that I'll serve as your guardian until Elliot recovers."

I paled, remembering the incident with Trenton.

"Thank you, uncle," I said. "Where do we need to go?"

"There are two nice guardsmen who will escort us down there," he replied. "Come along Royland." And with that, he led the two of us to the end of the hall.

Just as my uncle had predicted, two of the castle guardsmen broke away from the archway and fell in step with us. We descended a stairwell and after several turns entered a more sumptuous area of the keep. Although I had lived in Meadowfork for all of my fourteen years, I had rarely entered the keep itself. Oh, there were sometimes festivals or events in the inner ward, and all of the children found excuses to deliver messages and the like or to climb up to the curtain wall on a dare. But, the closest I had been to this part before was delivering sacks of flour to the lord's kitchen.

As we approached a large door, one of the guardsmen indicated that we should stop while his cohort walked up and rapped on it. A smaller door up at head height was thrown open from within, revealing a man's face. After a hurried conversation to which I wasn't privy, the guardsman returned to us and said: "Wait here, the lord's council will announce you presently."

"Royland," said my uncle "you need to stay right here when we're let in, alright? There's a good lad."

The older boy just shrugged and produced a small leather-bound book from the pocket of his tunic. As he sat on a plush bench nearby reading, I marveled that he owned such a rare item. I was not at all surprised that he could read it, despite the fact that most of my peers could not. I had a bit in common with Royland there. I could read since I was five. My father is a very learned man, and even when I was very young, he never spoke down to me. Other youngsters in town sometimes thought I was 'putting on airs' when I used words they didn't know. The problem was, I honestly didn't know which words those were.

While waiting, I tried to imagine what they would ask me. About the stone? Certainly, but all I could say about that was that I didn't know what had happened. Trenton was sure to be angry with me, but my only defense would paint him in a bad light, and that wouldn't lead anywhere pleasant. My stomach growled. I thought furiously about how to describe why I had tackled him. Father had always said it was important for the nobles to maintain their superiority at all times. I wondered if I could appeal to that somehow.

At last, we were announced and led into a well-appointed room. There were heraldic shields and tapestries depicting battles from the goblin wars. Lord Westarbor sat at its far end in an ornately carved chair up on a slightly raised platform. To either side of him sat many advisers and several of his knights who were in residence. His wife, the lady Westarbor, was not in attendance, so this was either to be low justice or perhaps merely a general inquest. I hoped for the latter, but was soon to be disappointed.

Uncle Robert's hand was on my shoulder, ushering me forward into the baron's presence. "Your lordship," he said, bowing low, "my nephew has regained his senses, and I have brought him as you required. I believe he has recovered enough to give his testimony of the events."

Remembering my manners, I followed suit and bowed low as well. As I straightened, I noticed a strange movement in a tapestry behind the assembled men.

"I have some questions for this witness, your lordship," interjected one of the advisers. I recognized him as the baron's chamberlain. He sometimes had business with my father keeping records of the mill's expenses and banalities.

"Proceed then, Gerrard," said the baron with a nod of affirmation.

"Did you, as reported and duly witnessed, lay hands on a nobleman of this kingdom in the person of the son of your liege?" he asked.

"I did, sir," I replied.

There arose a muttering among the assembled advisers. Uncle Robert's hand returned to my shoulder, and his grip tightened.

"And did this act of violence take the form of an unprovoked attack from behind?"

"No," I quickly denied.

This caused a greater stir, but they soon settled back down.

"There are witnesses that claim otherwise. Would you like to rethink your answer?"

"*Not* unprovoked," I responded.

Momentarily taken aback by this, the chamberlain soon rallied and asked in a disdainful tone: "What *provocation*, then do you claim could justify such an act?"

"The man I struck was threatening the son of my liege," I answered.

Confusion reigned for a moment, and then various responses emerged ranging from stifled gasps to open amusement before Lord Westarbor intervened. Rising to his feet, he drew all eyes to him and the babble subsided.

"This grows tedious," he announced. "What happened at the mill last night, boy?" he asked more simply.

I told of how the stone had dropped on my father while he was cleaning it. I described the clouds of dust, and how I had stumbled outside and met the men of the night watch. I then explained the dangers of an open flame, emphasizing that Sir Trenton's very life was imperiled by the lantern he bore. This seemed to astonish the baron, but I noted several of his advisers nodding thoughtfully. I went on to recount the strange lifting of the stone I had witnessed.

"Did you use magic to lift the stone?" asked the baron, staring at me intently.

"I don't know, your lordship."

"Was anyone else present in the mill, apart from my son or his men?"

"I believe the Cains had come over to help," I answered hesitantly, "but they were outside."

"Very well," he said. "In the matter of the stone, we are bringing an expert on magic. You will submit yourself to him tomorrow."

There was a brief pause as the baron moistened his lips and swallowed. "It is my further judgment that for laying hands on a nobleman, *whatever* your intentions, you shall spend two hours in the stockade this evening. As a father, you have my thanks. But such an insult cannot be ignored and permitted to fester."

*The stocks!* Petty thieves and liars were put in the stockade. I supposed it was better than being flogged and pilloried, but I felt my face burn with shame, nonetheless.

"Yes, your lordship," I mumbled hastily.

I felt Uncle Robert tense up. Looking over, I could see his jaw muscles working.

"Yes, your lordship," he ground out in a gruff voice as he cast his heated gaze firmly downward.

Sensing closure, we took our leave with the two guardsmen flanking us. As we exited, Royland stood up from where he had been reading and trailed along in our wake.

***

My two hours in the stockade were planned for later this evening, after the good folk had finished their daily labors and could come to gawk properly. This would also allow time for the harkers to announce the entertainment far and wide. It was too long past midday to get food at the keep's dining hall, and since we were not permitted to leave the premises prior to my punishment, uncle Robert had words with the guardsmen. One went down to the kitchens and ordered that food be brought up to our rooms. By the time there was a knock on my door, I was famished.

"Come in," I beckoned.

A maid entered bearing a large platter. She seemed young for the post, but I was certainly no expert on noble households.

"Just set it on the bed, please," I said, there being no table or other furnishings in my chamber.

The platter had me salivating. There was a loaf of fine white bread - not the usual brown fare, a hunk of cheese and several kinds of succulent fruit. There was also a tankard of what proved to be fresh milk. Folk in the keep dined well if this was but a simple repast.

As I sat down and prepared to feast, it did not escape my attention that the maid was making no movement to leave.

"They're calling it the miracle of the mill," she said.

"I'm sure I wouldn't know," I admonished, "as I have lain unconscious or been on trial since it happened."

19

"Did you tip Trenton into the mill race? Truly?" she continued with an impish grin.

This was no maid; I realized. Her hands did not bear the mark of drudgery, and her accent was too aristocratic. Moreover, a servant's use of Trenton's name without the honorific would be scandalous. She wore the habiliment of a servant, but, looking more closely, I recalled seeing her face on many prior occasions.

"I know you," I said in astonishment. "You're the lady Megan."

"Guilty," she replied. "I just *had* to meet the boy who floated the millstone. You are all the people are talking about."

Lady Megan, the daughter of the baron, was Sir Trenton's younger sister. At thirteen, she was already becoming a beauty. The distinctive, long black tresses that marked her as an Arenson were at present tucked beneath a plain servant's coif. She was perhaps most well known for leading the spring flower festival at Westarbor Keep.

"My lady, you *cannot* be in my room unescorted," I chided.

"Are you such a cad, then?" she replied coyly but then relented when I flinched at this rejoinder.

"In truth," she said with downcast eyes, "I came to apologize on behalf of my father. He knows you bear no blame for the mishap with Trenton. In fact your actions were most laudable."

"He said this?" I asked somewhat surprised, "then why . . . ?"

"Why are you being chastised?" she finished for me. "For several compelling reasons. Firstly, the baron cannot be seen as weak - ever. Trust me on this. There are those who would use this as an excuse to besiege my father both figuratively and perhaps even literally. Some already say that he gives his villeins far too much leeway and suggest that a stronger hand is required."

"And secondly?" I prompted as I took this in.

She sighed. She really was a lovely girl, even when her shoulders drooped.

"Trenton," she lamented. "He was raised to the stories of father's valor in the war. *Ever* has he sought to magnify himself and prove his *own* mettle. I think the absence of a real foe causes him to belittle others in a vain attempt to shore up his own reputation. I fear that your treatment of him at the mill will only be perceived as a challenge to his authority. And *that* is something he will not abide. Father knows this and seeks to disarm the situation with your public reprimand. It is wise but still unjust."

She spoke passionately, and I sensed real sorrow in her words and not the pitying kind that was all most nobles would allow themselves to express. Somehow, she made me wish I could console her, but having no sisters, I lacked the proper words.

"I understand," I said instead. "I shall endure it. And I thank your ladyship for her most charitable thoughts."

At this, her lips quirked upward and she accepted my gratitude with a tilt of her head and a shallow curtsy. Devilment again lit her eyes as she turned toward the door, assumed a stooped posture, and trudged back out into the hall.

After she was well gone, I descended ravenously upon the tray of food that had thus far eluded its unenviable fate.

***

Although mostly clear, the sky above was filled with billowy white clouds. As usual, the stockade had been placed in the courtyard beyond the keep's outer gate. The sun hung low in the sky, but at least my back was to it as I crouched shirtless in the torturesome device. My neck and wrists rested in circular depressions in a great wooden plank affixed to a raised platform by several beams. A second plank hinged atop it denied me the ability to withdraw my head, and my wrists were further fettered by iron shackles. The stocks required I be bent prostrate with my face prominently presented. The day had warmed, but I could still feel the sharp nip of the cold autumn breeze. Several guardsmen stood nearby projecting their authority over the gathering crowd. They were there ostensibly to protect me should the mob grow too riled. I took little heart from this because although they would shield me from thrown stones and the like, rotten vegetables, dirt, and all manner of other foul dreck were actually encouraged.

The people were restless, waiting for the harker to read out the list of my crimes. This would mark the beginning of the public shaming. I had attended too many such events in my short life. I myself had heckled and jeered at petty thieves and other ne'er-do-wells who had merited such attentions. Although I had drawn the line at actually flinging rubbish at them, I knew many who *were* so inclined and took great pleasure in the sport.

To my further embarrassment, I spotted many people that I knew well arriving to witness my humiliation. Right up in front stood Trenton and his fellow squires. It was generally considered beneath the dignity of the full knights or noblemen to attend such an assemblage. It was an affair aimed more toward the common folk's pleasure. Nonetheless, few, I think, would challenge his right to see my punishment meted out.

More strangely, I spied Lady Megan approaching to the left of the crowd. No longer reined in by a servant's coif, her lustrous raven locks were unmistakable. In a bright blue kirtle, she was difficult to miss. She was accompanied by two ladies in waiting, one of whom bore a large burlap sack. They did not join the crowd in the courtyard but stood to one side watching.

The harker chose this time to step up onto the platform. In large, sweeping arcs, he rang a brass hand-bell until the people stilled. Over the low susurrus of remaining babble he began to read from a parchment clenched firmly in his other hand.

"The condemned, Lucas Harper of Meadowfork," he began in a loud, sonorous voice. "has been found guilty with malice of forethought of laying hands in violence upon a noble of our great barony!"

Trenton and his cronies looked properly outraged by this but some others, like the bakers apprentices, merely seemed chagrined.

"Moo!" someone in the crowd interjected, and there was a tittering of laughter.

"As this is a first offense," the harker continued, looking slightly confused at the outburst, "he is sentenced to serve two hours in the stockade at the mercy of any of his peers who would rightly denounce such villainy! This sentence is to commence . . ." There was a slight pause as the harker quickly extricated himself from the platform. "Now!" he shouted at last.

"Moo!" I heard again, this time accompanied by the clangor of an old tin cowbell.

The noise of the crowd began to swell, but among the usual jeers and taunts I caught some laughter and more lowing sounds. As was inevitable, the first volley was hurled from somewhere near the back of the crowd. Some farmer's lad had apparently come equipped with a supply of cow dung which he eagerly launched in my direction. Fortunately for me, his first missile was off-center and struck the stocks to the left of my head with a soft squelching thud.

But then another peculiar thing happened. The swain with the eager arm was beset by several around him. With a chorus of moo's and a scuffle, he was hastily restrained and disarmed.

Trenton Arenson with his hands cupped to either side of his mouth shouted: "This will teach you to respect your betters, Harper. Remember this when . . ."

He was cut short by an even more vigorous "Moo!" followed by more laughter and the cow bell. His eyebrows descended in ire, and he turned and peered back through the milling spectators trying to single out the culprit. Still more laughter issued forth at this, but most in his line of sight were looking about in blank-faced innocence.

All at once, I thought I understood.

There's a story that the young farmers like to spread around at the tavern. According to them, cows sleep standing up. So, as a rite of passage, they like to creep up to a field late at night then run up on an unsuspecting cow and knock into her with their shoulder. This tips the cow over onto her side. Then the laughing, drunken perpetrators run away while the cow bellows in fright. A group of boys once convinced me to go along with them. It turns out that the following is true. Of the big animals, only horses sleep standing up. Cows are very wary of people approaching them. Cows are sturdier on their feet than one would imagine. And lastly, that drunken boys really like to see a fool try it.

Apparently, the story had made the rounds of what I had done to Trenton, and some genius had likened it to cow tipping. Once Trenton caught on, I was certain he would take it as a deadly insult. I knew an outward sign of mirth just now would only get me into greater trouble, but that served only to heighten the hilarity. I wanted to bray like a donkey at the ridiculous image this evoked. I was sure my face was as red as a beet, and tears glistened in the corners of my eyes as I clamped firmly down on the impulse to laugh.

I sobered up only when it began to dawn on me that few here genuinely wanted to see me shamed. Father and I had many friends among the good people of Meadowfork. And, despite the baser impulses of some, most were willing to rise in support of one of their own who had done no wrong. This was a testament to the kindness and wisdom of people in general.

Then another astonishing event transpired. Lady Megan and her handmaids began walking toward the front of those assembled. Reaching into the burlap sack, she withdrew from it a long-stemmed flower. Turning toward me and with a gentle smile gracing her countenance, she lofted the posy expertly to land at the base of the stockade. This captured the crowd's attention and her brother's as well. Holding forth the sack to those in the crowd, the ladies in waiting began to dispense all manner of autumn blooms. Those who had been holding themselves in check, suddenly had a way to participate in the event and express their good wishes. I was literally showered with flowers.

To say that Sir Trenton did not look amused would be to understate the matter. The burning gaze he leveled upon me promised a harsh reckoning to come. He made his way into the keep with his back held ramrod straight pursued by a chorus of lowing. Most of the other squires accompanied him, but rather surprisingly, several remained to join in our revelry. A festive atmosphere ensued and all present stood about conversing and gossiping for the remaining hours until sunset. Although I found myself well pleased by this outcome at the moment, I wondered if this was a prudent thing in the long haul. I considered what Lady Megan had told me about the barony and its detractors. If my punishment had not served its desired purpose, would this cause problems for Lord Westarbor?

After the sun had set and I had been released, I gave my back an all-around stretch. I was approached by many of the remaining townsfolk. Some had questions about the mill while others wished to offer their condolences regarding my father's injury. I shared my thoughts with the former and thanked the latter. When I was preparing to return to my room in the keep, I decided to scoop up a bunch of the blooms that had been tossed at me. Although it wasn't the kind of flower I was used to sweeping up, 'Waste not; want not' my father would say.

***

The following morning found me awake before the birds. I checked in on my sleeping father. Being determined to avoid crossing Trenton's path, I then quietly headed to the kitchens to beg some victuals. I was invited to join the castle servants for their breakfast of oatmeal porridge. There I was enjoined to regale my hosts with the tale of the rising millstone and my time in the stocks. From the ewery maid, I was offered a vase for my flowers which I gratefully accepted.

While returning to my bed chamber, I heard people talking in father's room. Royland was sitting nearby playing cat's cradle with a piece of string. His slender fingers twisted and writhed to produce the most amazing patterns. Interested, I stopped and asked him who was within.

"The baron," he said in a low voice, his eyes still riveted to the twine.

I was now even more curious, but continued on to my own room to drop off the vase. Quickly assessing my half-wilted blooms all in a heap, I took a few minutes to arrange some of the nicer ones and poured the remains of my morning wash water in as well to help keep them fresh.

Returning to my father's door, I screwed up my courage and knocked.

"Enter," said my father, that one word filling my heart with joy.

Elated that my father was at last awake, enter I did. Father was sitting up in his bed with uncle Robert behind him and the baron reclined in a chair at its foot. Recalling my manners, I bowed low and said, "your lordship."

The baron gave me that appraising stare that he wielded so easily.

"Well, young Harper, I see you are no worse for the wear," he observed.

"I still say that was a dirty trick," said uncle Robert belatedly adding: "your lordship."

I felt the weight of his gaze shift from me as he turned to my uncle.

"You *know* why it was necessary, Robert," replied the baron. "as doubtless does young Lucas himself. Don't you, Lucas?"

"The baron cannot be seen as weak, and his family must not lose the love of the people," I said in summary fashion.

My father's eyes popped, and uncle Robert looked poleaxed as the baron laughed. It was a pleasant sound, full-throated and warm with genuine mirth, yet somehow fierce like the baron himself.

"Direct, honest, and to the point," said Lord Westarbor, smiling. "I can see *your* influence there, Elliot. He would make a *terrible* courtier. Still, since the young man has stated the problem so succinctly, I shall endeavor not to meander overmuch in proposing its solution."

"Spare us the flibber-flabber, your lordship," said uncle Robert recovering his composure. "What do you have in mind?"

"After the incident at the mill, I sent a detachment to summon Elizar," replied the baron.

"I doubt he will come," argued my father. "Master Chadwick never leaves his flock untended."

"He shall have no alternative," the baron rebutted. "By royal decree, any who possess the gift are to be tested and apprenticed, and whether or not he would prefer it so, Elizar Chadwick is our local master. You know how urgently mages are needed to secure the kingdom. And you also know how the king *fears* any mage who might work against us."

A shadow seemed to cross over my uncle's face at the latter remark.

"Your lordship is well aware Isabel and I inherited no magery from our mother," stated uncle Robert. "We were tested many times."

"Indeed," the baron acknowledged, "however, the gift has been known to skip a generation as any *shepherd* will find is true of *black sheep* as well," he said with a peculiar emphasis that caused Robert's visage to darken even further.

"My experts inform me that the millstone weighs more than eighty stone," he continued. "As witnessed by a dozen men, my son among them, it rose into the air. Elliot was unconscious at the time; no one else was near; and immediately afterward, young Lucas here fell like a puppet with its strings cut. I would characterize that as a very strong act of emerging magic. And all *flibber-flabber* aside, it provides us the ideal opportunity. Lucas can apprentice and explore his gift for a year. Meanwhile, my son will cease to be distracted by misplaced thoughts of petty vengeance and begin focusing on winning his spurs and coming into his majority. It hinges only on the test."

My father looked unconvinced.

"Father," I said, drawing his attention. "What kind of man is Master Chadwick?"

"The best kind," my father replied.

"That he is," added uncle Robert. "He saved our skins many times over back in the day. Now he's retired to a sheep ranch in the north valley. A waste of good talent that, but, 'to each his own,' say I."

"Then I would *like* to find out whether I have the gift," I said. "I will take his test."

"There, you see?" said Lord Westarbor placatingly.

"What of the mill, then?" asked father in a tone of resignation.

"My Winifred and I can help out until you get back on your feet," uncle Robert offered. "And Royland won't be any trouble. He's a good lad and a right powerful help when you set him to a task. If your lordship will agree?"

The pleading look my uncle turned upon the baron was as out of character as it was effective.

Lord Westarbor looked discomfited for a moment. He then shrugged and said, "Undoubtedly, I can find a far more productive farmer to fill your tenancy," and then added with a surprising dash of familiarity, "you old goat."

Later that day, the famed old wizard arrived at the keep driving an oxcart. A light rain had kicked up. After the ox plodded through the main gate, it stopped directly in front of the stables where the grooms rushed forth to secure the animal from out of the drizzle. Master Chadwick stepped down and made his way unhurriedly toward the keep. He was an older gentleman, but fairly well muscled and with an erect posture. He had a white beard everywhere except on his lower lip and chin. I think the style was known as 'mutton chops,' which I thought was funny because he was a shepherd, after all. He wore work clothes just like a commoner if a little finer. He had no bejeweled staff, no funny hat, no long robe or high collar or cape. What marked him was that no rain was falling upon him. Not a drop. Oh, and the mud didn't seem to stick to his boots.

As he entered the keep, the wizard was greeted by a full honor guard which, of course, had to include the baron's family. I was kept well out of sight during all the pomp and circumstance. My test was to occur later that afternoon once the dining hall had cleared from the feast. After my own light meal, I waited nervously in a lower hall of the keep. My father was still recuperating, so I was accompanied by uncle Robert and my cousin. As usual, Royland kept mostly to himself quietly reading his book - a different one, I noted.

At last, the master was led down to the hall - by the baron himself, no less.

"Elizar," the baron said, indicating me with a sweeping gesture "may I present our suspected young prodigy, Lucas Harper. His uncle, the esteemed Robert Wagge, I believe you already know. Lucas, may I present Master Elizar Chadwick of Arborvale, master mage and breeder of fine white wool."

Master Chadwick first greeted my uncle. "Robert," he said with a slight tip of his head "Still playing soldier?"

"Ah," replied my uncle with a swipe of his hand, "I'm getting a bit long in the tooth for that game, master. I'm more focused on my trade and my family these days, but I still keep my spear sharp," he finished with a broad wink.

"And you, young sir. Are you Elliot and Isabel's child, then?" asked the old man.

"Just so, master," I replied.

"And for how long have you suspected you had the gift?" he asked with a hint of skepticism.

"For only two days now, master," I replied ruefully.

"That is a point in your favor," he assured. "It is best to begin one's journey into magic without any preconceived notions or false expectations."

"Well, I'll just leave you to it, then," interrupted the baron. "I have some duties of the keep awaiting me. But rest assured, I am most interested in the *proper* outcome here. *Most interested.*"

And with that, he turned on his heel and rapidly quit the hall, his boots clicking on the stone floor.

"That man hasn't changed a bit," mused Master Chadwick. "I do hope you pass the test, Lucas, so I can keep his bribe."

Uncle Robert looked scandalized.

***

Master Chadwick had my uncle bring two comfortable chairs over to a round wooden table in the hall. He sat in one and bade me to take the other.

"The task is simple, Lucas," began the wizard as he placed a fist-sized rock in the table's center. You shall lift this stone harnessing the power of your gift while I observe. It should prove a great deal easier than hefting that millstone, no?"

"How exactly am I to accomplish this?" I asked.

"Concentrate on the stone, boy," said Master Chadwick. "Study it. Keeping your eyes upon it, imagine your arm stretching out to it. Have you ever had a daydream?"

"All the time," I replied while remaining focused upon the stone. "Father says I spend too much time woolgathering."

"Does he indeed?" chuckled the old man, grinning as if at some private joke. "Now we mages use words in the old tongue to help train our minds. There is no power in the words themselves, but it helps us to focus on the task at hand. In time,

29

our minds begin to associate the words with a particular mindset, allowing us to engage it more readily. I want you to think about lifting the stone from the table just as you would do it with your own hand, while chanting the word 'levare.' It means 'lift' in the old tongue."

"Then why don't I chant 'lift'?" I asked.

"That would be most inconvenient," grumbled Master Chadwick, "Imagine if every time you said the word 'fire' you would unconsciously summon one. What would your life be like then, eh?"

I could see his point. So stretching out an imaginary hand, I began chanting 'levare,' 'leh-vaa-reh,' 'leh-vaa-reh' . . .

"Now, while continuing to lift up on the stone," said the old man in a low hypnotic voice as I continued to incant, "I want you to seek deep within yourself with your mind's eye. Some imagine it as a shining brightness within, while others envision a well of deep, still waters. This is your magic center. Whatever its source, you must draw from it; coax it out, just a trickle at first, and allow it to flow down your imaginary arm toward the stone. Then simply increase this flow to accomplish your task."

I definitely felt something, or had I only imagined it? The flicker of doubt warred with my credibility as I promptly lost the feeling. The stone lay unmoving, but for just a moment, I had felt its weight. What had it been like? I tried to recapture the vision, but it was elusive, like a half-remembered dream that vanishes as one wakens.

Calming my scattered thoughts and continuing my mantra, I had the impression of a blotch of green. It was small but fraught with possibility and potential. Rather than the 'trickle' that Master Chadwick was describing, when I coaxed it, it began to sprout. Slowly at first, but then with gathering speed, the sprout grew out into a thin vine-like tendril which proceeded to traverse my imaginary arm until it touched the stone. A suggestion of the stone's heft returned, but it was not a weight like one would feel in one's arm. Rather, it was more a sense of pressure at the base of my skull.

I could tell that the stone's weight was far too great for my fragile vine to overcome, so I drew more heavily on the patch of green. My vine began thickening, and several smaller tendrils grew twining about it along its length lending it further strength. All the while, my meager little verdant patch diminished. Before it was entirely spent, and with a final short bark of 'levare,' I increased my mental grip upon the stone and heaved upward.

The stone wobbled.

Bearing down, I heaved once more, this time continuing the pressure as my vine-like tendril frayed and began to unravel. Thinking about it more as hoisting with a pulley seemed to help stabilize and strengthen my mental construct. Even so, my paltry remaining green center had dwindled to a mere speck and was taking on an unhealthy pallor as the stone slowly rose a hand's width above the table.

With a groan, I released the stone, which promptly clattered back down upon the tabletop. I sagged back into my chair and heaved a sigh of relief with my head swimming.

"That was well done, Lucas," said Master Chadwick in a tone that lacked enthusiasm. "I can state with some conviction, that you are indeed a mage."

"Are you certain, Elizar?" asked my uncle.

"Mage sight doesn't lie, Robert," rejoined the old wizard. "That was purely Lucas' doing. I only wonder at the difficulty he had with this small rock. Perhaps he overextended himself on the millstone the other night. I should think he would have recovered by now, but magic can be a strange thing."

"Truer words," responded uncle Robert with a nod.

As I began processing the implications of what had just occurred, I noticed that Royland had finally set aside his book. He was rocking back and forth and moving his lips soundlessly as he so often did when unsettled. His gaze was locked upon the stone.

"Levare," he said once.

And, to the amazement of all in the room save for one, the stone lifted straight up to hover several feet above the table. It then gradually descended to touch down again lightly. With a crooked smile resting on his lips, Royland resumed his reading.

I had to pack in a hurry. Master Chadwick had agreed to take both Royland and me as apprentices. His small ranch in the north valley was only about a day's travel by oxcart. Though I would not be allowed to leave it during the year of my apprenticeship, I assured father and uncle Robert that I would write to them often. Uncle Robert was especially concerned about Royland going out on his own, and I had to promise him I would look out for my cousin.

At the keep, I owned nothing but a vase of flowers. Unable to take them with me, I wrote out a note on some borrowed stationary and begged a housemaid to deliver them to Lady Megan as a souvenir. In the note I thanked her for her kindly gesture and wished her and her family well.

I had to return to the mill to retrieve extra clothing and my few personal effects. On the way there, I encountered Gregor Cain and his father driving their wagons onto the road.

"Still here?" I shouted up to Gregor on the second wagon as he shortened the reins and brought it to a stop.

"I'll catch you up, pa!" Gregor hollered.

"Just leaving," he said, turning to look down at me. "We weren't allowed to go until everyone was questioned," Gregor complained. "My pa was pretty irked. We lost two whole days and never did get our corn milled."

"I'm sorry about that, Gregor," I said.

"Well don't fret over it," Gregor said with a lob-sided grin. "Grain keeps, and we've got hand mills aplenty at the stead. Pa says that rough grind is great for brewing corn spirits anyway. Well, best I mosey."

And with that, he took up the reins and goaded his oxen back into motion.

"Gregor," I said, causing him to look back. "you don't happen to own a cow bell, do you?"

He peered at me through squinted eyes for a moment and then continued on his way. "Moo!" I heard distantly, as he rolled up the lane.

# CHAPTER THREE

# The Squire

"It takes your enemy and your friend, working
together, to hurt you to the heart: the one to
slander you and the other to get the news to you."

*~ Mark Twain ~*

How *dare* she interfere so? I marched forward, careful to
adopt an upright bearing and maintain a steady pace. Decorum
needed to be preserved, after all. Hadn't that uncouth ruffian
been on the verge of tears? Had he not been practically wetting
himself with fear before my thrice-accursed sister intervened? I
was here to see justice meted out, but instead had witnessed a
travesty. A greater mockery of the law could hardly be contrived.
And what could be the purpose of those infuriating, mooing
sounds? I could hear them still at their boisterous braying as I
strode in courtly manner through the yawning mouth of the
keep's main gate. Well, fie on them. Fie on them one and all.

My fellow squires who accompanied me would scarcely meet
my gaze. Did they imagine my ire to be so great as to overcome
my honor? Had not our respective knights drilled it into us time
and again never to lash out in anger? 'Refer to the Code,' Sir
Declan would advise; the code is wise, and the code has stood
the test of time, *ad nauseam*. Two of our number had even
remained behind to *cavort* with the rabble. I might have

expected *Myles* to revel in my disappointment, but I had hoped for better from Reginald. Had we not been as brothers since the day we swore our vows as squires?

It was at this time that I parted ways with my three remaining companions. Hayden, ever the boldest of the three, asked if I should like to take a cup of ale ere we retired.

"Regrettably," I demurred, "I am moved to contemplate the day's events in solitude. In my absence, feel free to raise a cup to my good health. I am sore in need of such after *that* disgusting display."

Agreeing to do so and bidding me farewell, Hayden departed hastily to rejoin the others.

Finally alone with my thoughts and free of social obligation, I looked about. My eyes caught upon the stairway up to the curtain wall, and my feet soon followed its unspoken invitation. Ascending at a dignified pace, I arose to the battlement. In the last hours of daylight, the guardsmen posted here were restive in weary anticipation of relief by the night watch. The watch fires stood unlit but well-stocked with oiled logs. A vague smoky odor was the only testament to their recent use in yesterday's debacle. That had not been my first time standing the watch, but it would likely ever remain my most memorable.

The men straightened at my approach. At least the *soldiery* knew proper respect for a gentleman of station. I passed them by with a simple greeting of "Hail, the watch," making an effort to inject some false cheer, and strode onward. I soon found myself at the west tower. Sir Declan had once dubbed it my 'brooding place.' I thought of it rather as a bastion for silent meditation far above the cares and the burdens of the barony. It had a good vantage overlooking the courtyard. Below, the townspeople and the bumpkins from the outer farms still congregated about, their cackling merriment an unseemly repudiation of the solemn purpose for which the gathering had been called. The wind played gently through my hair as I looked down upon their vulgar spectacle.

"I sense a troubled soul," said the voice of my knight.

Sir Declan always seemed to know my mind. I had been attending him for nearly four years, but I had known him all of my life. He was with my father since the beginning, when the barony was first won. As he was the knight commander of our forces, it was considered a high honor to serve as his squire. I once overheard Myles insinuate that my assignment to this good knight was only in deference to my sire's wishes. I cared not for such envious tripe. Had I not bested Myles in both swordplay and the lance? For many reasons aside from the honor this accolade imparted, I was *glad* to attend upon Sir Declan. He exemplified all of the virtues to which our knighthood aspired. None could fault his honor. And he was a kind and patient master, always thoughtful and considerate of the dignity of others.

"I told you that you should not go," he continued as the silence stretched out.

"You did not forbid it, sir," I reminded. "I went only to witness the hand of justice fall upon one who had wronged me and dishonored my family by his misdeeds."

"Do you say so to convince me - or yourself?" he challenged, continuing before I could summon a response. "You went to gloat, Trenton, a pursuit most unbecoming a knight."

"I admit it," I confessed, shamefaced.

"Then there is hope," he said, "for the code enjoins us to be truthful first with oneself, and then to all other men. Look to your own conscience, Trenton, and allow justice to find its own course."

"Would that my sister had done likewise, my lord." I said, recalling her treacherous interference in the sordid affair. "She used her influence to ameliorate the penalty. Did this not warp the true course of justice?"

After a thoughtful pause, he began to instruct. "The lady Megan is well attuned to the mood of her people," he began. "She walks among them performing many acts of charity, and they adore her for it. But perhaps more importantly, she listens to them. There is much wisdom to be gleaned from the minds of the common folk, and it is their continued goodwill that drives the wheels of our barony. If your sister felt the need to intercede on behalf of the miller's son, then I deem it likely she did so for the sake of your family's reputation. It is not a bad thing for our liege to be perceived as kind and merciful. Would you detract from that?"

"I would rather he be seen as just and fair," I countered.

"Exactly." observed Sir Declan "And now our good liege can be viewed as both."

It sounded just like something my father would do. And how like Sir Declan to arrive at the heart of the matter so quickly. His canny wit and perception of the broader canvas more than the strength of his sword arm is what made him a great general.

"Soon you will no longer have my council, so I suggest you heed it well," said my knight. "Return to your chambers. Get cleaned up and cast off this melancholy. Tomorrow we will receive an important guest, and you are to be in the honor guard."

"Who is coming, my lord?" I asked, intrigued.

"It's no secret," he began. "Tomorrow there will be a feast to honor the arrival of Elizar Chadwick of Arborvale. He has been summoned to look into the extraordinary event at the mill yesterday eve."

The mill again, I thought ruefully. Not yet a full day had passed, and already I was heartily sick of the topic.

"You will be attending as the baron's son," he continued, "so I shall enlist young Derrick to act as my squire for the event. With your own knighthood soon to come upon us, there's no better time to start breaking in a replacement."

Derrick Lester was the son of one of our enfeoffed knights not in residence at Westarbor Keep. Derrick, a boy of thirteen summers, had been my sire's page since he had been seven. Always eager to please yet gentle, and only four years my junior, I regarded him almost as a younger brother. I was sure he would make a fine squire. The thought of him attending Sir Declan brought a smile to my weary heart and not a little envy at the journey he was about to undertake even as my own neared its ending.

"You still have a full hour before the sun quits the heavens, lad," declared my knight. "I shall expect my armor and equipment to be gleaming ere daybreak."

I groaned inwardly. Had I not already spent long hours cleaning the muck from my own greaves and hauberk due to my ill-fated encounter with the miller's brat? I glanced down at his supine form in the stockade and hoped that horseflies would find him before his sentence concluded. It was an uncharitable thought perhaps, but it lightened my step as I quit the battlement and resumed my duties.

***

I stood with my mother and father in the entry hall of Westarbor Keep. I almost missed my armor. It rarely chafed anymore, and I had become accustomed to its weight and protection. When I was a young page, my sire had instructed me that a highly embroidered velvet doublet such as the one I now sported was but armor of a different sort. How one is perceived in a social setting was important, and dangers far worse than a sword thrust could be deflected by meeting expected decorum. My father's lookouts had reported that Master Chadwick was in sight and should be arriving momentarily.

Mother was resplendent in a blue surcoat embroidered with silver thread in the pattern of swans. She and her handmaidens stood ready to receive the guest of honor. My sister arrived and was a fair sight to behold withal. Having known her since childhood, I had never thought of her as beautiful, but I knew that others did. I was made vaguely uncomfortable by the gazes she drew from my fellow squires. All six of the knights in residence along with their squires and ladies had turned out to greet the famous wizard of the western wild, as he was sometimes known.

I must confess to disappointment when the man finally arrived. It was raining, but rather than pull up to the grand entrance, Master Chadwick arrived instead at the stables down the way. The rickety old cart he drove was as run down as the beast that pulled it. He then trudged slowly through the muddy courtyard. Aged but still sound of body, he sprouted thick white whiskers strangely absent from his chin. As he entered, he threw off his cloak and handed it to a servant with a flourish. Beneath it he wore a homespun tunic and breaches with calf-length peasant's work boots - at least they were clean. Was this the great mage who had helped my sire to carve out a barony? I heard he had retired and owned a sheep ranch, but to look at him, one would think he was the shepherd himself. Also, the man smelled.

Striding forward, my sire clasped his hand most naturally and greeted him. Mother was a mere step behind. Rather than being repelled, she smiled as if receiving a rare treat and said in her sweet voice, "Elizar, it has been far too long."

"Lady Chamille," he replied with a more courtly bow than I would have credited. "you are still as lovely as the day we first met."

I noticed that several of the knights took umbrage at the familiar use of mother's first name. My sister could be called 'Lady Megan' because she lacked a title of her own, just as the other squires had to refer to me as 'Sir Trenton' as a courtesy title derived from being the son of a baron. Still, they sometimes said it chidingly, as though I were a baron's small child. I could hardly wait until after my dubbing. Then it would still be 'Sir Trenton,' but the 'Sir' would be my own.

As the gaff went unchallenged by my sire and by Sir Declan, who had first claim to be her champion, it was not deemed a faux pas. My introduction as 'Sir Trenton, first heir of Westarbor' merited only a head nod and a pleasant smile from the mage. My sister executed a low curtsy when announced. She had obviously been practicing. And again, I was made uncomfortable, this time by an undignified leer that slipped from behind the social mask of Myles Nieves, my nemesis and squire to Sir London McDaniel. Had I only imagined it? Introductions proceeded until each of our knights and their ladies had been named and pleasantries had been exchanged.

"You must wish to freshen up after your journey, Elizar," my mother supplied. "This is Sebastian. He will show you to your chambers and help you to prepare for dinner. If there is anything you need, you have only to ask and our household is at your disposal."

As Master Chadwick retired to his suite, I quietly remarked to my sire: "He seems to know courtly manners, my lord. One would think he would have the good sense to dress properly for the occasion. Who wears worsted wool garments to a baronial reception, after all?"

My father looked at me askance. "While wizards' ways can be strange, I'm certain he intended the slight as a mild rebuke. I'm afraid I was rather *insistent* that he come immediately. But do not let his looks deceive you, my son. Underestimate that man at your own peril, lest you find a wolf in those sheep's clothing."

And because my sire had said it, I knew it must be true, for his gaze could pierce the hearts of men.

***

" . . . So, *Sir Vincent*, then a young knight of only eighteen, but already a banneret, mind you, said to the king: 'I see a way to solve this problem and win the day.'"

"Pray do go on, Sir Nolan," prompted Sir Graham, "you tell it so well."

My family and most of the knights present had heard the story a hundred times. Stars above, half of them had *lived* through it. The squires and a few of the ladies, however, sat in rapt attention. And Sir Nolan was never one to disappoint a willing audience.

"Very well," continued Sir Nolan taking a deep drink from his goblet, "so, *Sir Vincent* pointed to the map and said, 'If the goblins can be pushed back beyond here,' meaning the valley that's now Arborvale, 'they can be held indefinitely, your majesty.' You could've heard a bird blink. Then the king started tugging on his beard and saying excitedly, 'Yes. That has promise, promise indeed!' So, given the king's blessing and aid, our good liege here assembled his knights and called many more to his banner with the promise of land to the west. I won't offend the ladies present with tales of bloody battles, but suffice it to say we reconquered the Downham lands that had been overrun as well as the new lands and founded Westarbor barony. For his insight and valor, our liege was raised up to baron. I myself was knighted that day," he said in conclusion.

The meal had been extravagant indeed. It included all manner of fish, fowl, and game animals and featured a whole roasted boar. Luscious fruits and a variety of cheeses had been available as well as the pure white loaves of bread which had gained such renown of late. We were well on to dessert courses, and the feast was beginning to wind down.

"If I may be so bold as to ask," began Hayden after a satisfied silence, "why is it that you do not have your own fiefdom then?"

"That's simple," replied Sir Nolan, taking no offense as none had been offered. "I chose to stay with my liege. He had a clever plan to keep half of the new barony in demesne - *not* broken into fiefs. To provide the lances owed to the king's service, we had to pool our resources and hire stipendiary knights. The first years were lean ones. Our chief export was timber, as we cleared out the woodlands to make grazing land. The eastern farms recaptured from the goblins sustained us in those times. My liege then encouraged his villeins to innovate by including them to some extent in the profits to be gained from novel ideas. Projects like the lords mill and the new copper mine to the east could not have been accomplished with the resources of but a single fief or with minds that were hidebound . . ."

"I think you are beginning to bore the ladies, Sir Nolan," interrupted the baron. "Please, no more talk of politics on a full stomach. Let us move on to more agreeable topics."

"I have one," ventured Myles, surprising us all, for squires rarely hazarded a new conversational gambit.

"Let's have it then, Myles," said our liege.

"Well it seems that the farmer's sons around here have a rather unique game they enjoy," he began with a sidelong glance up the table.

My sister's head snapped around, and before her manners could re-assert themselves, I caught a glimpse of fright. My fellow squires also seemed to be behaving strangely.

"They claim that cows sleep standing up," Myles continued. "So, they creep into a field at night and run into a moo cow to knock her over with their shoulders. The boy who knocks over the biggest *cow* wins the acclaim of the people. I thought it sounded *most* amusing."

He was staring straight at me as he finished with a smug grin. Reginald was looking at his plate, downcast. Hayden, Blake, and Jay were staring about guiltily. Only young Derrick seemed somewhat bemused. And did not my sister betray her own role in my humiliation? *Damn them.* My sire sat at the table's head with my mother and our guest. He *had* to recognize *exactly* what was being implied, but he just sat there with that agreeable smile casually taking a bite of his pie. Was he giving me a chance to handle the situation myself? I had no swift rejoinder. I was not clever like that. I would not stammer out some poor excuse for a witticism. Nor would I, I decided suddenly, disgrace myself with an angry outburst. I attempted to smooth my features.

"Are you unwell, Sir Trenton?" asked Sir Fletcher unhelpfully.

"I shall be fine presently," I managed to answer. "I found something at the table most disagreeable," I added with a pointed look at Myles Nieves.

From my father came a slight, almost imperceptible nod. My sister's face brightened as well.

"And do these boys," my father asked, oh so gently. "ever encounter a bull?"

"Not that I have heard, my lord," answered Myles. "But I am new to the game."

"Well," remarked my sister casually. "*I* think the *farmers* had best look after their son's welfare more carefully.

My sire yawned and stretched and slowly arose from the table.

"Ladies and gentle knights," said he. "I think the time has come to say goodnight and bid you all a pleasant rest. I have some important matters to discuss with our guest, so Lady Westarbor will see to your needs. Master Elizar, if you please?"

And with that, he and Master Chadwick quit the room. Thinking to do likewise, I headed toward the door. Sir Declan caught my arm.

"Trenton," he said, "give them a chance."

"Unhand me, sir," I growled.

Taken somewhat aback, he did so. And as young Derrick stared on in aggrieved confusion, I began to run down the darkened hallways.

***

My mind was awhirl with confusion. Myles had mocked me in open sight of all the gentry of the keep. Or had he? He had only laid bare what others already knew or suspected. No, his intent was surely but to goad me into disgracing myself; he had nearly succeeded so great was the betrayal I had felt. That accursed miller's son was the true architect of this scandal. I could envision him even now raising cups with his accomplices and sniggering. *It could not be born*. Why was my sire coddling the wretch? And why did my mentor and purported friends seek to withhold this outrage from my eyes? That is what stung the most grievously.

My reputation now hung in tatters. Had I done aught to deserve it? Entering my personal suite, I secured its door and cast about for a fitting distraction from this anguish. I desired no company this night, but I refused to just lay about wallowing in my woe. In frustration, I shed the gaudy doublet of a noble's son. I then considered my hauberk where it lay clean from yesterday's efforts and elected to seek the comfort of its cool embrace. I would one day have my own squire to assist in its donning, but such service could be eschewed if one knew the proper methods. And Sir Declan had insisted I be able to quickly gird myself for battle.

Grabbing inside the mail's shoulders, I lifted its unwieldy bulk straight above my head and allowed it to flow down my torso. I then wriggled and squirmed in a manner that we knights and squires choose not to see as undignified until it fitted snugly upon my form. The familiar activity served both to soothe my sullen thoughts and to affirm my desire for action. Donning my greaves and a pair of high leather boots took but a moment more. Finally, I belted on my sword and decided that a visit to my only true friend was the order of the afternoon.

Still in a mood too grim to suffer others, I thought to leave by a secret way. Westarbor Keep was old. It had stood long before the barony itself had arisen. Sir Nolan had once regaled us with the tale of how our liege and his knights had wrested it from the witch of the western wood. Back then it had lacked the curtain wall, the stables, and many of the other outbuildings and amenities it currently possessed, but this part of the main castle was said to be original.

Having grown up here, I had, of course, discovered its secret ways. One such led right here to my private chambers, but I had long since made it secure from inside. Retrieving the key I had stashed, I worked open the lock then pried off the false panel to reveal the opening into an ancient passage. No draft stirred within, and I caught the faint odor of mildew as I slipped into its semi-darkness.

Navigating with utmost care, I made my way to the exit that let out upon the scullery. It was near enough to my goal of quitting the castle unobserved. I peered through the peep hole only to spy our old household servant, Sebastian. Grizzled and bent with age, he knew his way around the keep like no other. I supposed this derived from his occupation. Sebastian had served as our chandler for as long as I can remember. He spent his days pottering about lighting and extinguishing the many candles required to illuminate various rooms and hallways. My sister used to engage him in an occasional game of chess, but I couldn't recall sharing more than two words with the man. When the way was clear, I emerged and skulked out through the servant's entrance. Not well practiced in the base art, I found it especially difficult to skulk wearing mail. I was successful, nonetheless.

Entering the stables, I stomped the mud from my boots on a thick mat of hay thrown down for the purpose. In my haste, I had neglected to wear my cloak, and though the rain had subsided, a chill mist still hung in the air and clung in droplets to my armor. A single lantern lit the stable. It hung about midway down the long double-row of stalls. Its dim glow barely augmented the pale light let in from the overcast sky, and it flickered irregularly. An equerry was at my elbow in a trice.

"Sir Trenton," greeted the man solicitously. "We didn't expect any from the castle to be rising from the feast so soon. Is there some urgent business I can help with?"

"I've come to take Tempest for a ride," I informed him. "Fetch me my saddle and an apple if you would be of service."

"It shall be done at once, it shall," he said before hurrying off.

I walked down the narrow avenue, my heart still deeply troubled. Westarbor Keep boasted perhaps twenty fine horses. Most were coursers or simple rounceys, shared among the knights and their squires, but the one I sought was a destrier. Originally, I had thought that father had bought the young stallion to be his own steed, but over time, I came to understand that he was meant for *me*. Had master Hart not trained him from a colt, insisting I participate in every step along the way? Save for the stable master himself, I was the only rider that Tempest would now permit. Parts of the training had been difficult. Some would even call them cruel, but the point was to teach the young stallion to stand up to his own fears: loud noises, the smell of blood, and all manner of provocations to which equines have aversion. It's what it took to make a fine warhorse.

Arriving at his stall, I beheld him once again. Tempest was a gray. Though his coat had been black when he was a foal, as he aged, it had lightened considerably and taken on a silvery sheen atop a slate gray color with dappling. This would not last, however, as over time he would lighten still further until those who didn't know better might deem him white. They would never make such a blunder if they could stand him next to Sir Declan's destrier, Angelo, whose coat and mane were as white as the wings of his namesake. My Tempest stood at sixteen hands tall but still had some growing to do. And he was beautiful.

I sensed the equerry returning. With the saddle balanced upon his shoulder, he presented the apple as though it were a trophy. I took it with a nod of gratitude.

Tempest was instantly alert. His ears pricked up and he moved eagerly forward in his stall. I could feel the gusts of his hot breath against my face as he smacked his lips. Relenting, I held out the treat, which he immediately accepted in no uncertain terms. As he munched the juicy morsel, I accepted the saddle from the equerry.

"You may resume your duties, goodman," I directed him.

I entered the stall and set about the task of saddling Tempest and fitting him with bit and bridle. I patted his neck and spoke gently to him. Still a bit wary of my intentions, he stamped and snorted, laying his ears back with implied threat. But we had performed this dance many times before, and it was well understood by now that I always led it. Should I bring the lance? It seemed a bit excessive for an afternoon trot about the courtyard, but it would be good for us both to practice balancing its heft. I kept my lance hung upon the rear wall of Tempest's stall. Retrieving it, I then led my restive steed toward the stable's doors.

"Moo!" I heard.

Startled, I whirled about, further unsettling Tempest in the process. My grip tightened upon my lance and my face heated as I spied the offender. There, in a stall at the end of the row stood Master Chadwick's flea-bitten animal shaking its horns from side to side and mocking me with its eyes. Would it always be thus? Would that sound forever call to mind the taunts I unknowingly endured from commoners and the falseness of my fellows? I needed to hie from this place lest I suffocate in such reminders of my shame.

And so I emerged from the stables, mounted my steed, and headed out through the main gate. My lance was shipped in an upright position, its heel resting in a special cup cleverly built into my saddle for the purpose. At a trot, its weight seemed to fall awkwardly as we posted, so I urged Tempest up to a canter and it smoothed out. I also missed the weight of a shield on my other arm to counterbalance the effect. Sometimes it is easier to carry two buckets than but one. Up ahead stood the very site of my disgrace: the mill. We gave it a wide berth and pressed on. Soon clear of the small town and its silent laughter, I signaled for greater speed, and Tempest did not disappoint.

Given a free rein, Tempest transitioned to a full gallop without further urging. The reckless tantivy suited my mood, and several miles slid by as the wind lashed the mane and tail of my mount. Onward we sailed out into the countryside, the main thoroughfare giving way to a less traveled trail that wound about the low hills of the western barony. This way lay the part of my liege's demesne not yet enfeoffed to any knight. Nonetheless, it was dotted with occasional fields and farmhouses of the tenants my father deigned to give writs. In their administration my sire cleverly sought to match the talents and predilections of each tenant to the needs of the barony. Here was a wheat field, and yet further on a sawmill, each element providing a needed resource and a suitable livelihood for the willing hands of his subjects.

His initial energy spent, I once again took charge and brought Tempest to a more restful walk. Overhead, the sky had begun to clear. Though still heavily overcast, here and there a sun ray pierced the low-lying mass of gray gloom, shedding its glory upon patches of distant landscape. The fresh air of the outdoors and the steady rhythm of hoof beats combined to lull me into a more contemplative frame of mind.

I considered the code and what it would have of me. 'To keep faith' seemed apt to my situation. Should I simply seek to endure the discourtesies done to me and use them as fuel to bolster the twin graces of modesty and humility? That may be part of the answer to my troubles, but it felt somehow incomplete. I ran through many other tenets of the code in similar fashion, but none seemed relevant until the admonishment to 'Never turn one's back to the foe.' Why did that one stand out so? Who was my foe?

Such were my thoughts when I encountered the maid. She was running across a field on a course set to intercept me while struggling to keep the hem of her long skirt above the sodden grasses of the meadow.

"Please, my lord, you must help us," she shouted as she approached, stopping to wave her arms about frantically.

Her frightened face was framed by the white bonnet customary to a milk maid, and the apron she wore over her bodice dress and blouse seemed to affirm this vocation. In turn, it was likely that she mistook me for a knight, for bearing a lance and upon such a fine steed, what else might I be?

"What is the trouble, and how may I be of service, goodwife?" I asked urgently while steering Tempest off the road to her side.

She forced out her reply between deep gasps of air. "A dangerous beast has descended upon our barn," she said pointing to a structure back behind a farmhouse. "It stalks our herd and threatens the children."

My heart was moved to pity by this and the imploring gaze she directed up at me.

"We shall see to this beast," I declared, wheeling in the direction she had indicated and driving my good steed forward.

When I rounded the farmhouse, I saw it from across an open field. The structure was in fact a pole barn with a back and two sides but completely open in front. Crouched within, stood a beast of legend over the bloodied carcass of a milk cow. Its body was that of a lion but of a size to rival a horse. Affixed to its shoulders sprouted the half-folded wings of a great eagle of a similar dimension, and instead of paws, its forelegs ended in talons. Its head was likewise that of an overlarge bird of prey. As I watched, it was tearing off long strips of flesh from its mangled kill with a cruel hooked beak.

Sensing our approach, the beast abandoned its gruesome feast and raised its great avian head in profile to regard us with one round, yellow eye. Realizing I would get no better opportunity, I decided to charge forward before the creature could win free of the barn and take to the sky. Lacking the spurs of a true knight, I nonetheless dug in and Tempest responded at once. The destrier first reared up and trumpeted his challenge to the heavens, pawing at the air with his hooves. I held my seat only by instincts born of long training.

As we swiftly transitioned to a full gallop across the short field, the beast was not idle. Its tawny hide rippled with the action of the coiled muscles beneath as it spun about and charged us in turn. I lowered my lance and tried to steady its tip while maintaining a firm grip on its stock. We met just at the open side of the barn. As it pounced, talons extended to rend, my lance took it just beneath the collarbone.

The blow was such that I felt a sharp wrenching in my shoulder, and my lance was torn free of my grip. The beast staggered back grievously wounded, but so too was Tempest thrown off his balance, desperately prancing to the left to avoid a fall. Spreading its wings for stability, the monstrous semi-avian arose and made as if to take flight. But Tempest was having none of it. Rearing and whinnying once more, he flailed at the gryphon, ending the maneuver by bringing both front hooves down heavily upon the creatures right wing.

This time, I was not so fortunate as to keep my seat. I tumbled from the saddle to the hardpacked earthen floor. The landing was painful, but I managed to use its momentum to roll back up to my feet. The gryphon now flailed about dragging one wing behind it, but Tempest had also suffered a wound in the exchange. Now riderless, he seemed hesitant to move in close. Instead, he stood his ground menacingly, snorting and stamping.

I unsheathed my sword and advanced upon our wounded adversary. With impossible speed, a talon flashed out to rake across my stomach. My hauberk protected me somewhat from a blow that would surely otherwise have laid me open wide. As its beak descended, I thrust out my sword, using its own downward force to impale it from neck to brain. Silently, the great beast toppled over on its side and stilled, never to rise again.

As the hot blood of the gryphon pooled upon the ground, I staggered over to lean exhausted against a post at the barn's entrance. From behind the farmhouse, a man wielding a pitchfork cautiously drew near. The milk maid and at least three wide-eyed children peered around the jam of the back door. Tempest, still in a high temper moved toward the man.

"Down," I commanded.

Tempest heeded. The dairy farmer nearly did as well. He dropped the pitchfork to one side and swept the broad-brimmed straw hat from his head which he bowed low. Finding his courage, he shouted a question.

"What is your name, my lord," he asked, "that I might commend it to all who would hear the tale when I bear witness to this deed."

"Trenton Arenson," I replied, eschewing the honorific so as not to cause misunderstanding of my rank, "squire to Sir Declan Highcastle."

Though bruised and battered, still I was jubilant. In the distance, I heard a cow lowing and even the now familiar tinkling of a cow bell. But this did nothing to darken my mood. The spell had lost its power over me. I would return to the keep and confront those who would see me laid low. If my friends doubted me, they would soon see the error of their ways. What had Sir Declan said to me? 'Give them a chance, Trenton.' And so I would. I realized that two beasts had been slain this day: the gryphon, and my own self-doubt.

***

In the days that followed, the word spread of my defense of the dairy farm and its denizens. Gryphons had not been seen in these lands for a generation, and I secretly held that providence had played a hand in this one's appearance. At first, the other squires were sheepish about the comments that Myles had made at the feast and their foreknowledge thereof. As Sir Declan later explained to me, the code tells us to 'guard the honor of our fellow knights,' and they thought that they were doing so by not speaking of the matter openly. Myles himself, it seemed, had had a falling out with Sir London over the affair. He had been dismissed from that gentle knight's service. After I made it clear to them all that I took no offense, my relations with them returned to normalcy.

To those closest to me, 'Moo' became a friendly greeting oft used to reference my heroics – not that other event. Reginald even found the courage to propose in jest that I use the cow in my knightly heraldry. But my sire would have none of this. He had his heart set on a gryphon rampant in Arenson blue. Rare was the knight who could rightly lay claim to such a potent symbol, but none could admonish a young knight for choosing a creature he had personally bested in combat. My liege even went so far as to announce the deed far and wide by pigeon.

While most other barons practiced the sport of falconry, Westarbor preferred his pigeons and doves. It was another of the strange innovations in which he had invested. He had heard tell of a recent widow of one of his tenant farmers who fancied birds. This was not a fowler, mind you, who trapped or hunted wild birds. We retained one of those as well. No, rather she *fancied* birds. It started with her chickens and then spread out to

49

include even the native birds in the area. She built little 'bird feeders' to give them seeds to eat and little 'bird houses' for them to live within. Most considered her mad, but my sire thought her brilliant. With the loss of her husband, and with five children to support, he offered her the management of a great project and provided her and her family living space within the keep. He also offered her something he called 'seed money' in a jesting tone, though in truth, I saw no humor in it, as she would obviously need to buy seed.

My liege then converted the entire east tower into a dovecote. It was riddled with holes the birds could use to fly in and out which were cleverly designed to double as arrow slits for defense of the keep. Within, it was divided into different roosts to keep the kings pigeons and those of other fanciers separate from our own. His advisers had argued against the expense until years later the project began to bear fruit. Quite a large number of fresh eggs were produced. Our chamberlain had an exact count, but it was considerable. Moreover, we could eat the birds themselves. They bred as quickly as mice. I had eaten several doves at the feast for Master Chadwick. Our cook prepares a wonderful plum sauce. More traditional fowl such as chickens, geese, and peacocks were kept in coops in the tower's base and cared for by the same family.

In the early years, the nearby farmers became quite irate. For you see, the kept pigeons and doves had a penchant for swarming down to the fields at spring seeding time and greatly shortening the goodmen's yields and tempers. These villeins were somewhat mollified when the baron began rewarding their forbearance by providing each with many sacks of colombine with which to condition their fields. You see, the birds even *shat* benefit for the barony.

But, in my liege's opinion, the greatest benefit of all was care for and separation of his homing pigeons. When I asked him, my liege explained it to me. These birds were amazing. They couldn't carry much - just a small scribbled message for the most part. But they flew straight to their 'home' with great reliability. Over distances as far as perhaps four hundred miles, the birds could usually deliver their tiny packets in just eight hours. As a ludicrous comparison, even if there were a smooth straight road running all the way to the same destination; a fast horse at its full gallop would require sixteen hours to do the same. We all know that any horse would be completely exhausted after but a three hour gallop. Stopping only to eat and sleep, the horse and its rider would in sooth require nearly a month to complete a four hundred mile trek, again along a straight road. Of course, one had to dispatch the rider eventually anyway to retrieve the birds, but the end result for my father was that he could correspond with the king and a select few others very swiftly indeed. The formerly mad bird woman had now become a trusted adviser and a prominent member of our community. It took one of my sire's wisdom to envision such a possibility.

The biggest problem remaining was my sister. She had been avoiding me since the night of the feast, and when we were forced to interact, she did so in a most indifferent manner. I resolved to seek her out and make an effort to rekindle her familial affections. I made my way to her suite of rooms which were near to mine in the rear wing of the castle. My knock upon her door was promptly acknowledged. The door swung half open, and I was met at its threshold by Agatha Grimbley, one of my mother's maids.

"How may I serve, my lord?" she asked.

"I have come to visit my sister," I informed her. "Is she within?"

"The lady Megan is not receiving visitors, my lord," she stated simply.

Oh. It was to be that cheeky game, was it?

"Then tell the lady," I said in a courtly cadence, "that the heir of Westarbor, her brother, desires a word with her and ask her when it might be convenient."

The door swung open further to reveal my sister standing at her guardian's side. Her eyes sought my own. They were the clear blue of our father's eyes, of a hue that I'd oft thought may have inspired the Arenson-blue of our heraldry. And like our sire's, there was an intensity to her gaze as though it could pierce right through to a man's soul.

"I will see him," she said. "You may leave us, Agatha."

The lady's maid paused for a moment, then quietly took her leave.

Opening the door still wider and stepping to one side, Megan asked: "What would you have of me, then?"

Directness often worked best with Megan, so I replied: "You've been avoiding me since the feast. I would know why."

"I've been avoiding *everyone*, Trenton," she said.

"Whatever is the matter?" I asked, growing concerned for my sibling.

"Let us just say I am out of sorts and leave it at that," she said dismissively. "Tell me what else is on your mind, dear brother, for I would rest."

"Why did you appease the mob at the stockade the other night?" I asked, stepping into her chambers. "Did our sire put you up to it?"

"I made father aware of my intent," she confessed. "But, no, Trenton, it was my own idea."

"Why, Megan?" I asked once again. "The lad is a ruffian and a malapert sorely in need of a lesson in manners."

"He is no such thing," she quickly refuted. "His actions saved your *life*, Trenton."

"I heard of the tale he concocted about flames and mill dust," I scoffed, "but I remain incredulous. There is something more you are not telling me."

"They believe he has the gift," Megan mused aloud. "You really should set aside your pride and consider that perhaps he only acted as was needful."

Something strange had happened at that mill. I had not witnessed it directly, as I had been extricating myself from an impromptu mud-bath. But I had seen the miller's boy flee like a jackrabbit from the scene of his offense and was told he had swooned like a frightened maid when finally cornered by my men. In truth, he *had* said something about the lantern, but he was being most ill-mannered at the time.

"Why, then," I asked, "did he boast of my . . . discomfiture, as Myles suggested?"

"Myles is a beast," she snapped, the fiery condemnation disproportionate even to my own feelings about the miscreant. "I'm sure he painted that scene in the worst light possible for poor Lucas."

She stopped, suddenly realizing her gaff.

"Poor Lucas, is it?" I said sternly. Not poor *Trenton*, I noticed. "Are we now on a first name basis with the oaf?"

As we had been speaking, my eyes had wandered over to an old vase that rested on my sister's dresser. Megan had always had a special affinity for flowers. She even made them the main theme of her embroidery work she was taught by our mother. It was commonplace to find fresh flowers in her suite. Strangely, though, the blooms in this vase were not fresh. They looked wilted and abused and not artfully arranged in the least. Moreover, they bore a note. Curious, I began to surreptitiously maneuver toward the dresser.

"I spoke with him just after the event," said Megan. "There is no malice or deceit in him, and he seemed as mystified as any about the incident at the mill. He appears to be just a sweet boy who was caught in a bad situation."

"Oh, he's sweet now as well?" I teased, and closing the remaining distance to the vase, I plucked up the note. Surprised and blushing furiously, Megan moved to snatch it away, but I quickly held it up above her reach. For just a moment, I glimpsed the old Megan, the young sister whom I loved from a time before she had put on courtly graces.

"Give it back, Trenton. That's *private*, you brute," she glowered.

The code instructs us to always 'Respect the honor of women.' I was almost certain that this did not prohibit the dutiful teasing of younger siblings. Then the moment passed. Her composure returned, and she peered at me in weary sufferance.

"You might as well read it, then," she said frostily. "It will only confirm what I just told you."

I regarded the letter:

Dear Lady Megan,

   Please accept these flowers as my thanks for your gracious gesture.  I thought you might enjoy a remembrance of a fellow suffering in durance not so vile.  I haven't anything to give that is of equal value to your kindness of that day, but should you ever find yourself in need of my assistance, I will do all in my power to aid you.  I wish you and your family well.

Forever Your Servant,

*Lucas Harper*

"Does he even *know* what a bouquet of oathbloom signifies?" I asked.

"I don't know," replied Megan, flustered. "We were gathering them for your oaths of knighthood. They were simply near to hand when I struck upon my plan to aid the boy. I didn't get the chance to talk to him again before he was whisked away to Arborvale. I doubt he did aught but collect them up from the ground and intended nothing apart from the simple gratitude he professes."

"And yet you keep them," I noted.

***

From the west tower, I looked out once more over the barony. The people of Meadowfork scurried about their tasks as the wind brought the first cold bite of winter. Snow blanketed the fields beyond, and any trees that lacked the grace of needles stood a stark and naked vigil, patiently awaiting the return of spring. The great wheel of the mill was turning once more after its long hiatus for repair and refurbishment. This was most timely. The bakers had nearly depleted their stores of flour, and we had all grown accustomed to the loaves that fine milling provided.

This brought my thoughts back to the miller's son. Should he prove to be a mage, that would place him on a social footing nearly equal to my own, but I still found him sorely lacking in character. Megan seemed to hold him in some esteem, and I knew her to possess good discernment of a person's worth. But could her judgment be trusted in this instance? Who could know what flights of fancy might twist the fickle heart of a maiden of her years? I hoped my sister wouldn't waste a moment mooning over 'Sweet Lucas.' The lout was hardly worth considering. This was doubtless one of the reasons my sire had him 'whisked away.' Good riddance. We had more weighty matters to consider.

The date of the ceremony had been set. At long last, I was to be granted the tremendous honor and responsibility of knighthood. While I had always known I was destined to be made a knight, the timing had been somewhat in doubt. Squires often saw as many as twenty-one seasons before they stood their vigil. My liege had left the matter firmly in the hands of my knight so that he could be petitioned and do the dubbing himself. Sir Declan had noted changes in me recently. It was more than the slaying of the gryphon, though that feat and why I had attempted it stood firmly in my favor. He said that I had a new-found confidence, and it showed in my treatment of my fellow squires and dealings with others. He also cited the restraint I had managed when provoked at the feast, deeming it a further sign of my readiness. With my eighteenth birthday but a fortnight away, it had been decided to combine the celebrations on the winter solstice. I could scarcely wait.

CHAPTER FOUR

# The Shepherd

"Let the great world spin for ever down the ringing grooves of change."

*~ Alfred Lord Tennyson ~*

When we first arrived, I thought that the modest, rustic cottage on the hill belonged to Master Chadwick, but I was soon to be disabused of this notion. The old wizard skillfully guided the cart through the double-doors of a large outbuilding. No sooner had we unhitched mister Strongback, than a stout woman of middle age came sweeping in. Actually, her voice preceded her by a few steps as her mouth was already running at a full gallop.

"Elizar," she crooned, "I hope you remembered to bring back my madder root and the other supplies from Meadowfork. And the roof is leaking again. I swear, you take better care of this barn than you do the house. If my mother were alive, she would weep for the mess in the parlor . . ."

As she caught sight of Royland and me, she paused in mid-tirade, placed her hands on her ample hips, and swung a questioning glare toward my mentor. Master Chadwick looked almost, well, *sheepish*, standing there with mister Strongback's harness slung across one arm.

"Tilda," he began gamely, "I would like to introduce Royland Wagge and Lucas Harper," indicating us each in turn. "These two young men have come to apprentice with me to learn the mystical arts. Boys, this is Goody Matilda Fowler, gracious owner of this domicile and mistress of the distaff."

As he spoke, she turned to regard us. Royland began fidgeting and staring at his boots.

"A pleasure to make your acquaintance, Goody Matilda," I supplied trying to attract her attention.

"Young man," she snapped, her scrutiny still locked upon my cousin. "don't you know it's only civil to meet a person's eyes when introduced?"

Royland wrestled his regard up from the floor to briefly meet that of the matron. Then he turned his head to one side, his face reddening.

"Oh, a shy one, eh?" she said, her expression thawing a bit. "Well, I'm pleased to meet you both as well, I suppose. And just call me Tilda. Everyone does."

"For how long will these young guests be staying, might I ask?" inquired Tilda.

"Not guests, Tilda," corrected Master Chadwick, handing me the harness, "*apprentices*. We could use a couple of strong backs around the ranch, could we not?"

"Must you always," she said in a tone of mild vexation, "deflect an honest question with another question of your own?"

Master Chadwick appeared to consider this for a moment then innocently replied, "Do I do that?"

Her jowls quivered, and she released a short bark of laughter as the tension eased from her frame.

"You are incorrigible, Elizar." she sniffed. "Why don't you get these two cleaned up while I go see what's in the pantry for their supper? I've already eaten at a *decent* hour. You can tell me all about it over evening tea."

Her single raised eyebrow threatened a more fulsome inquisition to follow. Master Chadwick began fishing about in the bed of the cart. His efforts soon produced a small bag which he proffered to Tilda with aplomb.

"Your madder root, madam," he announced.

Tilda's eyes sparkled as she accepted the blatant peace offering and headed back toward the cottage. She could still be heard muttering to no one in particular as she departed. "It's a wonder. He *does* listen sometimes. Still the old goat brings two new mouths to feed with nary a word of warning and expects I'll just be pleased as punch..."

"Pay her no mind," Master Chadwick advised, "Tilda spent a lot of time alone before I signed on here. Sometimes she just likes hearing the sound of her own voice."

We finished stowing mister Strongback's tack and harness on a set of hooks. An ox, being a castrated bull, combines the great strength of its more fully functioning brethren with a far milder temperament. Mister Strongback was no exception. Master Chadwick gently steered him to a stall in the back of the barn while Royland fell easily into step behind them. Showing unusual awareness of the world around himself, my cousin took the initiative to fill the feeder with some fresh hay. I had to remind myself that Roy had grown up on uncle Robert's farm; the familiar tasks of tending animals were probably second nature to him by now.

"Stop your woolgathering, Lucas," admonished Master Chadwick. "There shall be time enough for that in the spring."

So, we three marched out behind the barn, where sat an old well. It was ringed with mortared stones to a height well above my knees. Atop this stood a pair of sturdy wooden beams holding aloft a small peaked roof to ward away any detritus that might fall from above to taint it. Between the beams rested a rounded pole wound about with a hempen rope. A set of tin buckets hung from hooks on its eaves. Because the cottage was on a hilltop, I reasoned that the well must be fairly deep to reach the waters below. My assumption was proven when Master Chadwick released the pail at the rope's end to drop for four or five seconds before a hollow splash reverberated from its darkened depths.

"One of your tasks, Lucas," began my master, "will be to draw up water each day . . .

Master Chadwick was interrupted from his discourse by a mournful, trumpeting howl which descended in pitch into a set of short 'wuffs.' Bounding up the hill came a most unusual hound. His head and chest were stark white in hue, abruptly changing to a dingy gray at his shoulders and on all of his hindquarters beyond save for his four boots. His coat was a tangled mass of fur nearly as thick as the fleece of a sheep. Most striking was the long hair of his face and head. It hung down in thick bangs that I thought must surely deprive him of vision and framed his panting jowls.

The wizard smiled and slouched forward to present his upturned palm to meet the onrushing, hairy bundle of vitality. Just as I thought a collision was assured, the dog skidded to a full stop and, quivering all over, set about bathing Master Chadwick's hand with his tongue.

"Wuff," he said, sitting back on his haunches.

"Yes, I know, Sampson," said the old man gently in reply, "but I have returned now. How fares the flock?"

"Ehr-Wuff," whined Sampson cocking one ear erect.

"Very good," said Master Chadwick. "Sampson, these are Lucas and Royland, they will be working with us for a while. Boys, meet Sampson. Offer him your hand, so he can get your scent."

Reluctantly, I did so. Sampson approached to snuffle my palm. His nose was wet and slimy. Then circling around, he embarked upon a more thorough exploration of my anatomy than I felt was needful or proper. Seemingly satisfied, he then gave Royland the same treatment. I thought this would upset my cousin, but he didn't seem to mind it much.

"Now return to the flock," said Master Chadwick pointing his finger to a distant meadow. "I'll bring your dinner out after I've had my own."

And in an instant, the dog was surging back down the hillside with his stubby, white-tipped tail sweeping behind him.

"Does he understand what you say, master?" I asked.

The old man graced me with a good-natured grin.

"My boy, shepherds control sheep dogs through hand gestures," he explained. "Sometimes I speak to him aloud because it can get very lonely out on the meadow. Besides, who can say how much a dog might understand?"

I noticed that he had not directly answered my question and had then quickly posed one of his own. Tilda just might have the measure of the old fraud.

"Ah," I said intelligently, "that explains it then."

Dinner was a casual affair at Fowler Ranch. Tonight, it included a roasted haunch of lamb, some cornbread, and a small tankard of ale. Royland and I sat across from one another, each to one side of the master. After Tilda retreated to her kitchen, we ate in silence for a time. Royland mostly kept his eyes down on his plate. Master Chadwick only picked at his food, giving each of us an assessing glance from time to time. Finally, he spoke.

"It has been some time since I have had more than one apprentice," he said. "Royland will present a challenge with so much to unlearn, but I'm reasonably sure that he will respond nicely to my usual teaching methods. I confess I am somewhat at a loss as to where to begin *your* lessons, Lucas."

Royland paused and then continued eating.

"Why is that, master?" I asked.

"It's that your innate talents seem so potent," he replied. "I've never met a boy who could lift a sixteen-hundred pound millstone with no formal training. I dare say such a feat would tax even a master's powers."

Royland became attentive at this, his food forgotten, and gave me the briefest of glances.

"Yes, well..." I temporized, "I still don't know how that happened."

***

The practice field was little more than a large circle of dirt surrounded by a low fence. From its pungent bouquet, I suspected it might double as a holding pen for the sheep. At one end, stood a mannequin the like of which a dress-maker or armorer might use. A small cart rested on the other side of the fenced-in area filled with a variety of undressed field stones. These averaged about the size of my head. Master Chadwick walked over behind the cart with Royland and I in tow.

"The task is simple," he said. "You are to lift a stone and hurl it at the quintain using the power of your magic. Royland, please demonstrate."

At this, Royland thrust his chin up and half-lidded his eyes as his brow furrowed in concentration. 'Levare conicere,' he muttered. One of the larger stones atop the pile began to lift above the others. When it was clear of the stack, my cousin made a sweeping gesture with his arms toward the mannequin. As he did, the stone heaved forward spinning through the air to land a few paces to the right of the target with a dull thud.

"Well done boy," said the old man with an approving nod. "You need to work on your aim, but that was a fine effort. Now it's your turn, Lucas."

I stared at the pile of stones atop the cart and mentally selected a medium-sized one near its apex. I touched my magic center as I had been instructed and set about the task of hoisting the stone. 'Levare conicere,' I incanted. Though I felt the strain immediately, nothing happened. I pushed harder and was rewarded only with a dull ache at the back of my head.

"You may begin, Lucas," repeated Master Chadwick, "and holding your breath will not help."

Realizing that I had been doing just that abruptly broke my concentration on the task. I paused, took several slow, deep breaths, and focused on a much smaller stone from the pile. It took all of my mental strength and tricks to affect it. When it began to rise, I adopted a spread-legged stance and copied the sweeping gesture I'd seen Royland use, bearing down with all the mental force I could muster.

My little fist-sized rock gave a feeble hop toward the target, bouncing only a few feet from the bed of the cart.

Royland sniggered, then immediately look ashamedly down at his feet.

Master Chadwick scratched his ear and said with a bemused expression, "Where is all that power you used at the mill the other day? Describe what you were thinking at that time."

What indeed? I frantically searched my memory of those events. When the stone had fallen and trapped father's arm, I had been panic-stricken. I had strongly wished for the millstone to be lifted free. Hmm, to be lifted, but not necessarily by my power. Though the spindle had been disengaged, I had only ever seen the runner stone lifted from the bed stone by the turning power of the mill itself and by extension, the weight of the water turning the great wheel. My hasty prayer had been for some greater force to lift the stone.

I found this hard to put into words, but as my master drew out my halting explanation, his expression grew quizzical. "Not what I had expected," he muttered. "What you seem to be saying is that the force to lift the stone was already present, and your amazing feat was in somehow connecting to it. I must think upon this. For the present, you two continue the exercise. It never hurts to build up one's magical strength."

The morning progressed with Royland punishing the target dummy with head-sized stones while I lobbed the smaller rocks toward it with varying degrees of success. After studying and mimicking Royland's gestures and techniques for a while, my best 'throw' was about twelve yards. The ache at the back of my head had grown up and had children by the time the sun rose toward midday. My cousin also looked fatigued. When Tilda rang the triangle at noon, he lurched over to the fence and sat down with a groan.

"Hard work, that," sighed Royland, tiredly looking off into the sky.

Amazingly, the boy could speak three words together when he wanted to, it seemed. I only nodded, not wanting him to turtle up again. I walked over to the mannequin to see what damage had been wrought by Royland's barrage. It had certainly been under no threat from me. I had seen the target suffer solid hits repeatedly throughout the morning. Despite being made of wood, it seemed but little worse for wear. Running my hand over its smooth surface, I spotted Royland's head bobbing in a nod.

"Master Chadwick enchanted it," he explained. "It'd have to be hit a lot harder to muss it. Let's clean up and go get some lunch. Tilda'll scold us if we come in filthy."

Apparently, his dam had burst.

After a lunch of vegetable stew and buttery biscuits, the old wizard took us back to the practice pitch. He had a flat wooden box that floated effortlessly through the air behind him. Glancing balefully at my efforts scattered behind the cart he said, "Clearly you lack the considerable magical strength I had envisioned, but perhaps you possess a *different* genius."

Plucking the box from the air, he presented it to me lengthwise, its lid opening seemingly of its own accord. Inside rested a crossbow of the large, heavy variety used by some men at arms. I remembered that most of Lord Westarbor's soldiers had employed longbows for war. They maintained a few crossbows for the peasant levies manning the walls, however, because they were much simpler to operate without much training. My shoulders sagged in disappointment as I lifted the bow from its case. The crossbow was rather looked down upon for its limited speed of reloading.

"I had hoped to learn magic," I said.

"And so you shall," replied the old man, sending the empty case through the air with casual ease to settle on the back of the nearly empty cart. "But, for the remainder of the afternoon, I would like you to loose these quarrels into the target while Royland practices shielding it. Begin."

I hadn't actually ever discharged a crossbow before, but the principle seemed straightforward. This particular crossbow had a heavy steel cranequin. This is basically a gearbox hung by a noose over the rear stock of the bow. The front end hooks over the string to either side. A lever about half as long as my forearm sockets into the cranequin and can be turned with relative ease to pull back on the string. A quarrel is then fitted in front of the string, aimed, and released by pulling a trigger along the bottom. The only challenge, I discovered, was to perform any of these tasks at all quickly. Even aiming wasn't difficult. After the first couple of volleys, I found my distance and could hit the target regularly with little effort.

Then Royland stepped in. Standing about six feet to the left of the target, he would wait until I took aim then raise his hands palms-out with his thumbs and forefingers touching. As I released, he would incant an odd word that I would later learn was 'impedimente,' and a dim blue circular screen would briefly appear before the target. When my quarrel met the disc, it would stop in its forward flight and drop soundlessly to the ground. *When had he learned that trick?*

Master Chadwick watched me load and loose all twenty quarrels without comment. Although at first I was embarrassingly awkward, I felt I had gotten the hang of it and acquitted myself decently on the last half dozen or so shots. I ran over to retrieve the spent quarrels, most of which lay in an untidy pile just before the target.

When I returned, the old mage beckoned me over to where he sat upon a fence railing in the shade of a poplar tree.

"Take a break, Roy-boy!" he hollered. Royland took a long draw on his water skin as he lowered himself to a seated position. "As for you, Lucas, I would like to teach you a new spell. Hand me the crossbow."

As I did so, he stood up and cradled it in his left arm.

"This spell requires a certain manner of thought. These words and gestures will help you achieve that frame of mind. I hope they will eventually prove unnecessary. Watch and listen closely now."

The old man pointed at the cranequin with his right index finger which he began rotating in a circular fashion while softly chanting 'spacium girabit.' I could sort of see what he did with my developing mage sight, a kind of empathy we had for magic worked nearby when we had a chance to observe it closely.

Suddenly the crank handle began to spin madly, almost blurring from sight as the bow string creaked back into place. A wide grin split Master Chadwick's face as he pointed the crossbow up into the air. He pulled the trigger releasing the tension on the string as it loosed with a vibrant 'twang.'

"Now you try, young man," he commanded.

It looked easy. I soon found this impression was in error. As I centered my magic and dropped into focus, I tried repeating the gestures I'd seen while I spoke the words. At first, nothing happened. Then, as in a daydream, I began to see the shadow of a pinwheel turning in my mind's eye. I struggled to overlay the phantom wheel with the crank handle to move it. As I got close, suddenly the handle twitched, and I felt a jarring, ringing sensation in my ears, followed by a wave of dizziness and nausea, causing me to lose focus entirely. I fell to one knee and nearly dropped the crossbow.

"Almost - Try a slower pace," said Chadwick in his maddeningly patient tone.

Beginning anew was far more difficult, the words and motions immediately triggered a fresh wave of nausea and my gorge rose. I managed to suppress it and continue. I spoke more slowly this time, my finger describing lazy circles over the cranequin. Eventually, the shadowy pinwheel re-emerged, its blades turning much more slowly. Afraid to engage it again, this time I merely watched, trying to bring it into sharper focus. My mind began to drift and imagine other things that turned such as a wheel on the cart or my father's great waterwheel. That last image solidified and merged somehow with my pinwheel, granting it more power and substance. Holding it all together with a will, I latched this composite to the cranequin which began to turn in a stately rhythm.

I smiled as the string slowly drew back to the loading position and locked there. Banishing the spell construct, I was momentarily staggered once more. The ground and everything in my vision seemed to keep making little half-turns like that time I had drunk too much ale at the fall harvest celebration. But then everything seemed to firm up and stabilize.

"Well, I'll be," exclaimed Master Chadwick. "I've never seen anyone take to that spell so quickly before. You won't be needing this anymore."

And with that, the old man reached over and unsocketed the crank handle from the cranequin.

"I want twenty more quarrels shot into that target by supper time," he said. "Break's over, Roy-boy!" he then shouted. "Get on your feet and ready to shield!"

As the old fellow ambled back toward the cottage, I wondered how on earth I would manage that spell twenty more times this afternoon. I already felt drained and woozy from my earlier attempts. I supposed that at least Royland would have it easy, and it turned out that I was right. As my initial triumph waned, my loading time increased because it took me ever longer to recover my balance between shots. Royland just shrugged and used the extra time to carry all of the field stones back to the cart. He never failed with his kinetic shield to stop my quarrels from striking their target.

At dinner that evening, I ate lightly. It seemed the ache at the back of my head and his children had invited their neighbors over for a drunken barn dance.

Master Chadwick picked guiltily at his plate, finally saying, "So, you did it eh? All twenty?"

"Yes," I replied.

Royland nodded in earnest affirmation.

"Then there can be no doubt," said my master. "You, young sir, have a talent."

"A talent?" I asked.

"Yes, a talent," he said again. "It is rare enough for a man to be born a mage, but occasionally there is one among us who possesses a special talent, something beyond what other mages can do. You, Lucas, are a Winder."

He said this last word with a long 'I,' meaning to wind something up - not to blow like a breeze.

"A Winder? What's that?" I inquired.

"A Winder," Master Chadwick announced, "is a mage especially attuned to the turning force of the earth. For most, the 'spacium girabit' spell is well beyond journeyman difficulty. Although masters like myself can do it, we can't generally do it for long, and it takes a great deal out of us."

"Wait," I said. "Surely, just turning a crank is not such a major accomplishment."

"Indeed, it is not," he chuckled ruefully. "There are any number of lesser spells to apply physical force to an inanimate object. These use up the power you personally possess. Your stone hurling exercise from earlier today is one example. A mage of sufficient strength and finesse can simply 'grab' the knob to turn the lever. But 'spacium girabit' makes use of the turning force of the world, the same force that causes the stars to cross over the night sky. When I showed you the spell, I purposely misled you into thinking it was something simpler, because for you I suspected it could become so. I confess that after that one brief use of it, I have been napping all afternoon while the room spun about. Your recovery rate must be phenomenal and should only improve as your talent grows. Forgive me. As your master, I had to know whether you possessed this rare natural ability. Given sufficient training and using 'spacium girabit,' there may be no practical upper limit to the force that you can bring to bear on your surroundings."

For a long time thereafter, the only sound to disturb the silence was Royland's fork tapping his plate in deft, even strokes.

***

Royland and I were given the guest room of the cottage. It was small. One of its two beds had been built atop the other in a style the ranchers called bunks. My cousin quickly claimed the bottom-most, leaving me to climb up to the other. I had assured Master Chadwick we were both early risers. To my regret, I soon discovered that Royland, despite being so quiet throughout the day, snored most dreadfully. His nocturnal symphony disturbed my slumber and left me bleary-eyed and ill-rested on the following morn. When I bemoaned my plight to Master Chadwick, he simply grinned and suggested I count sheep.

Throughout the following weeks, my training regimen was much the same. Over time, the dizziness from winding my crossbow became only a fleeting effect. Although it helped, I no longer needed to incant the words aloud to achieve the special mental state of 'spacium girabit.' My hand gesture was abbreviated to one simple loop with my finger. It still tired me a bit, though. Better still, with practice, I found I could slow down or significantly accelerate the speed of rotation. I could now cock back that crossbow almost as fast as I could lay the quarrels into its tiller. Rather than dismissing the spell between shots, I learned to hold onto it and split my concentration to aim at the target, which I could then pepper with five or six shots in a row. Royland was soon overwhelmed when attempting to shield the target, but he always made a game effort. He began making weaker screens that he could hold for longer, depositing them at an angle so that my shots would glance off to one side or the other. I even began to look forward to my daily water hauling task. I found I could easily draw the pail up by turning the well's crank with my winding. The buckets were still heavy to carry after I'd filled them, but it really wasn't any great distance to the house or the barn.

Master Chadwick spent some time each day reviewing our progress and updating our assignments. He would now often give us something in the morning that burned up most of our magical power. However, unlike that first day, our afternoons were spent working on the ranch. We mended fences, found stray sheep, chopped firewood, and performed a myriad of other necessary tasks while he holed up in the warm cottage with his studies.

The animal husbandry proved both interesting and enjoyable. Through the winter we had to make sure the sheep had a break from the wind, access to water, and we set out an occasional bale of hay mixed with corn silage. We sometimes set out blocks of salt. The sheep never got cold. One morning after a heavy snowfall, I was amazed to see one walking around the meadow with five inches of snow resting upon its back. When I remarked on this, Master Chadwick just laughed and explained that sheep generated a lot of heat as they processed the plant fibers in their stomachs, and that their fleeces were excellent insulators. The number of books on our bookshelf began to multiply as Master Chadwick demanded we study many mundane topics as well as magical theory.

Watching over the flock day and night was the tireless old sheepdog. He could sometimes be seen bouncing around the edge of the meadow reining in strays, or perched up at a vantage point keeping a lazy eye on things. No matter how cold the day, Master Chadwick himself always brought dinner out to Sampson and spent some time out there on the meadows. Sometimes I'd swear the two were conversing.

As the days grew longer, new life began to return to the valley. The meadows showed the first hints of green. Many new tasks arose to be handled as we prepared for spring sheering and the lambing of the ewes. Perhaps due to the relaxed atmosphere of the ranch, Royland was starting to speak his mind more often. He was opening up, especially to the old man. Whatever the task, the young man stood ever at our master's side acting as a second pair of hands and even offering his advice upon occasion. Feeling the odd man out, I began to envy their close relationship. One day, when Royland was busy chopping wood for the hearth and Master Chadwick had enlisted my aid in examining the sheep for ticks, I decided to ask him about it.

"Master," I hesitantly began, "are you teaching Royland more because I am so weak in magic?"

"Eh?" he said, turning from the ewe he was probing as I held it still. "What makes you say that?"

"Well," I began, "you taught him that shielding spell on our first day, and he talks with you more than anyone else I've seen. He rarely spares two words for me."

"I see," the old man harrumphed. "Bring us another one, Sampson," he shouted over his shoulder as he stood from the ewe's side.

Taking that as my queue, I too arose and led the recalcitrant animal to the gate. I released her to happily rejoin her fellows in the meadow beyond the pen. Sampson skillfully cut a new ewe from among those huddled at the pen's far end. I noted no hand gestures were employed as the dog delivered this offering to Master Chadwick, who deftly brought the sheep to its belly and knelt beside her.

As he bent to his inspection, his hands running through the matted fleece of her back, neck and sides, he began to speak: "Your cousin has a lot to deal with, Lucas."

The ewe became unsettled, and I promptly dropped to my knees beside her and rolled her to her side. I had learned that when a sheep couldn't get her feet planted, she became much easier to manage. With an appreciative grunt, my master continued his probing and the sharing of his thoughts.

"From what I've gleaned thus far," he began, "Royland has been blessed, or perhaps one should say cursed, with an overabundance of magic. Since he was a little boy, he has been troubled by an incessant buzzing in his head. Over time, he found that by focusing intently on but a single task, he could overcome the distraction."

"That's terrible, master," I said with sympathy. I was suddenly glad that my little green patch was not so demanding.

"Moreover," continued the old mage, "Royland has a talent much like your winding. He can feel the emotions of others by touch or upon meeting their gaze. Since not all people have nice thoughts about him, he has learned to flinch away from such contact. It is very similar to a minor talent known to run along the Arenson line. *Another, Sampson, if you please.*"

As we swapped ewes again, I reflected on my cousin. It all made perfect sense. It explained why Royland, with so little interaction, always seemed to know who meant him ill and whom he could trust.

"Finally," Master Chadwick said, already busied with the next sheep, "have you noticed when your cousin seems to move his lips but no sound issues forth?"

"Indeed I have, master," I said, still reeling from these revelations. "He does it when he's upset."

"I believe that at such times," said our master, "Royland is accessing his magic to cast a personal spell that silences or greatly muffles the sounds and emotions which batter him. He has learned quite a few spells on his own and without the benefit of proper instruction. One of them is the shield spell you've seen him practicing. I am at present, trying to teach him to couple these abilities to words in the old tongue. For in his ignorance, he invokes them unconsciously whenever he says words like 'quiet,' 'stop,' or 'protect.' It's why he hesitates to speak much."

"How did he tell you all of this, master?" I asked.

"That was the key breakthrough, Lucas," Master Chadwick replied. "You see, Royland found that when his magic becomes exhausted, the buzzing ceases for a time. That is why I've been taking him off privately just after your morning workouts. Does this begin to answer your questions?"

"It's a lot to take in, master," I replied with new-found humility.

"Then take it as grist for your mill, Lucas," quipped the old man. "Do not doubt that your cousin loves you, and count yourself fortunate to be among his friends, for I predict that one day he will make a most fitting mage in the service of Osten. And rest assured that even as I get him sorted out, I am considering how best to nurture your own unique gifts. Ah . . . ," he paused.

Drawing forth a long, slender pair of forceps, he dug through the fleece to expose a bloated tick clinging fiercely to the ewe's neck.

"Praemium," he exclaimed while pointing his forefinger straight at the offending blister with his thumb held upright.

The tick burst asunder with a crimson splatter as the sheep bleated plaintively and kicked in fright.

***

Tilda was rarely idle. When not performing domestic chores around the cabin, she could be seen pottering around the place tilling up small gardens. She would mark each with a crossed set of sticks to indicate which herbs were seeded there. Most of these were not the familiar herbs for flavoring food. Indeed, some I knew to be quite poisonous. Instead, Tilda planted woad for making blue dye; turmeric and weld, for yellow, and so on. She encouraged several lichens as well for their use in making dyes.

Any heavy work, however, fell squarely upon my and Royland's narrow shoulders. After spending several days behind an ox-drawn plow, Master Chadwick taught us a new spell he called 'Earth furrow.' As expected, Royland's use of it proved far more effective than mine. Whereas he could churn up a ten-foot stretch of ground with a single casting, my efforts just punched through the hard-packed soil of last year's fields to produce a barely adequate mole hill. Still, a row of these proved a sufficient target for a handful of seeds or bulbs, so I was soon relegated to assisting Tilda with her herbaries.

I thanked the stars that this was a sheep ranch and not a full-fledged farm. Nevertheless, we spent a couple of weeks preparing the small fields and gardens that most any estate maintained to produce a modest spring crop of beans and barley. Master Chadwick filled his days 'inspecting the meadows' and otherwise tending to his flock. We also planted a whole large garden with flax and fenced it in. Apparently, the sheep liked to roll about in it, and this needed to be discouraged.

Though fairly isolated, the little valley did have its visitors. Wagons came out occasionally to restock us with food and other perishable items. Sometimes a neighboring rancher would come for dinner to negotiate grazing or watering rights or to offer the breeding services of a prized ram. My master explained that any flaws in the ewes could be overcome by breeding them to a superior ram. This gave rise to the sheep herder's mantra that 'the ram is half the flock.' Master Chadwick had several rams which exemplified the traits he hoped to breed into his flock. His favorite was 'Big Barney,' a snow white, fine-wool ram who was a very successful breeder. According to my master, the fine-wool sheep produced a much smaller fleece, but the quality of the resulting wool more than made up for its paucity. Fine-wool made garments that didn't itch when close to the skin, and thus could command a much higher price.

With the visitors came news from the village. My father was well on the road to recovery. The mill was back in operation, faithfully grinding out the lord's flour from stores in its granary. Batches were sufficient to keep the bakers happy and the lord's table full. Uncle Robert and his wife had moved in to assist my father while he convalesced. I wished I could visit them, but the terms of my apprenticeship did not allow me to leave the ranch for the first year. Somewhat surprisingly, Gregor Cain had asked to apprentice under my father in the miller's art. With my being away, I suppose there was a vacancy for a young set of arms and legs. If it worked out, I felt sorry for the bullfrogs at the mill pond. Their lazy days would be at an end.

Tilda received a letter from her sister, Karina, and recited it to us. I knew her as Goodwife Galloway, the town's main baker. Karina had been very busy. She had to prepare baked goods for a five-day feast in Meadowfork that led up to the knighting ceremony for the baron's son. Trenton, now Sir Trenton in truth, it seemed, had ridden out into the barony and slain a gryphon that was terrorizing the land. All of the knights of Westarbor had ridden in to welcome him into their noble ranks. There had even been an emissary from Guy Lord Downham from the east. Our good baron had had the gryphon stuffed and mounted in his council chamber. Karina assured Tilda that it was a fearsome sight indeed.

With the spring planting all but complete, and the breeding arrangements for the flock concluded, our lives began to settle into more relaxed patterns. Mornings were filled with new demanding exercises always of some practical use to the ranch. I often thought privately I was as much an apprentice shepherd as I was an apprentice mage. The ewes had begun to lamb, growing gravid and requiring more of Master Chadwick's attention, but he still made time each morning to line up and supervise our lessons.

One overcast morning while in the midst of an interesting exercise in splitting wood with the 'Force Axe' spell, Master Chadwick suddenly jumped up in uncharacteristic alarm. "There's trouble in the south meadow!" he declared urgently. "Arm yourselves and come quickly." With that, he sprinted off.

Royland turned to me with a dumbfounded expression that I was sure he saw reflected on my own face. The old man had never before seemed this startled by anything. I scooped up my crossbow with which I had practiced earlier. Royland's gaze cast about the yard and came to rest upon the wood cutter's axe he had been using during the initial stages of our lesson. He snatched it up, and we began running toward the south field in pursuit of our master.

I neared the hedge row that marked the edge of the south meadow out of breath and with the beginnings of a stitch in my side. Despite his long gangly strides Royland lagged behind several paces. As I burst through the hedge, I could tell immediately that something was amiss. The flock was all huddled at the near end of the field milling about and bleating nervously. On the far side of the meadow bordering a small wooded area, the great, shaggy dog, Sampson, was growling and yipping. With his head kept low to the ground and his hackles raised, he was bobbing and weaving about in a half circle around something I couldn't quite make out. He appeared to be favoring a paw.

Master Chadwick was about halfway across the field. He was frantically making the hand signals he used for Sampson to return, but the dog didn't disengage, so focused was he on something about the size of a wheel barrow.

I began forcing my way through the milling flock. As I thought of my crossbow, my training served me well. My mind slipped easily into 'spacium girabit,' and with barely a glance, the cranequin whirred as the string softly clicked into place. Finally emerging from the flock, I scrambled to set a quarrel into place while Royland ran ahead with his ax.

When at last his circling brought the dog to a vantage point to spy the old man, he cocked his head in sudden awareness and began bounding back toward him. Then the creature (for a creature it was) lurched into motion. Before my horrified eyes was the largest spider I had ever seen. It had been hunkered down in the weeds. Erect, it stood taller than Sampson, perhaps as high as my waist. It was brown and hairy with too many black orbs for eyes. Its brown and black-banded legs bristled with some kind of fur and splayed out to the length of an ox cart.

Even dragging its bulbous abdomen, it was fast - perhaps too fast for old Sampson, whose limp had grown more pronounced. In fear for the dog I took aim and let fly my bolt. Royland had halted his forward advance, staring at his axe in sudden distaste. Then many things happened all at once. Time seemed to slow for me as my first quarrel missed. I had neglected to shoot ahead of the now swiftly moving target. Without my conscious thought, the cranequin was already spinning up for a second shot. Emitting a sharp hiss, the monstrous arachnid sprang through the air toward the retreating canine. Royland had dropped his axe and adopted his shielding stance. I had never seen him succeed at such a distance, but fear must have lent urgency to his cast because a familiar pale blue disc flickered above and behind Sampson. As the airborne spider struck this meager protection, it was deflected to one side long enough for Samson to veer off and make his escape.

Master Chadwick, now only a few yards from the fray, stretched his hand forth, palm outward, and produced a long gout of crimson colored flame. As the fire played over the beast, it cringed back and attempted a hasty withdrawal toward the trees. It was moving awkwardly and seemed unsure of its direction. Setting a quarrel into the flight groove of my bow, I took aim and let loose. This time I was rewarded with a loud screech as my bolt slammed home behind the creature's ugly head. It wobbled and dipped to the ground. As it continued to drag itself slowly forward on twitching members, Master Chadwick advanced still brandishing his flame. The creature stilled, and its legs curled up as its roasting corpse rolled over onto its back.

A hand came to rest firmly on my shoulder. This jarred my attention from the spectacle before me. I glanced over to see Royland staring at my crossbow. He nodded once approvingly in my direction and then began jogging toward our master. The old man was leaning forward with his hands resting on his thighs drawing and expelling deep breaths. He scowled at the large carcass from which an oily black smoke still wafted. Chadwick quickly turned his attention to Sampson. The old dog looked to be on his last legs. Blood seeped from a deep gash in his front left shoulder marring the muddy gray of his coat. He took several trembling steps to his master and then lay down. I joined them in short order.

After a brief examination, Master Chadwick's frown deepened. "Poison," he pronounced. "I need to attend to him straightaway. Royland, help me get Sampson to the barn. Lucas, I'd like you to stay and tend the flock. Try to herd them back to the house. If you should spot another mygalom, retreat and get help."

"Alright, master," I replied. I decided that my many questions could wait when I heard the profound worry in his voice. With upraised palms, Master Chadwick caused the wounded hound to rise up from the ground. Royland cradled him in his arms, and they hustled away leaving me with my own set of problems.

Approaching the main flock, I spotted Big Barney. The ram had been placed in this meadow to breed the ewes here. A ram, especially in breeding season, could be overly aggressive and was not to be taken lightly. The sheep were still bleating restlessly. Worse, they had formed several splinter groups apart from the main huddle and some individuals had begun to stray off in panic from the smoke. I was sure that Sampson could have quickly restored order, but my master was counting on *me*. Cautious not to breech the animals' flight zone, I ran over to retrieve a water bucket that had been left out. I quickly emptied it and tossed in all of the loose pebbles I could find nearby.

Although it is true that sheep can be terribly ornery, and my luck with driving them anywhere was poor in the best of circumstances, I also recalled that most sheep will come along greedily when they think they are going to get grain to eat. Yes, they recognized me as I rattled the bucket and calmly approached. At first a few showed some curiosity, then more and more began to shoulder their way forward. I rattled the bucket enticingly again while clucking my tongue and backing away slowly. Before long the whole flock began to follow. It seemed my bluff had succeeded. I would have to make a point of getting them some actual grain when we arrived.

***

Back at the house, I saw Tilda harnessing mister Strongback. After coaxing the flock into a fenced-in field, I made good on my promise of grain for all then hurried over to help her. She explained that she was heading into town to inform the baron's men and to stay with her sister there. Royland and my master were in the barn tending to the injured sheepdog. After a careful look around, I headed in that direction.

"Master," I cried when I spotted them in a corner stall. "will Sampson be alright?" The old dog lay on his side with his chest rising and falling in a regular rhythm. A variety of tools lay strewn about. There were a pair of fleecing sheers, a bar of lye soap, a pile of blankets and a steaming bucket of water with a few damp rags hanging over its rim. As I watched, Master Chadwick was ministering to the unconscious animal with a damp cloth, and I noted the remnants of his magic lingering around the wound.

"He should recover," said Master Chadwick in a weary voice. "Mygalom venom is not usually lethal if treated promptly. It acts more to weaken and immobilize its victims. Sampson will sleep now and be quite feeble for a couple of days. He may have dizziness and vomit occasionally as the poison works its way through."

"Mygalom," I tasted the word. "You named it that earlier. Are they common around here?"

"Not for many years," the old man replied while wringing out the last rag over the bucket. I noticed the water was stained faintly pink with Sampson's blood. "Not since before the goblin wars. Mygalom infestations are a bane to ranchers and husbandmen. The hateful things are aggressive *and* social." He positioned several blankets around the sleeping dog before using one to cover him from neck to tail.

"When you say social, don't you mean antisocial?" I argued.

"No," he sighed, "by social, I mean there will be more of them. Perhaps a great many more . . ."

"By the moon and stars!" I exclaimed. "One was quite bad enough to deal with."

77

"Too right, my boy," said Chadwick, nodding. "Once Tilda alerts the town, I expect the lord's knights will take a great interest in helping to root them out. Both you and Royland acquitted yourselves very well out there today, and you have my thanks."

While collecting up the various accoutrements, Royland smiled.

"What was that fire spell you used?" I asked excitedly. "I hope you will be teaching us that soon!"

"Journeyman level magic, I'm afraid," said the wizard with a grimace. "I wouldn't be doing you any favors by introducing fire magic early. For that, you will need proper lessons at the academy."

I thought of the magical tasks that I could now but weakly perform. My mental catalog was not all that long. And although my magical strength had grown somewhat, it was still not very impressive. "Will they accept me, do you think?" I asked.

"Work hard and study harder," my master replied. "We've still the better part of a year to get you up to snuff, young Harper. For now, we must prepare to root out the mygaloms. I shall need you and your cousin to help guard the flock until Sampson is fit to resume his duties. We shall suspend your regular lessons for the duration of this crisis and take the opportunity to absorb some special teachings."

As good as his word, our master taught us several new spells to help us stand watch. There was one for wakefulness. I wasn't sure I was doing that one correctly because the morning's events had left me very wide awake already. He showed us a spell called 'visio tenebris' that let us see pretty well through darkness. After I had practiced it all afternoon in the barn, I found I was able to manage it pretty easily; it didn't take a great deal of power.

Then my cousin and I began taking it in shifts.

CHAPTER FIVE

# The Knight

"The weak can never forgive. Forgiveness is the attribute of the strong."

*~ Mahatma Gandhi ~*

Without his daily magical workout, Royland had reverted to his old quiet self. Nor did I see him very often as he, Master Chadwick, and I took it in turns to stand guard over the flock. We had transferred them to the north meadow as far from the tree line as possible. Big Barney was there, providing his dubious protection; as well as the other ram, Little Abe. The two would occasionally and quite literally butt heads over access to the ewes. This invariably resulted in Little Abe's exile to a remote corner of the meadow. Sometimes, we put the poor fellow in a stall in the barn to give his lambasted self-esteem (and cranium) a bit of relief.

It happened that of all present, only I could cook. My father and I had never depended wholly upon the grace of others for our supper. It was true the town bakers had often plied us with their goods to curry the favor of the mill, lavishing their loaves and pastries upon us. As a consequence of this, my culinary expertise extended only to a couple of basic stews and kickshaws that could be breaded and fried in a pan. My first attempt at cornbread was so badly burned that even the animals rejected it. As they formerly were off-limits, my use of Tilda's pantry and kitchen felt somehow irreverent. Indeed, devoid of her substantial presence, the entire cottage now reeked of abandonment.

Just as my master had predicted, Sampson was very feeble when he awoke. He could hobble over to his water, but was not ready for much else in the first several days. We all tried to encourage him to eat, because he needed his strength, but he was having trouble keeping food down. Mid-morning on the third day found me tempting him with a sausage, when suddenly he lifted both ears and became alert. Fearing another attack, I hefted my crossbow, which I had taken to carrying everywhere with me, and followed his silent regard. Sampson heaved himself up to his feet from amid his pile of blankets and made his way toward the barn door.

Then I heard it, a faint drumming in the distance. As it grew louder, I followed the dog out into the yard. Down the trail that passed for a road in these parts, I beheld a most welcome sight. Two men on horseback were approaching the ranch at a gallop. The first rode a palfrey. It was brown in color with a brown mane and tail withal; a coloring I believe the horsemen call a 'chestnut.' It preceded a large gray brute in white quilted barding ridden by a knight with a lance. He wore chain mail armor with a full closed helm and an argent shield with an image of a bird.

As they drew nigh, Master Chadwick emerged from the cottage peering curiously down the lane. Roy was still out in the north meadow standing his watch. On closer approach, the two men slowed their steeds and drew up side by side. I could now see the knight's shield actually bore the image of a gryphon. *Trenton?* I felt exposed and hugged my crossbow to my chest as it began to wind itself into ready position. Master Chadwick glanced over sharply and made a wry face as if I had just broken wind. Perhaps sensing my dismay, Sampson emitted a low rumble and took a few stiff-legged strides to the fore as the two horsemen clattered to a halt.

The fellow astride the chestnut palfrey was known to me as well. He was Derrick, the page of our good baron. As we were but a year apart in age, I had encountered him at many festivals and gatherings. Derrick was a gap-toothed boy with curly blond hair who ran messages and errands for our liege throughout the town. Always soft spoken and friendly, and the son of a knight, I knew several of the young girls of Meadowfork fancied him. But Derrick seemed to ignore such regard, ever diligently pursuing his tasks.

From atop his palfrey, Derrick cleared his throat. "Know ye all herein," he began in a clear tenor voice. "Your good liege, Lord Westarbor, has heard the call of his people and has sent forth his knights to confront the horrors that threaten the safety and peace of the barony. May I present one such knight in the person of Sir Trenton Arenson, the son of our liege, and *slayer of beasts*."

It was really most impressive, spoiled only at its close. For upon the final three words, the boy's voice cracked most inconveniently to his former soprano. I sympathized. My own voice had undergone the change but a season past. I had gone mostly silent for the better part of two weeks to forestall the exasperating mockery and teasing. How much worse if my job had entailed the making of announcements to the public? I kept a straight face and turned my attention to Trenton as I had been bidden.

With the lance still in hand, Trenton raised his visor with the corner of his shield to reveal his proud countenance. Swiveling from his saddle he expertly dropped from his mount, cushioning his landing with but a slight bend at the knees to once again stand erect. Derrick followed suit with somewhat less grace and hurried to gather the reins of both steeds. The big gray animal flattened his ears at this, and I began to fear for the boy's safety.

Sir Trenton's eyes passed mine over with no glint of recognition much less malice, and came to rest on Master Chadwick.

The old mage nodded and intoned: "Well met, Sir Trenton. It is good of our liege to respond so quickly to our need."

"Is it true that the mygaloms have returned?" asked Sir Trenton, leaning his lance in the crook of his elbow and working at the buckles that strapped the shield to his arm.

"It is, Sir Trenton," my master replied. "Fowler Ranch stands ready to aid the good servants of our liege in any way we may for the duration of the crisis. I believe you know my apprentice, Lucas Harper. My other apprentice, Royland Wagge, is at present guarding the flock."

Derrick had laid the horses' leads upon the ground. Both mounts proved well-behaved and stood rooted in their places. Derick then stepped up to relieve his knight of both shield and lance. Sir Trenton removed his helmet and swung his head first to one side and then the other, freeing his black locks from their closeness.

"We shall require bed and board for myself, my squire, and three others," Trenton began. "The remaining members of my lance are on their way and should arrive by nightfall. I rode ahead to assess the situation firsthand. Four other lances have been dispatched and will be arriving at other selected ranches in the area. We will all coordinate through Sir Fletcher Klein, who shall have ultimate authority for our force."

Sampson began to stalk forward to greet the newcomers. I dreaded Sir Trenton receiving Sampson's overfriendly welcome, but I needn't have worried. Turning to lock his eyes upon the hound, and with his helm tucked under one arm, Sir Trenton made a palms-down gesture with his other hand. The dog halted his advance, and after but a brief glance over to Master Chadwick, dropped down to his belly with his nose settled upon his forepaws.

Trenton deposited his helm atop the pile of gear in Derrick's arms to balance there precariously. With a curt little nod at the barn, he dismissed the boy. As Derrick began tottering toward the structure in question, I stepped forward to lend a hand. I was drawn short by a stern command.

"I will thank you, boy," said Trenton, "not to interfere with my squire in the performance of his duties. Instead, see to your own inadequate weaponry."

I clutched my crossbow a bit tighter. Behind Trenton, I could see my master purse his lips and shake his head in subtle negation, so I held my peace.

"Yes, my lord," I replied.

Trenton scowled. "Your student seeks to display his ignorance yet again, Master Chadwick. Only now he would elevate me to baron. Only my squire and those under my direct command may properly refer to me as 'my lord' before I achieve my majority, boy. Until that fine day, you will address me as Sir Trenton or merely 'sir' if you must speak at all."

"Yes, sir," I managed.

Evidently, Trenton still had it in for me.

***

Master Chadwick offered to show Trenton the cottage and its amenities. At a loss for what else to do, I trailed along behind. It was determined that Sir Trenton and his squire would lodge in Tilda's bed chamber, as it was the nicest. My master would retain his own room. Two of Trenton's men at arms would bunk in the guest quarters, displacing Royland and me to the hayloft of the barn. Trenton's remaining man at arms, an archer, would find accommodation in Tilda's parlor. Master Chadwick set me the task of making him a bed of straw to be covered with clean linens.

I went to the barn to begin packing the straw into bundles. Derrick already had the big gray horse in mister Strongback's former stall. The two stalls remaining were occupied. In one stood Little Abe munching contentedly on his hay. In the corner stall was Sampson sprawled out upon an old blanket. Derrick stood studying the situation as he held the reins of his brown palfrey.

"Ho, boy, Lucas is it?" he hailed me.

"Hey, Derrick," I acknowledged. "Congratulations on your promotion to squire."

Derrick's face split in a gap-toothed grin

"And quite a fine day it *was that I swore my vows*," he said, his voice cracking up an octave near the end. He cleared his throat noisily.

"If you'd like," I offered, ignoring the inadvertent duet, "I can move that ram out to the north meadow to free up a stall - if it won't interfere with your duties, that is."

He rolled his eyes and with an amiable shake of his head replied: "That would work for Blaze here, goodman, But there

83

will be another pack animal arriving with the rest of the lance this evening."

"Ehr-Wuff," simpered Sampson from the corner stall. And, looking much put out, he took up his blanket in his mouth and dragged it to the far corner of the barn, there to resettle. From the set of his shoulders and his doleful eyes, I began to see how the term 'hang-dog expression' may have come to be.

"And thus is one more problem resolved," I said.

It occurred to me that the 'board' part of 'bed and board' promised food. That meant that I would need to prepare dinner for eight men tonight, and I didn't have the foggiest idea of whether knights had some fussy special needs or protocols. I explained the problem to Derrick while I gathered up straw and he was stabling and unsaddling Blaze. As the baron's former page, Derrick proved to be a veritable fountain of useful information about the nobility and their dining pleasures, most of which proved to be irrelevant. Trenton would be the only nobleman present. The other men at arms were just tenants who were working off their military obligations to the baron. As such, they were used to dining rough. I did, however, pick up some useful tips on how to avoid annoying Trenton further. He was to be served first, and none were to eat until he began.

As predicted, the others drifted in shortly before sunset. The three men wore gambesons. The thick quilted jackets hung down to their knees. As I understood it, a gambeson was the layer of armor a knight wore underneath his metal plates when he girded for war. Its thick pads served to keep the bulkier pieces from chafing. By itself, the quilted jacket wouldn't stop the thrust of a sword, but it might blunt a slash or cushion a blow. The men leading this trio were Connor Dawson and Kyle Digby. Both had boar spears with broad-bladed heads and iron crossbars to prevent the beasts from traveling on up the spear when pierced through. I thought these weapons made good sense. If I had to face a mygalom, I would certainly want to keep it at arms length. The third man was Taylor Allen. He followed behind the other two, leading a bay horse with panniers that held all of their gear and equipment. Taylor was the archer for the lance. While the other two held the mygaloms pinned in place, he was to deal them death from afar with his longbow.

Over the course of dinner, I learned more about the men. Goodman Dawson was a dignified fellow sporting an upturned mustache that he obviously groomed with pride. His manners were impeccable. He was also the camp cook for the lance. After sampling my simple stew, Trenton tasked the man to 'take charge of this kitchen for the duration,' relieving me of the odious duty. Kyle Digby was a different sort. Somewhat scruffy and unkempt, he had a zest for life and a jolly way about him that put me in mind of a younger version of uncle Robert. I learned he was a huntsman and the tracker for the lance.

Of the archer, I had yet to form an opinion. He ate quietly, contributing very little to the conversation. Upon arriving, he had retrieved several cages full of pigeons from the pack horse. These he insisted on placing in the parlor near where his bed had been laid down. Apparently, the birds would be used to send messages to Westarbor Keep so that the baron could remain apprised of the campaign. At least the birds were not noisy. Their soft cooing was in sooth quite pleasing to the ear, but the mess they made in the parlor was most unseemly. If Tilda's deceased mother would weep over a bit of spilt water, she would surely be in hysterics over its condition now.

After the meal, the men of the lance began settling in at the old cabin. I prepared to relieve Royland in the meadow to allow him to sup on the stew I had set aside. Before doing so, I thought to draw up more water from the well. The eight of us would require extra for our morning ablutions. As I slipped into the now familiar mindset of 'spacium girabit,' the pail began its steady and effortless ascent from the depths below.

"So it's true then," came a familiar voice out of the darkened doorway to the kitchen.

I looked back while the well's handle continued to turn.

"You have become a mage," continued Trenton, stepping out from the shadows.

"So I have been told and so you can now see, Sir Trenton," I responded, hefting the pail over the lip of the well to pour into one of the two buckets.

"Know that I have not forgotten your rudeness at the mill, boy," he said, stepping closer. "Were it not for the current crisis,

I would have satisfaction for that – mage or no mage. But heed these words if you value your health: Lay hands on a nobleman again at your peril, for it shall be met with the harshest reprisal. As even an apprentice mage, you may enjoy a social standing commensurate to nobility; but, the code also enjoins us: 'Never to refuse a challenge from an equal.'

I considered this as I topped off the bucket before finally saying: "I will take your words to heart, sir."

I hefted the load and made my way toward the house. By the light of the half moon above, I could see in Trenton's expression a desire to say something more. As he gave way to let me pass by, his face grew more stern as though reaching a decision.

"What's more, I will thank you," he snapped, "to keep your unwelcome attentions and lecherous thoughts away from my sister. She neither wants nor requires any pledge of service and protection from the likes of *you*."

I was too dumbstruck to respond. Stepping into the kitchen, I set down the bucket, hastened through to the main room and out the front door of the cabin. I proceeded down the lane and across the yard into the north meadow, puzzling all the time on what Trenton could have meant. I barely even knew his sister. Had he somehow heard of her visit to my room at the keep? That was entirely *her* doing - and completely innocent as well. And what was this pledge of protection he spoke of? Could he have been referring to the note I sent her? That was but a simple thanks for her help at the stockade. I hadn't written anything that could be misconstrued as suggestive. *Had I?*

As I approached his vantage point, Royland stood up from the grass of the meadow, relief etched upon his weary face.

"Good night, Lucas," he croaked while stretching himself and gazing out over the flock.

Given that it was Royland, I took that as both a greeting and a status report with even a wasted word to boot. This was progress.

"Good evening yourself, Roy," I said. "I relieve you. Go and get some supper. I left a bit of stew and mutton near the fire, but eat it in the hayloft. I think the soldiers are trying to sleep. They plan to start tracking the spiders at first light."

"Stay warm," the slender boy entreated as he strode briskly toward the ranch.

I settled into Royland's blind before the ground there could give up all of its warmth. A blanket wouldn't have gone amiss. I took a moment to examine my magic center. With constant use, it had grown a bit. Instead of a small patch of green, it had now come to resemble a more respectable garden-sized plot. Drawing from it, I chanted 'visio tenebris.' This caused a small depletion of the field as a minute but steady flow of magic empowered the spell of darksight.

I looked out over the sheep, for I could now see each quite clearly. You would think they would huddle together against the night's chill, but sheep seemed unaffected by the cold except in the case of high winds. Instead, they grazed about facing all different directions in a disorganized mass very like my own muddled thoughts. Unlike we humans, any given sheep sleeps only about four hours per night. You can tell which ones by the way their heads droop. They stagger it out so that the rest of the flock can arouse them should any danger approach. It had been a long day, and I knew better than to count them for the old adage did have some truth to it. Instead, I let my eyes glide over the flock as a whole, alert for dangers or disturbances. I had to cast 'manent vigilate,' my wakefulness spell, no fewer than three times over the course of the evening to remain keen.

I was joined in the night by Sampson, whose furry presence quietly proclaimed his holiday to be at an end. I welcomed his warmth as he sat beside me, his vigilant gaze somehow piercing the hirsute curtain of his bangs. With his service, I felt free to engage in another time-honored pursuit of the shepherds of old. The moon had set, and the clear sky above proved ideal for stargazing. My spell of darksight seemed to render the stars at twofold their usual brightness and enhanced their colors withal. There was *Centaurus*, and over there, the fangs of *Draco*. Directly above the meadow, I could make out *Venandi the Hunter*. His was a sign that portended a successful hunt. Suddenly, as sometimes happens, I caught a flash of bright light trailing down from the sky. It proceeded from Venandi's bow to the horizon on my right. I took it as an omen that tomorrow's spider chase would prove fortuitous. I was mistaken.

When the triangle was sounded signifying that breakfast was prepared, the sun had yet to mount the sky. Tired but hungry, I looked over to my canine companion where he lay.

"You got this?" I asked.

"Wuff," the dog replied, not lifting his scrutiny from our charges.

Taking that as assent, I raised myself stiffly to a standing posture and stretched my back in the predawn light. It would be another clear day, I noted as I traipsed toward the cottage. On its stoop I was met by Master Chadwick, already awake and ready to greet the day.

"Since you are here, can I assume the flock is in good paws?" he asked.

"Sampson seems watchful and content, master," I replied.

The old man nodded and graced me with a cheerful smile.

"Excellent," he exclaimed. "He demolished a ham bone we gave him yesterday evening. The return of his appetite is a good sign indeed. Before long he'll be back to his old chipper self, I'll warrant."

"Well, master," I returned, "I'll be back to *my* old chipper self after I've eaten a hill of food and slept most of the day away."

Just as I was about to seek out the aforementioned hill, I caught sight of Royland making his sleepy way over from the barn, a wisp of hay caught in his fine brown hair.

"Good morning. Roy," I greeted. "Did you sleep well?"

"Well enough," he grunted. "I heard the breakfast bell."

"Well, then," said our master, "let us see what Goodman Dawson has concocted."

And with that, the three of us entered the cabin and shuffled over to the dining area. It was a tight fit, as Trenton and all of his men save for Connor were already seated about the barely adequate table. Sir Trenton, at its head, was giving instructions for the day to the members of his lance, young Derrick at his side. When he looked up, his gaze passed over Royland and me, and came to rest upon Master Chadwick, whom he greeted.

"Good morn, master wizard," said Sir Trenton. "After we break our fast, we shall review the scene of the first attack. The south meadow, I believe you said? I should like you to show us the way. I would also like to hear your thoughts about these mygalom creatures, for I confess I know not much about their habits."

"The mygaloms," began my master, "are a most perfidious scourge."

He approached Trenton and sat on the bench next to Taylor Allen. I leaned my crossbow against the wall and took a seat at the foot of the table. Royland did likewise.

"I fought them years ago," the old man continued. "When they infest an area, they start by depositing their eggs in a pit in some wooded stand. Upon hatching, they begin as small spiderlings no larger than my hand, but there can be hundreds of them in each hatching."

At this point, Connor Dawson arrived bearing a large steaming kettle from which a savory aroma issued, quickly filling the small room. He proceeded to the table's head and began to ladle out a large dollop of spiced, fried potatoes and wild onions with chunks of ham onto Trenton's plate.

"The mygaloms then begin to feed upon the creatures of the forest and upon one another until but a dozen or so remain," said my master. "But, these are larger, of a size to rival a small dog."

Connor made his way down the table giving each man a portion of the kettle's bounty, but none so great as that first portion, I noted.

"Next," continued Master Chadwick, "these larger mygaloms spread out somewhat, and each digs a shallow pit wherein they cover themselves with leaves and debris. From there they can emerge with lightning swiftness to trap and immobilize prey they sense wandering by."

Having completed his rounds, Connor exited back to the kitchen. My stomach growled urgently. Still, Trenton had made no move toward his food, and I was loath to break custom and partake before he. So, as my breakfast stood cooling on my plate, I endured.

"And finally," the old man said in an ominous tone, "after having attained a growth you will shortly see for yourselves, each mygalom strikes out on its own to form a new nest, and the cycle repeats. It is imperative that we put them down before this can happen."

Sir Trenton nodded thoughtfully and stroked his chin. "Well then, let's eat and be off," he said, stabbing into a large chunk of ham.

Once he began to chew I lay into my food with abandon, as did the other men of his lance. Royland ate mechanically, and Master Chadwick took indifferent bites, lost in thought.

After our hasty repast, my master made good on his promise to lead the lance to the south meadow. Although a soft bed of hay was calling to me, I was curious what Trenton would make of the beast we had slain. So, I pulled once again on my magical reserves to renew my wakefulness. My inner garden was looking a little overtaxed by this time, and I was finding that the spell had diminishing returns. But, soldiering on, I collected my crossbow and followed the men of the lance with Royland as my silent shadow.

Once we had surmounted the hedge row, the scorched spot in the meadow was visible from across the field. It was a great blackened oval whereupon lay the crumpled carcass of the mygalom now four days deceased. Within the blackness lay a writhing carpet of motility. As my master approached it, a swarm of angry carrion birds suddenly arose. This murder of crows became abruptly evident as they burst from the greater blackness and winged their protesting way upward to roost watchfully in the nearby trees. Upon the ground around the lifeless monstrosity, lay a small number of their brethren weakly twitching in the throes of death from the poison they had ingested during their ill-advised picnic.

When the lance took in the measure of the beast, all seemed at a loss for words until Derrick chimed in with: "Blimey, if that isn't the king of all spiders!"

At Sir Trenton's command, Kyle Digby was sent to scout around the spot while Taylor Allen bent to examine the great arachnid itself. Within and about its bloated abdomen squirmed maggots in their thousands. Goodman Allen was most careful to handle the carcass with his gauntleted left hand, as his right bore only the open-fingered glove of an archer. The hair had been singed from the mygalom's right side, and the corpse had been much abused by the rapacious avians under whose hungry regard we still stood. Rooting about, the archer retrieved my quarrel from the back of the beast's head with a squelching sound and examined it in the early light of dawn.

"Yours?" Trenton asked Master Chadwick.

"Lucas,'" my master replied with a nod in my direction.

Rubbing thoughtfully on his chin, Sir Trenton spared me a sideways glance.

"I can track it, m'lord," declared Goodman Digby, returning from his survey of the area. "A thing that big leaves a trail a mile wide."

"Don't be too certain," muttered Chadwick. "They can climb through the trees as readily as along the ground. But, by all means, let us try to trace it back from whence it came."

Turning to me, he said: "Lucas, go and get some sleep. I expect you and Royland to see to the ranch in our absence."

"We shall proceed on foot" said Sir Trenton, "as the horses would be a hindrance in the forest. Kyle and Connor will lead us, followed by the good mage and our archer. Derrick and I will provide a rear guard. Form up, men. We go to purge the mygaloms."

And with that, they marched into the woods, Kyle Digby blazing a trail and beating the bushes with his boar spear while the others followed warily. When I turned to head back to the barn, I spotted Royland leaning over the decaying mygalom husk. He was rocking back and forth as he stared at it intently.

"Are you coming, Roy?" I asked.

He didn't speak for a long moment, but finally looked up at the horizon and replied: "You go on ahead, Lucas. I want to see something."

He then returned to his silent scrutiny of the putrescent remains while I trudged back to the ranch seeking the gentle release from care that was sleep.

I lay abed until well after noon that day. I awoke to the soft nickering of the horses below and their contented munching of their daily feed. Royland had seen to all the animals and was likely out on the meadow caring for the flock. After a brief trip to the pantry to slake my own hunger and thirst, I sought a productive way to spend my afternoon. An idea struck me when I noticed that Tilda's garden was looking a bit shabby from her inattention of the prior week. I resolved to pull up the new weeds before they could establish firmer roots. So resolved, I knelt by the first row and set to work.

I hoped that my master, Trenton, and the others would all come back safely. I mentally reviewed the alarming battle we had with but one of the murderous mygaloms. I pictured Trenton skewering a dozen of the creatures upon his sword while his men held some at bay with their boar spears, and Taylor Allen peppered them with his arrows. Master Chadwick was powerful and resourceful, but I feared for him. He had oft seemed so tired of late.

Reaching the end of the row, I doubled back and began working my way down the second row. Something strange was occurring with the first row of woad I had weeded. Each had sprouted a slim stalk from its center, some of which had achieved a good six inches of height. From my reading on the subject at Tilda and Master Chadwick's direction, I had learned that woad was a biennial plant. As any good gardener knows, annuals like corn or peas grow to seed in but a single season and then perish, withering away to make way for next year's tilling and planting. Perennials such as turnips or asparagus grow and bloom over the spring and summer then die back every autumn and winter, only to return the following spring from their rootstock.

Biennials, however, live out a strange two-year cycle. During the first twelvemonth that the seed is planted, it produces roots and leaves and stores up its energy then dies back to just a short stem and low rosette of leaves through the winter months. Upon regrowing in the second year, it will bolt, sending up a long stalk which flowers and produces its seed. Carrots behave like this. Why, then, was the first row of woad, which Tilda and I had only just planted, bolting into stalks with clusters of delicate, yellow blooms before my very eyes?

Knowing that magic must be the cause, I looked within. Sure enough, without my knowledge or intent, my inner garden had sent up its vine-like tendrils to grow down my arms to my fingertips and even now were lapping playfully against the woad plant around which I was weeding. This must be a result of what my studies of magical theory had termed a 'magical affinity.'

As Master Chadwick had explained it, how one envisions his magic center often gives rise to specific magical gifts, or 'affinities.' By way of an example, my master had described his own magic center as a deep wellspring from which an aqueous substance could be drawn. He claimed it gave him a special affinity for performing water magic. Master Chadwick had demonstrated this by drawing water in a thin stream up from the well to fill a bucket without use of the pail and rope. He claimed that magic of this sort didn't tax him as much as it did others. I remember wondering at the time why he made *me* draw up the water each day, until discovery of my winding laid those uncharitable thoughts to rest.

So, continuing on my elective mission to uproot the undesirable flora, I began to whistle a merry tune. This is perhaps why I failed to notice I was being observed. When I turned about at the end of the second row, I was startled to see Royland watching me very closely. Unused to being the subject of his scrutiny, I was momentarily nonplussed. Then I realized that what I was doing must be fascinating to his mage sight, so I just forged ahead shamelessly.

When I began the fourth row, this one of welds, I noted that Roy's eyes had left me and were now fastened upon a two-foot long stalk of woad blooming in the first. He turned and met my gaze squarely, a broad smile forming on his narrow face. As I paused in my digging to savor this rare regard, he extended his forefinger to make a little perch. Moments later, a butterfly drifted over to alight upon it. After a brief pause, the butterfly moved to the woad stalk and began servicing the little yellow flowers one by one. It was soon joined by a bevy of its brethren in a variety of hues and patterns.

Master Chadwick had once shared with me that Royland's magic center seemed to be an overly large hive of angry hornets that he struggled to soothe and control. Mayhap this gave him an affinity for six-legged crawlers? In any event, I had rarely seen my cousin so joyful and at his ease as when marshaling this hoard of winged fluttering insects to pilfer and pollinate Tilda's beloved herbs. What a fearsome pair we had turned out to be, I mused. If magery didn't work out for us, I would imagine we could always hire out as expert gardeners. Although practical and not too disagreeable, I smothered this thought aborning. For I knew that Royland, at least, was meant for something greater.

***

Though my back was sore from all the bending, and my hands were near to cramping from the unaccustomed activity, my magic center sang and thrummed. Rather than being diminished by my efforts, it seemed more energized and ready to tackle still more. It was late afternoon, and my thoughts turned once again to the fate of the lance that had set out this morning. As we cleaned up, I was considering what to bring out to old Sampson for his dinner, when his wailing, mournful howl reached my ears. Fearing the worst, I plucked up my crossbow and cradled it in one arm. The cranequin whirred, automatically snapping the string back to ready.

Royland and I turned as one to the north meadow. But before we could take a step in that direction, we saw Sampson arrowing past to our right. Bypassing the cottage and its surrounds, he was making for the trees to the southeast. We turned and loped after him at a steady jog. Cresting a rise, I saw the lance. There was Trenton and Derrick marching in the lead. Behind them were Kyle and Connor with a litter stretched between them bearing a huddled figure covered by a cloak. Bringing up the rear was Taylor Allen. With many a glance backward to the trees, Taylor kept pace, an arrow nocked to string. Where was my master? I suspected I knew. Sampson quickly arrived beside the men and fell into step with the litter bearers. I turned and ran back to the cottage, stoked up the fire in the kitchen, and hung a kettle of water to heat.

I didn't have long to wait for the group to arrive. They found me busily digging through the linens for some clean rags.

"Put him in here," said Connor, indicating Taylor's straw mattress in the parlor. "He must be kept warm."

Derrick followed the group in, bearing several new logs for the parlor hearth. Royland stood in the doorway, his mouth working soundlessly. Master Chadwick was deposited on the bed where he twitched and moaned most pitiably, his breathing interrupted by a series of erratic gasps.

I started to remove his tunic, being as gentle as I could, but was making little headway. Kyle Digby thrust me aside and, brandishing a sharp dagger, hastily cut away the worsted wool garment. This exposed my master's thin but muscular chest. On his abdomen, just below his seventh rib, there was a swollen gash about four inches in length. There was little blood, but the edges of the wound looked nasty, already beginning to blacken. There was an angry redness all around the site and an unusual amount of swelling puckered the wound closed around a waxy yellow boil of flesh. This proved too much for Royland and he promptly turned around and fled the room.

"He's a goner I tell ya," said Kyle Digby. "The poison'll soon reach his heart."

"No," I quickly refuted, "Master Chadwick told us that mygalom venom is rarely fatal," *if promptly treated*, I did not add.

"Come Kyle," said Trenton in a hollow tone. "Let us leave the boy to tend to his master in peace. Your opinion is not helpful here. I shall draft a message to our liege relating this setback. Taylor, I shall need your services as scribe. Bring your quill set and meet us at the dining table."

And with that, they withdrew, leaving Connor and I to minister to the ailing mage. Derrick also remained. Having built up and banked the fire to provide maximum warmth, he asked what else he might do to help, so I requested he retrieve the kettle from the kitchen.

"What happened?" I asked Connor.

"It started well," he began. "Each time we discovered a mygalom burrow, the master wizard here would force it out using his fire. Kyle and I, standing to the fore, would seek to draw its attention and try to pin it with our spears. The aggressive curs never fled. I'll grant them that much. Then Sir Trenton would wade in with his sword while Taylor let loose with a volley of shafts. The beast would quickly expire under some combination of these, and we would dismember it to make certain."

When Derrick returned with the heated kettle, I applied fresh linens to the wound and bathed the area in warm water just as I had seen my master do for Sampson some five days gone. I recalled seeing residual magic about the dog's shaven and cut shoulder wound, but I knew of no magic for healing. Doubtless, Master Chadwick had somehow drawn the poison out using his water magic. So, I kept washing and patting around the inflamed lesion as best I could.

"We were clearing our third such burrow," Connor continued. "While we were engaged with the creature, another dropped from the trees above, choosing as its victim your master here. It happened so quickly that none were able to intervene before it was upon him and gnawing most savagely. Of course, it was roasted alive for this effrontery, but by then it was too late to avoid the venom. We brought him back here in all haste, but good Master Chadwick rapidly declined on the journey until he became as you see him now."

I felt a draft as the front door was thrown wide. The pigeons became unsettled and took up a fresh chorus of cooing as Royland made his hurried way over to the bedside.

"Stand aside, Lucas," he said in an impatient voice.

"I'm cleansing the wound, Roy," I retorted.

"You need to believe in me, cousin," he said in a more pleading voice while staring at our master. "I know what to do. You must hold him still."

"I think he means to lance it, son," declared Connor in a gentle tone. "I'll hold his shoulders, and you and Derrick take the legs."

No sooner had we shifted our placements to comply, than Royland, kneeling at our master's side, produced a small leather pouch and promptly overturned it directly upon the laceration. Out poured hundreds of wriggling maggots.

"Here now!" exclaimed Connor with a horrified expression.

"Steady, Connor," I urged. "Royland's ways may be strange, but he is a powerful mage, and likely our master's best hope."

At first nothing seemed to happen as my cousin began to rock forward and back chanting: 'sternetur tinea munda' over and over again. But then the nasty little devils began to bore into the old man's flesh, especially around the blackened area, and started to disappear from view. It was a sickening sight.

I was to learn later that common maggots, despite their disgusting habit of swarming through carrion, feed only upon dead tissue. Their tiny bites cleared away only such flesh as had been already killed by the poison, and their burrowing allowed them to follow its course through our master's body to remove all such. Moreover, it happens that maggot slime is a remarkable healing balm able to close off wounds and stop bleeding. All I knew at the time, as Master Chadwick began weakly thrashing about, was what my mage sight was telling me.

For on close observation, I could see my cousin's discrete little packets of magic buzzing about and guiding each maggot to consume more poisoned flesh. After a time, they began to reemerge, bloated and discolored and twitching in agony. The last of them came out in a rush as the swollen wound discharged its pus. Young Derrick lost his lunch to the floor at this point, and I couldn't honestly blame him, for there had been a foul stench when the pasty substance had spewed forth.

"Now you can clean it," Royland finally said as he met my eyes for the second time in a single day.

So, while Connor looked on in astonished distaste, and Derrick excused himself, I set about sponging away the filth from my master's abdomen. I thought the redness may have already lessened somewhat, and of the blackened skin there remained no trace. Royland collected all of the engorged maggots, living and dead, and flung them into the fire to sizzle and burst.

"What now?" asked Connor.

"If I remember correctly," I answered, "he will sleep for a long while as he burns off the remainder of the taint. He will be feeble for at least several days and have trouble keeping his food down. That is if all goes well. Go and rest, goodman. You've had a hard day. Royland and I can watch him tonight. Please accept our thanks for your efforts on my master's behalf."

Not long after, Taylor Allen stepped in with a tiny folded note. He retrieved a pigeon with a blue-banded leg and attached the note. Opening a window, he released the bird to take flight in a sudden burst of fluttering wings. This accomplished, he turned to us.

"How's your master, boy?" he asked in his quiet, neutral tone.

"We'll know better in the morning, goodman," I replied. "On behalf of my master, I would like to offer you his room for tonight, as I would prefer not to move him just now."

"Aye, then so it shall be," said the archer. "Perhaps you would be so kind as to help me resettle these cages in my new billet then?"

As we hauled the pigeons down the hall to Master Chadwick's room, I asked him why one of the pigeons had a purple band. He told me it was a secret code between him and the recipient in a tone that brooked no further questions. Upon returning to the pigeon-free parlor, Roy and I settled in for a long night of apprehension as the sun slid behind the ridge line to the west.

***

I awoke groggily at the foot of my master's bed. I must have dozed off for some time as the fire had died down to mere embers, and the faint light of false dawn was creeping through the parlor window. Royland was sitting in Tilda's rocking chair doing something with bits of straw purloined from the bedding. I went over and stoked the fire back to a livelier state and threw on several fresh logs. I next went to check on Master Chadwick. The old man had lain torpid throughout the night, but his chest still rose and fell steadily. I took this to be a good sign. To elicit more response from our master, perhaps I should lull Royland to sleep, for I believed his snoring could truly wake the dead, but I feared reprisals from the billeted soldiers.

With that morbid and unkind thought, I snatched up Roy's waterskin and brought it to Master Chadwick's parched lips. I carefully dribbled only a small amount so as not to cause him to choke. As I withdrew the receptacle, a curious thing happened. From even a foot away, a thin stream of water kept issuing forth from the waterskin into the old man's mouth. When I blocked the opening with my finger, he moaned and cracked open one unfocused eye. I removed my finger from the nipple, and the flow resumed. With mage sight, I could perceive a connection between the water and the old mage. He wasn't choking, so I decided to let him enjoy his fill. Royland was soon by my side, peering intently at the strange, miniature geyser. In less than a minute, the outflow abruptly ceased. Shortly thereafter, the old man began muttering quietly. I bent close and strained to hear.

"The lance . . . safe?" was all I could make out.

"Certainly, master," I assured him. "Sir Trenton and all his men arrived safely. They brought you home. Rest now, master. All is well," I soothed.

The deep lines of his haggard face smoothed somewhat at this, and he soon returned to his lethargic slumber. A half hour or so later, we made a new discovery. It began with a bit of clattering in the kitchen as Goodman Dawson prepared the morning meal. Master Chadwick once again bestirred himself. He seemed more clearheaded and was looking about. As we moved to assess his condition, we found that the old man, using his magic, could fill the chamber pot from clear across the room - with nary a splash. Before we could engage him in speech, he sagged back down into the mattress, already back in the land of dreams.

Royland and I took turns washing up at the well, and I used the opportunity to spin up more water for the kitchen. But, before breakfast could be served, I heard the familiar drumming sound I now recognized as hoofbeats approaching.

"Hello the house!" I heard when the rider was still some short distance off and slowing.

As I came around the side of the cottage, Trenton emerged onto its stoop, shielding his eyes from the morning sun.

"Well met, Hayden," he said. "How fares the Fletcher lance?"

"I've just come from the Tillerson ranch," replied Hayden, dismounting in a cloud of raised dust. "Sir Fletcher has already joined Sir Graham there, who reports the main enemy nest has been found."

I had met the Tillersons. They had joined us for dinner one evening a few months back. The kindly middle aged couple had brought along their daughter, Priscilla. Both she and her mother, Harriet, were members of Tilda's sewing circle. They were especially known for their fine weaving. The family had also bragged about their other grown son, Avery, who had become a cobbler in Meadowfork. I knew him as well. It was a small barony.

"What news of the ranchers?" queried Sir Trenton.

"It is dire, I'm afraid, sir," began Hayden. "The Tillersons' ox was found dead upon the road still harnessed to their abandoned wagon. And like many of the flock scattered about, it was completely drained of blood. Of the ranchers, there was no sign. All had either fled or perished."

Trenton grimaced. "Well come in and join us," he said. "We can break fast as you convey Sir Fletcher's orders."

Hayden was seated near Trenton at the table's head. While Royland was caring for our master, I decided to join the men to hear the news. Connor Dawson sat next to me after having served up a brief repast. Hayden produced a large rolled-up parchment and spread it out upon the table. On it was drawn a detailed map of the valley displaying all of the places the mygaloms had been encountered.

From what was discussed, I gathered that the other four lances were led by Sir Graham, Sir James, Sir Nolan and Sir Fletcher. All were to gather at the Tillerson Ranch to assault the mygalom lair that had been discovered there. The plan was to surround the wooded lot wherein the spiders nested then set it aflame and deal with the creatures on the open field. As such, the knights would be mounted, and their supporting lances would form into units all under the direction of Sir Fletcher. Any creatures that escaped would be tracked down individually and slain. I was ordered to locate and deliver all of the oil and animal renderings I could find at Fowler Ranch to be used to start the blaze. I did so as the men made ready for the brief journey to Tillerson Ranch just up the valley to the west.

I returned to the parlor, freeing my cousin to get some food. Not long thereafter, Master Chadwick began to stir. His face looked drawn and his eyes sunken, as he turned his head to regard me. My master always seemed so strong and sure, but now his frailty was made evident in his voice.

"Was the poison cleansed, then?" he wheezed.

"Royland's doing," I replied, sparing him the details. "How do you feel?"

"Weak. Dizzy. Foolish," replied the old man.

"Why foolish?" I asked, surprised.

"I should have known to watch the trees," he replied with chagrin.

"There is a saying my father often cites at such times," I returned. "He says, 'The mill cannot grind with water that has passed.'"

The old man's lips quirked up at this. "I like that," he said. "I shall have to remember it."

"Sometimes," I said, "he used it to admonish me not to bemoan something that had already happened. Occasionally, however, he said it in regard to a present decision. I think in those times, he was telling me to seize the moment and not to waste an opportunity. Master, I mean to go with the lance and see if I can help them. The mygaloms are my enemies too."

Master Chadwick was silent for a long moment. "What brought you to this decision?" he finally asked.

I explained what I had heard over breakfast, and went on to describe seeing the resolve in the brave men around me. They had all seen the enemy up close and had overcome their fears. They were going to risk themselves on our behalf. As a mage, I felt I should render what assistance I could. If nothing else, I could bear witness to the deed.

"When I was a younger man, I thought much as you do," said my master. "Even now, I would accompany them myself if I could but leave this bed. Very well, Lucas, I release you from your apprentice vow to stay here at the ranch. But be most cautious, for you have seen the mygaloms' malice."

I popped out to the dining room to let Roy know of my plans. I found him ignoring his food and hunched over the spread-out map instead. He was staring at it intently with his brow furrowed and taking various measurements using the outstretched thumb and pinkie finger of his left hand. I decided to tell him later, for there was no talking to him when he got like this.

***

From up on the hilltop, I could take in the lay of the land. The Tillerson's ranch sat abandoned to the southeast. There were several tilled fields breaking up the surrounding pasture land. A panicked remnant of the Tillerson flock wandered about in small clusters heedless of such boundaries. The exsanguinated carcasses of sheep lay about in the fields amid angry swarms of flies while vultures circled oppressively above still wary of their erstwhile benefactors.

The targeted area was a large copse of trees just to the north. It was bounded on its far side by a gurgling brook that wended its way west to feed a small pond. Outside of its boundaries lay the husks of several mygaloms leftover from the first attempts to scout the area. One such arrow-riddled carcass was in the process of being moved by a full-sized, living mygalom. This ambitious cannibal was dragging its deceased relative back toward the tree line presumably to feed on it in private.

Two lances each were lined up to the east and west of the small forest. Trenton's lance guarded the southern approach. Oil had been spread liberally by the scouts at the copse's edges.

"I tell you, I saw goblin sign," said Kyle Digby to Connor in a half whisper.

"Impossible," rebutted Connor, also in a low voice. "The goblins are quiescent. The watchtower has reported not a peep out of them for years."

"Well, then," grumped Kyle, "explain how someone very small wearin' hobnailed boots was wandering around in there."

"You said yourself the tracks were old," returned Connor. "Perhaps you . . ."

"Quiet in the ranks," snapped Trenton. "We don't want to miss the signal."

Then we heard it, the single, high, piercing note of Sir Fletcher's horn that was to begin the onslaught. The archers came to the fore, and lofted their flaming arrows high into the air to land at the forest's edge. Some of the oil ignited after the first volley, emitting a thin, black soot as it rapidly spread through the underbrush. As the green wood of the thicket began to wilt and catch, it crackled and the vapors thickened. Fed by a steady breeze from the west, the smoke soon transitioned to a billowy white mass drifting up and to the east. A low gray haze fell over the eastern field, making visibility poor where the forces of Sir Graham and Sir James were arrayed.

The ring of fire was incomplete, leaving several large gaps where the mygaloms were expected to emerge. And emerge they did. The first of the beasts stood little chance, for we were well prepared for them to sally forth. Separating the lances from the thicket lay a killing field of perhaps two-hundred yards. The bowmen, of which there were six, having switched to their standard ammunition, used this to good advantage to loose arrow after arrow upon the foe. The few that did not die immediately were so degraded that they staggered about aimlessly. One even fled back into the flames.

As more of the hairy brutes began to sense their peril, however, the thicket began to boil over with them. We could see many climbing up into the trees in a futile attempt to escape their would-be funeral pyre. As the number of escapees increased, archery alone became insufficient to discourage their emergence. Many of this second wave of mygaloms were of a smaller size - roughly that of a hound. Lower to the ground, more numerous, and more agile withal, they made far more difficult targets.

A second blast from Sir Fletcher's horn was heard, this one rising in tone near the end. That's when the knights took to the field. Spurring their mounts forward, the five lancers entered the fray. They began by targeting the larger mygaloms still on the field, their lances making quick work of the wounded behemoths. They then turned their attentions to the smaller spiders. They rode at groupings in an attempt to trample them. This tactic proved haphazard at best. The mygaloms, like their smaller cousins, seemed to have a heightened awareness of things that could crush them, and a penchant for making prodigious leaps to escape from such.

One of the creatures even jumped onto the haunches of Sir Nolan's mount, and he was forced to drop his lance and resort to the sword. I knew not how he managed to keep his seat half-turned in the saddle as his steed went wildly careening about. At a sound from the horn, now in Hayden's hands, the knights quit the field in good order; all except for Sir Nolan, who was finally unseated and arose to hobble shakily back to his men at the perimeter.

As ever more mygaloms gathered outside of the fiery death trap, some even using preternatural leaps from the treetops, they finally began to make headway toward the encircling men at arms. The knights had dismounted, their squires relieving them of their lances and removing the horses to a safer distance. The archers had withdrawn behind the sturdy line of soldiers armed with boar spears. They continued their salvos, becoming more successful as the range decreased. Though there were many large gaps in our perimeter through which the vile arachnids could have easily escaped, their natural aggression played them false, and they unerringly made a beeline to confront us to vent their ire.

I decided it was time to add my contribution. Dropping into my winding mindset, I began to lay quarrels to tiller as quickly as I could loose and rewind. Taylor Allen's bow sang with a repeating chup, chup, chup, in an even cadence that proved the requiem of many a foe. He gave me a strange, offended look when I began to match him bolt for arrow. Nor did my aim go astray often as the creatures were coming straight at us veering neither left nor right.

Sir Trenton was magnificent. Whirling here and there, he repelled a considerable number of the beasts. Though large, the spiders didn't weigh much, and he soon discovered he could send them flying back with a forceful sweep of his shield. He repeated this tactic all along the line while maiming or crippling others with his sword. Not one of the valiant men of Westarbor showed his back to the enemy, though we were hard pressed.

The flames from the wooded stand now climbed high into the sky. Occasionally, we would hear a crackling crash as a tree therein finally succumbed to the pull of the earth. Oddly, this only diminished the brightness of midday. Smoke rose in a high plume to waft about obscuring the sun, which took on a reddish cast. Ash began to drift down about us, some containing burning cinders. I felt certain that no mygaloms still survived in the inferno that was formerly their nesting ground, so all we had to face were those present now.

Then it happened. One of the beasts that Sir Trenton was sweeping away from Goodman Dawson chose instead to use his shield as a springboard. Soaring over our line, it landed directly atop Taylor Allen, sending his bow skittering away across the meadow. It clasped him close in its eight-legged embrace and bore him to the ground as he flailed his arms around wildly in a vain attempt to fend it off.

'Levare,' I said without delay and called upon my inner garden to hoist the creature free of the horrified archer. Young Derrick, standing back in reserve, saw his moment to rush forward, bare steel, and run the hovering creature through as it scrabbled to find purchase on naught but air. As satisfying as this small victory was, the brief cessation of archery had broader consequences to the lance. For in that moment, a remaining group of angry mygaloms were able to close the distance to our soldiers and outnumber them.

Trenton fought like a demon to free Goodman Dawson from a pile of three. As I resumed my loosing of quarrels, I prioritized the ones approaching Kyle Digby, but it was too little and too late. Having pinned one of the creatures with his spear, Kyle became outflanked by two others. Though I skewered one with a bolt, the other came upon him from behind and latched onto his throat with its mandibles. Derrick stepped in again, his sword flashing with the reflected light of the distant flames and ended the threat while I put a bolt through the head of the mygalom

Kyle had pinned. But as Derrick stepped back, Kyle slumped down and fell to the ground with his head at an awkward angle.

Respite came but a moment later as Sir James and his men came hustling over to our aid. Having finished the group to the east, they reinforced our southern lance and helped us to finish such remaining spiders as straggled in. Though he was exhausted, Sir Trenton's mail and helm had been proof against any wound the smaller mygaloms could inflict. Connor Dawson too was miraculously unscathed. His gambeson was rent in a few places, but it had saved him from the venom. Taylor Allen was another story. He had a gash on his cheek that was rapidly reddening, and his right eye was already swelling shut. Kyle Digby lay dead, his neck broken.

In all, two men had been killed in the battle, and seven more had been poisoned. Sir Nolan's horse had to be put down. The injured men were quickly loaded onto the wagon which Sir James had confiscated from Turner Ranch. They were to be driven straightaway to Fowler Ranch for a treatment I didn't envy. Work crews were assigned to make sure the fire didn't spread, to gather up the stray sheep and sheep carcasses, and a variety of other tasks. A few others and I were tasked with walking the battlefield to make certain each mygalom was truly dead. We disposed of their corpses, the diminishing fires of the former thicket making do as an expedient crematorium. Though grueling, it was a service I was only too happy to perform. We had to dismember some of the larger creatures to manage it.

***

The two casualties were wrapped in linens and returned home to Westarbor keep, there to lay in state and be buried with heroic honors. Fowler Ranch had become a makeshift hospital where those afflicted with the mygalom poison were subjected to the unorthodox but effective ministrations of my cousin, Royland. Most were mercifully unconscious for this repugnant remedy. All of the available beds and even the stalls in the barn were pressed into service for the seven enfeebled, recuperating men.

Sir Nolan had a badly sprained hip from his fall and would have to refrain from riding for the better part of two months. He did have a new story with which to regale his grandchildren who had grown tired of the retelling of the old ones. As he was presently without a steed, he deemed it a fair trade. His men boasted that the old codger had felled fully half of the mygaloms that attacked the western flank in revenge for his dignity. Sir Fletcher was not inclined to dispute or correct this exaggeration.

Three of the lances were dispatched to the western pass to verify the soundness of the defenses there. They returned to describe an alert but bored watchtower with an excellent vantage over the northern and southern ridge lines. No goblin force could hope to surmount their summits without being spotted. The pass itself was girded by an eighty-foot high stone wall bristling with defenses that was roundly deemed impregnable by all who had stood atop its high battlement. The watchtower also had a whole kit of the baron's pigeons ready to send word at the first sign of enemy hostility.

Master Chadwick had mostly recovered physically, but seemed to bear scars of a different nature. He wore his age as never before. He spent a lot of time out on the meadow away from the others. Royland and I had to pester him to take his meals. We lacked and sorely missed Tilda's sharp tongue and cinnamon muffins with which to rebuke and entice the old gentleman.

A final incident of note occurred before the other recuperating men had regained enough strength to be deemed fit to return to the service of their respective lances. The knights had stolen our practice pitch for their daily drills, being especially fond of the enchanted target dummy that could withstand their abuse. Royland and I took to sitting on the fence to watch their sparring. For after having seen Trenton in action, I wanted to understand how they had become such accomplished warriors. One day, we were sitting there with Derrick watching Sir Trenton spar with Hayden. Royland was being his old indefatigable self, playing still with his bits of straw. Derrick grew curious. Now a blooded veteran of battle, Derrick had lost a great deal of his carefree attitude. He was given to a more somber demeanor of late. It seemed that more than just his voice had changed in the past week.

"Ho there, boy, Royland is it?" he said. "What's that you're making, if I might ask?"

Roy gave him a sidelong glance, then bashfully held forth a woven tube about as big around as my thumb and three inches long. When the boy seemed perplexed, Royland took Derrick's hands and guided the forefinger of each into the ends of the tube, then suddenly jerked them apart. The tube contracted to coil more tightly around Derrick's fingers and stretched and thinned through its middle. No matter how hard Derrick tugged, the tube would not release him. It only coiled ever more tightly. Beginning to panic, he jumped down from the fence and began to look wildly about, doubtless for something with which to cut himself free. Taking pity, Royland held up a hand and approached. He took hold of Derrick's wrists and gently drew them together. The tube sagged and thickened, loosing the boy from his predicament.

"That's brilliant!" exclaimed Derrick. "Can I keep this one?"

Royland shrugged, then nodded agreement with a sly smile.

"I want to try it on Blake and Jay," Derrick confided. "Don't tell them, alright?"

"With Royland," I said, "I can assure you that mum's the word."

By this time, Sir Trenton and Hayden had finished their bout. The older squire had hopped the fence into the east holding pen. I vaguely recalled his saying something about relieving himself. As he approached a fence post and began to hike up his hauberk, I spotted Big Barney taking notice and beginning to make challenge signs, bobbing his head and backing up. It was breeding season, when rams were at their most irritable. Broken bones were common when an angry ram took one unawares.

"Hayden!" I hollered. "you cannot go in *there*. It's not . . ."

"Don't try to tell *me* where I can piss, you ill-mannered hayseed," returned Hayden.

I jumped into the pen. As Big Barney put his head down and began his run, I had just enough time to shove Hayden aside. We went down in a tangle of limbs as the ram struck the fence rail with a resounding crunch. Momentarily dazed, the ram shook his head and ambled away. Hayden sprang to his feet in a fury, his now wet breeches still tangled about his knees.

"Defend yourself, miscreant!" he shouted, waiting for me to arise.

My heartbeat quickened and I heard my crossbow wind from over on the fence where it leaned. Royland took up his shielding stance, and Derrick was staring at us agape.

"Stand down, squire," came Trenton's commanding voice, as a look of disbelief crossed Hayden's face. "You should pay heed to Lucas when he warns of danger, for it has been my experience that he often knows what of he speaks."

That was the first time I could ever recall Sir Trenton using my proper name. And though addressing Hayden, he was looking directly at me. Apology seemed foreign to the young knight standing before me. It went against his upbringing and his very nature. But his brown-eyed stare said all that was needed. It crinkled around the edges with mirth that did not extend to the rest of his face. But also within dwelt a palliative of forgiveness, and was that a modicum of respect?

## CHAPTER SIX

# The Milkmaid

"Any man who can drive safely while kissing a
pretty girl is simply not giving the kiss the attention
it deserves."

*~ Albert Einstein ~*


"Hurry, Lucas," said Master Chadwick.

The old mage was fidgeting by the door to the cottage. Royland was sweeping the last of the straw from the parlor, while I had been awarded the gratifying task of scraping the pigeon guano from its floor. How could such small birds make such a large mess? I took up the brush, and after liberally dousing the area with warm water, began to scrub. The white stuff just smeared around.

"There's no time for finesse, boy," pressed my master as he tipped over the entire bucket. "Put your back into it. She's almost here."

I scrubbed harder as the spreading ring of filthy water reached my knees and soaked into the cloth of my breeches. Royland was sliding the rocking chair back into the corner and giving it a final wipe down with a dust rag. As I heard the clatter of the approaching cart, the water on the floor reversed its course and began to trickle back upward in a brown slurry that arched back into the empty bucket. I hefted the bucket and hastily followed my master out onto the front stoop.

Pulling up to the cottage was a weary-looking mister Strongback lugging an overfull cart of goods with three passengers. In the driver's bench holding the reins sat the imposing figure of Tilda. Beside her was Harriet Tillerson, her friend from the nearby ranch where we had fought. Perched on the back was Harriet's daughter, Priscilla. A brace of cows ambled along behind the cart tied to lead ropes. The tinny chiming of their belled necks quieted as the entourage rattled to a rest.

Master Chadwick stepped to the fore. Before he could say a word, Tilda turned from a conversation she was having with Harriet to address him.

"Elizar," she began without preamble, "I took the liberty of offering these ladies our guest room. Avery and his son are going out to assess the damage caused by those *creatures*. I thought we should give them a few days to clean up the mess so these two could have a *proper* homecoming. Help a lady down, wont you?"

At this, she lifted her bulk from the driver's bench and looked expectantly at my master with her hand outstretched.

"Welcome home, madam," he said simply.

And taking her hand gently in his own, he guided her in one smooth, gliding step to lightly touch down on the stones of the walkway. My mage sight flared as he did so. He nudged me in the side with his elbow and indicated Goodwife Tillerson with a jerk of his head. So, with a brief 'levare' muttered under my breath, I sized her up. The spider attacking Taylor Allen had been relatively light. But I knew the willowy woman above, though not nearly as rotund as Tilda, would still outstrip the resources of my modest inner garden.

"Allow me, goodwife," I said in my most polite tone of voice, offering her my hand.

With a firm grip, I offered the strength of my good arm and used my magic only to assist. With a startled little moue and a quiet exclamation of 'oh,' she touched down rather lightly herself.

Unexpectedly, Royland then stepped forward. Staring at the cows behind the cart, he spared a sidelong glance for Priscilla up in its bed. "Jump," he urged.

The two older women seemed shocked by this impropriety, but Priscilla only narrowed her eyes at the challenge. With a brief pause for calculation, she made a credible leap toward the ground. With no pretense of offering his hand, Royland arrested her fall completely and brought the surprised woman slowly down to rest beside her mother. She stared over at my cousin, still in his silent contemplation of the cows, raised her hand to her lips, and giggled.

"No one likes a showoff, Roy," said my master in an indignant huff. But obviously, someone *did*.

"And what's this," asked Tilda looking hopefully at the bucket I had left out on the stoop, "a homecoming gift?"

"Uh . . . *yes*," said my crafty master with feigned brightness. "Lucas has devised a special treatment for your herb gardens, Tilda. We wanted to show you straight away. Show her, Lucas."

Not entirely certain what he had in mind, I retrieved the bucket and tried not to slosh its contents over the rim as I led a procession around to the side of the cottage. When Tilda's garden came into sight, I recalled how Royland and I had enhanced it. It hadn't seemed like so much at the time, but taken in all at once, I supposed it was kind of stunning. Tilda obviously thought so. As her eyes danced over the lush foliage of her rathe-ripe garden in full bloom, the delighted look on her face foretold that any mess remaining in the house would surely be forgiven. I remembered to tip the bucket's contents into the watering barrel to lend credence to my master's hasty fabrication.

"Bloomin' biennials!" she exclaimed, "I don't know what devil you've been tempting with your soul, Lucas, but I approve. I wasn't expecting to harvest any of this until June at the very earliest."

"Perhaps *we* should get some wizards for *our* ranch, Prissy," declared Goody Tillerson.

"We're a rather exclusive guild, madam," said Master Chadwick rubbing his chin thoughtfully, "but I suppose I could ask around . . ."

Tilda snorted. "Like I told you, Harriet," she said, "he's just *incorrigible*. Come to the kitchen, let's see what a *shambles* these *men* have wrought. Goodness knows what our liege's *knights* thought of the poor hospitality *those* three likely offered them. I'm surprised the baron hasn't asked for a formal apology . . .

Her voice trailed off as the three ladies took their leave of us. My master had the good sense to stay put and say no more. He just stood there looking a bit relieved and all too pleased with himself.

***

After unloading its contents onto the stoop, Royland and I moved the cart back into the barn. We unharnessed mister Strongback and got him settled, then we started to lead the two cows toward the remaining stalls. That's when Priscilla rejoined us. She walked over to mister Strongback's stall and scratched him between his ears.

"He worked hard all morning," she cooed. "He should rest and have oats. But Skye and Sarah here ought to be put out to graze for a bit. It's too early to bring *them* in."

So we ushered them out through the barn's rear doors and over to the south meadow. The twin bovines seemed to find the grasses agreeable and set right to converting them to cow plops. As we watched them, I noted that they were rather husky for kine and had horns just like their male kin.

"Where did you get the two milk cows, miss Priscilla?" I asked, climbing up to roost on a nearby fence rail.

"Just Prissy is fine, Lucas. Can I call you Luke?" she asked with an inquisitive tilt to her head. I nodded, assenting.

"They were a gift from the baron," she continued. "After we were forced from the ranch, father was thinking of packing it in, but he wasn't sure where to go that would be less dangerous. Hearing about the loss of our ox, our gracious liege offered to replace him to encourage us to stay."

"So why the cows, then?" I asked, puzzled.

"Well," she began, finding a fence rail of her own and hopping up. "they're not for milk, or rather, not *just* for milk. You see, my

114

father likes to make cheese. He has me milk all of the ewes. Do you know it is actually easiest to make cheese from ewe's milk? It's about twice as thick as cow's milk."

"You don't say," I remarked politely.

My attention was beginning to drift from the topic as she nattered on, but strangely, Royland seemed riveted by her tale.

"So, anyway," she said, "my father reasoned a pair of cows could be trained to the yoke and give milk as well, so he could experiment with different cheeses. Though not as strong as male oxen, he reckoned that as a team, Skye and Sarah would do in a pinch for the light carting and plowing we need. The baron approved the exchange. It happened that the good baron knew a dairy farmer who owed his son a big favor."

"So, will you milk these two while they're here?" I asked, indicating the heifers quietly grazing in the field.

"No, silly," she laughingly replied, "cows only give milk after they've calved. We made sure that farmer Cunningham gave us a matched pair of bred heifers. They're three-year-olds. Each will give birth this spring. Then their udders will fill. Father plans to gift the calves back to Baron Westarbor as veal for his table, then we shall have milk for about ten months if we keep at them."

It seemed kind of cruel to take the baby cows from their mothers, but I was coming to see that it was a cruel world. However, I was also beginning to tire of all this milk talk, so I tried for a change of topic.

"Speaking of children," I parried, "How is your brother, Avery junior?"

"He is well, Luke," she returned. "When he went to town to take up his profession, father didn't place much faith in it. He said A.J. was just 'milking the ram' with his talk of shoe-making."

"What made him take up cobblery, of all things?" I asked, being determined to depart from the lactation theme.

"That's a funny story," said she. "When A.J. was younger, he had this notion that our ranch was haunted by brownies. He claimed he had seen them out by the pond. Thinking to make use of them, he would put out a saucer of milk each evening along with some cut pieces of leather. He had heard in a story that if you make them such gifts the brownies might stitch you a pair of shoes."

"And did they?" asked Royland, entranced.

Mischief danced in the young woman's eyes as she continued the tale. "Well, he never got any shoes out of it, but some creature or other did drink the milk. Eventually, A.J. gathered his scraps and fashioned his own footwear. He grew quite proficient at it. Here is some of his latest handiwork."

And with that, Prissy dropped down to the spongy grass of the meadow, spun about, and bunched up her skirts in front. This revealed a set of calf-length, soft leather boots. The dark stained leather contrasted sharply with the creamy skin of her knees and lower extremities.

"What do you think?" she asked, shifting to a curtsy pose and smiling demurely. "Aren't these nice?"

The boots *did* look comfortable and well-made. They weren't all *that* fine, but I thought I should compliment her brother's work, especially as Royland had somehow grown upset, his mouth working like a fish.

"I think," said I, "that you should hide those away lest you be found in violation of the sumptuary laws."

"Aww," she gushed, "you say the sweetest things."

Royland was saved from comment by the ringing of the triangle that proclaimed supper to be ready.

***

After dinner, Royland and I were asked to go and search the barn. It turned out that mister Strongback had once been half of a team of oxen. His left-hand partner, Scott, had contracted some strange ailment years ago and had to be put down. Tilda had simply traded her wagon for the smaller cart she used today which could be pulled more readily by a solitary ox. But Tilda never threw anything away. The old magpie maintained heaps of equipment buried in crates at the back of the barn collecting cobwebs. Among these, she assured us, was Scott's and

Strongback's original, smaller yoke which would be just *perfect* for Skye and Sarah.

Mining through Tilda's trove of ancient treasures was a truly daunting task. However, empowered by a better meal than we had known in weeks, we persevered. Among the collected oddments of decades, I happened upon an item with which I was familiar. Packed in a dusty crate I found an old bull's-eye lantern. Thinking to clean it up a bit and have some fun with it, I took it up to the hayloft, to which Royland and I had once again been relegated. Finally, the yoke unearthed, we managed to pack everything else back up neatly and retire to our loft before the last of the day's light was spent.

Royland didn't go to sleep immediately as was his custom. Instead, he watched me clean the old lantern. I polished its glass and scraped most of the green corrosion from its working parts until the trigger could lift its shutter once more. When I pried out the little stub of a candle from its base, Royland reached out his hand and gave me an expectant look. I handed it over without comment.

Touching his index finger to the wick, Roy murmured: "digitus flamma," and it lit.

"Hey," I objected, "we're not supposed to be learning any fire magic yet, Roy."

He shrugged, then looking over to his right, he raised a finger to his lips in a shushing gesture as he handed me the lit candle. So, I ensconced it firmly back into the lantern and just accepted being an accomplice to his convenient misbehavior. I unshuttered the light and played it all around the barn casting eerie shadows and bothering the three bovines below.

"Give it here," whispered my cousin.

Accepting the lantern with a boyish grin, he locked its shutter wide open and set it down facing the back wall of our loft. He then proceeded to make a series of arcane hand gestures. I grew a little concerned. He looked like the very devil himself with his face lit from below and his chin, eyebrows and cheekbones cast in sharp relief. Shifting my focus to the wall, I was seized by a different humor. For upon it, portrayed in shadow, rested the large head of a wolf baying up at the moon.

A few moments later, the wolf became a bunny, twitching his ears and wriggling his small snout convincingly. I started to chuckle. But Roy had only just begun. He made a goat with horns and a little beard, then a stag. I began calling them out.

"Camel . . . Owl . . .Snail," I laughed. "Oh, not that Roy, it's too soon!" I exclaimed, for he had rendered an enormous spider that moved so realistically that I could feel my winding reflex stir.

A pair of moths, attracted by the light began flapping against the lantern. Looking down, Royland somehow persuaded them to join in his show. As they fluttered about, projecting their shadows upon the wall, Royland conjured the image of a hawk to pursue them, then a bat. When the bat shadow would touch a moth shadow, it would 'die' and fall from view, only to arise elsewhere in a few moments. We laughed into the night, me aloud and my cousin silently, until the candle finally gave out.

As I lay there in the hay, my sides still aching from laughter, I heard Royland's nocturnal cacophony commence. If only I had access to all of the lumber my cousin sawed at night, I could build my own cabin free from the distressing sound. But I knew I would sleep well this night nonetheless, for I was well and truly spent. As I drifted to the land of nod, I considered the many strange activities my poor cousin had mastered to gain relief from his inner hive. Although it was rather sad, at least he was getting over his aloofness. I felt honored he was beginning to share some of his eclectic but hard-won aptitudes with me.

***

The following morning over breakfast, Master Chadwick informed us that we would be separating the remnant of the Tillerson flock from our own. We had gathered and brought Goodman Avery's sheep here to provide for them until their owners could return. Tomorrow morning, my master would drive them back up to the Tillerson ranch so that Goodman Avery could resume their care.

The Tillerson ram, in defense of his flock had been among the first casualties of the mygalom invasion. My master observed that Big Barney was well up to the task of siring our next generation, so he offered Little Abe to Harriet. Initially, Goody Tillerson objected this was too fine a gift. My master insisted that he could easily select a few promising replacements from among the rams in the spring birthing and spare them the culling that would otherwise be their fate. Tilda made it clear that this was what good neighbors did for one another in tragic times, patting her friend's hand gently. With a promise to repay the kindness somehow, the teary-eyed matron finally accepted.

Diverging from his predictable pattern of following Master Chadwick around, Royland proved to be little help to us that day. I think Tilda commandeered his assistance in hauling and unpacking her purchases from town. In any event, I found myself doing double my usual work in wrangling the foreign ewes to the east holding pen. Sampson proved ruthlessly efficient at cutting them out from the flock, and my master would verify the identity and condition of each. To me, a sheep was a sheep, but the old shepherd knew his own on sight.

When we finally finished with this arduous assignment and were walking back toward the cottage, my master took notice of the small flax field we had planted. He wandered over for a more thorough inspection and harrumphed.

"Have you been weeding this patch as well, Lucas?" asked the old man.

"Yes, master," I replied earnestly. "I like weeding."

"Show me," he commanded with a droll little smile while gesturing toward the field.

Despite feeling a bit worn out from the day's activity, I rolled over the low fence, dropped to my knees and commenced plucking up the undesirables from amid the tall stalks. Their flowers were mostly gone since last time, having shriveled into little brown pods. Master Chadwick crouched down beside me to watch while absently scratching at a sideburn. I felt a little conspicuous with him observing me like an owl, but I soon found my usual rhythm in the simple and comforting task.

"Extraordinary," declared my master a few minutes later.

"I'm just pulling up weeds, master," I said. "Oh, I know my magic is bolstering the flax withal. It's my affinity. I encourage the plants to grow."

"It's not just that, Lucas," said the old man. "You seem able to instinctively discern which plants are wanted, and which are not. For those of us lacking your affinity, that is a very subtle and difficult spell to manage. Tell me, how do you feel right now?"

"I feel great," I said.

"Weren't you just hungry and tired a few minutes ago?" he asked.

Thinking on it, I had to agree that I was.

"This is what I think is happening," declared my master, holding up a dandelion I had pulled up and discarded. It was unnaturally wilted and shriveled. "When you lay eyes on a weed, you identify it as unwanted, then your mere touch siphons the life energy out of it to replenish your own magical store and general health. That scrape on your hand, for instance, is now almost healed. Once you become sated, you seem able to dump the excess energy into the plants you have deemed desirable. This is quite a remarkable gift. We must strive to get this under your conscious control."

That was interesting. I stopped weeding to stare at the old man's expectant face.

"Don't you see, Lucas?" said Master Chadwick excitedly. "What if you could siphon off a tree to heal someone?"

"I don't see how," I said after a brief pause for thought. "It's just something I do with the plants."

"We shall have to explore it later," said he, "For now, we have a field of flax to harvest. These are now fully ripened - about two months early, I might add."

We began by pulling up all the stalks by their roots and binding them into little sheaves. The flax grew to well above my waist, but the silky linen fibers within ran on down into the ground, so it couldn't be simply scythed like hay. During this phase of the operation, I was scolded more than once for withering the flax stalks, until I learned to consciously rein in my gift whilst uprooting them.

The little pods, that my master termed the 'bol' of the flax, would be separated out later by a rippler. He assured me each contained about six to ten seeds. Some we would reserve to plant next season's crop. The excess would be crushed to produce linseed oil for cooking and all kinds of other uses. For the time being, we just left them on the stalks.

"What's next?" I asked.

"Dinner," replied Master Chadwick with a tiredness I no longer felt. "We'll let them be retted by the sun and the dew for a while. Tilda usually takes over breaking, scutching, and hackling them.

I was behind on my reading. I'd have to look up these obscure horticultural terms when I again had access to the guest room. For now, I just helped my old master back to the cottage, cleaned up at the well, spun up some more water, and awaited the glorious spread I knew Tilda would put out whenever guests were present.

***

After dinner, I busied myself with this and that. Master Chadwick was taking tea with Tilda and Goody Tillerson. He seemed worn out. He mostly just sat there sipping at his cup and smiling amiably while Tilda ran on and Harriet tossed in an occasional word of encouragement. I took the opportunity to interrupt and beseech Tilda for a fresh candle, thinking I could perhaps cajole Royland into another dazzling display of shadow puppetry.

The sun was nearly down, so I headed out to the barn and began my climb up the ladder to our loft. As I reached the top, I was suddenly confronted by an image that would haunt my reverie for weeks to come. There lay Royland and Priscilla sprawled in the hay and locked in an embrace with their lips pressed together. Quickly reversing course, I managed to drop the candle. It clacked against the boards below while I descended the ladder two rungs at a time. As I went scurrying for the doors, I glimpsed two heads popping over the loft's edge.

Outside, the dying sun painted the distant cloudscape in fiery auburn hues. Of their own volition, my feet began to make their way toward the north meadow. I don't know why I was so perturbed over it. My cousin was eighteen, after all. I had just never thought about him spooning and sparking. The girls in town had long ago written him off as an idiot. To be fair, Roy had

121

always seemed to reciprocate those feelings and shun any attentions that did come his way. It kind of made sense in retrospect, knowing the young man could sense the feelings of others.

I found Sampson on his favorite hillock laying in a circle of beaten down grass.

"Move over," I directed.

"Wuff," he answered as he only minimally complied,

So, I flattened out my own space immediately adjacent to the hairy brute's verdant redoubt and settled myself down.

I supposed I should be happy my cousin had found someone who felt that way about him. I was sure that Roy wouldn't have kissed her if her feelings weren't honest. Royland was a decent fellow and deserved some happiness. But I still couldn't return to that hayloft. Nope, some things you just couldn't unsee.

We had just a quick breakfast the next day before our guests set off. I had to endure Royland and Prissy making sheep's eyes at one another over the table. One time when Prissy noticed my grim regard, she quickly turned away and hid a smile. My ears burned at the awkwardness. Fortunately, the two older women kept up a steady patter of conversation throughout the meal and my master seemed too deep in thought to follow much of the byplay.

They soon set out for Tillerson Ranch. With Sampson driving the small flock before them and the sun at their backs, Master Chadwick, Harriet, and Priscilla departed on foot. My master was carrying his shepherd's crook. I had rarely seen him actually make use of it to manage the sheep. He preferred to command Sampson to perform the equivalent of most of its uses. The two ladies led their new pair of cows. Across the necks of the would-be oxen lay the yoke that Roy and I had uncovered in Tilda's horde. It had cleaned up very nicely. It was essentially a big, thick, sturdy wooden timber with indentations that rested just in front of the animals' shoulders. From it descended two large u-shaped iron bars that fitted around their necks. It put me somewhat in mind of the stockade it had been my dubious distinction to attend. The animals lugged no load. They were not even shod as yet. The point of the coupling was merely to begin teaching them to walk in unison and respond to simple commands. The pair bawled their protestations about being made to leave so abruptly from their warm, comfortable barn. I could certainly sympathize.

As the group trod off toward the west, Tilda, Royland and I saw them off. My cousin surprised me again by shouting: "Bye! Come visit again soon!" Tilda and I turned to marvel at this wonder. Farewells seemed foreign to his usual, self-absorbed nature, and we hadn't even been aware that the boy *could* shout.

# CHAPTER SEVEN

# The Spinster

"By all means, marry. If you get a good wife, you'll become happy; if you get a bad one, you'll become a philosopher."

*~ Socrates ~*

In the following days, our magic lessons resumed. After much experimentation, we found that I could indeed borrow the energy from a tree. I couldn't heal others apart from plants, and any self-healing I personally derived from the process seemed limited to dispelling exhaustion and slightly speeding up the normal healing of cuts and bruises. I could top off my small magical reserve but couldn't exceed it. So, although I could now chuck rocks for a long time, they were still not the big ones that Roy could throw. Also, I felt kind of bad about borrowing the strength from a tree, and always made sure to pay it back later, often with interest. No, my green thumb seemed doomed to remain but a minor talent like Master Chadwick's water tricks or Roy's insect mastery, useful at times but nothing awe-inspiring.

With the return of our morning workout came Royland's rare garrulous moments. If you caught him after an especially taxing exercise, the boy could be downright chatty. On one such day, just after a tiring session in our training area, he approached me.

"Lucas," he said while rubbing his neck, "about me and Prissy..."

"It's alright, Roy," I interrupted. "I know that you love her. I won't make fun of it."

Royland reared his head back in surprise. "We're not in love, Lucas," he said, bemused. "She just likes smooching. She was showing me how."

Roy swung up onto the fence to the holding pen.

"You see, Lucas," he continued, tapping his finger to his temple, "in here, women are just like you and me. They like . . . things . . . just like we do, only they have to be a lot more careful."

" . . . to not get with child," I supplied. Royland blushed.

"Well that, I suppose" he allowed, "but I meant: to guard their reputations. You see, for whatever reason, when fellas get the idea that a girl's been around, they get all jealous and don't want her. It's stupid, but it's a fact. Other women are even worse about it. They spread gossip around maybe to improve their own chances? I don't know. Anyway, I just wanted to tell you not to say stuff about anything you might have seen. If you do, and Prissy gets her feelings hurt, I'll have bees sting you somewhere unpleasant."

I believed he could do it. Moreover, the very vagueness of the threat combined with what I knew of Royland's superb imagination gave me pause. Then he broke into an amused expression and awkwardly patted my shoulder.

Master Chadwick soon arrived with Sampson at his heels. Yesterday, our master had collected most, if not all, of the pregnant ewes into the east holding pen just behind us.

"The task is simple," our master began.

Roy and I immediately let out audible groans. We had learned that our master inevitably began thus when he had some new torture to heap upon us. I thought he did it to trick us into a state of calm and to embolden us to strive our best, but we had long since become aware of what the phrase portended. Realizing he had been caught out, the old man looked even more sheepish than he typically did and, with a sly grin, began anew.

"The task is as follows," he said. "Spring sheering is long overdue, thanks to that arachnid business. I found two more cast sheep last night alone."

A cast sheep was one that somehow got rolled over onto her back and couldn't get up without a helping hand. The first time I saw one like that, I thought it looked absurd, pawing at the air with four little hooves. But the sheep could die if left that way. Something bad happens with the gases in their bowels or the fluid in their bladders. Sheep aren't meant to be upside-down. Nor could Sampson flip them back. The best he could do was to keep the crows off them and bark for help. It happened mostly to the ones expecting lambs and especially when their fleeces were full and wet.

Master Chadwick stood in the pen, fleecing sheers in hand, and began to demonstrate how to harvest a sheep's wool.

"To properly fleece a ewe," Master Chadwick began to lecture, "first we employ a short length of rope to tie the ewe's foreleg to her opposite hind leg. Then we work our way around, flipping her this way and that. Then snip here . . . and here, and we're done."

The entire process took about ten minutes, but the old man was already looking fatigued. And that was with a veteran sheep. Our master assured us that the uninitiated yearlings struggled in 'sheer terror' the whole time. He expected us to laugh at his pun, but Roy and I just narrowed our eyes at the old man, refusing to give him the satisfaction. The ewe looked funny lacking the bulk of her wool which now lay in one great fleece across the fence railing.

Although he seemed to be slightly shy about it, Master Chadwick had invented a highly useful, personal spell specifically to sheer the wool off of a sheep. Of course, he made us each do one in the traditional way first. It went about how you'd expect and resulted in two tattered, near-mangled 'fleeces' and two very unsettled ewes. Then we huddled closer to watch our master perform 'radet ovium.' He made a gesture flexing all ten fingers in tandem as he chanted, and after a minute, the fleece practically fell off of the next ewe.

We took turns until all the little expectant mothers had been shorn, then our master left us to haul the fleeces away and stack them in the barn. Tomorrow morning would be more of the same, after we had brought in another batch from the meadow. This didn't seem so bad. We didn't yet appreciate how much work lay ahead for each of those fleeces.

Rough cleaning of the fleeces took days. Royland and I had to pick through each one to remove bits of dung and straw that had woven their way deeply into the curly, natty wool. It was kind of like weeding but without the nice energy boost to which I had grown accustomed. Nor did Master Chadwick offer any handy, magical solution. So, with fingers aching and cramping, we placed these small offerings on the compost heap for next year's gardens.

Next, we were introduced to the fine art of washing the fleece. At this point, we were given over to the tender mercies of Tilda, while our master returned to the meadow to attend to the lambing that had commenced. Under her guidance, Roy and I had to wash each fleece, sometimes repeatedly, with heated, soapy water in large tubs. You couldn't even scrub the dirt out for fear the wool would felt - just rinse and soak, rinse and soak. I was getting dizzy from winding up the water alone. I began to long for the back-breaking days of just grinding flour.

After washing, we set the fleeces up on racks to dry out in the sun before soaking the next bunch. Once dry, we were set about beating the fleeces with willow branches. This willeying was also hard work, but it did allow us to avenge ourselves somewhat upon the tangled mats we were gradually coming to detest. Now that we knew the process, Tilda abandoned us to it and took the first fruits of our labor over beside the cottage. She began separating and sorting through them by some mysterious method known only to her, and to arrange them into piles. I could see no escape from the endless mound of fleeces we had so easily shorn from the ewes in those first several days.

***

On nice days, Tilda's rocking chair made its way out to her area beside the cottage. There she would sit with two strange flat brushes, running the clumps of woolly fleece from one to the other and back until it began to resemble the soft, puffy stuff of clouds. Soon, there were great, ropy wisps of the stuff hanging from a line in the barn. All the while, Royland and I kept to our daily chore of soaking, drying and beating the fleeces. Although I didn't really notice it anymore, I felt certain I would never get the pungent stink of sheep out of my very skin. When the weather turned bleak, the old woman would instead work in her garden. Stalks and leaves of the weld, woad, and other plants were harvested, sorted, and put out to dry in various places about the house. Sometimes, she would impose upon our master to assist. He had a cunning knack for extracting most of the moisture from the cuttings.

It happened one day when I was passing by the parlor on my way to the well, that I heard a soft clicking sound. I peered within and spied Tilda astride a step stool before a most marvelous device. In one hand she held aloft a short rod atop which a cap reined in a big, fluffy tuft of woolen strands. I was no stranger to the distaff. Most of the women in town did some home spinning of linen or wool. I would often see them sitting with the distaff in one hand and their spindle hanging down from the other, twirling away as they drew out the fibers to make their homespun threads and yarn.

The sight I now beheld was different. Instead of an ordinary spindle, the threads that Tilda plucked forth were fed into a horizontal spindle spun by a flywheel she turned by means of two foot-peddles. I had heard of spinning wheels, of course, but the reality of the vision struck a resonant chord within me. It automatically invoked my 'spacium girabit' mindset and called to me. As the rest of the room seemed to lose all color, the mesmerizing wheel drew me in.

The feelings that it invoked in me are perhaps best described as sounds that were felt rather than heard. It was as though an alluring aria issued forth from the device. There was a deep, resonant tone from beneath my very feet. The flywheel blared a triumphant, harmonic fanfare like a set of brass instruments while the little spindle fluted out a set of counterpoints which danced up and down my spine. It wasn't perfect. A few 'notes' sounded off somehow. But, it was beautiful, nonetheless.

When Tilda looked up from her work with a distracted expression, the music ground to a halt. I let out a shuddering breath and sagged forward.

"Did you want something, Lucas?" asked the old matron.

"I was just seeing what you were doing, Tilda," I replied.

"I'm trying," she said while making some adjustment to the instrument, "to get this cantankerous old thing set up for the season. Can you hand me that jar of olive oil? I think I heard a squeak in the whorl."

"Oh," I said, handing her the jar, "you're calibrating it."

"I suppose so," she grunted, applying a bit of the oil with her fingers. "You and your ten-penny words, child. I swear, you must have taken all of the chatter from your cousin when you were in your cribs, the way you go on and he doesn't."

She was a fine one to talk, I thought. Lowering her bulk back down to the stool she soon had another go at spinning. As before, I became immediately enraptured by the process. It felt to me as though she were a virtuoso playing her harp as the bobbin turned and the threads spun together in an enchanting, synchronous melody. Then, she struck a series of sour notes.

"I don't think you're doing that quite right," I noted.

Flustered, Tilda set down the distaff and began to work out a snarl that had developed at the orifice where the threads went in.

"Oh," she said in a tone of mild frustration, "and now you'd teach your granny to suck eggs, would you? Perhaps you'd like to give it a whirl, mister smarty-britches?"

Before my brain could gauge the depth of her sarcasm, my head was nodding eagerly, prompted by my lingering desire for the music of the wheel.

A sour look graced Tilda's face then transformed into a wicked smile as she lifted herself up, dusted off the stool and made a beckoning gesture.

"Come on, then," she said in a sickly sweet voice, "show old Tilda the error of her ways. I'll draw up all the water from the well tomorrow if you can produce so much as a foot of good yarn."

Now unsure, I felt my stomach tighten and flinch as I took my seat. I needn't have worried, for as soon as I raised up the distaff, I felt a connection to the amazing apparatus. With only a few false starts, I got the wheel spinning and learned to draw out the fibers between a thumb and forefinger. As the spinning got underway, I again heard the notes that seemed slightly 'off' in some way. My attention was drawn from the wheel to the threads themselves. As they twisted together, some of the little fibers' ends were left sticking out. I gently began correcting this by turning them inward to catch upon others. Also, where one group of threads would end and another would begin, there would sometimes be a slight bump in the yarn. I quickly found that this could be smoothed out by how I drew from the distaff. Soon, instead of a single, long draw, I found myself making a series of shorter tugs followed by one long; until each transition happened as smoothly as changing partners at a barn dance. All the while, I modulated the speed of the wheel to perfect the music that only I could hear. I wasn't really using the foot pedals, or treadles, anymore. I was just resting my feet on them to better feel the rhythm.

Suddenly, something felt wrong. As I reached for more threads, I noted a strange absence of fulfillment. Stilling the wheel, I looked over to find the distaff nearly empty. To my left, I was surprised to find an astonished-looking Tilda leaned over to where we were practically cheek to cheek. She stepped up to the spinning wheel, released the bobbin, and drew forth a double-arm's length of yarn, inspecting it closely. She then looped it about her meaty fists and gave an experimental tug. Eyebrows lowered with determination, I saw the muscles of her not inconsiderable forearms bulge as she sought the limits of the strength of my strands. The yarn defied her efforts and held. She looked over at me in consternation. I had rarely seen Tilda go silent before.

"Your master must see this," she finally said.

Plucking up an empty skein from nearby she promptly began unrolling the bobbin and winding its contents thereupon.

We took the half-skein of yarn out into the fields where my master stood overseeing the new lambs and their mothers. The first-time mothers ordinarily had only one lamb. But the veteran ewes could drop up to three at once. To assure that the nursing ewes didn't get overtaxed, Master Chadwick would sometimes have to take a lamb from one ewe and foster it onto another.

Most of the baby lambs were sleeping. A few were nursing, and a little pack of four were frolicking about, gamboling from one end of the pen to the other.

"How comes the culling?" shouted Tilda as we approached.

"Just about as usual," replied my master with a shrug. "I must confess that this is my least favorite part of the job. Who am *I*, after all, to decide who is too far past their prime to be of further use?"

"Ah, just use your usual ratio of seven to one," said Tilda, "It's served us well in the past. You'd better make up your mind soon in any event. Goodman Verney is due to come calling most any day now."

"I suppose you're right, madam," returned the old man listlessly. "At least there are no black sheep this year as yet. I find it hard to condemn a lamb and its dame whose only sin is growing wool deemed unsuitable for your dyes."

"Speaking of wool," she said, handing him the half-skein of yarn, "tell me what you make of this."

The old man stroked the lustrous fibers, his touch lingering in the center to pluck forth a couple of strands to play between his fingers.

"I told you that old wheel had a few good years in it," he praised. "I do believe this is your finest work to date, madam."

"I was afraid you might say that," groused Tilda. "And I'd have to agree with you if it were indeed my handiwork you were fondling there."

Confusion washed over my master's face as he looked back and forth between the two of us.

"Lucas?" he asked in an astonished voice. Tilda nodded.

"I should like to conscript your apprentice for the next few weeks to explore this new-found talent," she said. "*Honestly*, Elizar, I knew the boy could work *magic*, but it never occurred to me he could be *useful*."

I managed to feel both very gratified *and* insulted. And just like that, I was promoted from menial to head spinner. Master Chadwick continued with his lambing and culling. Tilda began carding the wool full-time, sitting in her rocker and showing me the ropes. Only Royland seemed dissatisfied. He now had to wash all the remaining fleeces by himself. I would see him on occasion with his fingers pruning up beating the tar out of those fleeces with his willeying stick. Under Tilda's tutelage, I learned all of the variations of spinning of which the wheel was capable. We made everything from thick, fluffy yarn for knitting and crochet, to the delicate, tight threads preferred by the weavers, heavily favoring the latter.

True to her word, Tilda had drawn up and hauled all the water from the well on the following day. When Royland tried to step in and help, he was briskly shooed away. The Fowler pride was not to be sullied. And though I took care to wash and drink only sparingly, I thought the water had never tasted so sweet.

***

As the days passed by, my spinning became second nature, freeing my mind to pursue other thoughts. I would ruminate on this and that, sometimes asking Tilda her opinion on a matter. Once she realized I was no longer subject to distraction, she began sharing many interesting facts and stories. Carding wasn't very mentally demanding either.

One afternoon, she was telling me about how my master first came to be here. Apparently, just after the war, the king was worried that the goblins would reunite under a new leader to contest the border. The kingdom's mages were spread thin, but one would be needed to keep watch in Westarbor. Tilda, then a tender young woman of twenty had just lost her parents, who had been among the first of the new settlers. They died of a plague that had swept the region just four years after the war. She was already very accomplished in dying, carding, and spinning the wool but knew very little about managing the animals. This had been her father's forte. Being free ranchers, possession of the land and its chattels had come to her and her sister, who had already moved to town. Alone, Tilda struggled through the next several years to make the ranch work, but the flock had suffered.

Along came Master Elizar Chadwick. Young and hale at thirty-six, and fresh from the wars, he sought a place in the new barony where he could keep watch upon the goblins. The first blocks of the watchtower at the pass were just being laid, as were the curtain wall and other improvements to Westarbor Keep.  The newly-minted baron wanted the famous wizard to reside at one or the other, but  Master Chadwick had something else in mind.  He was tired of the politics and bureaucracy of the mages and nobles, and even the exciting battles.  He desired nothing more than a quiet place to think, live a simple life, and develop his magery in peace.  He had always wanted to try his hand at breeding animals.  His parents had managed a herd of cattle when he was a boy.  Thinking to take part in the sheep ranching industry springing up in the western barony, he went out to survey the recently deforested land.

He could have had his own land grant in an instant.  He could have bought some stock and started fresh, but when he saw Fowler Ranch and its distressed flock, he was charmed by it.  His offer to buy out the owner 'land, stock and buildings' was met with a stubborn refusal.  Instead, the arrogant mage was offered a shepherd's wage and a trial period in which to prove himself.  Amused, he accepted and only rose to the status of full partner many years later.

I was engrossed by the tale, and the hypnotic turning of the wool left me prone to speaking my thoughts as they occurred to me.

"Tilda, do you love Master Chadwick?" I blurted.

The carding brushes ceased their rhythmic scraping.

"Does this have anything to do with Priscilla?" she asked in a cutting voice.  "I saw you making eyes at her the day they left.  A pretty young thing she may be, Lucas, but she's too old for you.  You should set your sights on a girl more your own age."

I was gobsmacked.  The yarn I was making developed a snarl which promptly bunched up in the orifice.  The wheel made several more full rotations before lurching to a stop.  I would have to tread cautiously here lest Royland sting my unmentionables.

"Certainly not," I protested.  "I just wondered . . . ."

"Well, if you're going to be a nosy parker, you should expect to get some back," said Tilda, resuming her brush strokes with great vigor.

As I worked to free the errant yarn, she continued in a calmer tone: "Although Elizar did cut a fine figure back in the day, he was a confirmed old bachelor long before I met him for reasons that are his own to share. I do love the old goat, Lucas, but more like a father. Mind you, I once had a few romantic notions of my own. There was even a certain butcher who shall remain nameless that came courting once, but I didn't want that life. No, I've long since resigned myself to remaining unmarried. It's less complicated, and one of the few ways in this world that a woman can stay independent and free to make her own choices."

***

The next day, Tilda was absent from the parlor. Looking about, I found her and Roy setting up the big cauldron in the side yard. I should've known better than to seek them out, for I was immediately put to work hauling water. They built up a low fire and heated the water to which Tilda began adding various ground herbs and tinctures. The fumes that issued forth had a cloyingly floral fragrance with strongly astringent and rotten overtones.

Royland had rewound the skeins into big loops of yarn and loosely twisted them into hanks. These he had submerged in a cold bath of liquid that Tilda called the mordant. It was supposed to make the wool accept the dye more readily and keep its colors bright. I found it best not to ask what all went into it. I had seen the old woman collecting sheep urine among other things. Deeming them ready, Tilda took an armful of these braids, and set them within the heated cauldron which she then moved off of the fire. As the cauldron bubbled and steamed, Tilda stood dunking the wool with a long wooden paddle. She looked like a storybook witch stirring her pot. She would need only to recite some rhymes and cackle a bit to complete the picture.

"What are you smirking at, child?" she said. "Best we get you back to your spinning before you lose the knack."

It was at this point that my master came from around the back of the cottage.

"I think it is time," he announced, "that these two return to their morning lessons. You've had your two weeks and then

135

some.  You have yarn enough for your current projects.  There'll be plenty of time to spin the rest."

"I tell you, Elizar," Tilda wheedled, "that boy could spin straw into gold if he put his mind to it.  We should let him keep at it.  He seems to have taken to the work."

"That is as may be, madam," replied my master, "but the lad is here to apprentice as a mage.  It is high time he resumed his primary calling.  It's not as though we have much of a market for the fine cloth this will produce.  I doubt that the sumptuary laws will even permit its donning by the folks around here anyway."

"Don't quote me the sumptuary laws," said Tilda, throwing up her hands and rolling her eyes skyward.  "Heaven forbid we hard-working lowborn have anything nice to show for all our efforts.  It's as though they fear an uprising if we're allowed any bit of fun."

"You're not far wrong, Tilda," said Master Chadwick.  "The baron is far more lenient and progressive than most.  If you lived over in Downham, I doubt you would be permitted to dress even as finely as you do."

"Well, what about the nobles themselves, then?" countered Tilda.  "Although not quite as elegant as their imported silks and ermine, surely they would want such cloth for a warm winter garment or two.  And let's not forget about the knights and their ladies.  They like to prance about in their frippery."

"I shall discuss it with our liege," promised my master, obviously amused by her tenacity.  "At the very least, I imagine we could export such cloth to bring some extra coin into the barony.  Meanwhile, Lucas will return to morning lessons with Roy.  He can spin for you if he so desires after any other afternoon chores I assign him.  I'm afraid I must insist."

Tilda looked a bit deflated by this.

"Well, I suppose I do have enough to be getting on with at that," she said grudgingly as she turned back to check on her cauldron.  "Lucas, feel free to come use the wheel whenever you get the itch.  It was nice to have some company."

And, just like that, it was back to the practice pitch and the tossing of small rocks.  I watched in envy as Royland now hefted two of the larger stones at once and dealt double the destruction upon our poor wooden adversary.  My strength had grown somewhat.  I could now at least manage a decent distance.  But I was missing the spinning wheel already.  Just thinking about it left my vines in a twist.

Without warning, I was struck by a novel solution to my shortcomings.  I had to sit down and carefully consider this audacious epiphany.  Royland shot me a black look, no doubt thinking I was shirking already, then continued his assault.  I settled my inner garden.  Then, instead of the biggest, thickest vine I could manage, I caused it to extrude as many thin, wispy vines as possible from my puny parcel.  I drew them out long and slender, stretching outward as far as they could reach.  Then I turned my 'spacium girabit' mindset inward upon them and wound them into a single, great, ropy composite cord.  It consumed all of the resources of my magic center.  And although the resulting construct was really no larger than the biggest single vine I could foster, I felt its fibrous strength eagerly awaiting my will.  Standing as I turned to the cart, I selected a large stone, and with a cry of 'levare conicere,' swept it toward the target dummy.

I finally understood what Royland and our master must feel when a mighty deed was *not* beyond their means.  For rooted in a hundred places and wound like yarn, *this* vine was up to the task.  Take that, wooden foe!  Royland looked at me in confusion for a moment, then stepped over closer shielding his eyes from the sun.

"Good one, Lucas," he praised as a smile played across his lips.  "Can you do it again?"

I wondered if I had another one in me.  My mental construct still seemed firm, but it was rapidly depleting my reserves.  If I rested to recover, I would have to start all over again.

"Sorry, tree," I said as I leaned against the nearby poplar's furrowed bark.

With a rush, I felt its energies fill my inner field with green.  Weeds were but a snack compared to the refreshing feast of timber.  In response, the tree began to drop seed pods, thinking autumn had come.  Prior experimentation had already caused it to flower early.  I refocused on the stones as the seeds gently drifted downwind on their fluffy white sails.  I would have to put this to rights later lest the poor thing die.  Its sagging, leafy arms had already begun to resemble those of a weeping willow.

As I hefted a second stone and readied to throw, my cousin stepped in the way.  Believing he meant to test his shield, I went easy on him and lofted the small boulder in a high arc toward the target.  But the familiar blue shield never materialized.  Instead, Royland called out 'capturam petram,' and made an underhanded gripping gesture with both hands.  The stone halted in mid-air as though frozen, bobbed there for a moment, and then smoothly descended to rest in the dirt.  Intrigued, I invoked my mage sight and tossed him another.  Watching closely, I could kind of make out how he had accomplished the new spell.  This time, Roy did not set the stone down.  With a cry of 'conicere,' and a familiar sweeping gesture he sent the stone back my way.

"Capturam petram," I cried as I struggled to repeat my cousin's feat.

And thus began the strangest game of 'catch' in which it had ever been my privilege to participate.  With frequent stops to rest and recharge while Royland waited impatiently, I honed my skill in mustering my newfound strength.  Our master found us still at it when later he ambled by toward the barn, a lamb slung over his shoulders like some kind of living stole.  After a brief pause for assessment, he grinned from ear to ear and continued on his way.  Our wooden target heaved a figurative sigh of relief as it was spared from further bombardment that morning.

I did arrange to spin a bit for Tilda that evening despite a heavy list of assigned afternoon reading.  I found the parlor adorned with a glorious array of braided yarns ranging from the pale yellow of pure weld to the deep gold that resulted when Tilda modified it with powdered copper, and several shades in between.  Tilda blushed prettily at my effusive praise and agreed that this had been a good run as she rubbed her dye-jaundiced hands upon her apron.  I viewed the spinning session as extra practice for my magic.  The yarn had taught me much.

***

Several days later, an ocean of woad-blue yarn had joined 'mount yellow' in the parlor.  They were bordered by a veritable forest of Lincoln green, made by over-dying one upon the other.

This was Tilda's mainstay. Though she dabbled with the red of madder root and some other exotic colors and combinations, by and large, her pallet tended toward the hues of the sea and the sand. Over breakfast, Tilda informed us that her sewing circle would be meeting at the Tillerson's for the next few days and we would be on our own for meals. Woebegone, the other two looked over at me and I sighed.

"Are you quite sure, Tilda?" teased Master Chadwick. "Word has just reached me from the Turner Ranch that Goodman Verney will be arriving here on the morrow. You know we always get the best deals when you bat your eyelashes at him."

"I'm sure I don't know to what you are referring, Elizar," she responded, taking a prim little sip of her morning tea. "On another matter, I just realized that today is *measuring* day. In the Fowler tradition, all residents below the age of twenty are to report to the barn immediately following the morning meal. I will expect you there shortly."

Gulping down the remains of her tea, Tilda heaved herself up and sauntered out the front door.

"What's measuring day?" I asked Master Chadwick under my breath.

"I don't know," said my master. "Be wary, Lucas. That woman may spin a fine yarn, but I sense she is up to something."

Royland narrowed his eyes and nodded. I thought my master was just using the opportunity to enact one of his horrible puns, but Roy's verdict caused me to rethink it. I had learned to trust his instincts about people.

"Don't worry, master," I returned. "We won't let her pull the wool over our eyes."

That actually drew an appreciative smile and a nod of acknowledgment from the old gent before he also excused himself and stalked off, undoubtedly bound for the lambing pens.

Tilda met us right at the barn door, which she had opened all the way until its handle touched the outside wall. It was propped open with a stone so as not to swing back shut. I had never really paid attention to all the scratches on its inward side before, but there were indeed a set of organized marks thereupon. Taking me by the arm, she marched me right over to one side of the door. Producing a small paring knife from her apron, she then scratched a deep gouge right where the top of my head met the wood.

"I mark you at five feet and four inches," she said, as she hastily scratched out 'Lucas XIV' on the wood.

The new gouge rested about three fingers below an older mark that said 'Tilda XIX.' Doing the math, I realized this was very near when her parents had passed on. I started to argue that I was almost fifteen, but she 'tut, tutted' me to silence as she stalked over to claim Royland. She had to berate him once for slouching, and twice for flinching before arriving at a verdict of 'five feet and eleven inches.' It seemed I was catching up some.

"What's the prize for second place?" I quickly asked.

"No prizes, child," she said, eyes atwinkle, "but everyone gets to leave his mark."

And, with no further ado, Tilda turned and walked off to prepare for her trip. It wasn't much of a ceremony, but I reckoned that Roy and I were now honorary Fowlers.

***

Goodman Verney's wagon was a massive thing, more like a portable pen for livestock than a proper wagon. With high, slatted sides, it was pulled by two teams of oxen. Though not under much load at present, the good butcher nevertheless took his time navigating the rutted, bumpy trail we called a road. Behind this, came another, smaller wagon, pulled by a single team. This was driven by the apprentice butcher, Goodman Verney's son, Otto.

"Hello the house!" bellowed the butcher on closer approach.

He needn't have bothered, for we were expecting him and had heard him coming. The household, such as it was, had already turned out to greet him at the end of the lane.

Once the man had shortened his reins and come to a complete stop, Master Chadwick addressed him. "Well met, Nathaniel. It was good of you to come. You can just leave the wagons out here, and we'll go have a look at the animals."

Nodding affably, Goodman Verney climbed down from the driver's seat and gave Otto a brief instruction to 'see to the oxen,' and we made our way to the pens. Royland opted to stay to assist Otto with the animals.

"And where's Tillie this fine day?" asked the butcher, peering beyond us toward the house.

"Out on business of her own, I'm afraid," replied my master. "She told me to pass along her apology for missing your visit. Ah, here we are. There are fifteen mature ewes and sixty six young lambs. If you were to butcher half the young lambs now, the ewes could provide for the rest until you've got spring lambs in a month or so. All are healthy and most are unblemished."

And there, in the east pen, stood the condemned. Master Chadwick had gathered up all of the sheep to be culled from the flock. There were all of the male lambs save for two he had held back as potential breeders for the day Big Barney was retired. Of the female lambs, he had kept but thirty: fifteen for our own table over the next season, and fifteen to join the flock on a more permanent basis. The mature ewes in the cull included most of those over five years of age, or those who had proven poor at lambing or had borne lambs with traits my master didn't favor. The poor things didn't even get a last meal. The old man had explained that It was better to starve them a bit before the slaughter lest the contents of their entrails taint the meat.

After a thorough inspection of the pens, Goodman Verney and my master retired to the cottage to discuss terms. Coin was rarely used in the barony for such transactions. Instead, men dickered over all manner of debts and obligations, sometimes using a few coins to balance out the end deal. It was fascinating to watch. Although I knew differently, one would think the two men didn't like one another, the way they denigrated and scoffed at each other's goods and services. Goodman Verney drove a hard bargain. He insisted that we give him the pelts and intestines of any lambs that we home-butchered for our own use. In turn, my master held out for more meat deliveries throughout the season, and a provision to keep some of the intestines saying: 'you're not the only one who needs sausage casings, you know.'

In the end, the good butcher agreed to take all of the sheep to be culled.  In exchange, he would offload some bacon and other cured cuts from his smokehouse which he had brought in his second wagon.  Several additional deliveries were detailed and arranged to occur throughout the remainder of the year.  These would contain a variety of fresh and cured meats.  The first delivery seemed strange.  Goodman Verney was to bring us a number of delicacies along with a dressed lamb spitted whole so as to be roasted over a fire pit.  When I asked about it, Master Chadwick looked put off and absently explained that Tilda was hosting her sewing circle here in about two weeks.  I started looking forward to the event.  There were only four or five of the ladies and a few of their children.  By my reckoning, that left the better part of a whole lamb for me, my cousin, and my master.

Business accomplished, Master Chadwick called in Sampson and together we drove about half of the culling out to Goodman Verney's wagon.  He would have to send Otto back to collect the rest tomorrow while he butchered this first lot.  We arrived at the wagon to find Otto regaling Roy about how he killed the animals for his father.  According to him, one swift blow to the back of the head with a hammer was the proper way because it could spoil the flavor of the meat should the animal suffer.  In this instance, my cousin was proving to be a good listener, nodding and tossing in words of encouragement while the younger boy gesticulated wildly to illustrate his tale.  It was satisfying to see Roy making new friends.

"Otto, quit your lollygagging and put down the ramp," barked the butcher.  "These lambs aren't going to kill themselves, you know."

While Otto complied, Goodman Verney leaned upon his wagon's wheel and turned to Master Chadwick.

"It's a shame about the Tillerson flock," he said with a sigh. "I was out there last week. Avery and his son managed to salvage a fair number of fleeces and hides. I ran the hides over to Dylan Turner on the next run and got him some credit for them."

"I must have just missed you, Nathan," said my master.  "I made a quick visit there four or five days ago. Avery said it was depressing sheering all the dead sheep, but 'wool is wool.' That was a good thought about the skins. I imagine Dylan will have his work cut out for him stretching them all into parchments this summer. In any event, I'm sure the Tillersons will get it all put back to rights. Ah... load them up, Sampson."

The dog had difficulty getting all of the lambs up the ramp. Although properly frightened by the menacing mutt, the new lambs didn't react like veteran sheep. Sometimes one would try to escape. Others would freeze in place or lie down and just shiver. But soon, with my and Roy's help, Otto was closing off the tail gait on the last of them. Packed in tight and huddled together, the little lambs were ready for their final journey. So we bade them farewell as Goodman Verney and his new charges, so recently arrived at Fowler Ranch, departed down the lane.

***

The next few weeks passed in a blur. Whenever I found a free moment, it seemed that Tilda or my master would sense it, and assign to it a chore. Ever since Tilda had returned from her sewing circle, she had been in a tizzy to get the ranch in condition for her friends' visit. Roy seemed more capable every day. As the constant practice gave him greater control over his magic, he was slowly beginning to emerge from his self-imposed exile from humanity. Or perhaps he was just looking forward to seeing Prissy again.

With just a few days remaining, the hullabaloo grew still more fevered. Otto delivered the spitted lamb which we stored in the cold cellar, and Tilda busied herself cooking all manner of delicacies. Their tempting aromas only deepened my disappointment with the meager fare that was presented at our quick, basic meals. It wasn't clear to me just what project the circle would be working on, and Tilda was being tight-lipped about it, so I just followed my master's good example of keeping his head low and doing as he was told.

Finally, the big day dawned. The very first thing we did was to start up a raging fire in the pit where Tilda often hung her big cauldron. Once it had died down to coals, this would be used for the spitted lamb. The butchers had done a fine job of tying the roast tightly to the spit with twine, and Master Chadwick had all of the basting and seasoning items prepared. Once we got it

143

set up, I couldn't resist using the 'turning force of the earth' to play with it a bit. The long-suffering look on my master's face was well worth the scolding I got for it.

"Lucas don't you know it's considered rude to play with one's food," he admonished, "and even more so when it's *my* food? This will need to roast here for at least five hours. Let us minimize the chances of a mishap by agreeing to forego the horseplay."

Earlier than expected, the ladies began to arrive. The Tillersons arrived first with Skye and Sarah pulling their wagon. The two animals didn't yet have their teamwork mastered, but seemed to be learning well. They both responded quite nicely to Goodman Avery's command of 'whoa.' Royland rushed over to help Prissy down. I noticed that he did offer his hand this time.

"Well met, Avery," said Tilda. "Who's watching the sheep?"

"I had Junior stay over to do a shift so I could attend this shindig, goody. I hope I'm not intruding."

"Not at all. You're most welcome. I'm sure Elizar will appreciate the company while we ladies get about our *business*," she said with an exaggerated wink.

"In that case," he said while stepping down and turning to give Harriet an assist, "I'll just set these animals loose to graze and seek the old fella out. Where's he roosting these days?"

"You almost got it, Avery," she said. He's in the side yard, but he's 'roasting,' not roosting. Lucas will help you with your team and show you the way."

"Or I could just follow the smell of burnt meat, I suppose," he said with a grin, "My thanks, goody."

Turning to me he said, "I'm very pleased to meet *you*, Lucas. I've heard a *lot* about *you*. I understand you stood with the knights when they cleared my land."

"I did at that, Goodman Avery."

"Just call me Avery, lad. That was no small thing you did. I saw one of those beasts up close. Killed my ox right out from under my goad, it did. We were lucky to get out on foot. Well, a

Tillerson always pays his debts.  For starters, there's a wheel of my best cheese on the back of this cart with your name on it."

"There's no debt, Avery," I said as I began unfastening Skye from her harness.  "I helped the knights because they were protecting all of us.  Let's get these ladies some grass.  I know a spot they like."

When I returned, I found that the Turner ladies had also arrived.  If Tilda was their expert spinner and dyer, and the Tillersons were weavers, then the Turners were their seamstresses and embroiderers.  I had even seen some of their work in a shop in town once.  Dylan Turner's mother, Lydia, went by 'Granny.'  Granny Turner was one of the first settlers of the western barony when she was a young woman and was now almost as old as Master Chadwick.  Her daughter-in-law, who went simply by 'Kay' had brought along her three young children.

Sampson seemed overjoyed by the many new guests whose acquaintance he could make with his intrusive wet snout.  He snuffled about underfoot until he was cruelly banished to the meadow by Tilda.

I noted a curious lack of wool as many food dishes and a few lumpy sacks were unloaded from the wagons.  When Tilda had gone out to the Tillersons, she had brought nearly her whole stock of yarn along.  I laughed when It turned out that Avery's large cheese wheel did have my name on it.  It literally had 'LUCAS' carved into the top.

To quiet the children down, Granny Turner told them that if they were nice, they could visit the lambing pen.  This didn't have the desired effect.  As ranchers' kids, they had a lambing pen of their own at home.  Royland came to the rescue. Producing some loops of brightly colored yarn, he made several interesting cat's cradles.  Soon, he and Prissy and the kids were all sitting quietly in a circle learning to play it with two people at a time.

"So this is the wizard who winds wool," said Granny Turner when things had settled down a bit.

I desperately hoped *that* one would not catch on, and was gratified that my old master wasn't here to remember it.

"I suppose I am," I said, "but I have heard tell of your wizardry as well, Granny."

"He's a charmer, Tilda. Keep him."

"I intend to," Tilda quickly asserted, "if that old goat will let me."

The small talk ran on for a while more and still I could detect no movement toward sewing of any kind. There was food preparation. Tables were set up, and the ladies looked very cheery.

When the children were engaged with one another, I saw Roy and Prissy begin to extricate themselves from the mini-sewing circle.

Just for meanness, I said to the kids, "Hey, you should ask Roy to show you the ghost shadows up in the hayloft."

My cousin cast me a baleful look, but it was far too late for *him*. While the two youngest ones, Hollie and Ronnie, attached themselves to Royland's shins, the older one jumped up on his back. The well-coordinated attack had the look of long practice. I would wager that their father, Dylan, was either very strong or a complete physical wreck by now. In any event, I was delighted to see Royland forced to duck-walk over to the barn, Prissy at his side. For a young man who didn't like to be touched, he was making a lot of exceptions of late: animals; small children; very forward young ladies.

When Roy reached the barn doors and opened one, his body language showed astonishment, even encumbered as he was by three riders. A shout rang out from all sides: "Surprise! Happy Birthday, Lucas!" And out from the barn walked uncle Robert, aunt Winnie, and my father. They were followed by Goody Galloway, the town baker who was Tilda's sister.

"I guess we wont be sewing then," I said with belated suspicion.

"I thought he had us when he saw his name on the cheese," Harriet tittered.

Over the rest of the resulting hubbub, I realized I was witnessing a pretty amazing scene unfold. Uncle Robert was standing stock still. Before him stood his shy son with a girl in hand, bedecked by children, smiling, and staring him straight in the eye.  Aunt Winnie looked like she was about to cry, but they must have been tears of joy, because Royland dove right in and gave her an unusual quadruple hug that included a number of squirming Turners.

For my part, I had not seen my father on his feet since the accident.  He looked just like his old self, and I realized in that moment how much I had missed him.  Letters just weren't the same as the man.  I found my vision blurring and was having trouble swallowing past a strange lump in my throat.  I would not cry.  I am the wizard who winds wool, dammit!  And with that bizarre thought, I jumped up and ran to his side.  Hugs are okay. Hugs are manly (as long as you thump them on the back).

***

It was late in the afternoon, verging upon evening, when the lamb was finally ready.  My master's estimate of five hours had been woefully misguided.  Time had sped past as we enjoyed our happy reunions with family and good neighbors, spoiled only by the tantalizing aromas that wafted occasionally over from the slow cooking mutton to torment us.  I wished my master would give in to temptation and simply finish it off with mage fire. Karina returned to her bakery wagon which they had hidden down the lane for my surprise.  From it, she fetched a goodly assortment of breads and pastries to slake our appetites while we awaited the main courses.  I shared my cheese wheel, which now read only: 'L U C /.'

We all turned to acknowledge a clamor that arose at the cottage.  On its stoop stood Master Chadwick with a large spoon gleefully striking within the triangle which hung from the eaves.  He was not normally permitted to ring the triangle.  Tilda had always insisted that this was a privilege reserved only for the cook, but, with the hours he had put in on the roast, it would be heartless to deny him this one small victory.

Hustling to the kitchen, the ladies of Arborvale retrieved their dishes and began to lay them upon the outdoor tables.  As my master brought forth a platter heaped with roasted lamb, and Tilda uncovered her savory sweet potatoes, she was bothered by a fly.  Indeed, several of the pesky things had descended to sample from any exposed dish.   Turning from a low conversation with Uncle Robert, Royland rose to his feet and gave the tables a long, stern glare.  Suddenly, all the flies found that there was someplace else they would really rather be.  Looking up at him, Tilda beamed, and, instead of turning aside, Roy executed a short, dignified half-bow before resuming his seat.

Dinner was amazing, and well worth the long wait.  Even the children were silent as we earnestly dug in to a meal the likes of which we had rarely enjoyed.  Kay Turner urged me to rein in my reckless pace with hints that Tilda's sister had baked me a cake for dessert.  Three layers deep it was, each layer a different flavor and dripping with honey.  On top, written out in icing, it read: 'Happy XV.'  After somewhat over-partaking, I finally sat back in drowsy satisfaction.

Then out came the gifts.  So they wouldn't feel left out, Royland gave each of his three minions a straw finger trap.  When their small digits proved to be of insufficient girth to trigger them, the  devices were happily re-christened 'thumb traps.'  If he had been their knight before, now he was their liege.  We soon saw 'uncle' Roy and his loyal followers armed with preserving jars set out to the meadow to wage war upon the fireflies.  I could only imagine how their general would tease them with his command of all things insectile.

"Happy birthday, Lucas," said Tilda as she proudly presented me with a rather large package.

"We of the circle," began Granny Turner in a solemn tone, "would like to thank you for helping to free our lands and also to acknowledge your skilled spinning.  With your yarn, we are able to craft cloth of unusual fineness.  We thought it fitting that you should share in its bounty."

As I opened the package to reveal a gorgeous, green tunic, Harriet Tillerson chimed in.

"It also occurred to us that wizards of any stripe are exempt from the sumptuary restrictions, so what better way to showcase our best work than to have you represent it for us?"

I held up the garment by its shoulders.  It was Lincoln green and had a sheen to it like the finer satins and silks I had seen on the nobles and the knights.  The weft and weave was so fine as to be nearly invisible.  It was stitched and embroidered with a yellow thread so deep in hue as to be almost golden in the pattern of leaves and vines.

"A.J. wanted you to have these to go with it," said Prissy, presenting a pair of low, leather boots.  "They're like mine only shorter."

Overwhelmed, I tried to rise to the occasion and give the gifts their proper homage.

"Thank you all.  And A.J. as well.  I think you are right that the laws would classify this fine a garment as a luxury.  And whether or not I am fit to don such a delight, I assure you that I will remember each and every one of you whenever I wear it."

"Put it on," spouted Tilda.  "I want to see if I took your measurements right.  We waited until after dinner so you wouldn't spill gravy on it."

I wanted to protest, but looking down, I could plainly see the evidence of her prescience.  Honorary Fowler indeed, I thought, as I blushingly tried to demur.  But the ladies were not to be denied.  As my old master laughingly savored my dismay, his reverie was cut short.

"There's one for you as well, Elizar," said Tilda.  "I took your measure long ago."

Granny Turner, shoving a similar package toward him said, "Go try yours on too."

He took his time opening the package and holding the kirtle up for display.  His was a deep woad-blue with cloud patterns embroidered thereon.  He bowed his head humbly before he spoke.

"As you all know, I stand in solidarity with my neighbors against the sumptuary laws which seek to keep us low.  It is the company we keep, not the finery we flaunt, that makes occasions such as this so sweet.  I would rather be here among friends and family than at the finest feast at the barons own table, where privilege and bickering oft spoil the broth.  I shall keep this fine gift and wear it with pride should the baron's men once again come banging on my door in the middle of the night demanding my presence.  Until then, I will wear only the humble cloth permitted to my true peers."

"Hear, hear," supplied Uncle Robert.

"How long did it take you to think that one up?" I asked under my breath as I walked past his chair toward the cottage to get dressed.

Amused, my master replied in a similar whisper, "Well, I don't have to play dress up, do I?  Go get changed, birthday boy."

Upon my return I was greeted by many 'oohs' and 'aahs' and a smattering of applause led by Uncle Robert.  I was descended upon as if by a covey of quail given a fresh handful of scratch.  I was poked and prodded most intimately as my new attire was tugged and pinched into place.  Next came the pins.  All the while, Avery, Uncle Robert, my master, and my father looked on with sympathy.

"This looks so splendid on you, Lucas," said Prissy.  "I hope you will spin some more, but whatever you decide is alright by us."

"Is it not every young man's dream," observed Master Chadwick, "to be surrounded by ladies who don't care whether he spins them yarns?"

Avery Tillerson had to be helped back up from the ground where he had lain in a fit of helpless laughter while the older women served my master with their grim glares.  When the merriment died down, Uncle Robert and my father approached with a box.  I opened it to reveal a sleek, new crossbow.

"Let me explain something first," said my father as I reached for the beautiful thing.  "From your letters and from the tales brought back by the knights, I understand that you control a very powerful magic to make things turn.  Thank you for lifting the millstone, by the way."

This was greeted with laughter by all.

"Now as it happens," he continued, "I know the keep's artillator.  He crafts all of the crossbows,  quarrels, arrows, and spears for our liege.  He also helps me build and replace parts of the millworks from time to time."

"Oh, you mean Javier Lewis," I supplied.

"Yes, Javier.  I'm not sure he believed me when I told him of your abilities, but, as a favor, he took the commission to build you this.  It's made from witchwood and is therefore nigh unbreakable.  Though rare, witchwood can still be found in limited quantities throughout the barony.  I use a piece to anchor the main shaft of the mill.  Your uncle here located some while clearing a field in his tenancy.  Javier assures me that it would take a team of oxen to crank back the string on this."

"Well let's find out, say I," declared Uncle Robert.  "I wore through three good pickaxes tryin' to pry up that stump."

Taking up the weapon, I first tried the crank.  It was tight. After only two rotations, I could turn it no more.  The string had barely moved an inch.  I unsocketed the crank handle from the shiny, new cranequin and set it aside.  I then laid my will upon the instrument.  I could feel the great resistance, but knew it to be inconsequential when pitted against the 'turning force of the earth.'  I looked on with pleasure as the string slowly creaked back -- then *snapped*.

"I was afraid of that," said my father with a dejected sigh.

"Alas," lamented Master Chadwick with a grin, "If only we knew someone who could craft us an extremely strong string."

"My yarn?"

"Wool's too stretchy," he said quickly.  "Linen is the answer, my boy.  Furthermore, you will need to study up on reverse twisted bundling, I think."

Words were insufficient.  Setting down the precious gift, I hugged my father once more.  Then I drew Uncle Robert in as well.

"Well, thank you all," I finally managed.

"Umm, there's one more," said Karina.  "I was told to deliver something into your care.  Wait.  I'll go get it."

As she stepped over to and into the barn, I wondered how this day could get any better.  She emerged holding a bird cage in her arms.  Within were two of the blue-banded birds like the ones Taylor Allen had used.

"Who's it from?" I asked.

"I'm not sure," said Karina, "Servants from the keep brought it; they heard I was coming out this way.  It came with a letter and a big bag of seed."

"Those stay in the barn this time, Lucas," grumbled Tilda.

"Yes ma'am."

Curiosity ate away at my resolve to open the letter in private until none remained.  So I cracked the seal and scanned through it by the light of the candles on our table.

"Well, who sent it, son?" asked my father.

"It's from Lady Megan," I replied, perplexed.  "What does R.S.V.P. mean?"

My father looked at me askance saying, "Reply soon via pigeon, of course."

I managed to fend off the curiosity that the letter invoked and tucked it away in the pocket of my tunic for later perusal just as the children returned from the meadow with Roy.  I had never before seen such a successful hunt.  Each child held a jar that was positively aglow and teeming with its tiny captives. Royland's three stooges stepped forward as one and set their hostages on the table before us. Then one by one, they removed the lids.

"Happy," said Willow.

"Birthday," said Ronnie.

"Lucas," chirped Hollie.

And as the fireflies reclaimed their freedom to take flight once more into the night sky above Fowler Ranch, their commander formed their serried ranks into a gigantic number fifteen and bade them to all blink in unison.  This time, I led the applause and Uncle Robert added a two fingered whistle as the others joined in.

CHAPTER EIGHT

# The Artillator

"Until the great mass of the people shall be filled
with the sense of responsibility for each other's
welfare, social justice can never be attained."

*~ Helen Keller ~*

"That's not quite right, dear," said my mother. "For the split stitch, the needle must pierce the preceding stitch."

"Well its supposed to have a mistake, isn't it?" asked Lynette.

"It's meant to have an *intentional flaw*," mother clarified. "That is very different than a dropped stitch. Besides, accidents don't count. Look what Megan is doing. Her floral border goes all around the cloak. Do you see where that one tulip is sideways in the purfle? *That's* her flaw."

"I don't see why we have to make a *flaw*," complained Constance. "They'd be perfectly beautiful without them."

Mother sighed.

"No thing and no one is perfect," she said. "That's the point. All of us have flaws, and we must learn to be beautiful *with* them. The cloak is more interesting this way, and it's thus more attractive to one with an eye for *true* beauty."

This struck home with Constance who cocked her head in thought. Lynette, however, was likely a lost cause. She just couldn't see how the embroidery was supposed to reflect the soul of the artist, not merely serve as an embellishment to its wearer. My two companions could scarcely be more different: Lynette with the attention span of a gnat and Constance who, living up to her name, could sit for tedious hours making a rigid pattern of fleur-de-lis but was challenged by any notion of whimsy.

"I think we're done for the day," said mother. "We're losing the light."

I turned the cloak over onto its back and carefully ran the remaining thread underneath a line of tight stitches of a similar hue. Lynette, eager to be done, turned her piece over and began to tie a knot.

"Knots are a crutch, Lynette," my mother chided. "The back of your piece will look unrefined."

"It's just the back, my lady," groused Lynette. "No one looks underneath a place mat."

"You'd be surprised," returned mother.

"And it'll be all bumpy," supplied Constance with a superior air.

I held my peace. Long had I known that what lay underneath was far more important than what was on the surface. When I was but a small girl, I didn't understand. People would often say one thing but mean quite a different thing. I didn't like the people who did that. When I was five, my father took me aside and finally explained it. He said it was a game that everyone played, in fact *the* game. One facet of 'the game' was called etiquette. It had very strict rules which I was already learning from my mother and her ladies in waiting. It was why the servants all used the same genteel forms of address and mannerisms no matter what they might be feeling inside. Another more important part of the game was called diplomacy. My father said he would teach me that.

"Are you ready, my lady?" asked Constance, breaking my reverie. "It's time for our lesson in the harp."

Constance was not looking forward to the activity but was speaking with false cheer for the sake of good manners. I could recognize this by the timbre of her voice and the set of her shoulders even despite my recent problem.

Truth be told, I wasn't looking forward to the lesson much either.

Lynette could play the harp like an angel. This was a natural talent she had picked up on her own whilst growing up on her father's farming fief. It was the primary reason she had been chosen as my companion, since all ladies of good breeding were expected to pursue music. But although Lynette had an exceptional talent, it certainly wasn't for teaching. Her 'lessons' consisted of sitting us down before the great thing and bidding us to pick at it, all the while smirking and shaking her head when we failed to produce something resembling a tune.

Constance had discovered a book in father's library that described the instrument and all of its parts. She would name each string as she plucked and had managed to find a few harmonious outcomes. I had no doubt that she would eventually achieve a mechanical competence of a sort but never the flowing brilliance that Lynette so gracefully wrought.

So, packing up my project, I headed off for a weary hour of discord.

***

The hour was late by the time I made my excuses and set off to see my father. When I arrived at the council chambers, the guards let me pass right through unannounced. Seated at the far end of the room were father and Sir Declan deep in discussion of the barony's business.

Both men stood, and my father said with a sappy grin, "Well, if it isn't the little lady of the castle. And where are your merry maids?"

"I came alone, father. I have something private to discuss with you."

"Perhaps I should withdraw, my liege," said Declan with a deferential half-bow.

"Nonsense," replied my father. "You know we can discuss anything in front of Megan. We should finish. It's growing late, and I shall have no time in the morning. Megan, bide a bit while I have a word with my good knight commander."

And so, as the two men reseated themselves to resume their discussion, I cast my eyes about the room.

Of course, the first thing that called to my attention was the gryphon. It sat proudly on its haunches with one foretalon raised to strike. The wings were arranged artfully. Its hooked beak gaped open wide in challenge, and its eyes gleamed most wickedly. Every time I saw the thing, I broke out in gooseflesh. When Trenton had bested the creature, father had promptly ordered it brought to the keep to be stuffed and mounted. The inner ward where it had been eviscerated had stunk for days, and a full watch had been required to keep away the scavenger birds. Finally, filled with sawdust and stitched back together whole, it had barely fit through the chamber's broad door.

"It has been verified, my liege," said Declan, "the stones marking the border cannot be found. I sent scouts to check, but they appear to have been missing for some time."

"Likely, this is Lord Downham's doing," returned my father. "He seeks to reclaim some of his lost lands and to cast doubt on the ownership of the copper deposit. All the while, he overtaxes us to ship the refined metal and indeed all our goods through his lands."

"The men I sent to the capital to retrieve new pigeons are overdue," announced Sir Declan. "How fared your entreaties to his majesty?"

"The king is being cagey, my friend," father replied. "He will send an adjudicator to reassess the border. I know what he wants. His majesty feels that perhaps he didn't make the best of deals when the barony was founded. He thinks he could do better than the twenty lances pledged to his service from Westarbor. Reading between the lines of his messages, I infer that an increase to twenty-five might see the matter of the border resolved in our favor."

"Twenty-five? Can we afford it, my liege?"

"Barely. And we can *not* afford to lose our investment in the copper mine. Gerrard assures me that way lies ruin. I had hoped to use the excess to reinvest and build up the treasury. There's a man in the north valley who stretches sheep hides into parchment as smooth as a baby's bum. Dylan Turner, I believe is his name. I was thinking to sponsor a book bindery here at the keep. I'm certain that Elliot could contrive such a device now that the mill is back up and running. Just imagine it, Declan - our own book binding shop. Who would be a provincial barony then, eh? And I know just the man to operate it . . ."

"Mayhap, my liege," said Declan, folding his hands before him, "we could lay that aside for now and consider the matters at hand. You were saying earlier that Lord Downham was withdrawing his lances from farther east and was likely to position them along our border. How do you know this is true?"

"A little bird told me," my father replied with an enigmatic smile.

"This is disturbing, sire. Moreover, word has reached me that Myles Nieves, upon returning to his family in Downham has been raised up to the knighthood."

"Payment for services rendered, no doubt," said father with distaste. "Maybe we shouldn't have held the little viper to our bosom for quite so long, but I couldn't squander the opportunity to send misinformation. In any event, Sir London will be far better served by his new squire. It was burdensome for the man to pretend for so long."

I was appalled. Myles was now 'Sir' Myles?

Back when father had first taught me the game of diplomacy, I had learned that only he and I could plainly see when another was being untruthful or disingenuous. Others had to rely on 'tells' in a person's voice, face, or manner. I learned that if you caught someone in a lie, it was better to let them think you had not so that you might find out why. I learned to say things I didn't mean convincingly, either as part of etiquette or for some other advantage in the game. I didn't care for that part much, so I further learned how to simply mislead. After I had learned the tells of everyone around me, I developed and practiced a set of false tells for myself. Mother didn't need to teach me the art of creating an intentional flaw; I was already a master at it.

"On a final note, my liege, I feel that Sir Fletcher performed outstandingly in leading the battle against the mygaloms," observed Sir Declan.

Before continuing, he leveled his gaze in my direction where I stood contemplating the one heraldic shield displayed in the hall that was hung upside-down.

"I think it's time for me to step aside, and for him to become your new knight commander."

"Is this why you have taken no new squire, my friend?"

"You knew it was coming, my liege. Time is a relentless enemy to which we all must eventually succumb. The code instructs us 'to fight for the welfare of all,' and I believe that the welfare of the barony would be better served by my successor. Do not forget that one day soon he will be serving your son, and it would be best if the new baron had not been a squire to his knight commander."

Trenton was very bad at *the game*. So my father had taken him as a page and taught him the code of chivalry instead. Father said that sticking to the code would keep Trenton out of mischief. The code was very difficult to reconcile with the game. It was more a belief system; a set of little truths that, if adhered to, would make a person just and honorable. I had read it, but Sir Declan lived it, and every day he seemed to draw new meaning from its rather simple themes. Father told me that a ruler must place the welfare of his people foremost, or he must at least be able to fake it from time to time. He wanted Trenton to stand among the former.

"If you are certain," said my father looking rather glum, "then I'll begin to make arrangements. What are your plans?"

"I thought I might take you up on your offer of a fiefdom in Arborvale," said the knight. We've had an amazing journey together, my liege. I would end mine as a country knight with vineyards."

"I must think on this further, we can take it up again at a later time," said father. "Do not bring it up in the council tomorrow, but come prepared to discuss the Downham matters."

"Yes, my lord."

As the knight took his leave, my gaze was drawn once again to the stuffed gryphon perched upon its low pedestal. I found it difficult to shake off a sense of foreboding from the matters discussed as menace rained down from its cruel eyes.

His business concluded, father finally turned to me.

"It's a marvel, is it not?" he said indicating Trenton's trophy.

"Very lifelike," I replied. "I feel as though it is watching me and ready to pounce."

"I thought it was just me," said father, "but others have said the same. I found that one of our own groomsmen at the stables practices taxidermy for hunting trophies and the like. He does excellent work. It's nicely intimidating. One day, when your brother sits in this chair, it will serve as a useful reminder of his prowess. He shall need every advantage we can give him, I fear. What's on your mind, poppet?"

"Father, it's about our gift," I began.

"We don't have the gift," he quickly corrected. "If we did, we would be made to apprentice and become mages. No, my sweet, we Arensons are blessed by what the mages term a 'wild talent,' and a very useful one at that."

"Well then," I began anew, "my *wild talent* has been oft absent of late. It comes and goes; there are times when I can't discern what a person is feeling. It frightens me, father. It's as if at any moment I could be rendered blind.

He rested his chin upon his fist and gave me an appraising stare.

After a few moments he said, "Well, I don't know how it is for women, but when I entered my own adolescent years, I found that my talent retreated for a time until the changes had settled down. I was so busy earning my knighthood that I barely even noticed. I should have thought to warn you, poppet, but it just didn't occur. You don't have anything to worry about, I should think."

"For how long is 'a time,' father?"

"A couple of months give or take. For how long have you been affected?"

"Since before the solstice."

With a sympathetic smile, he arose and crossed over to where I stood.

"There, you see? You should be right as rain in no time, poppet. It's all part of the game."

"You know, you shall have to stop calling me 'poppet,' father," I said with a sigh.

"You shall always be my poppet," said he, folding me into his arms.

I rested my head upon his shoulder, and, for the first time in months, I felt truly safe.

***

Mornings at the keep lately had become a bothersome fuss. My companions liked to watch the knights spar in the inner ward. Since the knights arose early to do so, the girls insisted on arising earlier still so that they might prepare and be seen at their best. To keep them happy, I would usually permit them to dress me at an ungodly hour. Then we would convene on the balcony to root for our favorites, or in Lynette's case, her current favorites.

On this particular morning, I felt my eyelids required a more lengthy inspection from within. I claimed to be indisposed and bade the two to go on without me. They could help me dress for breakfast afterward. Constance argued that her proper place was to stay by my side, but she eventually acceded to my wishes after some further grumpy urging.

For once, I allowed myself to wallow in the comfort of my bed. Like so many pleasant things, however, my carefree reprieve was not to last. Accustomed to our early schedule, the servants were wont to freshen the room shortly after sunrise. Our usual chambermaid must have been otherwise occupied, because today I was visited by Mollie Green, our ewery maid. The girl knocked upon the door but seemed startled when someone actually invited her to enter. She stood at my threshold blinking and uncertain.

"Well come ahead, Mollie, and be about your business," I said, sitting up.

"Yes, m'lady," she submitted with eyes downcast.

Then she briskly strode over to the window, spread the draperies to their hooks and threw open the shutters. As I smoothed my nightgown and stretched my back and arms, she made short work of the chamber pot, emptying its contents straight out the window. She refilled it with the stale water from our washbasin, swirled it around and then emptied in again.

"Fresh rushes today, m'lady" reported Mollie with a snaggle-toothed smile.

Ordinarily, the servants didn't initiate conversations with me, but I allowed for Mollie's special status. The girl was the daughter of Patrick Green who was our nearest farming tenant. Being both simple-minded and rather plain, Mollie had few prospects for either marriage or a profession. One day, when Goodman Green had come to once again air his grievance about the pigeons taking the spring seed out of his fields, my father took note of Mollie standing patiently behind him. Father inquired of Farmer Green, whether she might be available for work at the keep. He hired her on the spot and made her head of our ewery. The grateful farmer never complained again. Mollie spends her days cheerfully collecting, cleaning, and replacing all of our wash lavers, chamber pots, vases, and the like.

She peeled up the rush mat at the threshold and replaced it with a new one she had brought. The rushes were newly woven and appeared to be fresh from the mill's tail race where they were grown. Mollie sprinkled a double-handful of ground herbs over the mat and graced me once again with her frightful smile when she noticed me watching her.

"I suppose Olivia shan't be coming today then?" I put forth.

"No, m'lady," said the girl, refilling the wash basin and setting out a fresh pitcher. "Livie's da done took ill, and she's tendin' to him. I told her I would do her chores today."

I vacated my bed when I saw Mollie begin to make up those of my companions, fluffing the pillows and smoothing the sheets. She stopped when she spied the flowers on my dresser.

"Are you done with these, m'lady?" she said taking up the vase of withered oathbloom. "Hey, I know this one. This is the one I gave Lucas."

"Oh?" I said, at once curious "How do you know the miller's son?"

"Well, he was here, wasn't he?" she said excitedly. "One day we was all talkin' about the miracle and the strange party they had at the stocks when the boy himself comes walkin' in. Then he sits down to breakfast with us humble as pie and shares his story. Near to broke my heart, it did."

Then the simple girl, feeling she had spoken too familiarly, pursed her lips and returned to making the beds. Some of the servants could be quite good at the game, but not this poor lamb.

"I want to keep the flowers, Mollie," I said, "you may dust them if you're careful."

After the girl left, I crossed to the dresser. In a lower drawer under lock and key, I kept several of my cherished possessions. I retrieved the key and worked the lock. On my sixth birthday, mother had given me a book for pressing my flowers. Drawing it forth from amid several lesser treasures, I sat in my chair and flipped through its pages. I smiled at my early efforts labeled in childish handwriting. 'DAISY' and 'TULIP' were my first. It went on like this for a while. I hadn't added a new one in years - until last autumn. Flipping to the back, I found it: 'Oathbloom' in the more florid script I used today. I had added the notation, 'Used ceremonially to seal an oath, a promise of steadfast service and protection.' I probably shouldn't have written the boy. I did so because I just *had* to know what he meant by the flowers.

After tucking the book back in its niche, I lay back down. The early summer breeze and the scent of fresh rushes stirred my memories of that day. I had gone to his room to find out exactly what had happened. Father seemed uncertain. Trenton was furious, and all the townspeople were going on about signs and miracles.

The boy was not what I had expected. He was either very bad at the game or a genius at it. The boy wore his feelings openly upon his face. The rate at which his expressions altered as we spoke told me he had a first rate mind that caught and analyzed everything said and its implications. But underlying that was no deceit whatsoever, only genuine and honest feelings. As I tested and teased him, sending false tells, he quickly met each with an honorable response. Finally, I told him the bald truth of the matter. Rather than being incensed at his unjust situation, he seemed more concerned with me and *my* feelings than his own upcoming punishment. I decided to help him.

When I arrived at the stockade, the boy was unhappy but underneath lay acceptance and then, amusement? From Trenton and his boon companions, I sensed an ugly, predatory anticipation, but the rest of the crowd seemed to have great sympathy for the boy's plight. Empathy and good spirits began to dominate their mood even well before I made my move. And when I did, the outpouring of affection was overwhelming, far exceeding any outcome I had envisioned. I had come to manipulate the masses, but instead felt myself swept away helplessly in the tide of their goodwill.

And I understood in that moment that this was no 'game' but, rather, the lives and fates of real people. My heart was touched in a way it had never been before, and perhaps changed forever. How had the girl put it? 'Near to broke my heart, it did.' Was this Lucas' gift? Even my brother had come back a changed man from his subsequent trip to that ranch. Much of this was due to losing a man of his command, but through the grief, I caught his tells when Lucas was mentioned. His attitude toward the boy had definitely softened. Of course, by this time, I was well into my problem and unable to invoke my talent, so I could no longer be certain. I sighed.

" . . . But only yesterday you said that Sir London was the fiercest and now you favor Sir Fletcher?"

"I can bestow my favor as I want," Lynette contended. "You're just jealous because he winked at me."

"The sun was in his eyes, you loon," returned Constance, "That wasn't a wink."

"Oh, look," said Lynette upon entering the room. "She's mooning again."

"Who is it this time, my lady?" she asked as she flounced onto her newly made bed. "You should tell us. We're supposed to be your secret keepers, after all."

If I had a dire secret to keep, (and, indeed, I had several), I would do as well to tell the harkers directly than to give it in trust to Lynette. Constance might be suited for the role of secret keeper unless she felt compelled to inform my mother for my own good. No, I had best shut this down ere it sprouted wings.

"I bet it's that Derrick," Lynette guessed. "He's a charming one now that he's been properly raised up to squire."

Since it seemed to be expected, I called upon one of my false tells to blush. It had taken weeks before a mirror to get it just right, and I was rather proud of it.

"It *is* Derrick," she tittered kicking her feet to make a further mess of her bedspread.

"Let us get my lady prepared for the day," said Constance, closing in upon me with a hairbrush. "Lynette, make yourself useful and go select an outfit."

Thus, another day began.

***

As the summer progressed, the weather turned balmy and the people of Meadowfork went contentedly about their tasks. Crops stood abundant in the fields, and the celerity of spring gave way to the lackadaisical pace of longer days. When I received Lucas' response to my polite inquiry, I was somewhat disappointed. In tiny but exquisitely precise writing, he asked if oathbloom were the 'orange ones,' and claimed he had selected them because they were 'the prettiest.' I don't know why I had expected the boy to know aught of floriography. It was a rare subject, after all. Even so, he had promised to send a more fulsome reply in a letter once traffic permitted. It was nice to have someone of my own age with whom to correspond.

Constance and Lynette were all agog about 'the new cloth.' At first, I thought the caravan from the east had finally arrived, but I was told it had not. It was a good three weeks overdue. No, apparently some industrious spinsters in our own barony had struck upon a technique for making a very fine woolen weave to rival satin in its smoothness. It came in blue, green, yellow, and the off-white of natural wool. Mother had immediately bought up most of the blue and much of the fine yarn to use as embroidery floss.

Father had taken Trenton under his wing and finally began teaching him the game.

"It is time for you to take your place in my councils," said he. "I am well pleased with your new knightly bearing. You should have several worthy years of errantry before shouldering the burdens of your majority, but we must prepare you. In but a few years hence, we will have to set off for the capital to confirm you as my heir before the peerage. I have asked Megan here to teach you the subtle signs by which men's demeanors betray their true intent. She will sit by your side, so you may benefit from her rede."

And so it was that I found myself in the stifling council chamber at my brother's elbow under the grotesque gaze of a stuffed gryphon. We were seated a ways back from the raised dais upon which father and his advisers conducted their daily business so that I might quietly coach my sibling in how to spot tells.

On one such day, as Gerrard Keaton was droning on about the low revenues this season due to the scarcity of merchant traffic from the east, there came a commotion at the entrance. Elsa Lawson, known to some as 'the formerly mad bird woman,' arrived in a bother pushing her way past my fathers guardsmen. Her cheeks were flushed, and I spotted a white feather sticking to the back of her wimple.

"I apologize for my tardiness, your lordship," she said, waving a small slip of paper in her hand, "but I bear urgent news."

"The gist, madam," prompted my father.

"A pigeon has just arrived from the watchtower. As we have long feared, the goblins amass in the hills beyond the pass. Their war drums can be heard, and many campfires light the night."

There was dismay written on every face around the council table as the woman closed the distance to the dais with a spry stride that belied her advanced age.

"Let me see the message," said father with his hand outstretched.

She presented the folded scrap of parchment with a deferential bow and made her way to her seat. There she took up a fan made of peacock feathers and employed it with deft strokes to help ease the swelter. My father took a moment to frown at the tiny writing as he confirmed its contents. After the briefest glance to Sir Declan, he looked over at Sir Fletcher and passed him the note.

"You've been out to the pass recently, Sir Fletcher. Are our defenses there sufficient?"

"I believe so, my lord," replied the knight as he also perused the note. "If we man the bastion immediately, I don't see how the clans could mount much of a threat."

"We can ill afford to draw in many of our forces from the eastern barony just now," father declared, dabbing at his forehead with a kerchief. "Damn but we seem beset from all sides. Here is how it shall play. Declan, you shall rally the knights of the eastern fiefs. Do not bring them here, but have them make ready to ride hither at a moments notice."

"It shall be done, sire."

"Sir Trenton and Sir James will remain at the keep to deal with any local emergencies."

Both men nodded their acquiescence.

"Sir Fletcher, you will lead the remaining four lances to reinforce the pass. On your way there, rouse the old mage and have him attempt to parley. He speaks their foul tongue; perhaps we can find out what's gotten them riled up and appease them. Does anyone else have aught to suggest?"

Trenton stood and declared, "We should dispatch a force of archers to encamp upon the northern and southern ridge lines. They can make the enemy pay a stiff price for any attempt to come over the mountains. This could also serve as a relief force should the pass come under prolonged assault."

"That's a good thought. Take it up with Sir Fletcher. And if he approves, you have my leave to call up thirty levies. Very well, our course is set. I shall expect regular updates on the situation."

"Elsa," said father, turning to the woman, "have your pigeon handlers set to depart at first light. We shall need cages sufficient for the watchtower, and some to accompany Sir Declan.

"Certainly, my lord. I will make preparations at once."

And with that, the old woman arose and departed in a flurry, leaving only a single white feather adrift in her wake.

***

With my brother out mustering archers and the other knights on a trek to the western pass, I found myself free of my recent role in father's council. Constance and Lynette were most pleased by my increased availability. They both sought ways to lighten my heart and counseled me to enjoy my newfound freedom while it lasted. But my mood had shifted to one of ominous foreboding. Something oppressive hung in the air. The townspeople felt it as well. They currently went about their tasks lacking the cheer I normally felt from them. It was as though a sense of dread effused the very rays of the somber summer sun.

Inspiration came in the unexpected form of a package from Lucas:

Lady Megan,

I hope this letter finds you in good health. As always, Fowler Ranch is keeping me very busy. Between my studies and learning the wool trade, I rarely have time to just go out and do something fun anymore. My birthday party was amazing. Seeing my father again was the highlight of my entire spring.

Your letter and the pigeons you sent were a rare and unexpected treat. I hope you received my RSVPigeon. I'm saving the second one for a special occasion. She cheers up the barn with her gentle cooing and makes me think of you each time I go out to feed her.

My father gifted me a special crossbow with which I can finally punch through Royland's shield spell. If you should see Javier Lewis, your keep's good artillator, please mention to him that I said his craftsmanship is superb. Enclosed, you will find several fine bow strings I spun from the linen we derived from our flax. If it pleases your ladyship, convey them with my compliments to Javier as proof that I have overcome the problem with string breakage. And give one to Taylor Allen with my thanks for his kind words.

Master Chadwick was just called away to the pass by Sir Fletcher and some other knights. Royland, Tilda and I await his safe return and pray he will prove able to suss out what the matter is with our diminutive neighbors to the west.

*Wishing You Well,*

*Lucas Harper*

As rumors flew far and wide about the threat of invasion, the common folk felt helpless and subject to the whims of fate. While father and his advisers anxiously awaited news from the knights, the good people of Meadowfork needed a distraction, a way they could contribute to the outcome. The people needed what I needed: a way to feel useful.

The letter from Lucas had given me an idea. I placed it in the box in my dresser. This very day, I would make it a point to seek out the artillator. I felt the beginnings of my plan take shape, and this would be the first step. I would have to go alone because it would be difficult enough to get Javier's proper attention, and I wanted to be very careful about how I presented my request.

Javier Lewis was an odd duck. Originally from a small town in the duchy of Freemark to the south, the man had a reputation as a premier architect and a worker of wonders with all things made of stone, wood or metal. My father had enlisted his aid years ago to draft the plans for several of his pet projects. He had helped to refit the east tower into a dovecote. More recently, he had worked on the construction of the lord's mill, but Elliot Harper had to be tapped to bring the project to fruition. Javier was long on ideas, but when left to his own devices, the man never seemed to make substantial progress on a task before tearing it back down to make unplanned improvements. Javier was a dreamer, which was why my father liked him so.

I waited until late in the afternoon, when my two companions were engaged with private lessons, to approach the artillator's workplace in the base of the west tower. This served as an armory for our good knights, but father had made a generous allowance of space for Javier's many experiments and half-finished ideas in a bid to retain the man's services. Javier's private domicile was in the rooms above.

I tugged on the bell-pull at the tower's entrance and heard a distant, muffled chime sound from within. There was no immediate response. The knights often complained that Javier was slow to answer when they came for their training gear, being caught up in one of his undertakings and failing to show the respect due their station. Father had solved the matter by the simple expedient of placing a key to the armory under the mat that graced its door and bidding the knights to help themselves when required. This breech in the keep's security served me now when, after an overly protracted delay, I bent and retrieved said key.

The interior of the tower was lit only by a dim lamp resting on a far table. My eyes began adjusting to the diminished illumination as I made my way through a clutter of swords, shields and other paraphernalia neatly racked in front.

"Hello?"

My hail was answered by an echoing stillness. The tower's base was one, big circular room about fifty feet in diameter. Some parts were partitioned off by old tapestries or wooden frames from which hung a variety of different professional tools. If memory served, the stairway to the upper levels began somewhere off to my right, spiraling against the outer wall. A cleared area in the room's center seized my attention. I thought I had detected movement over there. As I approached, I noticed a grouping of tall, wooden dominoes arrayed in a large circle. Most stood up on their edges, but several lay flat upon the even, stone floor. I was bending to examine one of these when a hand gripped my arm.

"Get back, my lady," said the voice attached to the hand in a tone of urgency.

Initially, I was annoyed by such presumption, as I was roughly tugged backward in a most unseemly manner. But then my widening eyes caught sight of a massive stone swinging directly toward me on a rope. It slowed to a stop at the circle's edge, just where my head had been a moment before, then began to silently retreat in the opposite direction.

I turned to my benefactor who belatedly released his hold upon me and mumbled, "your pardon, my lady."

Javier was a man of middling height with an aquiline nose and a head of wavy hair the color of straw, fading to grey about the temples. To say he was clean-shaven would be to misrepresent the day-old shadow of a beard that almost constantly graced his cheeks and chin. He wore a soot-stained smock over his rumpled but otherwise fine raiment. Most prominent were his eyebrows which danced and bobbed above his slate grey eyes whenever he spoke. Those brows were currently knit together in concern.

"It's a pendulum," he said in a failed attempt to answer my unspoken question.

I could tell the man was bursting to explain. As the stone swung back toward us, I noted a pointy thing attached to the bottom which descended nearly to the level of the floor. Following the rope upward with my eyes, I saw a circular hole had been sawed into the ceiling above to accommodate its swing, and unless I was mistaken, a smaller hole in the floor above that. I decided to play along.

"Well, what is its purpose, then?" I asked.

"It is to measure the turning of the earth," he declared gyrating his finger in the air.

I thought the gesture would have better matched the statement had he targeted his own ear with that finger.

"You see," he continued with evident pride, "I release it precisely at midday, and the course it traverses changes minutely with each swing. It should complete a full rotation in one day, but I think my rope is too thick, for it presently takes a day and a third."

As he spoke, the 'pen-du-lum' came back again, this time knocking over the next domino in line with its pointy thing while Javier waggled his eyebrows at me in triumph.

"Perhaps you're onto something there," I said. "Maybe the weight is being pulled by the sun as it circles about us in the same manner as the moon governs the tides."

"An interesting proposition, young one. But why then does it matter not where I start the rotation, hmmm? No, I think it is the world that is turning, and the sun and other bodies of the heavens remain still, only *appearing* to move as we turn with it."

His madness was full upon him today which boded ill for the servicing of my request. Anyone with eyes could see that the sun moved across the sky. Still, father said it was best to humor him when he was taken with such an idea.

"So, what's this then?" I asked crossing over to a lesser 'pendulum' by the wall that merely swung back and forth on a long pole.

Overhead, the pole was attached to a set of gears and springs and finally led up to an arrow set into a disc. Around the rim of the disc were a series of numerals from 'I' to 'X.'

"Ah, my lady," he said stepping over, "that is a device for measuring time itself. I call it a temporal gauge. I was hoping to calibrate it from the large pendulum once it's perfected. The arrow is turning very gradually. When it is midnight, it will point to five. By the next midday, it will be pointing back up to ten, and the cycle will begin anew."

"That's going to need a better name if you want it to catch on."

"What would my lady suggest?"

"I don't know - something more memorable like a 'hickory dickery' or some such."

Whatever could such a preposterous device be used for? Anyone could plainly see when it was midday. A different question occurred to me.

"But there are twelve hours each day and twelve more each night," I protested. "Why not mark the proper hours upon your disc like the sundial the watchmen use?"

"Why not indeed?" he mused raising one eyebrow for emphasis. "My lady is perceptive. I had thought that since the creator of all had endowed us each with ten digits, why should we not divide our day into ten equal parts rather than twenty some odd. Each one-tenth of a day will be called a 'javier,' which would be about two and a half hours long."

We were straying pretty far afield. The problem with the moon-touched such as Javier was that they tended to draw others into their madness bit by bit like moths drawn to the flame of their genius. It was time to focus the man upon my request. But how should I phrase it?

"Well, I imagine you have some spare time whilst waiting for the next 'javier' to fall," I began.

The man smiled encouragingly and nodded, apparently pleased by my tacit acceptance of his new unit of measure.

"Are you aware that the goblins are stirring, Javier?"

"I had heard something of the sort, my lady. It's no concern of mine."

"It will be when they're upon your doorstep upsetting your experiments," I warned.

This gave the man pause.

Maintaining the momentum of my argument, I continued, "The people are sore afraid and need something to keep them busy and make them feel safer. Tell me, how many crossbows do you have available?"

"At present, my lady, there are seven ready for use. There are another six fine instruments lacking only a cranequin, and four more somewhat disassembled due to a recent project I conducted for Goodman Harper."

Harper? Of course, Lucas' new bow.

"The keep will require as many of the devices as you can put into service."

"Do not the knights prefer their longbows, my lady?"

"They do," I confirmed. "But these are not for the knights. I shall be offering to train all of the common folk in their use so that should push come to shove, they can feel they have a say in their own destinies."

"You say 'I,'" he noted with his eyebrows drawn together in suspicion like two caterpillars attempting to mate. "Does your father back this plan?"

"He will, goodman," I replied, hoping it was the truth. "Oh, and lest I forget, Lucas Harper asked me to give you these."

I fished about in my pocket to find the bowstrings the boy had sent.

"He said to tell you that your craftsmanship is superb, and that these are to show he has solved the problem with breakage."

The man lit up at the praise, proof that my talent was once again briefly functioning. Taking the strings, he drew one forth and examined it closely. The man let out a low whistle, and it required no special talent on my part to mark his wonderment.

"The lad may be as clever as his father," said Javier as he turned to watch his pendulum swing. "I shall have to evaluate them, but I can already confirm their superior quality. I can imagine many fascinating uses for lines of this strength. Very well, my lady. Provide me with more of these, and you shall have your crossbows."

I let out a breath I hadn't realized I'd been holding. Here I'd struggled to determine how to convince the man when all it took was a few bits of string.

****

In due course, father approved my plan. Word had come by pigeon, that the wizard's peace offering had been rejected by the goblins. Details were sparse, but the full tale was to arrive by messenger within the next several days.

When all was in readiness, the harkers went forth into the town to announce a new entertainment. Any who wished could gather in the outer courtyard to partake. We had a dozen crossbows with a promise of more to come. Constance had obtained numerous bales of straw from Farmer Green and had them stacked up against the wall of the keep. Over these were stretched squares of canvas on which Lynette had crudely depicted goblins.

There was scant participation at first; it was chiefly the younger boys. Once Lynette's 'goblins' started sprouting quarrels, however, it became a different matter. Over the course of several days, word spread and more showed up to watch and to join in. It was people you mightn't expect. Elderly matrons had a turn, as did a quiet green grocer, a nervous lapidary, and all manner of folk from the town and beyond. Swaggering toughs from the tavern stood beside modest maids from the country to cheer on their neighbor's efforts.

In an unusual reversal, men at arms and the remaining knights from the keep came out to watch. They were not permitted to bring their longbows. Taylor Allen soon took charge of those who proved unable to turn the crank of a crossbow. He set up a table to the side where he taught them the art of fletching. Under his direction, the very young or otherwise infirm were dispatched to the dovecote, where Elsa Lawson helped them to collect suitable feathers, and to the west tower, where Javier Lewis provided fresh shafts of a proper length to make quarrels. Some of their efforts were quite sub-standard, but Taylor would laughingly place these in his own quiver (to quietly rework later).

The people, upon seeing their fears and worries objectified and given form, began to confront them. The blanket of oppression which had lain over the community began to dissipate. It was Lynette's idea to organize a tournament at the week's end with prizes. Trenton agreed to act as judge. The winners were each awarded a chit that could be presented to the artillator to borrow a crossbow for the day. There were twelve such. The grand prize was ownership of a fine crossbow, and was won by Gregor Cain, a new boy at the mill.

Word soon arrived from Sir Declan that the knights of the eastern fiefs stood ready to come should their aid be required. Regular reports that flew in from the watch tower stated that little had changed there. When the messenger arrived with the complete story of Master Chadwick's efforts, not a great deal more was learned. The current leader of the Broken Mountain Clan called himself Chief Ravenbald. He railed against our people, preaching of wrongs done in the past. When the wizard sent out a peace offering of six flawless sheep and offered to parley, they were cut down by goblin archers screaming 'death to the blue king,' and left untouched to rot in the pass. 'The blue king' was their name for my father since the Arensons often wore blue. Our good wizard further wrote that he had sensed powerful shamans within their ranks. Though disappointing, the news was hardly unexpected, and we remained firm in our belief that there was little the clans could do to break our defenses. Let them howl their fury and vent their spleens; it would avail them naught.

***

With the tournament concluded and the people wary but less fearful, my maids and I decided we needed a day to ourselves. Lynette was already bored, and Constance, though loath to admit it, was missing the excitement. Noting that our rooms were devoid of fresh blooms, I thought a day of flower gathering might provide the balm for which our weary souls longed.

Constance seemed indifferent to the idea, but when I suggested a trip out to the lake, she perked up. Constance had a deep, abiding love of horses. She had grown up at the Baldwin fief surrounded by the herd her father kept. Sir Bailey Baldwin provided most of the fine chargers for my father's stables, and Constance visited them frequently, never missing an opportunity to ride.

So while Constance arranged for a picnic lunch, and I packed up some baskets appropriate for our use, Lynette begged a boon of her half-brother, Blake. After getting permission from his knight, he agreed to accompany us and serve as our escort. Blake too was the son of Sir Powell, but by his first wife, and was presently a squire to Sir James.

The stable was nearly emptied of its charges. The better chargers had all gone out with the knights, and several of those remaining were reserved for the harkers. They were at the ready to swiftly bear my father's orders to his forces arrayed throughout the land. Nonetheless, Constance managed to retrieve a set of three palfreys suitable for ladies to ride in the country. Blake secured a more spirited rouncey for his ride.

To my disappointment but as I should have expected, the palfreys were equipped with sidesaddles. Although I was no rider, it still irked me to be so patronized. It seemed that with each new day, another activity that used to be fun was deemed 'unladylike.' Though easier on my bottom, riding thus would leave a strange crimp in my spine and altogether remove the sense of unity I should feel with my mount. Leave it to Constance to prioritize propriety over enjoyment.

As we set off through the town with Blake in the lead and we three ladies strung out behind, I could feel the improved spirits of the people. It showed in their bearing and in all the little things they did. Hats were doffed and heads were bowed as our procession moved down the lane. Up ahead I spied a group of young girls. They had a length of rope stretched across the street which the ones on the ends whirled about. Others of their number took turns running into the middle and skipping over the rope as it made its lazy circuit above them and the group chanted:

Tinker, Tailor, Soldier, Sailor,
Rich man, Poor man, Beggar man, Thief,
Or what about a Knight, or a Ploughman, or a Jailer,
Apothecary, Chancellor, Goblin-Chief!


I had heard about skipping rope, but I had never done it. I believe if one missed a jump and the rope snared one's legs, the last word chanted would indicate one's future husband. It was such a silly game, but I envied it. I only knew one game, and father's game was anything but silly. Due to my station, I had never been truly a part of a group of my peers. When I was their age, I was sat down and given embroidery work to pass the time among my mothers older ladies. Even now, my companions were selected for me and expected to be deferential. The unruly group scattered and parted as I and my ladies paraded past their position, only to reform once we had properly passed them by.

After we had cleared the town, our formation fanned out a bit. We followed the eastern road at a slow walk with Blake still in the lead and Constance bringing up the rear.

"Perhaps we could go a bit faster," I suggested, eager for some excitement.

"If we do," warned Lynette, "it'll go rougher on our posteriors, and Connie's chest might just jiggle its way loose from her bodice."

"That was unkind, sis," said Blake from up ahead. "Such remarks are neither courteous nor befitting a woman of your station."

"Pay her no mind, Blake," enjoined Constance, whose cheeks had reddened, nonetheless. "I've suffered worse from the spiteful little thing. It's just plain envy talking, nothing more."

Lynette made an indignant noise as she glanced briefly down at her own budding assets for reassurance. We had come a fair distance, despite our leisurely pace and were approaching Danstonshire, a semi-wooded stretch that separated Meadowfork and its surrounds from the eastern farmlands. Therein lay Lake Ganymede upon the shores of which I hoped to find some blue flag iris. If we were lucky, there might also be some water lily, not to mention arrowhead, pickerel, and various other blooms to liven up our chambers.

I could still make out the keep in the distance brightly reflecting the morning sun. Out from it, there arose a brownish plume of dust which was familiar to me. It was being thrown up from the road by a fast-moving horse. I remarked on it to Blake, who called us to a halt.

"They're definitely coming our way," he said, frowning. "Let's wait and see who it is."

We didn't have long to wait. Whoever it was, he was making good time. Before long, we could make out the rider. He wore the heraldry of my father's men. Upon sighting us, he began swinging his arm rhythmically and we heard the peeling clangor of the harker's bell. Finally, the man slowed his lathered horse to a walk and approached us. He stowed away his bell and addressed me directly.

"Lady Megan, I come bearing a message," he said. "It arrived during the night at the dovecote, and Elsa bade me bring it to you posthaste ere you had wandered out beyond our reach."

"Thank you, Phillip," I replied, "that was most gracious."

He handed me a tiny note, and I quickly took in its contents.

"We must return at once," I proclaimed in stunned agitation. "Blake, take us back at best speed."

The squire looked nonplussed, but recognized an order when he heard one. So, taking our horse's leads he began to turn us about as my maids peppered me with questions about the note. I had barely begun formulating a response when Constance's palfrey suddenly reared up, upsetting the lot of us. My eyes widened in horror as I identified the cause. Her horse's neck had sprouted a shaft of wood with fletchings. We were under attack!

As Constance struggled to regain control of her badly wounded mount, it began to slump to one side and jostled against mine. Incensed by the ruckus and in a panic, Lynette's steed separated itself from the cluster and began to run uncontrolled off the side of the road. The girl was clinging to her saddle-bow for dear life. My own mount, though more placid in its response, nonetheless shifted unexpectedly, and I felt my foot slip from the stirrup. Over backwards I somersaulted. My brief tumble was arrested when it encountered the brutally solid surface of the road. I tasted blood and was having trouble inhaling.

From atop his unpanicked war steed, Blake had been peering toward the trees in the distance behind us. He turned to Phillip.

"See to her," he commanded, pointing at Lynette and her runaway horse.

In the mean while, Constance had leapt clear of her obviously dying steed as it fell. She rushed to my side. Without a word, she hoisted me up and thrust me toward the waiting arms of the squire.

"Flee, Blake, get my lady to safety!" she implored.

As he took me about my waist and drew me upward, I saw Constance rending her skirt asunder. Black spots danced in my periphery.  As I finally managed to draw in a breath, I was set awkwardly in front of Blake with my arms draped about his neck and his left arm tightly around my midsection. Peering over his shoulder, I felt a sharp pang of guilt as we sped away. Would Constance be left to confront the bandits alone? My heart leapt when I saw the girl stalk my own former steed and leap astride it with a smooth, practiced ease. Though the saddle was wrong and lacked one of its stirrups, Constance managed to get the horse to wheel about and urged it up to speed with a skill a knight should envy.

Looking to my left, I could see that the harker had overtaken Lynette as well. They were even now turning toward the keep and away from the treacherous tree line. I shuddered to think what might have happened had we not turned back when we did. But then I thought of Lucas' note and its contents and realized: we weren't quite 'out of the woods' just yet.

***

Our group had coalesced into a single unit. As we passed back through the town, the people stared at us aghast. We must have certainly looked a sight. I was wrapped about a squire in the vanguard, my back covered with dirt from the road.

Constance rode beside us astride her mount in torn skirts glaring protectively to the left and right. Bringing up the rear was our harker leading Lynette whose white-knuckled grip on her saddle did little to ease the bone-jarring impacts as she bounced upon it. Decorum be damned. We had to quickly reach my father, so we navigated the streets at a trot. When we approached the main gate, the guardsmen there didn't know how to respond.

"Make way," shouted Blake, not slowing a whit.

At the keep's entrance, Constance dismounted and hurried over to help me down. By now the guardsmen had determined something out of the ordinary was afoot and had sent runners ahead to warn their superiors. I could hear Lynette's quiet sobs as she climbed shakily down.

"Can you walk, mistress?" asked Constance.

"I can run if need be," I lisped.

My answer sounded oddly stilted, coming as it did through a lip that was swollen where I had bitten it. Still, I tried to inject a note of urgency as I eased myself from her grip and made for the doors. Blake, having dismounted and handed off his reins, stepped quickly to my side and offered his arm, which I took gratefully.

"Hath the baron'th counthil convened yet?" I asked of the ranking soldier present.

"It has, my lady. Runners have been sent to clear your way. Allow us to escort you hence if that is the destination you have in mind."

I simply nodded, my tongue having betrayed me. When we reached the council chamber, we found the door waiting open wide. My father's eyes met mine across the hall, and a wealth of information passed between us in that one swift glance. All of his male advisers rose to their feet at my approach.

"How do you find yourself to be in such a disheveled state?" my father asked worriedly.

Looking back, I saw Constance modestly holding her skirts together in front with Lynette's hand resting supportively upon her shoulder. Lynette's eyes were red-rimmed and swollen from shed tears. Not trusting my voice, I nudged Blake in the ribs.

"We were set upon by a brigand, my lord," he reported. "He or they loosed an arrow at us just west of Danstonshire. All escaped without injury save for the loss of one of the palfreys. We'd have taken a moment to clean up, but Lady Megan insisted we seek you out immediately with her urgent news."

"Brigands in my barony?" said my father in obvious disbelief. "Go to your knight. Have him assemble your lance and apprehend this fellow."

"At once, my liege."

"I shall do the same, sire," said Trenton as Blake exited the chamber.

"Hold, son," said our father. "If it is an ordinary bandit, Sir James will soon see him detained. And I believe your lance still lacks a tracker."

Trenton winced as if struck by a physical blow. We would have to begin working on suppressing his tells.

"Moreover," continued my father, "if this was instead an attempt aimed specifically to capture or harm your sister, we'd be fools to send the first heir into their clutches."

Turning to me he asked, "What news, my daughter?"

I handed him the note. He squinted at it then I felt a burst of surprise from him, though this was not in any way reflected in his manner. His eyes sought mine again, and I silently confirmed my belief in the note. He began reading it aloud.

"At the Tillerson Ranch we spied a large army of goblins with ogres spewing from the mouth of a tunnel. They mean to march on the pass from the east. Tell your father he *cannot* allow our troops to remain there! -Lucas"

"If our enemies have a tunnel and can amass a horde within our borders," he began hesitantly, "then a whole new strategy is required. We must withdraw to a position of relative safety. Thoughts?"

My father's chamberlain, Gerrard Keaton stepped forward.

The old bean counter looked discomfited and said, "What if this is a ploy by our enemies to convince us to withdraw our troops from the west?"

Trenton snorted.

"No, it's from Lucas," he assured. "That is *precisely* the impudent tone he strikes when he lectures his betters on a course of action. He's usually right about it, though."

I had to agree with this assessment, so I nodded sadly. Thus vouchsafed, the note was passed around the table. There was but a limited discussion among the advisers before my father came to a decision and began issuing instructions.

"I wish I had Declan's advice right about now," my father said ruefully. "I see but one plan of action. Phillip, you are to ride this very day to the Donovan fief. There you will find Sir Declan being hosted by Sir Killian and his wife. Tell him that war is upon us and that he is to summon forth the eastern lances."

"As you command, your lordship."

"Gerrard, you will draft a letter for the remaining harkers. Send them out to all tenants in the western barony and instruct the people to fall back to the safety of the keep. It is to be a scorched-earth policy. If we cannot hold the goblins at the pass, at least we can do all we may to lengthen their supply lines and slow their advance. Leave nothing that the goblins might use in their war effort. Bring all animals and early crops to stock our larders. Destroy anything that cannot be borne hither. Taint wells. Retreat here in an orderly fashion. All will be provided for; all will have their lord's protection."

"It will be done, my lord."

"Elsa, send word to the king. Inform him of our need. If he would hold together the realm of Osten, he will send aid to Westarbor."

"At once, my liege"

As the others began scrambling to their assigned tasks, my father's eyes fell upon Trenton.

"I shall rely upon you, my son, for the most dangerous task of all. I need you to ride with all haste to the pass, skirting the enemy force, and lead the troops there home by a circuitous route. You must go alone for haste is required and your men would only slow you down."

I could sense Trenton's sudden pride to be entrusted with such a mission after what he had perceived earlier as a rebuke.

"Do not be tempted to harry the goblin army with an inferior force. It may seem as though you could loose some arrows and retreat on horseback, but shaman have been reported among our foes. I have seen the devastating results when unprotected men are assailed by magic. Just bring the men home swiftly and safely. We shall need each one of them behind these walls."

"Yes, my liege," Sir Trenton acknowledged.

I feared for my brother who had been given such a frightful mission, but then again, I feared for us all in the times soon to come. As I collected my two companions and headed for the door, I noticed my father contemplating the gryphon. Was he weighing his son's worth?

"I pray there is still time," I heard him mutter.

CHAPTER NINE

# The Equerry

"I can make more generals, but horses cost money."

~ *Abraham Lincoln* ~


"Olivia, be a dear and fetch another heated kettle to warm my lady's bath."

"Right away, madam Constance."

I could practically *hear* the curtsy, I could. Even from behind the walls, I smelled the floral mix of the scented herbs and bath oils infused in the warm tub. Rodents were blessed with very keen olfactory perception, a fact which I had until recently been regretting. The stench of death surrounded me. This one was getting a little too ripe and would soon need to be replaced.

"I was thinking," said Lady Megan, "that since the tournament has concluded we might take a day to go flower gathering."

"I suppose, my lady," said the other girl in a perfunctory way.

"Well, don't get *too* excited about it, Constance."

All this 'girl talk' was wearisome, it was. But one never knew what might turn up useful. The lady was known to be deep in her father's confidence. She might let slip a few secrets to her close companion. I needed *something* to report to Lord Downham to justify taking his coin. His plan was already shaping up nicely and soon my time here would be at an end.

"Where were you thinking of going, my lady? Jenkins Meadow again?"

"I had something a bit more exotic in mind. The summer blooms at Lake Ganymede should be flowering by now. I haven't yet found a blue flag iris of sufficient quality for my book."

"But that's in the *Danstonshire*, my lady. Your father would never grant us leave to go gallivanting way out there."

"That's why I sent Lynette to ask her brother if he'd escort us. We could set off in the morning and make a whole day of it."

Now *this* was intriguing. The baron's daughter might go east protected only by a single young pup of a squire and would not be expected back for the entire day. This called for some initiative on my part, it did. What an attractive target of opportunity. I was sure that Downham would approve. The more chaos the better. Perhaps I could arrange for an 'accident' to befall them?

"Oh. I like Blake, my lady, even if he *is* related to that saucy little fluff-head."

"Hmm. 'Constance Powell.' It has a nice ring to it. You have my blessing," the lady said teasingly.

"Well don't go offering up my dowry just yet, my lady. I said I *liked* the boy, that's all. Would we be riding, then?" the companion asked with sudden enthusiasm.

"Even so. You didn't truly imagine we would *walk* all that way? After we've been given permission, I'd like you to assemble a picnic lunch for the four of us and then round up the finest fillies Master Hart can spare."

"My lady, he said yes!" burst in a third voice

"Congratulations," muttered Connie, "I'm sure you and the gardener will make a very handsome couple."

"What? *Eww.* You are a hateful old cow, Constance Baldwin. I mean Blake got permission from Sir James to escort us tomorrow."

The calmer voice of her little ladyship followed, "Thank you, Lynette, I shall seek father's approval over dinner tonight. Yes, come in, Olivia. That hot water will be most welcome."

"Oh, me next."

"As the *senior* lady's maid, *I* shall have the second turn in the tub. It's only proper."

"But the water will go tepid," the 'Lynette' girl groused.

"If you don't like it, then you may remain as unwashed as a commoner. But not to worry, Livie will fetch us yet *another* steaming kettle-full. If you help our lady to dry and dress, I'll promise to be quick."

I heard a sloshing sound and decided I ought to have a peek - since I was here and all. I scrabbled up the lathe boards of the passage's wall toward the peep hole I had chewed earlier. Although I had eliminated all feelings of pain, the rat corpse I was presently 'riding' could still taste and feel the splinters in its teeth. It was an unpleasant sensation, it was. As I crept toward the opening, I suddenly sensed the light brightening off to my left. The rigor mortis slowed my reactions too much. As I stiffly turned to the right and tried to scurry back down, I felt myself batted from the wall. Looking up, I saw the sole of a boot descending. Just above the boot loomed the scowling visage of that grizzled old chandler. Then I saw no more.

***

I regained my senses where I lay in the loft. Riding a dead thing always took a bit out of me. Sitting up, I worked my shoulders and rubbed my thighs to restore the circulation. My magic center was a bit depleted but should recover with time. I'd best check my stores of poison as well. I needed some new rat carcasses, and it was best if they didn't die by violence. They were much more believable that way.

Damn that Sebastian. Always creeping about, he was. I had run afoul of the man on two prior occasions, him being one of the few castle denizens to frequent the secret ways. I couldn't figure it. Since the passages were unlighted, he really had no business prowling about in there. Ah well, I'd best be getting back to my own business before anyone noticed. I stood and made my way to the ladder. Before descending it, I shouldered a hefty bag of oats. Best to look busy, it was.

My poor luck persisted this fine morning, for when I stepped off the ladder I ran square into the stable master himself,

Alexander Hart. 'Play the part,' I reminded myself. It won't be for much longer.

"You're not fooling anyone, Truman. What's the matter? Too late a night at the tavern, was it?"

"I'm not sure what you mean, Master Hart."

"Did I not tell you to muck out these stalls? Since the commoners' 'tournament' has kept us all cooped up in here, the place has begun to reek like Master Verney's pens. All we need is for some of our charges to come up lame from standing in their own filth. When I first appointed you, your work was exemplary. But lately I've noticed a certain . . . lack of effort, shall we say? Your frequent absences have grown wearisome. Do not think that because you won the baron's favor by stuffing his pet beast you can slack off from your main duties."

"About that. I was just thinking. With all these empty stalls from five lances being out, we should use the time to clean them up proper-like."

"That would be sensible," said he. When the knights return, it will become an extremely hectic time for us all."

*They're not coming back, you fool.*

"I'm sure you're right," I said, nodding along.

"I'm taking Tempest out for some exercise. I'd ask you to do it, but he'll suffer no one apart from Trenton or me to manage him. I'll be riding him out to Farmer Green's pastures and turning him out with some of the mares. I trust I will find things in better order here upon my return. Otherwise, I may have to rethink the permanency of your position. Am I making myself clear?"

"As clear as glass, master. You can depend on me. When you get back, nothing will tickle your nose-hairs but the fresh scent of hay, and even the flies will sparkle."

This was *perfect*. With the master away, I would have ample time to make my arrangements.

"Speaking of exercise," I said, "I'm sure several of these other fine animals could use a good turning out as well. Perhaps I could do it this evening after you return. When will that be, might I ask?"

"There may be hope for you yet," said Master Hart. "I could be quite some time, as Patrick and his wife invited me to join them for dinner. He wishes to discuss the use of his field on a more constant basis to rotate our increasing stock. If you are willing to work late tonight, it will go a long way toward assuring me my confidence was not misplaced."

The great gray brute was in his usual temper. After the battle of wills that resulted from saddling Tempest, Master Hart took his leave. Whistling happily, I made for the tack room after first making certain I was completely alone. I closed and latched the door to guarantee no one would disturb me or come upon me unawares.

It was time to check in on his lordship.

Taxidermy was my singular art. One might say I had a special 'affinity' for making the lifeless appear more natural. Ever since the emergence of my gift, I could sense the presence of the recently deceased. Now I could even possess them and have them do my bidding. But I had always been too cautious to reveal my abilities. Although most would have boldly proclaimed their powers to any who would listen, I was quick to suspect that my particular gift would go unappreciated. Nor was I wrong to so surmise.

A bit of quiet inquiry into the matter taught me that the kingdom's mages, who were always looking to add to their number, would at *best* frown upon a necromancer. The hypocrites would applaud someone who could burn a man down where he stood but to play around with his corpse afterward was evil? Who needed the stuck up bunch of old prigs? No, I remained ever careful to hide my gift and taught *myself* its uses. The hardest part was enchantment, but I had finally gotten the knack of that, I had.

You see, once a dead thing starts to decay, it gets progressively more difficult to manage. In the end, it quits being a dead thing and becomes just a thing, inert and immobile. I could ride a corpse for about six days before it became untenable. Even after four days it was hardly worth the effort. But using enchantment; that was a horse of a different coat. It took a great deal of effort and preparation. I found the eyes and ears of a creature, when properly preserved and treated by my magic, could remain sympathetic to my powers nearly indefinitely. I offered my taxidermy services for a pittance; I did, claiming with some truth that I merely enjoyed the work. As a result, I had eyes and ears all throughout the castle and much of the town withal.

My greatest triumph was the gryphon I had mounted for the baron. It sat within the very heart of his own most private sanctum and had provided a wealth of information since its placement there last winter. In the privacy of my tack room, I settled myself and began to seek union with it. Adrift in my private cemetery, I absently noted an alley cat that must have been run over by a wagon nearby. Although fairly fresh, I didn't see much use for it with its neck all twisted like that.

The first time I'd been here was at the funeral of my old man, may the devil take his soul. He was all laid out on the bier, and when I went up to pretend to pay my respects, I was suddenly looking up at my own face. Kind of disconcerting, that was. When I tried telling my mum about it, she just looked at me all sad-like. In hindsight, it was a lucky thing she didn't believe me at the time.

I focused in on my private collection of enchantments. Each was marked by a tombstone of my own making. And there stood the gryphon, proudest of all. Melding with her, I found myself transported to the chamber of the baron's council.

*** 

The upside-down shield in the hall was galling, it was. And yet it always presented itself first when I viewed the room. They just *had* to place the gryphon directly overlooking the distasteful thing. It was my father's shield, you see, from back in the days when he was Sir Geoffrey Wilkins. They claimed he was a coward, that his courage failed him during the battle of Arborvale. He had shown his heels to the enemy and proven himself a poltroon, leaving his fellow knights in dire distress. My father described it differently. He said their position had been overrun, and he and his lance attempted a strategic retreat to regroup with the other knights. The truth could be a ticklish thing when stories were retold. I didn't know in which version the truth rested. I only knew that the version in which I had to live was one where my father had been drubbed out of the knighthood to die a broken and dishonored man pushing a plow for his 'noble lord.' It was one where my mother, forsaking even his name, was reduced to begging in the streets (and god knows what else) to provide our daily sustenance.

On the very day the old man had passed, I discovered my own dark gift. This couldn't have been mere coincidence. I was sure it was a sign from the powers that be. I was meant to wield it to achieve vengeance for my family's disgrace. Now I could wreck my revenge upon all the perpetrators of the vile treatment I had received. Father had paid his penance, but should his sins be visited upon me? Never. I should be among those living amid luxuries with servants to wait upon me, an armiger of a noble enfeoffed line . . .

The baron suddenly looked up from his scribblings and straight at me. Damn those Arenson's eyes. On second thought, just damn those Arensons entirely. I had come to realize that his lordship often sensed when I was present, especially when I was most impassioned. The daughter had the same keen perception, she did. Fortunately, I had a counter. Drawing from my gift, I called upon 'motis cessabit,' the calm of the grave. It was a personal spell I had developed to suppress my emotions. Forthwith, I felt the fire in my gut subside; all that remained was dispassionate logic and peace. This was how I had gotten close to the baron and his family unnoticed when so many others had failed. It was also useful playing cards.

There's nothing to see here - just a big stuffed toy. Return to your papers; there's a good fellow.

"Did you just feel a draft, Gerrard?"

"No, my lord," replied the only other occupant of the chamber. "I would welcome such. If anything, it feels overly confined in here today."

Gerrard Keaton was a right wound-up git. He was the baron's chamberlain, chancellor and treasurer all wrapped into one. If this were the king's court instead of a modest barony, he'd be obliged to *share* some of those honors. Gerrard was constantly demanding we count things. Once he asked me how many pounds of manure were produced each day at the lord's stables. Wasn't it unpleasant enough I had to muck out all those box stalls? Did he want me to weigh the dreck as well? I heard the kitchen staff had taken to calling him 'the bean counter' for something similar he'd asked of them. That was jolly good fun, that was.

"These numbers don't add up, my liege. The increased taxation through Downham barony would account for much of it, but what of our own men who haven't returned?"

"Add to that," observed the baron, "the higher taxes will only lower Downham's revenues due to the decrease in merchant traffic. What does he gain by stifling trade? We're being cut off from the kingdom, Gerrard. I can feel the noose tightening even as we speak. But why? What's the man's game?"

What indeed? You'll presently have your answers, little lordling, and I doubt they'll be to your liking.

After a brief knock, the door at the far end of the chamber creaked partway open.

"If it pleases my lord," said a guardsman, "pardon the intrusion, but the chandler requests admittance. He claims to have business with your chamberlain."

"I wonder what *he* wants," remarked the baron with a glance up to the fully lit chandelier. "Very well, send him in."

The two men grew more perplexed when the door opened completely to admit the stooped form of Sebastian. He shambled his way across the chamber to approach the raised area at the back where the baron and his chamberlain sat. Clenched in his right fist was the tail of a rat from which descended the crushed carcass of the rat itself.

"Your lordship," he wheezed with a necessarily shallow bow that almost tipped him over.

"This is most unseemly, Sebastian," sputtered the chamberlain. "Are you a cat then, to bring us such a prize?"

Sebastian raised a rheumy eye to Gerrard and replied, "I got another one. The problem grows worse. Like I told you earlier, we're getting downright infested, Master Keaton."

"Phew, when did you kill it - last week?" asked Gerrard, waving his hand before his wrinkled up nose.

"They're getting bold, I tell ya. I caught this one gnawing his way into the wall."

"Is this true, Gerrard?" inquired the baron. "Do we need to engage with a rat-catcher?"

"It's true enough, my lord. I was made aware of the problem, but it hadn't become a priority. We had enough rats of the two-legged variety to be keeping up with."

"Well, I'm loath to become known as lord over a rat-infested castle. I trust you will deal with the matter promptly and quietly. See if you can get that pied piper fellow. It's said he can work wonders."

"I doubt we can afford his fee, my lord."

"Send for him anyway. I'm sure we can work something out in lieu of payment."

"Very well, my liege," said the chamberlain, turning once again to regard the elderly chandler. "Your complaint has been registered, Sebastian. Now dispose of that repugnant thing, preferably somewhere far from here - and downwind."

I readied to return to my body in the tack room. There was nothing more to learn here. They had become suspicious, but it was far too late for them to prepare a meaningful response.

'Reawakening,' I took a moment to review my plans. I should expect a visit soon from little Connie. It had been a foresightful move on my part to befriend the lass. With Master Hart away, that left me in charge. I pondered the side saddles buried in the back. It should be short work to convince her. If there was one thing Constance cherished above riding, it was being all proper-like. Then like lambs to the slaughter they'd go. I unlatched and threw open the door. Rolling up my sleeves, I hefted a pitchfork. I'd best get a move on. I was no stranger to honest labor, but I detested it, I did.

***

The crickets were in fulsome voice this eve. As I wended my way forward, I wondered if the good farmer would note my absence. I had ridden the baron's own steed out to the field unimaginatively named 'Green Pasture.' There I had turned him out along with two of the rounceys and the remaining pack animals. There they would stretch out and graze for a bit. Next, I had waited around for night to fall before heading out on foot to my clandestine rendezvous.

A breeze would have been nice, but I resigned myself to suffering the stagnant air of mid-summer. At least the heat of the day had begun to dissipate. Directly ahead lay my destination, the gentle roll of land that was known as Meadowfork Memorial Hill. I hoped there would be no mourners present at this late an hour. People didn't normally visit the dead at night, but with all the odd characters in this town, one could never tell. Arriving at the foot of the hill, I espied the dirt path that spiraled about it up to its summit.

Visitors were supposed to tread the entire path, but I saw no reason to do so and opted instead to climb straight to the top over the graves of the dead. They wouldn't mind; I should know. First came the most common plots, those of vagrants and criminals. But soon I found myself among the more cherished graves. These were better tended and some sported markers. These grew more elaborate as I crossed the path again into the resting places of the more well-to-do. Even nearer the crest of the hill, almost on the plaza itself, I spotted two recent graves. This was the section where Westarbor honored its fallen soldiers, especially those who had died in the line of duty.

I remembered having to come here in my sables for the burial some three months past. The two had been inhumed with full honors. *Stars* what a boring affair *that* had been. Sir Trenton had blathered on endlessly about the fallen, their valor, and all manner of personal details about which I didn't give a hoot. I had to keep up my 'motis cessabit' spell the whole time because the baron himself was present, watching us all with those eyes of his. If I were delivering the eulogy, I'd have just gone straight to the point: 'bitten to death by large spiders - the end,' and put them in the ground. That would have been refreshing, it would.

"It's about time you got here," came a petulant voice from the plaza above. The voice had a hollow, metallic quality because the speaker wore a fully enclosed helm and never raised its visor. He fancied himself a black knight, he did, hiding his heraldry beneath a leather shield cover. I didn't expect this chicanery would deceive anyone. There were only so many knights wandering about out here. It was good that he was here waiting though, for it meant I could conclude my business and make it back in time to allay suspicion.

"Ill met by moonlight," I quipped.

The man exhibited no recognition whatsoever, the heathen. To be fair, it wasn't much of a moon; just a skinny little sliver remained.

"It's a pity you were ostracized after that fiasco at the feast," I continued as I stepped up onto the cobbles. "Otherwise, our meetings could be arranged much more simple-like."

On the plaza that graced the hill's summit stood the crypts in which the bones of the nobles were interred. Each crypt bore the family heraldry of its inhabitants. It was here where my father would have gained a place had he remained face to the foe as he rightly should have. I deemed it an apt venue for plotting my revenge.

"That was a most inauspicious gambit," bemoaned the knight. "Had it worked as it ought, the little poppinjay would have disgraced himself and would *never* have been raised up to knight so soon."

"Don't tell me you still hold to that antiquated system of honor?" I scoffed.

"The code? Of course not," he said dismissively, "but *they* do."

"In any event, it was best you were discovered when you were. And you were lucky to leave with your skin intact. I have since learned that your true loyalties have been well-known for some time. It follows that any intelligence you may have gleaned from your time among them is tainted and should be reassessed. Take *that* back to your liege."

"*Our* liege," he practically shouted, "and you'd do well to remember it lest your secret be exposed, *necromancer*."

Right. To business then.

"What news?" I inquired.

"The border is now completely secured; none shall pass in or out of this doomed barony."

"And the goblins? Does all continue in accordance with our liege's plan?"

"The deal has been struck," said he. "Once the goblin army has retaken their ancestral lands, our liege will send in his forces. We shall 'ride to the rescue' of the eastern fiefs and sue for peace."

"And what of the king?"

"His majesty shall have no option but to accept the new border; it will be a *fait accompli* by the time any of his forces can arrive. That is, provided you can manage your final mission.

"Don't worry about my part. I will get to it shortly; I will. But first, I have identified an opportunity to sow a bit more confusion. On the morrow, Lady Megan intends to ride east into the Danstonshire accompanied only by her maids and with but a solitary squire as escort. I was thinking you could lay in wait to take her captive."

"Who is the squire?" he asked sharply in that ringing voice.

"Blake Powell, I believe."

"Blake? I can handle Blake," he said with an undertone of menace.

"The other knights have been sent out to meet their ends at the watch tower save for Sir James and the upstart baron's brat. Pursuit should be minimal, and if need be, you can always just kill the girl. Oh, and I've assured that all the maids will be riding side saddle. *That* should make it a simpler matter to round them all up."

"You have a devious mind," the knight said approvingly. "That almost takes all the sport out of it. Very well, it shall be as you say. I misdoubt me not our liege will be well pleased by the bonus. Here is the payment agreed upon."

So saying, he dropped a plump purse at my feet that jingled pleasingly.

"The balance of your guerdon will be forthcoming when the deed is done. You may collect it at our liege's castle at Downburry."

I had insisted on half in advance, knowing my part in these maneuverings put me in a prime position to blackmail 'our liege.' And that was a dangerous place to be. Were I fool enough to try to collect my 'final payment,' I expect it would be paid swiftly and with steel. No, I would content myself with my revenge and the coin I had amassed thus far. Truman Wilkins had already reinvented himself once as Truman Huber, the equerry. I would do so again, I would. The not inconsiderable payment I had just received would set me up well in the south.

"Until I see you again at Downburry, then," I said, turning a mock bow into a quick snatch for the purse. "Perhaps I'll treat you to a drink at Nester's Flagon."

With my business thus concluded, I turned and headed back down the hill stepping all the way upon the graves of Meadowfork's dead.

***

"Something urgent I can help you with there, Phillip?" I asked.

"Not urgent, exactly," he said "I need to run an errand for Madam Elsa."

The bird lady? I didn't see how that old bat merited a 'madam.' If I understood right, she was a farmer's wife, a nobody. But since the baron had taken a shine to her and her family, I guess she rated now. I'd seen her in the baron's council chamber shoving and ordering the guards about like a high and mighty.

"Well, you can take out Old Blinkey. He's all saddled and ready to go, he is. Per our good liege's instructions, we are to always have a mount ready to serve his harkers."

"My thanks, goodman," he said. "Tell me. How long ago did Lady Megan and her entourage depart?"

This could be trouble looking to happen; it could.

"Ah, they left not a half an hour ago," I said, thinking quickly. "I believe they were heading out the south road to Jenkins Field to pick flowers or some such."

"I distinctly heard the lady specify Lake Ganymede," came a voice from behind me.

"I thank you, Master Hart," said Phillip, putting foot to stirrup. "That was my understanding as well."

"Oh. Right. Ganymede," I sputtered, "I must have misremembered it."

After the man had ridden off, Master Hart came around to stare me in the face.

"Are you feeling quite alright, Truman?" he asked all solicitous-like.

"Maybe just a little tired, master," I answered, yawning to sell it.

"Listen. About the other day - I might have come down a bit hard on you. This goblin menace has got us all on tenterhooks. You've performed admirably in cleaning up around here, and turning the horses out last night went above and beyond. Keep up the good work, but don't push yourself too hard. My wife tells me I need to 'get down off my high horse' from time to time. Peradventure, you and I could share a drink at the tavern this evening?"

Just the *last* thing I needed: a heart to heart with Hart.

"Wives are wise, they are," I chuckled. "And I'd be honored to make merry with you later this evening, master. Let me get Ironshod saddled up. It wouldn't do for another harker to come pecking in and have to wait for his mount."

"Very good, Truman," said he. "Perhaps we can try our hand at a gentleman's game of darts."

Before I saddled up the next rouncey, I gathered up my poisons and my coin purse just to be ready. A feeling of foreboding began to bunch up the muscles in my shoulders. I suspected no good would come of the harker's mission. Nor was I mistaken. About a half an hour later, there was a commotion at the main gate.

"Make way," I heard over the clatter of hooves.

I stepped out into the inner ward where other curious onlookers were also emerging. The squire, encumbered by her little ladyship was making his way swiftly up to the castle's grand entrance. He was followed by Phillip and the other maids looking considerably worse for wear. Had they bested Sir Myles? Had the fool given me up? I had to find out what had happened. I needed to hide myself away in a place from which I could observe the chatter, but where? The tack room was no good. The two palfreys along with Blinkey and Blake's rouncey were even now being led back toward the stables. From the looks of them, they'd need a good rub down; they would, and I suspected I knew the bloke who'd be saddled with that task.

I slunk my way quietly to the west tower. Ignoring its bell pull, I retrieved the key from under the mat. It was child's play to then slip within and re-lock the heavy door while retaining its key. The baron hadn't thought this one through very well. I lay down amidst assorted weapons and training gear and sought out my gryphon.

The council chamber came quickly into focus. They were all aroused and that Blake fellow was saying something about 'urgent news.'

"...Brigands in my barony? Go to your knight. Have him assemble your lance and apprehend this fellow."

"At once, my liege."

Next came a kerfuffle with the first heir wanting to go haring off, but the baron squashed that idea proper quick.

"...What news, my daughter?"

Now we were getting to the meat of it. Stepping up to him with a noticeable fat lip, the girl silently handed the baron a note, which after a moment he read aloud. Somehow, they had gotten wind of the goblin's tunnel. This was unfortunate; I would need to accelerate my plans. Taking note of the baron's orders, I garnered the following. Phillip was heading east to rouse the enfeoffed knights. Gerrard would set the other harkers to calling in all of the tenants. Elsa would send word to the king. I had heard enough. I knew where my priorities lay. I would need to act swiftly; I would.

As I released my connection to the gryphon, the baron's eyes locked with mine. I felt their clear blue gaze pierce the veil of anonymity I usually enjoyed as he sensed the depravity of the deed I intended. Good. Let him stew in it.

Arising in the shadowed alcove of the tower, I sought about for a suitable implement. A sword? Absolutely not, too messy. A mace? Too difficult to conceal. Then I spotted the ideal weapon. I took up the truncheon and tested its heft - perfect. I exited the tower, relocked its door, and cast the key away. I then advanced into the inner ward assured in the knowledge I could still strike from surprise.

I saw Elsa emerge from the entrance to the castle, fending off guardsmen with a shooing gesture as she stepped briskly past. She then strutted hurriedly toward her dovecote. Phillip, astride Ironshod was already making his way through the checkpoint at the main gate. Sir James and his squire were queued up at the stables, hastily assembling their lance and making preparations to ride in pursuit of the 'brigand.' It would take them some time as the men were sent for and a harried-looking Master Hart was conveniently short-handed for preparing their steeds.

It was difficult to slow my steps and saunter nonchalantly past them with my head averted. The milling crowd of murmuring yokels provided some cover as I slipped past. Elsa was just entering the east tower. I walked sedately in quiet pursuit to cries of 'Where *is* that blasted horse-hostler?' from behind me. Consider this my resignation, you sanctimonious twit.

Within, the tower's gloom was alleviated by dozens of rays from the morning sun which slanted in through the many holes piercing its thick, stone walls. It smelled of its occupants whose droppings bespeckled the dingy floor. I turned to the right and ascended the spiraling stairway to the chambers above. Moving silently, I spotted Elsa. She was already seated before her work table scratching away with an over-sized plume for a quill. I raised my truncheon and closed the distance.

"Is that you, Peter?" were her last words.

Upon receiving no reply, in the final moment the old woman turned her head around. Her eyes widened with fright to find me looming above her. Then the truncheon descended with a dull crunch as she let out her last strangled gasp. I heard bones snap as her cheek caved in. Not the cleanest kill, I noted as a thin trail of blood dribbled down to her chin, but it got the job done; it did. The old woman slumped to the side and as the light left her eyes, I was overtaken by a thrill of exhilaration. My magic center flared with the influx of energy as my private cemetery welcomed its latest resident. I hadn't felt that wonderful feeling for what seemed like ages. There was no time to revel in it; there was work still to be done.

I quickly pocketed the note she had been working on. Surveying my surroundings, I located a bag of birdseed. Retrieving it, I slathered the contents of a poison vial into its neck and thoroughly mixed it in. The roost for the 'royal' pigeons was nearby. Those were the ones sporting a purple band whose cage had no egress to the outside. Swiftly and precisely I deposited my tainted seed in a tidy pile within, removing all other feed. I smirked with satisfaction when several of the silly little blighters eagerly hove to at once.

Exiting the tower, I made my way toward the main gate. Sir James and some of his fellows were attempting to equip themselves at the west tower. They were beating upon its locked door most vigorously. His squire was doing his best to saddle up three horses out in front of the stables where Trenton was now demanding that Master Hart retrieve Tempest and his gear. A timely distraction that was. At the main gate, a guardsman stepped in my way.

"Advance and be recognized," said he in a wary tone that showed him to be at high alert.

"It is I, Truman Huber."

"Your master has been looking for you, goodman," he said disapprovingly.

"Aye, that he has," I glibly confirmed. "He caught up to me just a few moments ago. He ordered me to run into town and fetch him some urgently needed supplies for Sir James; he did."

"Then you'd best be about it, man. Off you go," he exhorted me.

*Idiot.*

I hustled up the main thoroughfare until the guards were lost from view, then cut off the road into the tall rushes growing beside the tail race. There I settled myself in and slowed my breathing. Now came the more challenging part. Focusing inward, I once again entered my private cemetery.

***

Elsa was there, and nearby her little bird friends were starting to emerge. As I was unsure whether the body had been discovered as yet, I first entered a pigeon. Inclining its head from the floor of the cage, I peered about. It was fun how my neck could swivel so far around. Nothing seemed to have changed from when I had left a few minutes prior, so I released the bird and entered the old woman herself.

Not yet stiff from the clench of death, I found the body to be a bit less responsive than normal, nonetheless. Old age will do that to you, I supposed. I stood slowly, getting accustomed to the balance of my new form, and examined the royal roost. Most of the birds had partaken of my lethal feast as evinced by their macabre thrashing about. One little mother, however, was huddled serenely in her nest warming her eggs. I reached in and adroitly wrung her neck. It would be unprofessional not to make certain; it would.

I felt a strange weight at my thigh and was delighted to discover the old bat kept a slim dagger hidden beneath my skirts. Nice to know.

Shambling toward the door, I chanced upon the woman's dresser. I took up a hand mirror and noted the ghastly condition of my face. Blood stained my wimple from temple to chin. And although there was little swelling or bruising due to death, a deep crease was evident where the cheek had been staved in. A flap of skin hung down to reveal several yellowed and cracked back molars. This wouldn't do.

Rummaging through her drawers, I found another wimple to wear over the bloodstained one. I thought the face would still present a problem until I espied a large, peacock-feather fan hanging from a hook nearby. I took it up and practiced fluttering it in a manner to conceal the left-hand side of my face. It would have to do; it would.

Creeping down the stairs, I exited the dovecote and headed for the main gate - *again.* This would be the difficult part. You see, I hadn't yet managed to produce intelligible speech when 'riding' a corpse. I never quite grasped why because the tongue didn't swell up and protrude until days after death, but I went with what I knew. As I approached the gate, I had attained enough experience of how this body moved to try to imitate the chicken-walk that Elsa oft adopted when in a hurry.

"Advance and be recognized," said the sentry.

Instead of slowing, I made the imperious 'shooing away' gesture I'd seen Elsa execute when confronted by guardsmen. For a wonder, it worked; it did. The man retreated several steps and motioned me on through with a look of consternation upon his face.

*Idiot.*

As I strutted up the thoroughfare, careful to flutter my fan in front of my ruined face, I considered where might be a suitable place for Elsa to suffer her grisly, accidental death. Directly ahead lay the mill. Surely, I could do no better than that. The wheel was still. Otherwise, I would have promptly thrown myself upon it and gone round a couple times. Wouldn't that have been a memorable sight? As I approached, I noted that a sturdy railing fence had been newly installed on the little wooden bridge that crossed the race. I stepped over the bridge craning my neck to see if anyone was within.

The door stood ajar and all manner of equipment was strewn about. In the back, I saw a man bent over the famous stone, scraping away at it with a stiff brush. I paused. This might work even better. How delicious. I drew my blade from beneath my skirts and moved in silent as death. He must have seen my shadow, for he stood and turned to face me when I was yet a few paces away. It was Elliot Harper, the miller.

"Can I help you?" he said with a bewildered look at my knife.

I lowered the fan and stepped in quickly when I saw his eyes widen in horror. I plunged the knife at his throat, but was annoyed when he received the blow on his forearm instead. I had forgotten the man had been a soldier; I had. The old miller swiftly retreated clasping his left arm to staunch the flow of blood, whilst bellowing for aid. I stalked grimly forward until I heard a shout from up above.

"Back away from Master Harper unless you're wanting to be food for the crows!"

Curious despite myself, I made the mistake of looking up. The boy stood on the floor above with a loaded crossbow at the ready. When he saw my face, he let out a yelp. But then, to his credit, he released a quarrel at me. The shot was dead-on, I thought with morbid humor. My right eye, through which the bolt had slammed home, was no longer functional. No matter. I had another. As I resumed my pursuit of the miller, I heard another shout, this time off to my right.

"Stay away from her, Elliot. She ain't natural."

So saying, the fool failed to follow his own advice and rushed forward. This was the brother-in-law. He was armed only with a long pole which he thrust at me. He must have had some training as well, for he easily defeated my defense, pitched me backwards and swept my feet from beneath me. I thought I might play opossum where I had sprawled out and see whether I could draw them in. But before I had a chance to do so, the miller reached over and pulled a lever which lowered the millstone, trapping my arm.

This fight was over and I had triumphed. There was only one thing more to be done. Although I couldn't make intelligible speech, I could fill my lungs with the air they no longer needed. I let out the most piercing, gurgling wail I could manage to attract as many witnesses as possible before allowing Elsa to 'expire' at the hands of those murderous millers. I fancied I could still hear it echoing as I sat up amid the rushes.

I joined the hasty exodus from the keep as watchmen and citizens alike ran up toward the mill to offer their assistance and to see what had been the cause of that bone-chilling caterwaul. When enough guardsmen had arrived to enforce some semblance of order, I politely gave way and edged to the back of the spectators. Sir James was among them. Good. This should slow down his pursuit of the 'bandit' nicely. I slunk away and out through the town and headed up the eastern road to the sound of the alarm bell's tocsin.

It was nearing midday when I came upon a palfrey lying dead upon the road with an arrow sticking out from its neck. Things were looking up, I thought as I searched the animal. Someone had packed me a picnic lunch - how thoughtful. There was enough to outfit me for at least three or four days if I were careful. Suspicion would fall upon the miller and that son of a witch, Robert. I would be long gone by the time they figured it out.

Out from the keep, there arose two brownish plumes of dust. It seemed that Sir James would not be so easily dissuaded from his pursuit of the mysterious marauder. I weighed my odds. I should have time enough. What was life without taking a few risks? Rooting through my travel bag, I retrieved a set of leather cords. I lay upon the road and began tying myself to the sidesaddle of the dead animal. I then shifted my consciousness to the palfrey. It was a struggle to stand with a man's weight upon my back, but fortunately I was well versed in quadrupedal locomotion.

Presumably, Sir James would first wish to survey the scene of the attack. Wouldn't he be astonished to find that the horse had just gotten up and walked away? I would follow the road through the Danstonshire and then cut across the open fields of the eastern fiefs. I began to trot, bouncing the man upon my back. I was sure I'd feel that later, I would. I transitioned to a smooth canter then clear up to a rolling gallop. It might be a little tricky getting past Downham's pickets, but I was sure I'd come up with something by then.

As for Sir James, let him give chase. His steed would soon give out whereas mine would remain tireless. He had at best two or three hours to try to overtake me. With the head start I had, his task was hopeless. No, he'd soon find it was no use trying to beat a dead horse.

# CHAPTER TEN

# The Butcher

"Governments need to have both shepherds and butchers."

*~ Voltaire ~*

"Ehr-Wuff!"

"Yeah, well I miss him too, but he's not here. We'll just have to manage the best we can. The others are depending on us."

"Ehr..."

It had not yet been a single day since we had fled the Tillerson's ranch. It had started when Royland came running into the parlor to interrupt our spinning session. I hadn't seen him so upset in months and had all but forgotten how he could become tongue-tied by his own spell of silence.

"Well, spit it out if you don't like the taste of it," Tilda had grumbled with an air of frustration. "Let us be the judges."

Royland had looked at me pleadingly. Now that he would meet my gaze, it sometimes felt eerie when he did so.

"The Tillersons are in grave danger; we all are," he finally managed.

He went on to explain how he had determined the goblins had a presence at Tillerson Ranch. His suspicions seemed to be based upon a lot of flimsy evidence, the sketchy bits and pieces of which rested on shaky ground. As he went on about mygalom placements, geology, and brownies at the pond among other things, I had trouble following his line of reasoning. I wasn't used to that. But I sensed his conviction ran deep, so I decided to believe in him.

Tilda went off to brew some tea to calm us all down. Presuming it was true, what could we do about it? Master Chadwick was still away, so the decision rested with us. The obvious thing to do was to extract the Tillersons. If the goblins had stayed their hand thus far, then it stood to reason they were trying to remain hidden. They wouldn't do anything blatant and risk exposure. However, we had no guarantee this would remain the case. As we began discussing the matter, Royland settled down and quickly became as calm and collected as I had ever seen him. Though the specter of worry yet haunted his face, the fear that we might doubt him had been exorcised. Tilda's ready acceptance of Royland's theory surprised me. I had expected her to scoff and to take more convincing, but she obviously shared my opinion of Roy's perspicacity and trustworthy nature. He was never a boy to cry 'wolf' unless canus lupus lurked nearby.

The plan we settled upon was for just one of us (me) to go down the road and warn our neighbors. Tilda would pack up the cart with as many supplies as would fit therein while Roy and Sampson began driving the sheep east toward the Turners. After all, the Tillersons were only just up the road. If goblins were there, we were all in danger.

Goodman Avery proved remarkably easy to convince. Having escaped peril once this year already, he was extremely concerned for the safety of his wife and daughter. 'A Fowler's word is as good as gold to a Tillerson,' he had declared when I had revealed to him the danger we suspected. Although honorary, it was nice to know my title still carried some weight. So as Harriet and Priscilla hitched up their team and packed up their belongings, Avery and I made ready to move the flock.

Avery wished he could say his flock had been decimated. That would have implied a loss of but one sheep out of every ten. No, the Tillerson flock had been *devastated* by the mygalom infestation. Only around thirty mature ewes remained. Thanks to Big Barney's fine efforts, and Little Abe's withal, most of these had lambed. Nor had Avery culled any of the females, hoping to increase his numbers as quickly as possible. This was a problem. More than half of his flock consisted of lambs no older than four months. Although they had at least progressed to eating grass, not many were in good condition for a hard drive anywhere. I supposed it couldn't be helped.

"Where exactly did Royland claim those goblins were roostin'?" asked Avery as we headed out to the west field.

"He said they were somewhere near the big pond," I replied. "He wasn't specific."

"Worse luck as it happens. I've got the whole flock waterin' down at that very pond."

"Maybe we should just leave the sheep and make our own way out, Avery."

"A Tillerson looks after his own, Lucas. I forsook them once and look where that got me. No, if there's a chance to save the flock, I have to take it. You stay up here. If there are eyes watchin', let 'em suppose I'm just movin' the flock up to the east field. I do that every now and then."

"If you're sure, Avery, then I'll observe from up on the overlook here. If you hear me whistle, run like hell."

I discovered a good vantage point and concealed myself.

Avery, crook in hand, strolled bravely down the hill with a feigned nonchalance that would do a thespian proud. I'd also give him this; Avery was very adroit in his handling of his flock. Little Abe stepped protectively to the fore but issued no challenge. Avery got them ambling along without much fuss, resorting to the crook only on a few stubborn ones nearest the water. Like a sluggish, white river, they flowed steadily up the trail and out of sight to the east.

To the west, the sun had mostly set behind the ridge line that had always faithfully kept our bellicose neighbors at bay. In the gathering gloom, I invoked 'visio tenebris.' Just as I was about to turn and follow the flock, I thought I detected movement in a thicket across the pond. Hunkering back down, I peered more intently at the spot. From amid the thick brambles that covered a stretch of treacherous, rocky ground, I caught it once again. It was a subtle, creeping movement that strangely caused nary a branch to stir. I was about to dismiss it as a raccoon or some other natural creature of the land, but my mage sight was prompting me to take a sharper look. For in the failing light of the fallen sun aided but poorly by the waning, crescent moon, the entire thicket began to emit a soft glow.

Under my continued scrutiny, the branches and vines that were tangled and matted throughout the rocky stretch seemed to peel back and fade into wispy images. Layer by layer this progressed until I could make out a dark circle near the center. The ghostly thicket was still present, but had been revealed as but a pale mockery of vegetation. A deceptive enchantment had become transparent under the auspices of my darksight.

And what it revealed was appalling. Within the 'thicket' stood two little men in leather jerkins staring avidly up the path where Avery and his charges had just departed. Never had I been so disheartened to see Royland proven right. Their eyes had a reddish gleam which called to mind those of an animal whose orbs reflected the light of a fire. Each was armed with a bow. These resembled the longbows employed by our knights but were sized smaller to suit their owners' diminished statures. The goblins' over-sized heads made them appear almost childlike, but the way they moved banished this notion at once.

For moving they were. Warily casting about, the two little sentries crept away from the dark cave they were flanking and out of the faux thicket entirely. Two others emerged to replace them at their erstwhile post. As the first pair made their way across the shallow brook below the pond and started up the hill, I considered whistling for Avery to run. I was glad I decided against the action when the two took up station about halfway up the trail.

It was then that I began hearing voices. The little men at the cave were exchanging words with someone deeper within. They were strange words full of fricatives and gurgling 'g's.' It was the language my master called 'gobbledygook.' He had learned it from captives taken back during the goblin wars. I supposed I should start calling them the first goblin wars now. 'It's always worthwhile to recognize what your enemy is saying,' he had lectured. I regretted not having his services now as I struggled to comprehend what the tiny men intended. I was given no further time to consider the matter as the cave began to disgorge dozens of the creatures.

Startled, I wanted to run. But I clamped down on this desire and chose instead to remain motionless to witness what I could. My position on the hilltop was relatively distant from the frightening force that was gathering, and I suspected that stealth remained my best ally. To my considerable relief, the goblins issuing from that unwholesome crevasse were being directed away from where I lay. They began to move off farther beyond the brook and formed up in serried ranks marching to the west. The pass! Master Chadwick was out there. Our men must be warned.

Just when I thought I had seen enough and began to back slowly away, something even more dire emerged from the cave. It was hunched over and barely fit through the opening so great was its girth. From my readings, I recognized an ogre. Books didn't do the massive creature justice. Standing erect, he was half again the height of a man and muscles bulged upon every leathery inch of him. His head had a sloping brow and an over-sized jaw from which protruded a set of tusks framing a bulbous nose. He wore only a great, ragged loincloth that could have been the pelt of an entire deer, and he was armed with a huge club. This he rested with ease upon a brawny shoulder. The ogre was followed by another that could have been his twin. The great brutes were goaded into motion by a gabbling goblin who directed them to join the others on the field. As they lumbered off, still more of their immense ilk continued to pour forth.

I had tarried here overlong. I felt that Avery should be well clear by now. I hoped he and the ladies would swiftly reach Turner Ranch, for I sensed the goblins were done with their hiding. I belly-crawled backwards making as little noise as I could manage and half-stood as soon as I dared. Crouching low and aided by darksight, I paced steadily out to the road and toward safety.

Eventually, we had all arrived here at Turner Ranch. I had released my final pigeon with a message bound for the baron. I hoped he had some way to signal the men at the watchtower. I was glad we had gotten the flock out of there too. I felt sure that was what my master would have wanted - double entendre and all. The sheep were watering at Turner's Pond while we considered our next move. Dylan Turner thought we should hunker down here until help could arrive, but having seen our foes, I felt we were too vulnerable and should try to head farther east. Granny Turner had echoed my sentiment, saying the goblin scouts would assuredly be out soon and then their horde would sweep across the barony. We should make for the safety of our liege's keep.

So here I sat in the morning light calmly reviewing my options with my master's mutt.

***

Ehr-Wuff!

Sampson cocked his head and arose to all fours. Peering intently down the road to the east, he announced that we were about to have visitors. I stood as well, arising to both twos. Looking out over the fields, I could see nothing apart from the dozens of little lean-tos that stood upon Goodman Dylan's land. Stretched out on frames were the scraped and drying hides of sheep angled to better absorb the rays of the sun. Each day, the man would go out among them, tighten all the tenterhooks, and pumice and powder the drying skins. They were thus gradually transformed by his art into parchment suitable for writing.

When the wagon came into view, I was relieved to note that the visitor was friendly and familiar. I experienced a sense of déjà vu as I saw the heavy wagon drawn by its two teams carefully navigating the rutted road.

"Hello the house!" rang out the voice of Otto Verney as he approached.

The boy seemed nonplussed when a dozen ranchers rushed out to greet him. He had been sent out to make a delivery of cured meat to the Turners and to collect a large bundle of Dylan's parchments for sale in town. When we shared our unwelcome news, the boy was most distressed and wanted to leave immediately, but we begged him to stay. There was safety in numbers, after all. And his wagon would be essential to transport the younger lambs or those sheep that might come up lame during a long migration.

The Fowler and Tillerson flocks were not yet well-rested after their nighttime treks from their respective meadows. They had at least had water, however, and had grazed enough on the lush Turner pastures to recover some strength. A brief consultation with Otto on the condition of the roads revealed that they were 'abysmal as always, but no worse than usual.' A southerly wind had picked up, scattering debris before it in irregular gusts which might indicate a summer squall was brewing. Nonetheless, it was decided we would attempt to herd the sheep farther east.

It was our hope that by day's end we might reach the relative safety of the Cain farmstead, there to take our rest before traveling onward. Otto assured us that the Cain compound was very secure, being fenced all around and protected by the many men of their extended family. He was uncertain of what welcome we could expect. He had invariably made his deliveries to the front gate, never being invited within or feted there.

The combined flock of hundreds was made ready to depart. Our drovers included Roy and Sampson on the right flank and Dylan and Avery on the left. The four wagons would follow up the center of the road. First came Tilda driving the lighter, Fowler cart. Next was the Turner Wagon driven by Kay with Granny on the bench beside her. These were followed by Harriet and Prissy driving the Tillerson wagon. Bringing up the rear was Otto's massive meat wagon loaded with all of the sheep deemed too young or ill-rested to keep up the pace. Also aboard it were the Turner children who would care for the little lambs in transit. As I had the least facility with the handling of animals, it fell to me to lead our exodus, scouting the road ahead for hazards and prepared to confront danger with my crossbow.

We set out a bit later than we had hoped due to the last-minute delays and problems that always plagued any enterprise of this magnitude: a broken harness strap; an essential supply to retrieve; and sundry other such last-minute snarls. Dylan was loath to leave the hides he had been drying in the fields, but there was neither space on the wagons nor time to collect them.

He sulked to think the goblins might reap the fruits of his long summer's labor until Avery admonished him saying: 'Quit your bellyaching, man. Would you rather our wee enemies take your hides or *our hides*?'

As we meandered along the road east toward perceived safety, the rumble of distant thunder did little to ease our apprehension. I could almost *feel* the eyes of the goblin scouts on my back pressing me forward. Granny Turner posited they were following our progress unseen. Her husband, Ephraim, had been a soldier during the wars. He had shared with her some of the tactics of our foes from those earlier days. Their main force was presently engaged trying to pin down and crush our countrymen at the pass. So we hoped a small band of their scouts wouldn't risk an engagement with an unknown convoy of our size. Such hopes were to be dashed later that very afternoon.

It began when the flock arrived at Bradlebury Bridge. This marked the midpoint of our planned day's journey. This stout, wooden bridge, which spanned a steep gully, was considered to be the boundary marker between Arborvale and Westarbor proper. The flock had spread out across hundreds of yards, and our drovers were hard-pressed to consolidate them to make the crossing. Our teamsters all shortened their reins and came to a stop to await their turn upon the bridge. Some stepped down to stretch or otherwise relieve themselves. Sampson was sent across early on to manage the sheep as they gathered on the far side.

It was at this time that our furry friend let loose his sharp wail of warning. Before we could react, three goblins stood from behind some shrubbery off to the right of our formation. From their small bows, they loosed a flight of arrows into our flank while three more of their brethren gained the road directly to our rear.

Royland adopted his shielding stance, but the damage had already been done. Otto's wagon had sprouted a black-fletched arrow and his right lead ox was bellowing in anguish. There being too many targets to protect, Royland made the sensible decision to erect a blue screen directly in front of the archers, suppressing their second volley entirely. I could only assume that the first round of arrows was to insure we couldn't flee, and that our enemies were confident they could overcome a bunch of mere shepherds by force *majeure*. By the looks on their formerly smug faces as their subsequent flight rebounded, I imagined they hadn't suspected that mages lurked among our number.

As the ox went down to his knees, dragging his left-hand partner along by the yoke, I targeted the three fiends dashing at us with bared steel. My first quarrel took one in the leg, spinning him about and introducing him to the taste of the road. Avery and Dylan came rushing toward the fray with their shepherd's crooks in hand, but they didn't look as though they'd make it before the little cretins reached the wagons. My second shot split a wooden shield asunder, so great was its impact. The bearer of said shield was lifted bodily and tumbled back a step to end up sitting in the dirt staring dazedly at his left forearm from which the jagged end of my quarrel protruded.

By this time, the three archers had gathered their wits. Forsaking their cover, they separated. Roy could no longer manage all three with his shielding spell. Howling, they advanced, sending their shafts with a single-minded fury at the erstwhile source of their frustration. Backing away, Roy hastily erected a protective barrier from which this dire volley splattered. I was jostled as a grey-white blur swept past me from behind. With a low rumble from deep within his chest, Sampson took to the field, bearing down upon one of the archers. It was then I was forced to make the painful decision to shift my attention to another of the archers to even Roy's odds. I had to trust that Avery and Dylan could stand against the lone combatant rushing down the road.

As my quarrel sunk home in the archer's chest, I saw that last runner dash past the shepherds. He scrambled up the wagon's high, slatted sides to drop into its bed beyond. Dylan almost got him with the hook of his crook, but the slippery little devil had won free. The courage of the remaining two archers fled, as did they but a moment later. Roy was making the return signal for Sampson who was ferociously harrying their retreating forms. The goblins I had crippled earlier were also limping away. From Otto's wagon, there arose a sorrowful wail and the sound of sobbing.

I didn't witness the events that transpired in the bed of that wagon. I was told only later when my blood had cooled. It was a grim tale that took place in the space of several heartbeats but seemed an eternity to those involved. It was the story of seven-year-old Ronnie Turner who, seeing a goblin drop from above to threaten his sisters, rose to confront it brandishing only a willeying stick. It was the tale of a butcher's son's brave leap into the fray from atop the driver's bench of the wagon. Choosing the smaller foe, the goblin had lashed out aiming to skewer the child, only to be felled by a single, precise blow to the base of his skull dealt by a hammer that had slain a thousand sheep. The holder of said hammer had immediately crumpled into a weeping heap, overcome by remorse. As for Ronnie, he had deflected the blow. Fortunately, the sons of Arborvale get *a lot* of practice willeying those fleeces.

***

The ramp had been lowered from the butcher's wagon. The dead goblin was gone, and the Turner children were being comforted by their frantic parents. Hollie straddled her mother's hip, and Willow and Ronnie bracketed Dylan who had his arms draped protectively around each. Otto had not arisen from the bed of the cart where he sat quietly weeping.

"Quit your blubbering, boy," admonished Avery. "It's over. Cheer up. We won."

Granny Turner scowled and scolded the man saying, "No one wins in war, Avery Tillerson. And killing *should* cause you to feel this way. My Ephraim, stars rest his soul, knew a few for whom it didn't, and you wouldn't want *them* by your side."

Granny stepped up into the bed of the wagon and eased herself down beside the distraught boy. Placing a hand on his shoulder, she looked him square in the face.

"It gets better, child," she soothed. "Not all at once, nor will you ever completely forget, but in fits and starts it'll fade until the better parts of your life come to the fore again. My Ephraim bore what you're feeling when he came back from the wars. I did what I could to comfort him, but he was haunted for *years* by the things he was forced to do. Crying it out now is a *good* thing - as much as you can. So cry. There's no shame in it, despite what some *ignorant* people might advise."

"Even so," she continued with a sigh, "we need to move on now. We're all still in danger and we need your strength. Your lead ox, Murphy, is dead. We unhitched him, but the way you've got your harnesses rigged, Marc's gonna need a partner. Tilda thinks mister Strongback can fill in. If she sits on the bench with you, do you think you can drive this wagon?"

As she spoke, the boy's jaw had firmed. And even though tears still formed to run down his cheeks, he managed a nod and climbed to his feet.

I wished I had the luxury to have a good cry myself. I felt nothing for the two goblins I had wounded. They had brought that upon themselves. However, even though the same could be said of that last one who had died with my quarrel in his chest, somehow it was different. I had claimed a life. I wondered whether he had an ugly little goblin wife and a few vicious little children who would forever remain waiting at home for him. Despite Granny Lydia's advice, I set it aside for now.

The sheep had scattered during our mad skirmish with the goblins, but they hadn't gone far. Dylan and Prissy were rounding them up and had already herded most across the bridge where Sampson was keeping them contained. In their panic, a few had rolled down into the gully. Royland lifted these back up with 'levare' and Avery assisted by dragging them back to the edge using his crook. Floating sheep look like funny little clouds. It was a good thing the wind was toward us, or they'd have drifted clean away.

The best we could do for the deceased mister Murphy was to utter a few solemn words and tumble him over the edge. As mister Strongback was fitted into Murphy's former harness, the Fowler cart met the same fate. Tilda's belongings were split between the already overloaded Tillerson and Turner wagons, but she fumed to think her cart might be pressed into service as a goblin war machine. I launched it over the edge myself using 'spacium girabit' on its wheels.

Some of the men were in favor of giving the dead goblins the same treatment, but I insisted on a bit more reverence. Though they were our enemies and would probably not respect *our* dead, I thought we needed to stick by our principles and bury them properly. So Royland churned up a big strip of ground to one side of the road using 'terram aratro,' the earth furrow spell. Over their mother's halfhearted objections, Willow and Ronnie were awarded the goblins' tiny swords and bows, the first spoils of the Second Goblin Wars.

Having attended to all of this and after completing our crossing, we decided that the bridge should not be left intact. Roy and I set to work on its beams with 'gloriabitur securis,' the force axe spell. I had to deplete three nearby saplings before the deed was accomplished. The absence of a reliable bridge would by no means hamper the goblin scouting parties, but hopefully it would slow their army's advance. One day the bards would sing of the 'Battle of Bradlebury Bridge.' I was quite certain this aftermath would be ignored, despite the fact that we had used far more magic than during the battle itself.

Underway once again, we were desperately behind schedule. In spite of the longer days, it would be a miracle if we should arrive at the Cain 'stead before the fall of night. Although we had thwarted the goblins' attack, Granny believed they were still present and mightn't be as completely cowed as we would wish. If they could gather more of their compatriots, they could be up for a second attempt. Worse luck, there would be no moon this night. Only Royland, Sampson and I could sense our surroundings in the dark. Should they attack again, I felt certain they wouldn't target the oxen first. The thought of it felt like a persistent itch between my shoulder blades.

It could be worse, I thought. At least that storm had passed us by.

After a few hours, we met a harker upon the road. His instructions were long-winded and filled with reassurances that our liege had our best interests in mind. Boiled down, they commanded us to make all haste for the keep, destroying anything we couldn't carry. We asked him whether he had delivered his message to the Cains and he assured us that he had. We thanked the man and told him that there were no other uninformed tenancies farther to the west. We also reported the destruction of the bridge. He was skeptical about our claim of victory at said bridge. That is, until we showed him the goblin weapons Willow and Ronnie had acquired. His duty discharged, the harker turned and headed back east at a pace we couldn't hope to match.

It could be worse, I thought. At least the baron had received my message, and he believed me.

When night did fall, our progress slowed. It was hard enough in the full light of day to keep the tired sheep moving along. In the last lingering dregs of a moonless twilight, the strain of doing so became almost palpable. As the long shadows faded and the night insects took up their doleful, rhythmic chorus, even Sampson's boundless energy seemed to be flagging. I didn't know the road out here as well as the others, but each time I asked, I was quietly assured that the Cain lands were 'just around the bend.' I became increasingly certain this was rancher-speak for 'we don't exactly know either.' I went ranging farther ahead in an attempt to find out for myself.

Not long after I had invoked both wakefulness and my darksight, I spotted an ominous figure lurking upon the roadway ahead. He was fairly tall and thickset in a way that suggested strength. His broad shoulders were hunched forward strangely, his weight resting on the balls of his feet and the butt of a spear he gripped in his left hand. I waived in a friendly manner and started to approach with my crossbow pointed non-threateningly off to one side.

In an abrupt burst of motion, the man spun about and thrust an odd contraption in my direction. With a sudden snap, the area to my right was bathed in bright light, momentarily overwhelming my enhanced vision. When my eyes cleared, they beheld a pair of goblins blinking and fanning their hands before them to ward off the revealing radiance. Before my next breath, two men emerged from the darkness behind them and thrust spears into their unprotected backs. I now understood how the frog must feel when it was gigged.

"You there," grunted the first man, turning the light to shine directly at me, "had better explain why you're creeping through Cain land in the dark of night unless you're wanting some of the same."

The words could have been Gregor's if you deepened his voice by an octave and added some growl. I hastily raised up my hands as much as the crossbow allowed and the itch between my shoulder blades intensified.

"I'm Lucas Harper," I said in the steadiest voice I could manage. "Some neighbors from Arborvale and I are fleeing the goblin army that's arisen in the west. We've got three wagons and a couple of hundred sheep."

"We've got eyes on them as well," declared the man. "You may pass through."

"We had hoped you could provide us some shelter for the night. Surely you heard the harker. We're all to make for the keep. But these sheep are on their last legs, as are the rest of us."

"You chose an inauspicious night to come calling, Lucas Harper. It's the night of the new moon - the night of the *curse*."

He said this last word in a long drawn out fashion that descended to a low rumble.

"I am not familiar with this curse of which you speak."

"No?" he growled. "You should ask your uncle; he bears the blame for it. Very well, Lucas Harper, approach and behold your grandmother's handiwork. Tell me *then* if you and your ilk would pass this night among the Cains."

With that, the light was shuttered, and my vision began to clear. I took several shaky steps forward, trying to ignore the shuffling sounds from behind. As his features became more evident, I was shocked to discover that the man sported tusks. Coarse, prickly hair covered most of his visible features in dirty grey-brown patches. His snout was elongated and turned up at its end, and his wide-set eyes were rimmed with yellow where their whites should be. Those eyes stared down at me unblinkingly as I stepped up to the man. I shifted my crossbow to cradle it in my left arm and extended my right hand.

"I don't believe I caught your name. Mine's Lucas, as I said."

He squinted at me and craned his neck forward to loom above.

"We know who you are, boy," he said in that rough baritone, hooking the lantern on his belt.

Then he clasped my proffered hand awkwardly with his own. His palm felt heavily calloused but smooth and leathery like the pads of Sampson's paws. They sprouted large, stubby fingers fused together to the first knuckle. From these, thickened, flat nails extended almost to the point of merging with one another. His grip was firm and steady, but I felt a restrained tension as his glowering glare went on unabated.

"Gregor mentioned you were well-schooled in manners. He didn't cite you were a stickler for 'em, though. You surprise me. Since you asked, I am Uriah, patriarch of clan Cain."

"Can you grant us a night of safety from the goblins, Uriah?"

"From the goblins, maybe, if your need be dire. I can't insure safety for your animals, though. Alright then, I suppose there's yet time enough. Gideon! Silas! Go throw open the gates. We are about to have *guests*."

Turning back to me he said, "Go and speak to your people. *Explain* it to them. If they agree, you must be quick. The refuge we offer will only be possible in the next hour. No longer."

So, as Gideon and Silas loped eastward down the road, I retraced my steps west toward the bleating of the flock.

***

I hurried back to the wagons and repeated the Cains' offer to the others after sharing what I had experienced. Since time was limited, I forestalled their questions and objections and urged them to get moving.

We soon reached the spot where I had encountered Uriah and his men. The dead goblins were no longer in evidence, but the smell of blood still lingered in the air, and I noticed that the sheep were skittishly avoiding the spot. About a furlong farther down the road, a lane opened up to our left which led to a tall, solid fence, the heavy gates of which were open wide. Where the lane met the road was a painted sign which read: 'Cain Farmstead - Trespassers will be persecuted!' I didn't think it was a misspelling. Sniffing at the base of the signpost, Sampson whined and retreated several paces.

"Well, go on," I said, pointing to the gates. "Get the sheep in there."

He gave me that hangdog expression but soon set about reluctantly complying.

Avery also drew up short and asked, "Are you certain this is safe?"

I told him I was certain it was not but that it was safer than out here.

At the gates we were met by another of the beast-men, the first that the other ranchers had seen. Although expecting it, some nearly balked at the reality. The fearsome nature of the man was partly offset by the incongruous straw hat perched rakishly atop his hairy pate.

"Evenin' Lucas and friends," said a voice I belatedly realized was that of Otis Cain. "Be welcome, but be quick."

Once the sheep were all in, they were herded into a large, fenced-in yard that looked like it might normally have held a variety of the Cain's animals. These, we were to soon discover, had all been locked securely in their barn.

Perhaps 'barn' was an understatement. It was a massive building made from heavy timbers and planks reinforced every ten feet or so. Once its fortified front doors had been breached, all of the gear and supplies from our wagons were placed therein at one end of an entire warehouse of crated goods that put Tilda's mighty horde to shame. The pig-men worked diligently and in concert like a fireman's brigade to accomplish this task before we could even get the oxen unhitched.

Our animals were given space in the few stalls that remained unoccupied in a stable that rivaled the baron's in size. When I informed Sampson he was to stay here with mister Strongback and company, he stalked indignantly back into a corner and flopped down with nary a backwards glance. Avery had thought to include the rams with our six oxen and two cows. Ushering us back outside, one of the Cains locked and barred the doors from within and then climbed down from the hayloft doors which he also secured.

One of the beast-boys snarled at us and began to approach menacingly, dropping nearly to all fours, but he was promptly wrestled to the ground and restrained by two others.

"Best we get these good folk situated," said Uriah. "It looks like we done lost Grindall already."

As Uriah led us over to the house, we huddled close, keeping the children at the center of our group as an occasional, unnerving grunt or snort broke the stillness of the night.

Inside the house, our lumbering host led us back through a cavernous kitchen with multiple hearths. He stopped at a heavy but narrow door on which he rapped gently with his thick, flattened, hoof-like nails.

"Are you decent?" he hailed.

"We're all dressed, Uriah Cain; that'll have to do," came a rich, contralto reply from within. "Are you sane?"

"No less than usual, but I feel it comin' on, so best you open up quick."

"Or you'll huff and you'll puff?" the voice teasingly recited.

"Tarnation, woman! At least get your story straight. It's supposed t' be the other way around. Just open her up for some guests I brought you."

There was a pause while this was absorbed, then a series of clicking and clunking sounds I presumed were deadbolts being thrown back.

"Then come ahead quick-like, but no false moves."

The doorway opened to reveal a narrow stairway that headed downward to a cold-cellar of gigantic proportions. Goodman Cain bade us enter, but he remained at the threshold either by custom or for fear of getting his broad shoulders wedged within the tight opening.

***

As we descended, Uriah said from atop the stairs, "I brought you these visitors, my sweet. I figured they could stay in the men's bunker. We won't be needin' it on this of all nights. The short one is Lucas; the one Gregor spoke so highly of. These others are ranchers caught up in the comin' storm the harker was rambling on about. I agreed we could shelter 'em. They'll move on come morning."

223

Short one? I had Ronnie beat by a foot and a half at least. At the bottom of the stairs stood an old woman with a pitchfork at the ready. In the back of the low-ceilinged but otherwise spacious cellar huddled a gaggle of other women of all various ages. Once we had arrived and entered the room, the woman, who I was to learn was named Bethiah Cain, ascended the stairwell sans pitchfork. She dropped a wooden bar into place and secured several other deadbolt latches before turning to confront us.

By the light of bright lanterns placed about the dug out area, I spotted nearly a dozen beds and quite a few homey touches that would do any lady's parlor proud. There were nine Cain women in all. Dressed in their night gowns, they seemed to come in three sizes. There were five more junior girls whose ages varied from nine or ten up to about my own. Additionally, there were three more mature women, none perhaps quite so old as Tilda. Finally, there was our more elderly hostess, Bethiah, to whom all the others seemed to defer. Introductions were made all around, but I found it difficult to remember all the names, much less assign each to its proper owner.

When I was introduced, I caught the gleam of recognition on several of the girls' upturned faces.

"Gregor never cited he was so purdy," observed one of the older girls with her hands clasped behind her back.

"Now, you mind your manners, Mercy Cain," scolded Bethiah. "That's no way to talk to strangers."

The girl looked down at her feet but wore an unrepentant smirk that gave the lie to her contrition. Before long she was whispering something to her sister that had them both laughing silently.

"Gramma, *boys* can't be down here," announced the smallest one chidingly. "Boys are *bad* on the night of the dark moon."

"These are boys from outside, Lisbeth," returned the matriarch patiently. "They'll be safe enough tonight. They'll sleep in the boy's bunker. Comfort and Mercy, please show them where they can put down their mats whilst I get these ladies settled."

We were led back to an adjacent excavation similar to the first but which sported fewer comforts. The low ceilings were somewhat off-putting, and I was gratified I *wasn't* tall like Royland. My cousin's slouch was more pronounced than usual, and he kept glancing nervously upward from time to time. There were eight bunks in this room, which was separated from the other by only a thick curtain that could be pulled across an opening. We were led over to a cabinet from which we could select blankets and pillows. I detected a faint musty odor which told me this room and its bunks didn't serve as the men's usual sleeping quarters.

"Men stay in here," said Comfort Cain as she and her sister departed drawing the curtain closed behind them. "G'night."

I had about a hundred questions, but was just grateful for the hospitality, even if it did seem a bit abrupt. As I made up my sleeping pallet and lay down, I thought I might fall asleep immediately. However, a series of unexplained noises from above soon put me on edge. There were grunts and howls, bumps, thumps, galloping noises and a loud squeal. These came at odd intervals interspersed with eerie silences, only to return with increased intensity.

"Rest now - it begins. There will be no peace until morning," whispered Bethiah from beyond the curtain.

"Gramma, tell us a story," came a frightened sounding voice.

"Which story would you like, sweetheart?"

"The farmer in the del."

The request was taken up and repeated by several other young voices in a most hopeful and eager manner.

"There once was a young farmer who worked for a mighty baron in the kingdom of Osten," she began. "But the baron was cruel, forcing him to work in the fields all day long and taking most of his crops for his rent."

There arose a chorus of hissing and tongue-clucking at this.

"Nevertheless, the farmer worked very hard and soon thought he had enough saved up, so the farmer took a wife."

"Was she purdy?" came a new voice.

"Quiet, Mercy. No jumping ahead. The woman was not unhandsome, but to the farmer, she was the 'purdiest blossom in the orchard.' What did the baron do? Why, he raised the farmers taxes since there were now two people instead of just the one."

"So both the farmer and his wife worked very hard on their little farm, paid all their taxes and finally saved up enough. And the wife got with child. Nine months later, little Otis was born. What did that mean old baron do?"

"Raised their taxes," returned the chorus of girlish voices.

But I noticed several voices had dropped out by this time. Whatever was going on? This wasn't how I had heard the story. It was rather oddly specific to boot. It was no wonder Goodman Otis had been so suspicious of our banalaty at the mill.

"Otis grew into a fine, strong boy who helped on the farm and was soon joined by his younger brothers, Silas and Gideon. And with each new child, what did the baron do?"

"Raised their taxes," returned a few yawning voices.

"'Tarnation!' said the farmer. 'We have to work so hard for the baron's protection that we'd be better off protecting our own selves.' So the farmer took his purdy wife and his three strong sons and snuck off one night. They settled in the western wild where there was no baron to tax them and carved out a little farm of their own in Arbordell . . ."

I must have drifted off, for I was suddenly awakened by a shrill scream. Realizing where I was, I sat up and reached for my crossbow.

"One of those *boys* is turning *bad*," sobbed the childlike voice of Lisbeth.

"That's just snoring, Chick-pea," Bethiah said. "You've heard Caleb snore before. Now go back to sleep."

*Royland.* That's not the impression I had hoped we'd make. I quietly arose and padded over to my cousin's bedside. He had also been awakened by the scream and now lay quiescent and close-mouthed upon his pallet. Nevertheless, I forced him over onto his stomach; it sometimes helped.

"Tell us another story," the girl entreated.

"It's late, Lisbeth, and Gramma's tired."

"Nother story," the girl sullenly insisted as fresh rounds of strange sounds erupted from above.

"What story would you like?" the matron acquiesced with a sigh.

"The witch."

This time, when the familiar pleading chorus commenced, I felt like joining in, but I held my peace and listened.

"When Abigail first arrived and took over the ruins of the old castle, the clan welcomed her and her two young children. For she was a witcher-woman who provided them with healing herbs and help with childbirth. By this time, Otis, Silas and Gideon had each brought a wife to the dell, freeing each from the wrongs she had suffered under that old baron."

"When asked about her own children's father, Abigail looked so sad. But she would never reply directly. 'I'm a free witch,' she would say or, 'Those days are behind us now.'"

"From time to time, knights from the kingdom to the east would arrive and begin clearing the forest. But always they or their servants would meet with a mysterious accident or be driven off in some other way. When all else failed, any structure they attempted to build would be flattened by a great shaking of the earth."

"This was seen as a good thing, for the knights were always greedy for land and never seemed to care whether people not from their kingdom were already living somewhere. Rumors spread of the witch of the western wood, and wise men learned not to cross her."

"Even the goblins who lived to the west of the mountains ceased their poaching and pilferage. They soon learned that they could hunt the forest if they did so in peace. But they could make no settlement, however temporary, without drawing the attention and ire of the witch. Over time, the clan all came to work for the witch at her castle, for now it was grand and elegant."

"One day, when the witch was very old and weary, her son, Robert came to the servants. 'She's gone batshit crazy, say I' the boy told them. He told them he needed to take his younger sister to safety, and if they knew what was good for them they would all light out from that castle as well."

"So light out from it they did. But seeing most of her servants abandoning her, the witch grew angry. Before the clan could escape, the witch called down a mighty curse on them. From here on out, the men of the clan would change into savage beasts each darkening of the moon."

Uncle Robert? Grandma Abbey? No wonder Uriah had said they knew all about me. There was likely a bedtime story called: 'Lucas, whom nobody bothered to inform.' I wondered how *that* one read. I lay awake long into the night before the cares and exhaustion of the day conveyed me once more into a fitful slumber.

***

When we emerged from that bunker on the following morning, the compound looked like a storm had hit it. The men were all bustling about setting things back in order. Bethiah and some of her women set right to work getting a breakfast readied. I think they were secretly pleased to have guests but were unsure of the proper protocols. So the ladies of the Arborvale circle stepped in to lend a hand and place them at their ease. The younger girls seemed fascinated by five-year-old Hollie, not having had any children that young around for a while.

The sheep had all been provided grain and the watering trough had been freshly filled. We suspected some were missing because of the suspicious bloodstains at the pen's far end. But we thought It would be impolite and ungrateful to bring the matter up, so we didn't inquire. The rest of them looked pretty spooked. I think if we had any black sheep, they would have been scared white by the night they put in.

When the doors to the barn were opened, Sampson streaked out and didn't stop running until he was all the way to the road past the signpost. There he sat panting and staring back toward the compound with his hackles raised. We let him be, and I made a point to bring him food and some water from our wagons' supplies. Our wagons had suffered some abuse. I could see a few new gouges in their sides, and one of the Cain men was replacing a wheel on the Turner's even as the Tillerson's was being reloaded. Avery and Otto were retrieving our oxen while Dylan oversaw the repair.

"Morning," said Uriah.

By the light of day and without the affliction brought on by the curse, he looked careworn. With a full grey beard, bushy eyebrows and sun-browned skin, he appeared every inch an elderly clan patriarch. But even with his sclera back to a normal hue, his eyes still captured ones attention. They were a little bit wild, those eyes, but could suddenly spear you like those of a predator.

"I suppose you folks will want to clear out early," he said suggestively. "Feel free to have some breakfast with the women folk. They don't get to entertain much. As to last night, we don't speak of such things in town. As a guest, I *expect* you to honor that tradition. Best of luck to you."

"Aren't you going to break fast with us, Uriah?"

The man looked uncomfortable and said, "I had a little something last night."

"When are you folk falling back to the keep?"

"We won't."

"Didn't you hear that harker yesterday? I saw their horde with my own eyes, Uriah, or part of it at least. It won't be a couple of their scouts coming down that road the next time you see them; let's get behind the baron's wall and help out as best we can."

The man sighed.

"We can't stay here either, of course. But every time I rely on someone else for protection, it takes a bad turn. The Cains look after their own now."

And there were those eyes again, examining me from head to toe.

"Perhaps I'll join you at breakfast after all, Lucas Harper," he said.

The ladies had prepared a plentiful meal of wholesome fare. After we had partaken, Uriah called in the Cain men and made a pronouncement. The clan would be 'buggering out,' an eventuality for which they had long prepared. There was some murmuring among the Cains, but none seemed truly surprised. Uriah's plan was to pack up some wagons and make for the Danstonshire highlands. He declared his lordship shouldn't begrudge a bit of 'polite poaching' on these lands during the crisis, and the goblins wouldn't likely range that far east before the keep was overrun. Perhaps they could return when everything had 'cooled back down a might.'

He offered to convoy with us ranchers, accompanying us for mutual protection at least as far as the keep. From there, we could follow our own hearts and choose whatever we thought was best. After only a brief discussion, we accepted; we'd be fools to decline such a fine offer. I suspected such protection would be more one-sided than truly mutual.

The people of the Cain family set immediately to work. All knew their tasks and performed them expeditiously as though from long practice. This notion was confirmed when Uriah reminded them: 'it's for real this time, so step lively.' It was then that Gregor's words from that night at the mill pond returned to me. 'Our family's only magic is in being prepared for the unexpected,' he had said. And it did seem to be a sort of magic the way everyone came together so quickly as though they had planned this for months. They worked like ants moving crates from the barn to their bunker, diverting one occasionally to their four sturdy wagons which were hastily assembled in the compound.

"Aren't you going to destroy the extra supplies?" I asked Otis when he seemed to have a moment.

"Nope, we're gonna hide 'em; you'll see," he replied.

"Have you given any thought to what conditions will be like at the keep?" he asked of me in turn.

"I'm afraid we haven't had the time since we started running, Otis."

He looked at me with disappointment evident upon his face.

"*Think*, son. I couldn't help but notice your gear seemed to lack in particulars. Did you bring any chamber pots?"

"They weren't the first items on our list, Otis. We packed food and valuables . . ."

"Forget valuables! What're valuable now are things you need to survive. Likely the baron will confiscate anything you bring to portion back out 'fairly.' He'll then crowd all the folks down into the lower halls where there'll be little privacy and even less of everything else. You'll get a meager ration of food and water and access to a hole in the ground for a privy. So you may as well load your wagons with equipment useful for those conditions in the hopes that some of it will be used for your benefit."

He was right. We'd all just been reacting in blind panic. I asked whether he could assist us, and he agreed. We ranchers all huddled around as fully two-thirds of our gear was stripped away and conducted to the Cain's massive cellar. It was replaced by goods that Otis and his kin recommended. Humbled by this grand gift, we were assured that the Cains had many more items of a similar nature than they would ever likely need. Tilda was teary-eyed to see her mother's elegant tea set crated up and carted off, but was thankful that it would be well cared for. She was promised she could retrieve it if and after the current mess was favorably concluded. In its place, we received an entire crate of utilitarian tin and ceramic tankards.

I thought they still had a ways to go when Uriah pronounced the packing to be complete. There were still uncountable crates in the barn. These, we were told, were purposeful. There was nothing of particular use in them, and upon finding such a trove, the goblins should look no further. Moreover, the neatly labeled foodstuffs among the useless items had been cleverly sabotaged. They placed them out when they suspected thieves. At first it would seem alright and would even be tasty. However, after eating it for a couple of meals, one would develop severe stomach cramps and begin voiding ones bowels uncontrollably for days on end. This was based on the addition of an undisclosed herb that was found to be detrimental to the Cain's cattle. No sir, the Cains weren't a family to cross lightly.

When all was in readiness, the Cains returned to their kitchen. One of their fireplaces therein was slid over, hearth and all, to cover and completely conceal the narrow doorway that led down into their bunker. Once locked firmly into place, there was no evidence whatsoever that the rooms below existed. We were told that one could even stoke a fire in its small firebox, though its flue would draw poorly and its use would likely be eschewed in favor of using one of the others.

The Cains turned out from their barn all of the animals that were not going with them. These could fend for themselves, or if not, it couldn't be helped. By early afternoon we set out. Sampson refused to help with the sheep until we had cleared the compound, and even then he took pains to avoid the Cain men and their carts.

***

Instead of walking, I rode in the wagon driven by Goodman Otis and his wife, Loretta. We stayed on the winding road just in advance of the flock. I sat atop the load of equipment in its bed accompanied by their two daughters, Comfort and Mercy. It turned out Comfort was my same age with Mercy only a year behind her. This lofty perch commanded a considerable view of the way ahead and would allow me to ply my crossbow to good advantage if the bumping and swaying didn't spoil my aim.

"Do you know how to use that thing, Lucas?" asked the girls' mother as we rattled along.

"I get by," I said, smiling.

"I'm only asking because you don't have the crank set," she noted, pursing her lips in disapproval.

In reply, I wound it up and released a few times without setting a quarrel.

"I get by," I repeated.

Mercy nudged Comfort and whispered, "Told ya."

"Lucas, since you're a witch like your gramma, can you lift the curse off our men?" asked the older girl, eyes flashing.

The courage of the statement was held together only by the fragile thread of hope in her voice. I didn't want to spin that thread the wrong way.

232

"I'm only an apprentice . . . witch," I carefully replied. "I haven't been taught any curses. Have you asked Master Chadwick?"

As the girls seemed to deflate, Otis pulled his hat down more firmly upon his head.

"That old quack told us that killing the witch should have ended her curse," he said. "Yet when the new baron seized her castle, they never actually saw her die. She'd have to be *really* old by now, so we're still hopeful."

"Hey, while we're on the topic, how is it that Gregor can be in town?" I asked.

"Gregor thinks he can live among the 'decent folk' and they'll accept him. Thinks he can learn a trade and have a normal life. Since he's the eldest child of the patriarch's eldest, Uriah gave him a year to try. Your uncle promised to keep him locked in the cellar during the three days of the dark moon."

"He's a good man, your uncle," added Loretta, "We're going to miss him as a neighbor. That's his old place just over yonder. I don't like the new tenants, though. They call our compound a spite fence."

"Fools don't know it's for keeping us in, not them out," Otis said. "It used to be different before the curse. When I courted Loretta here, I was offering to release her from servitude. It was a hardscrabble life to be sure, but we were free. Nowadays, how could a boy ask a woman to join our clan? How could he ask her to bear children with this affliction?"

"Most people are good at heart and might understand," I said, though I had to concede the latter point. "Maybe your sign at the road is a little off-putting? Wait. Why lock Gregor in the cellar *three* nights?"

"Just to be on the safe side," said Mercy. "The night before and the night after they change too, but it isn't so drastic. They keep their minds; it just changes their looks. Some of us cite it's a betterment."

"Ha ha," Otis intoned sarcastically. "Just for that, missy, you get a big, sloppy pig kiss tonight."

This earned him only an eye roll from the girl.

As it was getting late, Otis turned the wagon and led our convoy far off the road into a nice, flat, fallow field to form a secure circle. The sheep could rest and graze. The Cain men could hide their condition from passers-by. And, having set substantial watches, we hoped the goblins wouldn't molest an armed group of our size. Tomorrow we'd reach the keep and, with regret, part ways with the Cains. After we set up camp and posted our sentries, I heard the by-now-familiar request from Lisbeth.

"Gramma, tell us a story."

"Which story shall I tell, Sweet-pea?"

"The Three Little Pigs," said the girl to all-around clamoring and grunts of approval. Even the Turner children and the Cain boys who had begun to transform joined in the ruckus. In the cheery light of our crackling campfire, she began.

"After they had fled the witch's castle, Otis, Silas, and Gideon started looking for a new place where the clan could live. So each took his purdy wife and set out into Arbordell forest. Loretta, already heavy with child . . ."

All of us settled down and passed a peaceful night with the exception of Otto, who awoke disoriented several times from nightmares. I wondered what was wrong with me that it didn't affect me as much. Maybe the distance granted by the crossbow made it less personal. Or perhaps people were just different.

***

As we approached Meadowfork, we were joined by many others. There were a great number of loaded wagons heading for the keep. Prissy pointed out where the Cunningham's dairy farm now stood abandoned. There was still activity at the sawmill a bit farther on as wagons arrived and departed laden with loads of wood, both cut and uncut, bound for the keep. As we were slowed by the sheep, we often had to give way and wait at the side of the road for others to pass. At one such stop, the Cains bade us a final farewell and proceeded on without us. Now among many other neighbors, we felt well enough protected. I hoped the strange family would find their way to safety farther east and wished them well. Otis bade me to tell

Gregor to 'seek the house of straw.' The boy would know from this how to find and rejoin his wayward clan.

On a closer approach, we saw many towering plumes of smoke above the town, enough to make us wonder whether Meadowfork had caught fire. The next time we encountered the driver of a wagon returning to the sawmill, we asked about it. He told us all meat from the inbound herds was being cooked up or fast-cured for the coming siege. What's more, the bakers ovens were running at all hours to process all of the flour into consumables.

The stream of refugees thickened toward the edge of town. We were stopped by a pair of armed guardsmen who escorted us over to an officious clerk sitting on a crate. He had a long scroll and a quill and ink pot. The fenced fields beyond him contained all manner of herds and flocks similar to our own.

"Name?" said the clerk in a way that sounded more like a command than a question.

"I am Avery Tillerson, and these good folk are . . ."

"No, I refer to the sheep," said the man dismissively. "To whom should I say they belong?"

"Just put down 'Arborvale,'" asserted Dylan."We can sort out the difference later."

"Count?" said the clerk after scratching this down.

"More 'n two hundred head and shy of three," said Avery.

"You don't have an exact count?" said the clerk with a look of distaste. "How am I to assign you a proper pen?"

As Avery simmered, Dylan stepped in once more saying, "We had an exact count when we set out, but we've lost some on the long drive here. Between two and three hundred should be near enough. We'll tally them going into the pen, and I'll let you know it when we're done. Will that be alright?"

"Paddock five," said the clerk. "Your animals will be slaughtered for their meat to stock the keep's larders. You will be compensated for them to some extent after the current crisis has passed. Some exceptional specimens will be spared and driven east to repopulate the barony after the event. These will be returned to you if possible. If you accept these terms, sign here. If not, good luck keeping them safe from the goblins yourselves."

I had heard auctioneers speak slower and with more emotion. While Avery fumed, Dylan stepped forward and quickly made his mark with the proffered quill.

"I will rely on you for that count, goodman," said the clerk. "Master Gerrard takes a dim view of sloppy bookkeeping. Otherwise, good day."

After we had herded all two hundred and forty-six sheep into the indicated corral, the guardsmen escorted us back to the end of a long line of wagons awaiting admission to town. This line was moving very slowly. Up at its head, we saw Master Keaton himself peering into the wagons and ordering a bevy of his clerks and teamsters about while he furiously jotted notes on a very long scroll indeed. Piles of gear were unloaded and cast to one side as other wagons were passed through.

As Master Keaton made his way down the line, I noticed one of the buildings off to our right was being used as a makeshift slaughterhouse. Up its ramp moved a line of animals liberated from the very paddocks where we had housed our flock. There wasn't even any effort to separate the sheep from the goats. Out of the other side of the long building, which may once have been a farmer's barn, came blood-covered men hauling skinned carcasses (or parts thereof). Some others emerged bearing hides that were crudely stacked upon a fly-covered wagon or buckets of entrails bound for a pit at the field's far end. When the breeze shifted in our direction, it brought a charnel stench. It was little wonder the animals on the ramp were so balky as they were driven harshly forward.

"Father!" I heard from behind us, and Otto's wagon slid out of line.

And indeed, there was Goodman Verney approaching the building in a blood-stained apron with his cleaver in hand. As Otto's wagon was empty, I saw no problem with his departure. But I noticed Granny Lydia climbing down from the Turner wagon and hustling after him, so I followed as well.

"There you are, Otto. We were so worried," said the butcher, his booming voice fraught with emotion. "I'd kill a fatted calf, but it seems they've all been spoken for. As you can see, we could sure use your help today. Go fetch your hammer and get on in there, son."

"I don't think that's the best idea just now," contended Granny. "Nathaniel, a word, if I may?"

As she took the butcher aside for a rapid, whispered conversation, Otto's cheeks burned bright red and his lower lip began to quiver as he stared disconsolately at the ground beneath his feet. A few minutes later, the two returned.

"Otto, I'm sorry you had to go through all of that," began the butcher. "I think for now, you should stick with these good folks and find somewhere else to lend a hand. Leave the wagon with us; we can certainly make use of it. Just take your time sorting out what's what, and I'll see you at home later on, alright?"

The boy looked up and silently nodded in solemn gratitude.

CHAPTER ELEVEN

# The Baker

"Eat to please thyself, but dress to please others."

*~ Benjamin Franklin ~*


Granny, Otto and I returned to our two remaining wagons. Several carts ahead of us in the line, Farmer Jenkins was arguing with Gerrard Keaton about the disposition of his wares. Jeffrey Jenkins kept extensive orchards on his tenancy. His first wagon was loaded with early apples, the kind that ripened in June or July. His main crop wouldn't be in until later this fall. That wagon was passed without question. Apples kept well and would be a welcome addition to the supplies needed for a siege. It was the second wagon that was the subject of the heated exchange.

Farmer Jenkins was the village apiary. He kept hives of bees to pollinate his apples, pears, and plums. These he also lent out to other local farmers in need of their services. It was for this reason that he allowed a broad swath of his land to lie fallow and grew many wild blooms thereupon. In his second wagon were dozens of jars of honey which would also be much appreciated in the upcoming days, but also there were stacks of boxes containing his hives. From these emanated a persistent droning, and the other wagons kept well back as the hives' tiny occupants flitted excitedly in and out.

"We'll take the honey, but you will need to leave the bees out here," the chancellor insisted.

"I can't just leave them," returned the farmer. "It took me years to establish these colonies."

"Well, they can't enter the keep; we have enough problems without bee stings to treat."

At this, Farmer Jenkins took a dollop of honey with his index finger and smeared it liberally upon his chin. Before long, he had developed a very credible beard of bees.

"These little darlings only sting as a last resort," he said, blowing one overcurious insect out of his mouth where it had flown as he spoke. "If they sting ya, they die, so that keeps em cautious. Besides, I promised your chandler the wax from these hives at the season's end. How're you gonna *read* that scroll of yours when the keep runs shy of candles?"

Disconcerted but fascinated despite himself, Gerrard's face took on a stubborn set but then softened as he glanced eastward.

"Very well, said the chancellor, you may house them in the east tower where the royal pigeons formerly dwelt. Ask Peter. He'll show you where to place them. Doubtless they can conduct their business through the dovecote's many holes. But I'll hold you to your promise that they will do no harm. Carry on."

When it was our turn, Gerrard's face lit up with pleasure.

"Finally a group with some sense," he said as he began cataloging our wares. "How many wheels of cheese is that?"

"Fifty-seven large and forty-three dinner-sized," said Avery with pride.

Gerrard began marking it down, then frowned at his scroll. The wretched thing had notes and figures scrawled all over its margins both front and back. It was a palimpsest I would be loath to decrypt.

"Pass this one straight through to the keep," he called to a teamster. Unload it with the gear destined for the refugee areas."

"Right away, Master Keaton," the man replied, stepping up to the buckboard.

Before he pulled away with the Tillerson wagon, we had retrieved the sturdy backpacks the Cains had insisted we take. They were chock full of essential items and supplies that I had yet to inventory in full. It took some of the sting out of having our wagons seized.

When we peeled back the canvas over the Turner wagon, Master Keaton was even more delighted to discover among all the other useful equipment several heavy stacks of blank parchment. He called over his clerks and began to gleefully distribute them at once. Goodman Dylan looked on, his expression an odd mixture pride and weary resignation.

Now wagonless, we were told we could report to the keep for refugee placement if we lacked other accommodations in town. Tilda planned to first seek out her sister, Karina. Clearly, the bakery was busy, and perhaps she and the ladies of Arborvale could offer a hand. It had been several months since Royland and I had seen our parents, so we would head straight for the mill while Avery, Dylan and Otto staked our claim at the keep. As Roy and I moved out, Sampson began to trail along, but Tilda called him back.

***

Royland and I hustled through the crowded town. I had never seen its streets so busy. Eagerly anticipating a reunion with our parents, we didn't pause for chit-chat. Nevertheless, I glimpsed many familiar faces among the passers by. They were all bustling about with their own concerns in the teeming, hectic hamlet. The mill wheel was turning at a steady pace, dipping its paddles one after another to taste of the happily flowing waters in its channel. Approaching along the main thoroughfare, I noted with amusement that a sturdy wooden railing had been installed on the short bridge over the race. Rushing across, I spotted him hunched over the tentering apparatus with a tool in hand.

"Father," I cried.

"Eh?" said the stranger, turning from his work and flinching back from my hastily aborted hug.

Not quite a stranger, I realized. It was the artillator who stood before me with bushy brows raised in alarm by my sudden entrance and uncomfortable proximity.

"Lucas?" said the man, rapidly recovering from his erstwhile startlement. "Ah, good. I shall finally have some *competent* assistance with the mill.

So saying, he glared pointedly upward. As Royland entered the mill floor at a more sedate pace, I followed Javier's gaze upward to find an unfamiliar boy peering over the railing of the sack floor above. He was covered in flour dust from head to toe, and only upon second glance did recognition dawn. Trenton had been right. Working in the mill *did* give one the semblance of a jester.

"Hello, Kevin," I greeted. "Or is it Evan?"

The Monohan brothers were identical twins. The confusion thus engendered was only exacerbated by the fact that both had chosen to apprentice under the town baker. Ordinarily, I could tell one apart from the other, but the current circumstances were hardly ideal.

"Hey Lucas," the boy replied. "And you had it right the first time 'round."

This was all very curious, and it begged the question: 'Where were father and Uncle Robert?'

Turning back to Javier, I asked, "What are you doing here?"

It was the wrong question, for the man then launched into a technical lecture about force and torque that I could barely follow from my father's earlier instruction. But I gathered from his answer that these intended corrections might take quite some time.

"Well, shouldn't you close off the sluice gates while you're doing that?" I asked. "The water in the mill pond is not infinite, you know."

Javier smacked his forehead with the palm of his hand, a gesture I thought must arise from his southern upbringing. Unfortunately, this had no effect on the two furry caterpillars that twitched and fretfully danced above the man's eyes.

"Of course," he said. "You must go and do so at once. This is why I require an able assistant; to attend to such minor details while I am preoccupied with weighty thoughts."

"Alright," I agreed as the man turned distractedly back to his adjustments. "I'll get right on that. But tell me, Javier, where can Royland and I find our fathers?"

"I believe they are in my lord's dungeon," said Javier matter-of-factly as he blithely continued to tinker.

Roy looked astonished, and I could tell he was struggling not to be struck dumb by the news. As he began to form a retort, I took charge and steered him toward the door. If memory served, getting satisfying answers from Javier when he was working would be like trying to pull a recalcitrant ram away from a bucket of corn. Instead, I hollered up to Kevin above.

"Kevin, come help us with the sluice gates. We'll meet you out front."

We'd get to the bottom of this soon enough. But if there was one thing I had learned from the Cains, it was to gather information and prepare before running wildly off. When Kevin emerged, Roy and I bracketed him.

"Spill it, Kevin," growled Roy. "Why're our fathers in the dungeon? And where's my mother?"

Kevin looked surprised and turned to me.

"Since when does *he* talk?"

"Since he's very concerned for his father," I replied with as much patience as I could muster. "Please, Kevin, just tell us what's going on while we attend to the sluice gate."

As I turned and headed up the hill, Kevin fell into step behind me with Roy looming over him from behind sporting a scowl.

"We know your dads didn't kill that old bird. It's just those nobles sticking up for their own again. I'm sure it was all a misunderstanding like when you accidentally knocked Trenton down. Still, the whole town is buzzing about the 'murder at the mill.' How your dad dropped the millstone on her while his dad held her down and smashed in her skull. All the while that creepy Cain boy was using her for target practice. I'm sure it was him that did it all. The castle guard had to haul him away kicking and fussing all the way to the keep."

This sounded seriously bad.

As Kevin prattled on, I learned that this had all happened the day before yesterday. If I was counting my days properly, that was just before the night of the dark moon. I prayed silently that they hadn't placed Gregor in a cell with my father and uncle. Apparently, Roy had the same thought as he quickened his pace up the hill. Before even reaching the sluice gate, I was turning its wheel to close it off. I paused by the edge of the pond as the water in the race rapidly ebbed, the last of it trickling away as the story also wound down.

" . . . I think your mum went to visit them this morning. Anyways, I want you to know I'm with you this time. I know just how we can free your dads and spare them from the noose."

"You do?" I prompted hopefully.

"It's simple," said the boy. "We bake a key into a loaf of bread and take it to their cell, then they just walk out when the guards are distracted."

"You have a key to the dungeon?" asked Roy, his voice brimming with sudden skepticism.

"Well, we'd have to get that first, obviously." replied Kevin.

I'd never seen Roy smack someone before, but I think he stayed his hand only with tremendous difficulty.

"This will take some thought," I said. "To begin with, we must get in to see them to find out what *really* happened."

If we wanted to be taken seriously, we would need to dress with more refinement. So I thanked Kevin for his information and his unwavering support and headed for the barn to change. I thought the fine green tunic in my backpack would make a more suitable impression at the keep. Royland had been given a similar gift just one month prior. His was the yellow of weld embroidered with interlocked hexagons reminiscent of a honeycomb.

Kevin followed us into the barn. We couldn't shake the boy. He seemed serious about wanting to help. So despite Roy's disinclination to do so, I let him tag along. We couldn't afford to turn away any help freely offered. The young baker informed us his brother, Evan, was due to relieve him shortly as Javier's assistant. I told the boy that when this happened and after he'd gotten cleaned up, he could come and seek us out at the keep's main gate.

***

When we regained the thoroughfare, it was more crowded than ever. In the short time we had been at the mill, a line of refugees had grown out from the main gate and had almost reached the mill itself. Moreover, a heavy flow of wagons and carts passed by in both directions to cries of 'Make way!' Fortunately, it appeared the clothes did make the man. As Roy and I passed down the avenue, no one barred our way. Necks were craned, and fingers were pointed in our direction by those waiting in line, and I suspected we were the subject of many a hushed conversation. But none challenged our right to move on past. I spotted Avery and Dylan waiting with Otto about midway to the gate. I waved to them, but we dared not stop for fear of being diverted from our mission.

Our confident march down the lane was brought to an abrupt halt as we reached the gate itself. One of the baron's soldiers stepped directly into our path.

"State your business," he said in a no-nonsense tone of voice.

"We're here to see our fathers who are within," I said, trying to inject some of the hauteur I had heard from the knights and their squires.

"If you've already been processed," he said, "state your name and occupation and I'll check. Otherwise, no one goes in or out without special leave from his lordship."

"We've not yet been *processed*," I replied, "but our business is quite urgent. Do you know who we are?"

"In that case, you can move right to the back of the line. And yes, I am quite aware of who you are," declared the man with somewhat less civility. "I don't care how finely you're dressed. You aren't getting any special privileges from me. You *or* your idiot cousin."

A moment later, the man flinched and quickly slapped his hand to the back of his muscular neck. He brought his hand around to reveal the gooey remains of a crushed horsefly which he shook off with a look of disgust. I glanced over at Roy, who returned my gaze with a blank-faced stare. He then shrugged and cocked one eyebrow.

"You may let them pass, sergeant," said Megan.

The young woman stood beyond the gate and had spoken in a commanding tone, the casual assurance of which I was sure I could never equal. The slightly impatient glare she directed at the sergeant prompted the man to respond at once.

"Pass," he said begrudgingly as he turned back to impassively resume his station.

Not questioning our good luck, Roy and I hastened on through to emerge beside the girl in the inner ward.

"It's good to see you again, Lucas," began Megan staring at us with wide-eyed intensity. "And this must be your cousin, Royland, the mage of the mighty blue shield about whom you've written."

"Lady Megan, I . . ."

"Your fathers are both safe and well," she interrupted.

These tidings were like a soothing salve to my feverish thoughts and were especially well received coming as they did right out of the gate, as it were. How was it that she could so quickly banish my worries like so much chaff threshed from the grain? As the lady led us off to one side, Roy looked at me strangely. He too had relaxed at Megan's news, but he now wore a cautious look as though waiting for the other hooves to be shod. We were standing near the doors to the stables. As a man strode busily by, he stopped to make a brief obeisance.

"Your ladyship," said the man, doffing his hat and bowing his head.

"Alex," she succinctly acknowledged before the man hurried on.

Taking my queue from the man, I did likewise. Having no hat to doff, I settled for a respectful bow saying, "my lady."

From behind a disappointed frown, Megan said "Mages don't have to do that, Lucas, nor do friends."

"Ah, but am I not your ladyship's humble servant?" I said, straightening. "I've been studying up on oathbloom since your letter; horticulture has become somewhat of a hobby of mine of late."

*There* was that impish grin I remembered so well.

"Very well, my loyal retainer," she intoned, her blue eyes alight with mirth. "I shall conduct you into the presence of our liege where all will be explained. It's not what you think, but I can't tell you about it right now; the walls may have ears. Father wants to see you straight away."

When we were halfway across the inner ward, Kevin Monohan came rushing over to join us. The boy had cleaned himself up and had donned a floppy baker's hat. This was not the apprentice cap I had often seen him wear but that of a full journeyman. It looked like a muffin was growing out of his head. It reminded me that I hadn't eaten yet, and it was now past midday. When Kevin noticed who was accompanying us, the muffin came off.

"Your ladyship," he submitted, bowing low.

"Kevin," she acknowledged, staring at the boy with a bemused expression. "What mayhem are you planning?"

"He's sort of with us," I hastily admitted. "How did you get past the main gate, anyway?"

At this, the boy produced a small wooden chit with an arrow painted upon it.

"I told them I came to pick up my crossbow," said the boy with a smirk. "They still have to honor these as special leave from his lordship."

"As well they should," said Megan, nodding her approval. "That's part two of my plan. If Sergeant Gaines should give you any trouble about it, remind him that the program has father's full backing."

She continued toward the grand entrance, and we followed. When we arrived, a senior guardsman stepped forward and paid his respects.

"Would your ladyship like an escort?"

"That shan't be necessary, Tomas," said Megan, startling me by taking hold of my arm. "I have my protector present today."

My feet stepped automatically along as the girl tugged me past the astonished guardsmen and down the grand hall.

"Uh, Megan?" I said. "About those oathblooms, you know that I just . . ."

Her rich mellifluous laughter belied the girl's petite stature as she chortled like a bubbling brook in spring. I grew intimately aware of her sides shaking before she finally released my arm.

"I'm sorry to have startled you so. There is a purpose to my ploy, Lucas," she said with a final hiccuping sniffle. Tomas will now put the word all about and you shall soon have free run of the castle. You'll see; it's all part of the game called etiquette.

Although that could be quite handy, I thought it rather deceitful of the girl. Roy's sly appreciative smile as he looked back at the castle guardsmen's sudden, serious discussion convinced me of the truth of her statement. Like a man adrift on a sea of doubt, I felt quite out of my depth in such matters. So I clung to her earlier statement that 'all will be explained' and followed the lady's lead.

Several turnings beyond the grand hall, we came upon an alcove out of which stepped a bent old gentleman bearing a bundle of candles. He grinned to reveal an incomplete set of teeth, and though well dressed, his grooming left a bit to be desired. I thought his wispy white hair could use a comb and his face a sharper razor.

"Greetings your ladyship, and little master as well," he wheezed while staring directly at me.

"Sebastian," Megan responded almost as a question.

"I'm just an apprentice, goodman," I said, fingering the fine embroidery of my tunic.

"You are *my* master, young one," he said, widening his grin. "Long have I waited for your coming. I will tell you more when the time is ripe. Just know that old Sebastian is on your side and your obedient servant. Until later, then, I bid you good day."

And with that he turned on his heel and retreated silently back into the alcove. When we passed by it a moment later, there was no sign of the old codger. Megan stared at the empty alcove with a perplexed look.

"The strange thing is, he meant every word," she said.

Narrowing his eyes, Royland nodded his agreement. I began to feel overwhelmed by the day's events thus far. It was bad enough to be surrounded by mind readers and embroiled in castle intrigue, but now creepy old servants were literally crawling out of the woodwork. Only Kevin seemed more bewildered than I. He was staring this way and that as if second guessing his offer of assistance and seeking a path to escape this bedlam.

***

After several more turnings through the maze that was Westarbor Keep, I had completely lost my bearings, but Megan led the way forward with a sure step. The surroundings grew more lavish as we advanced until we arrived at a familiar door bracketed by two of the baron's henchmen. The last time I was in this place, I had been in no frame of mind to take in many details, but the hunger and worry for my father gnawing at my stomach lining were the same. One of the attentive guardsmen turned to Megan to await instruction while his foresighted brother at arms rapped smartly upon the door.

"You may announce us, Duncan. I'm sure you recognize Westarbor's two newest mages. Our fourth is *Kevin* Monohan, one of Meadowfork's bakers."

As these particulars were passed within, the lady made no move toward the plush bench, obviously anticipating only a brief delay. Nor was she in error as the door soon swung inward admitting us to the tail end of our announcement. The far end of the council chamber was filled with the baron's advisers. Sitting among them, I recognized Sir James and his squire, Blake. Even the audience chamber brimmed with spectators hopeful for some bit of news about the advancing goblin horde. I found the heat of so many bodies to be oppressive.

The gryphon about which I had heard so much was on full display on the left-hand side toward the room's front. It was far larger than I had imagined and was every bit as terrifying as Karina's letter had described. I had thought that Derrick may have been exaggerating when he had related its dimensions to Royland and me. My respect for Trenton went up a notch to have confronted such a creature alone. After acknowledging our entrance with but a brief glance at Megan, the baron continued giving instructions to the harried looking scribe at his side.

"He would have us bide," muttered Megan, taking hold of my arm once again.

Up at the front of those assembled sat a group of well-dressed women. I was later to learn they were the ladies of the knights in residence, those who had passed through Fowler Ranch on their way to the pass. They wore somber expressions, and many were fanning themselves to relieve the closeness of the room's confines. Among them sat the baron's wife herself, Lady Westarbor. A pair of maidens detached themselves from this group and approached us down the long aisle. I recognized them as the two who had accompanied Lady Megan at the stockade.

"Come and join us, my lady," said the petite blonde one. "He's about to issue us our instructions regarding succor for the evacuees."

"I believe introductions are in order first," insisted the more buxom brunette in a tone of mild vexation.

Following Kevin's lead, Royland and I bowed when introduced to 'Constance Baldwin' and 'Lynette Powell.' Both pointedly noticed that Lady Megan had yet to release my arm. They conducted us up to the front past the more humble attendees and ushered us into seats.

"I want you to double all of these rations," the baron was saying to his scribe as he poured over the contents of the scroll.

"My liege, Master Keaton provided these figures as the optimal apportionment to sustain the evacuees for as long as would be possible."

"What good will it do us to have all this half-cured meat spoiling in storage?" asked Lord Westarbor. "Let my people get some fat on their bones so they may better suffer the privation that is to come and perhaps resist the ravages of the pestilence that is sure to follow after that. If Gerrard causes you any trouble over it, tell him that his baron so commands. Now off with you."

"Yes sire," snapped the scribe in a tremulous voice as he leapt up and fled the hall.

"Daughter," he then said, turning to address Megan. "Assemble a detail from among the guardsmen to conduct these two to retrieve their parents and the Cain boy from the dungeons. You may inform them of all the salient facts of the case and *anything else* you deem appropriate. Then you and your maids are to ready the guest quarters where they are to remain under house arrest until such time as I can see to them personally."

Not a face muscle twitched as Megan received these instructions, but she surreptitiously took my hand in hers as she returned the baron's unyielding gaze.

The baron blinked.

"Additionally," he said, "open up the mages quarters in the rear of the keep. The boys *themselves* may, of course, stay *there* to await their master's return."

"Yes father," said Megan as she arose and began to lead us out.

We were only halfway to the door when the harker there began another announcement.

"The postmaster, Peter Lawson, would enter bearing urgent news for his lordship."

All eyes turned to the door and the baron nodded. Peter was Madam Elsa's eldest son who lived in the east tower with his brother and sisters as caretakers of the baron's fowlery. When the broad door swung inward once more, Peter came breezing in intent on quickly reaching the front of the room. Upon encountering us, he stumbled a half step and shot me a scowl of pure hatred before shaking it off and continuing forward. As we made way, Megan gave my hand a squeeze and turned back to face the council.

"Your lordship," Peter called out, executing only a cursory bow on his fast approach. "We have received word from your son."

The baron turned anxious eyes upon the young man and gestured for him to continue.

"It was difficult to find because it arrived amid a whole flock of other blue-banded birds. I think all of the rookery at the watchtower was released. The note claims that all are well, but they had to abandon the pass in a hurry. They'll return as soon as they may."

Gasps, cheers and sobs accompanied the news in a chaotic cacophony throughout the hall. As the baron retrieved the note, I noticed that Royland had wandered off. His lordship read from the note and passed it to his councilmen.

"And the royal pigeon?" prompted the baron. "Has it been located?"

"Nary a peep, your lordship. We've searched high and low, but there aren't any more purple banded. It must've escaped during the *incident*," said Peter with an odd catch in his voice.

"Well keep looking lad," returned the baron. "When Gerrard said the count was off, I became hopeful."

While they discussed the matter, I spotted Roy scrutinizing the gryphon with his signature rocking back and forth stare. Just as the hall began settling down to await the baron's next proclamation, my cousin spoke up.

"Your lordship," he said in an alarmed tone. "Were you aware the eyes and ears of this thing are enchanted?"

After a pause wherein the baron's eyes bore in to those of my cousin who seemed to wither under their baleful glare, the baron spoke.

"That . . . would explain a great deal."

"All the leaks and our missing equerry, to name a few," exclaimed Sir James in a wroth tone.

"James, you are to summon a work detail at once. I want that thing out of here. Take it to the trophy room. We'll need to examine all of them later."

Megan began urging me once again toward the door. Accompanied by her maids and with Kevin in tow, we barely won free of the room before a mass exodus ensued. I worried for Roy who didn't care much for crowds, but supposed he had brought it upon himself. Megan ordered one of the guardsmen in the corridor to fetch a couple of his fellows. While waiting for them to arrive, we rescued Roy from the room's outflow. Constance seemed almost offended by the disorder we had engendered, but both Kevin and Lynette appeared excited by the mayhem. I caught them exchanging mischievous grins.

***

It was dark down in the dungeons. Duncan led the way with a lantern down the many winding steps. The other guard, Nick, brought up the rear of our procession with Kevin, Royland and I sandwiched in-between. As we descended, I began hearing occasional drips of water accentuated by their echoes. It sounded as though they were striking a liquid surface almost like a musical note. On the bright side, it was refreshingly cool so far beneath the earth.

Lady Megan had informed us that our fathers were under no suspicion whatsoever; the baron knew better. Rumors, however, could not be squelched overnight, especially in the current, tense environment. So for their own protection, they had been placed under arrest and kept in the keep. As for the dungeons, that was for Gregor's sake. It seemed the baron was familiar with the Cains and their curse. Because the mayhem at the mill had unfortunately occurred just at the darkening of the moon, the baron had deemed the dungeons to be the best place to keep the boy safe. Our fathers had elected to keep him company through his rough stretch.

As the curse should have run its course by now, we had been sent to retrieve the 'suspects' and conduct them to better accommodations. The baron planned to later announce they had been cleared by Sir James' inquest and were above reproach. Not having apprehended the actual culprit would make it difficult to allay all suspicion, however, so the baron wanted to allow more time for tempers to cool. His lordship suspected that his former equerry, now thought to be an undisclosed mage as well, was somehow involved. I felt sorry for Peter, who had lost his mother and didn't know whom to blame.

At last, we spied a light up ahead and began to hear voices.

"I think I favor bein' in the iron maiden over the rack," said Gregor.

"A sentence I never imagined I'd hear uttered," returned the voice of my father. "Do you have any eight's?"

"It's just that thrashin' around on the rack leaves rope burns on my wrists the next morning," said Gregor. "Go fish."

"Well, it's lucky for you the baron doesn't hold with torture," said Uncle Robert, "him having better ways to get at the truth. My mother would've happily stretched you out right proper on that thing just on suspicion. Do you have any . . . Hold on, I hear someone coming."

Rounding a final bend, we were confronted by a most curious diorama. There sat my father, my uncle and Gregor on upside-down buckets playing cards across a torture rack by the light of an old lantern. In the corner rested what must have been this 'iron maiden.' It resembled a big bell with rounded doors, currently hinged apart, and had an opening on top where a person's face must stick out. On the floor nearby rested my father's tool box, a jar of oil, and some rust-stained rags which told me it must have taken some effort to put the old girl back into service. Uncle Robert was the first to break the silence.

"Lucas," he said excitedly, "and there's my Roy! And they've brought us . . . a baker? Ah. Doubtless so we can order our last meal before we all swing."

"Enough with the gallows humor, Robert," said my father. "Can't you see it's upsetting them?"

"We were really worried, father," I said as I moved up to the bars. "What's wrong with your arm?"

"Oh, this?" he said, indicating the sling on his left arm.

"That's just a little nick he picked up in a knife fight with a zombie," declared Uncle Robert.

"Robert, stop I said."

"It's the truth, isn't it?" said my uncle "No need to coddle them, Elliot; they're mages now. They can handle themselves."

Kevin's eyes widened further with each word, and the guards didn't know *what* to make of the byplay.

"Son, the truth is we're here for Gregor. You see, the Cains ... "

I was fitting the cell's key into the lock as he spoke. When he hesitated, I jumped in with: "We know about the Cain curse, father. Two days ago, we spent the night in their bunker."

"You did?" burst from Gregor.

"Your sister, Mercy, thinks Lucas is *purdy*," Royland added unhelpfully with a sinister glint in his eyes.

Roy, you're a bastard, I thought as Gregor's astonishment transformed into a dangerous squint leveled in my direction.

"It wasn't *like* that, Gregor," I blurted, seriously considering withdrawing the key from the lock as the large boy stood up from his bucket. "We only slept with your sisters because of the goblins."

I probably should have thought that one through a little bit better. Gregor began to shake, then a snort emerged. This was followed by a belly-laugh the likes of which I had only seen Goodman Avery approach in magnitude. It was the hearty guffaw my uncle had once christened a 'gut buster.' To the boy's credit, he managed to stay upright throughout, merely leaning on the wall for support. As the tremors subsided, he was finally able to draw breath and resume speech.

"Just when I thought you couldn't get any funnier," said Gregor. "The things you get up to. One day you'll have to tell me how you convinced Grampa Uriah of that one. He must've taken quite a shine to *you*."

Turning the key, I swung the door open on its squeaky hinges.

Kevin removed his hat and drew forth from it a greasy wad of dough. Casting it aside, he declared, "I guess I won't need this after all."

The guardsmen now looked doubly perplexed. Nonetheless, after the former prisoners had collected their belongings, they began leading us back the long and winding ascent to the castle above.

"Evidently, we have a lot of catching up to do," said my father, "but, for now, tell me how conditions are up top."

"Well, the goblins are on the move, and the baron is preparing for a siege," I advised. "Oh, and Javier is running the mill."

"Is he running it or 'ruining' it?" he asked. "I can just imagine. You know I must remain here at the keep, son. Please go and assist Javier once we get squared away. I'm not sure I trust the man not to burn the place down."

"I will, father," I promised, "but there's a matter I need to attend to first. Oh, and Gregor? You shouldn't run off until after the baron's announcement; that'd make you look guilty. But if you want to catch up with your clan, they said you should seek out the house of straw."

"Hmm. The Danstonshire. Smart. I'm much obliged."

***

Most of the shops along Baker's Row stood abandoned. The bakeries were operating, but were not servicing the public. Instead, they produced tray upon tray of dry, hard bread. The priority was not to please the palette, but rather to resist succumbing to mold for as long as might be possible. The resulting thick-crusted, brown loaves had barely cooled from the ovens before they were packed into tall wicker-baskets with lids. These in turn were promptly loaded on carts bound for our lord's larders at the keep. All the while, the busy bakers themselves suffered the sultry singe of summer without relief in the relentless radiance of their own ovens.

I witnessed one man on a ladder nailing closed the shutters of his shopfront, as though by this simple act he could thwart the designs of an invading army. I suppose hope does spring eternal. I trod on past many a similar scene as shops not yet fully forsaken received final, loving benedictions by their anxious owners. These were not my destination, however; that lay

256

ahead. At the end of the street, was one business still receiving a thriving custom. In these times when survival was uncertain, hoarding ones coin was considered the cautious game of fools. So weary soldiers and parched bakers alike were willing to pay a premium for a seat at the town tavern. There they could sing of the end of days, pass the time in good fellowship or perhaps, find the solace of oblivion at the bottom of a glass.

The bawdy music issuing forth from within served as an open invitation to enter unbidden. Though not a frequenter of such dubious delights, I nevertheless found myself answering this unseemly summons. Within, the babble of the crowd combined with occasional spikes of raucous laughter to create a wall of sound underscored by the odor of the unwashed. Amid a sea of tables teeming with patrons whose sobriety was little in evidence, I spied the man whom I sought. I wended my way carefully over to the island where he had parked his skiff.

" . . . And so her ladyship to spite 'er 'usband and to lift the onerous tax agrees to ride starkers through the whole of the town!"

"What, *naked*?" asked a soldier.

"Nary a stitch," replied the storyteller.

Around the table reclined gruff men of Westarbor's hastily levied soldiery who had attained various levels of inebriated comfort, doubtless with the last of their week's pay. To one side and quiet as always sat Taylor Allen.

"Were she sidesaddle or astride?" asked a second soldier who appeared to be deep in his cups as I moved a step closer.

"Of course she was sidesaddle you nit. I said she was a *lady*, didn't I?" berated the storyteller as he turned to size me up. "What's this, then? Bugger off, laddie. I was just gettin' to the good part."

"Isn't that the boy from the stocks? The one that flew over the mill or something?"

"Naw. He's the one whose murderin' old man done in the mad bird woman. Isn't that right, boy?"

Apparently, fame was fleeting, but notoriety lingered on. I ignored the barbs, intent on my task and the men soon returned to their earlier pursuits. The archer, however, looked up as though he knew why I'd come.

"She were a right strumpet if she flashed 'er unmentionables all about town."

"She used her long hair to cover up her naughty bits, of course."

"Taylor, I would like a private word," I said.

"Wait. Where is all this supposed to have happened?"

"Coventry."

Goodman Allen drained his tankard. Sliding back his stool, he dropped a few coins on the table before joining me on the way to the door.

"Is that down in Freemark?"

"Mercia; a different kingdom entirely."

The hubbub thankfully subsided as we stepped out onto the street. A refreshing breeze revived our suppressed sensibilities from the cloying clutches of the tavern's tainted air.

"How may I be of service, Lucas?" asked the archer leaning heavily on the railing as he stared down the street of the dying town.

Taking a page from my master's book, I decided to respond to him with an inquiry of my own.

"That's the question; isn't it, Taylor?"

After an overlong silence, I continued.

"You know, the birds the baron uses to communicate with his majesty are all dead. If only one had survived, it might've meant the difference between timely aid for Westarbor or a long, drawn-out siege and further ruin."

Still, no words were forthcoming.

"My father used to say to me: 'the mill cannot grind with water that has passed.' It's about considering ones actions very carefully. Sometimes one only gets a single chance to do the right thing or a lifetime of regret for choosing wrongly in the present moment."

"Put that way," said Taylor, finally breaking his silence, "I suppose there's really no choice at all. You know espionage is a capital offense, don't you, Lucas?"

"I know the baron," I said. "People can sometimes surprise you. If you come forth now, and he sees contrition in your heart, I think you may find there is clemency in his. Besides, his lordship is never one to waste a possible resource. I'm sure he'd much rather you died fighting the goblins than swinging from a gibbet."

The gallows humor that my father so detested won me a short bark of laughter from the quiet archer as side by side we retraced my steps back toward the keep.

Taylor Allen confessed that afternoon to the baron in private. He had been taking the king's coin to keep his majesty objectively apprised of the doings in Westarbor Barony. He produced the last royal pigeon from among those in the private cages he always kept near his bedside. I don't know what deal was struck, but the man was to continue his service in Trenton's lance. And if that service was in some additional capacity, I felt it was better that I remain unawares.

As the sun set over the crowded keep, the baron released his message of hope from the battlement into its last lingering rays. It was uncomfortable to realize that our best chance for rescue now lay written on a thin strip of paper borne aloft by the fragile wings of a fifteen-ounce bird. I prayed the winds of fortune would prove favorable.

CHAPTER TWELVE

# The Candlestick Maker

"If your opponent is of choleric temper, irritate
him."

*~ Sun Tzu ~*

Joy was evident from the people of Westarbor when Sir
Fletcher's horn announced the return of the knights in residence
from their foray out to the pass. Led by Sir Trenton and with my
old master in its vanguard, the formation marched through the
gates to cheers and whistles. They were followed by ranks of
soldiers who had been stationed at the watchtower as well as
the other archers that had been encamped upon the ridge. Roy
and I were witness to many tearful reunions as the knights were
greeted by their loving families and stalwart retainers. Almost as
heartwarming was Sampson's soulful howl as he tugged his way
free of my grip and arrowed straight to his master's side. The
knights of the east were soon to follow. A dozen lances strong,
and led by Sir Declan, they were received with no less acclaim
by the appreciative populace. Their arrival filled the lord's
stables near to bursting.

As the last remaining people and supplies from the deserted
town of Meadowfork were tucked away, a small armed
detachment was gathered. They were to escort some of the
children and ladies to the eastern fiefs, there to be hosted well

away from the looming threat. They took with them all of the palfreys and pack animals. This left only the knight's war steeds and alleviated the crowding to a degree. The majority of the supplies, however, had been stowed here at the keep. And the eastern fiefs could only play host to so many, especially lacking the bulk of their fighting force to keep order. So the keep remained overcrowded and apprehensive.

Master Chadwick was ushered into the castle and to the baron's council. Weariness from his long journey was written in hard lines upon our master's face. After a debriefing by the baron, he was assigned Sebastian as a personal manservant. Per the baron's earlier instructions, Megan and her maids had readied the lavish mage's suite in the rear wing of the castle near to the Arenson family's own chambers. I had never before dwelt in such luxury and felt rather guilty knowing that most of the evacuees were packed into the lower halls lacking such comforts.

The castle's servants were at our beck and call and Sebastian proved to be zealously attentive to our needs when his other duties permitted. He moved some belongings into the meanest room of our suite and even attended to Sampson's special requirements. Master Chadwick seemed to take all this as his due and dressed to meet expectations in the finery he had eschewed as a shepherd. At Sir Trenton's insistence, Roy and I were also provided with several new outfits to match our raised stations. I hadn't given it much thought before, but it seemed the sumptuary laws worked in both directions.

Much of our master's time was taken up in consultation with the baron. The weather was still cooperating with our foes, the clear skies above granting them swift passage through our lord's domain. Our scouts reported that the hoard's leading elements had already been sighted in Westarbor proper and were fast approaching. We could expect contact on the morrow or the day after at the very latest. By this time, the keep had been buttoned up securely, and Meadowfork had become a ghost town from which anything of value had been retrieved. We all waited in tense anticipation of the conflict to come.

That night, Master Chadwick took Roy and I aside after Sebastian had served us dinner in our quarters. I still found the old gentleman somewhat unsettling. Though he served us all with impeccable manners, I would occasionally find him staring at me with a quizzical expression. Upon noting my regard, he would grin and grace me with a bob of his grizzled old head that seemed overly respectful somehow, like we were sharing a private joke of which I remained blissfully incognizant.

"It's past time I brought you two up to speed regarding a mage's role in warfare," said our master with a grimace.

We waited patiently for him to gather his thoughts and continue while Sebastian cleared the small table.

"The task is *not* simple," he began in a humorless tone, despite the twist. "The first item of which you should be made aware is that the goblin shamans almost invariably envision their magic centers as flames. It is primarily for this reason that I was chosen to safeguard the west, my magic being antithetical to theirs. The second thing to keep in mind is that in any battle between mages, the conflict almost always devolves to an internal one. Your opponent will seek to undermine or destroy your magic center. I do not have the time to instruct you properly in how to defend against this. Such advanced instruction is normally imparted to journeyman mages."

"So they'll try to burn out my inner hive?" inquired Roy in a tone the menace of which challenged the wisdom of any enemy who might dare such a deed.

"Undoubtedly," replied our master. "I shall endeavor to provide what protection I may, but should their shaman engage, it would be best for you to withdraw so that I might focus more fully upon the foe."

"Can't you just snuff out their fires with your water, master?" I asked.

"In my younger days, I may have been up for such a challenge," he replied. "Even now, I'm rather certain I could prevail over the many trifling candles that accompany the enemy host. But there is one who leads them in whom I fear I may have met my match. In his great bonfire I have sensed the seeds of my possible undoing. Perhaps if we could wear him down ere the final reckoning, I might quench the conflagration he harbors within. It is for this reason we must marshal our strength and act only sparingly in defense of the others."

Our master's final piece of advice related to 'grand workings' which only master mages employed. Since we had never witnessed such, he took us out to the keep's main gates which he intended to enchant. He explained the enchantment would be similar to the one he had placed upon the quintain that stood in our practice yard back at Fowler Ranch. Due to the massive scale of the undertaking, a lot more power would be required and the protection wouldn't be as complete. Still, it would be better than nothing.

Grand workings differed from more ordinary spells in that they drew power from the surrounding area to augment and amplify a mage's internal strength. Such a draw was not without its cost, however, as directing more energy than one properly controlled was an exhausting and dangerous exploit. Its practitioner would emerge from the effort as weak as a newborn kitten and might not even survive such an ordeal should it be performed incorrectly. Add to that; the grand working our master intended was also to be an enchantment, sustaining itself from the magic present in the environment thereafter. As such, it would stand among the most advanced pieces of spellwork known to magedom. Our master had only agreed to undertake the feat at the baron's behest because the gates were the weak point in our defense against invasion.

Master Chadwick bade us to stand well back but to observe closely. He only allowed us to be present because he wanted us to experience its effect upon our magic centers. The goblin shaman might employ a grand working in the upcoming conflict. Our master felt that attending him now would help prepare us for such an eventuality. With my mage sight fully engaged, the first thing I noted was my master's magic center begin to pucker inward strangely. Whereas normally he drew up 'water' from his 'well,' in this instance, ripples flowed toward his well as though a great underground aquifer were being tapped and drawn in. My inner garden began to erode and fray about its edges as these ripples passed by and through. It was an uncomfortable feeling like having my teeth scraped by a metal file. This feeling grew in intensity until a great geyser of water began issuing from my master's well. The awful ache grew even worse, and I clung fiercely to the paltry remnants of my little green patch which were still falling away like wet sand through clenching hands, leaving me only a pittance.

It was at this time that my master began to chant in a voice so strong as I had never heard from him before. 'Inexsuperabilis permanens lignea!' he said over and over in a rhythm that the stars must hear and believe. The words beat into my head and my poor abused mage sight beheld the geyser arc into the keep's great gates. Onward rushed the outpouring of eldritch energies, beating like the waves at high tide upon the shores of those great doors until at last, having achieved the pinnacle of pressure, they began to subside. Here and I had thought tossing stones was tough.

Royland looked as battered as I, but he retained the presence of mind to run forward and catch our old master as he slumped forward spent. Dilatorily dutiful, I ran forward and took one of my master's arms over my shoulder as well. To my mage sight, the gates appeared to suck in the light around themselves and I didn't like standing too near them.

"Try and burn that down, Shastageheggin," croaked our master in a drunken voice, finally naming the goblin shaman whom he feared.

With his head lolling about and his eyes unfocused, Master Chadwick smacked his lips and offered several more incomprehensible tidbits and opinions. Roy and I half dragged the good mage back to our rooms in the castle to recover from his delirium with the dignity he deserved.

***

The baron still had scouts posted out in hidden redoubts all about Westarbor keeping tabs on the enemy. These brave woodsmen equipped with their cages of messenger birds were to stay hidden and report on the goblins' movements. Lamentably, some had gone silent, a mute testimony to the likely fate of the brave. Those that remained had reported our enemy on the march and approaching Meadowfork's borders. The valiant soldiery of Westarbor Keep stood poised to confront them from atop its walls. Royland and I had won a place on the battlement by virtue of being mages. We stood with our master all resplendent in our tunics of blue, green and gold.

First came the drums. Long before the enemy came into view, we heard their strident cadence growing ever louder. Bum. Bum. Bum-bum-ba-dum! Bum. Bum. Bum-bum-ba-dum! It grew almost hypnotic as the first elements of their forces crested the rise beyond the mill. As the drummers hammered on, the goblin horde continued to unfold in their hundreds, supplemented here and there by groups of ogres. The fearsome giants' intimidating size was only magnified, contrasted as it was to the throngs of diminutive goblins surrounding each such group. There was a commotion to the left as one of the brutes, clutching his gut, broke formation to squat in the middle of the thoroughfare.

"I wonder why that ogre is relieving himself on the march?" said Master Chadwick with a furrowed brow.

"I believe, master," I observed with a grin, "that is compliments of Clan Cain."

"Well, their troops will all come down with cholera if they don't exercise better discipline and sanitation than that," he said, no less perplexed. "In that happy event, perhaps we will not need to combat them at all."

We all knew, however, that my master's fanciful wish was no more than just that. The numerous foes arrayed against us continued to reveal themselves as they surmounted the hill and spread out just beyond the range of our archers. I considered loosing a few quarrels from my superior weapon to teach them some caution, but we had been told in no uncertain terms that all were to await orders from Sir Declan, our battle marshal, before commencing any hostilities.

All throughout our enemy's display of force, their drums continued to pound out their doleful beat. So it was somewhat of a shock when in unison they all stilled and an eerie silence ensued. Our foemen stood quietly in a frozen tableau spoiled only by the sight of several more of them breaking formation to noisily relieve themselves. Up from their ranks came a standard-bearer. He bore a spear upon which was tied a long, white strip of linen. Beside him, marched a rather plump, stern-faced goblin adorned in a multitude of clashing colors which I suspected only a goblin's eye might find fetching. This must be their leader, Chief Ravenbald.

I had been instructed that it was customary to parley before a conflict in the hopes of coming to peaceful terms and obviating the need for battle altogether. Being aware of this tradition, the goblins frequently chose to partake of it. In their case, this was done not to actually seek peaceful terms, but rather to puff up the eminence of their leaders in the eyes of their troops. Nevertheless, since it was our own custom, it behooved us to grant it since to refuse would place our honor at risk. Besides, there was always hope.

So as the goblin duo strode purposefully forward down the hill, the strings of our archers lay slack and empty awaiting the posturing harangue that was sure to follow. Instead, when the prismatic pair had achieved half the distance to our walls, our harkers raised long trumpets skyward and blew out a triumphant fanfare. As they did so, the baron strode forth upon the battlement accompanied by my master. He was fully armored and bedecked in blue with his heraldry prominent upon his shield. I thought Master Chadwick also cut a striking figure with his woad surcoat shimmering in elegant counterpoint to the baron's azure hue.

The world seemed to pause as the goblins swaggered to a stop a mere stone's throw away as though daring our men to forswear their oaths. As the aggressor, it fell to the chief to make the opening offer. In a shrill voice that scratched at our ears but carried easily over the hush that had descended, he vented a stream of invective in his harsh, chattering speech. Master Chadwick was muttering a translation to the baron as this progressed. Once the chief ground to a halt, his standard-bearer took up the task and began repeating the chief's words. In a ringing voice no less irritating for being in a tongue more suited for human ears, he rendered the following proclamation.

"Blue King, the mighty Chief Ravenbald of the broken mountain people brings your doom upon you. Our generous and handsome chief may spare your women and your young ones if you surrender now and quit all claim to the lands of Arbordell which you so foully stole from our fathers in days gone by."

I didn't think much of it as first offers went. And I could tell I wasn't alone in this assessment as jaws clenched and grips firmed on weapons all down our line. With our indignation bubbling near the surface of our thoughts, we awaited our liege's response.

"It is worthy that you offer mercy for the meek, and your status in our eyes is raised thereby," began the baron. "Still, I must refuse this offer for I hold these lands in sacred trust for the great king of Osten far to the south. It is to him you must appeal for any adjustment of borders. My knights and I are sworn to keep these lands and defend them by his auspices. I propose the following compromise. Return your army to your own lands west of the mountains and I shall host you here at my castle. You may air your grievances under an armistice, and we shall see what may be done to advance the welfare of both our peoples with trade and mutual respect. If, however, you remain set upon conquest, know that you shall find Westarbor a most difficult nut to crack."

As the standard-bearer whispered to his scowling chief, Master Chadwick began to gabble in an uncharacteristically high-pitched voice what I assumed to be a faithful rendition of the baron's words in gobbledygook. He paused in several places with a look of consternation before soldiering on to conclude with an emphatic gesture, slamming his fist into the palm of his opposing hand.

After a pause for reflection, the chief began anew. A fresh stream of shrill gibberish escaped his lips with a more impassioned fervor than previously. He made a sweeping arm gesture encompassing his troops up on the hill then continued for a bit more before winding down with menacing overtones. When the translation came, it proved less than ideal.

"Our magnificent chief is offended by your sniveling offer to live in your castle with you and would have it be known he prefers only women. They, in turn, are always most satisfied with him and favor his advances. We shall crack your nuts, blue king. We have brought many nutcrackers from all our clans. Still, since this was better than your first insult of sheep, the mighty Chief Ravenbald will grant you one final chance to surrender your castle and its lands. Your high walls will not protect you forever."

The baron stared daggers at my master who, wearing a mortified moue and shaking his head in negation, raised his upturned palms and shrugged.

"Mayhap you should try to avoid idioms, sire," I overheard him to remark.

Gathering himself, the baron tried again saying, "I once again reject your offer that we surrender. Think most carefully chief. You may possess the numbers to threaten us now, but what will you do when all the king's horses and all the king's men arrive here to drive you away?"

With a derisive sneer, the goblin's pudgy little chieftain uttered a brief statement and tossed down a small bundle before our gates. He and his translator then turned to walk casually back up the hill.

"What did he say?" asked the baron as he stared at the goblins' retreating forms.

"No help is coming for you," answered Master Chadwick.

"Levare colligentes," he intoned, causing the bundle to rise and come into his outstretched hand.

As he delivered it to the baron, a look of dismay crossed our liege's features. For cupped in his hand and pierced through with a black-fletched arrow lay the mangled remains of a pigeon sporting a purple band.

***

Moments after Chief Ravenbald returned to his troops, the drumming resumed. This was not the marching cadence we had heard previously, but a more ominous rhythm that spoke of anticipation. Bum! bum-bum-bum. Bum! bum-bum-bum. This went on for a weary minute or so, setting our teeth on edge before we heard above it an urgent, shrill command that launched the onslaught. Hundreds of goblin voices blended together in a sustained disharmonious chorus as the drums fell silent once more. The cry rose to a crescendo as the horde charged down the hill, blanketing the thoroughfare like angry soldier ants.

"Steady, men," entreated Sir Declan, his eyes riveted upon our foes' chaotic advance.

All down our line, the archers had nocked arrows to strings, prepared to loose when the order was given. I set a quarrel in the tiller and sought a target of my own. The leather-clad soldiers in the enemy's vanguard looked fierce, but I thought they would prove rather impotent when they struck our wall. The teams carrying long scaling ladders were more tempting, but I was sure that others were targeting them. I settled on a group of archers gathering by the mill race as I believed they presented the most imminent threat. I focused on the one appearing to issue commands. From our superior position atop the wall and with our longer bows, our forces could easily strike at the goblins' archers. I suspected that all else was merely a distraction at this point. When the command was given to 'loose at will,' I joined in the first volley. Without even tracking my results, I continued to rewind and release quarrels from my dread instrument as rapidly as the seasoned archers could ply their bows.

At first, it was sheer slaughter as the little men received death from above unanswered by their kindred. However, when the number of archers they fielded reached some critical number, they began returning our deadly barrage. Goblins bearing overly large shields provided some cover for their archers. The shots taken by my fellows became fewer as they were forced to take cover themselves behind the regular crenellations of our battlement.

Most of our force was deployed across this front wall, the sole approach to the keep where a large force could gather and be brought to bear. The sides and back of the keep were also girded by a curtain wall no less formidable. Moreover, the keep sat atop a hill whose sheer embankment made it folly to attempt such an approach. Even so, Sir Declan had spared some sentinels and archers there to ward against shaman-levitated troops or small groups with a grapnel attaining our walls to cause mischief. The focus of the battle, however, remained upon the frontal approach, designed as it was to allow egress to the keep, and the only point where a breech might prove disastrous.

Royland soon earned a place of distinction. As the exchanges of archery settled into a pattern predictable only by him, he set about erecting his barrier all up and down the line in brief, opportune placements. It saved many of our men from injury and frustrated many a goblin archer. This would later become known as 'Arenson's deliverance' or 'The accursed shield of the blue king,' depending on which side you were on.

We finally began seeing the tops of scaling ladders surmount our battlement. I had been firmly instructed to ignore these. There were men among our ranks whose specific job it was to handle such. Sir Declan didn't want any ladders shoved over prematurely. His men were to wait until a certain number of goblins were committed to climbing upon one before doing so. These also provided an ideal opportunity to pour out a bucket of boiling pitch whilst our foemen were nicely lined up. So I continued to seek a way to uniquely contribute with my witchwood crossbow. Perhaps I could fell an ogre or two. The large brutes seemed to be holding back atop the hill and were not yet engaging in the mayhem below.

Then I saw them. Just beyond the mill past the ogres stood a goblin dressed in a scarlet tunic. He bore a long (for him) staff and was surrounded by a group of acolytes wearing red capes. Even at this distance, my mage sight prompted me to take note of them. Up to this point, I had detected no magic from the enemy camp. This had changed but a moment ago as I now sensed something brewing up on that hill.

Pointing his staff, the central goblin unleashed something that to my mage sight resembled a fiery bird or bat. A moment later, one of our men hauling a bucket of pitch was scorched and dropped his bucket which had ignited. Its contents spewed all about the area he was traversing to create a flaming pool and splattered many droplets which stuck to and singed his fellows. My master stepped forth at once. With a one-handed swirling gesture and a brief cry of 'aqua exstinguit,' he caused water to arise from a barrel nearby and descend in a sizzling torrent upon the errant flames. Thoroughly doused, but mostly unharmed, the blistered men resumed their tasks with a warier step. I had wondered earlier why Sir Declan had so many barrels of water lugged up here. Now I could see it was likely for my master's benefit.

That must be this 'Shastageheggin' up on the hill. Unbeknownst to many, I had the range. How wonderful would it be if I could end his threat in one surprise stroke? I wound my witchwood and aimed most carefully. I feared he might flee my range or hide behind the ogres once he sensed his peril, so I was determined to make this first shot count. On release, I prayed my aim was true as my quarrel took flight directly at that goblin's evil heart. Empowered by the turning force of the earth itself, my harbinger of death soared toward my foe and . . . burnt to ashes which sprinkled leisurely down upon him and his acolytes. Apparently, it wasn't to be so simple.

The retaliation, when it came, was swift and fierce. I would like to say that our eyes met across that field, but at such a distance, that just wasn't possible. Something akin to that occurred involving our mage sight, and he singled me out from the throng. As my cranequin whined, his staff descended to point directly at me. As my string locked into ready position, it promptly scorched and snapped, its little frayed ends cringing and blackening. I remember seeing my bow burst into bright flames and hearing my master's cry of 'Lucas!' before my vision was drawn within. What was occurring in there terrified me. My inner garden was all awash in flames. Ropy vines emerged here and there beating blindly at the unholy blaze, but they were fast becoming singed and blackened by their ineffectual efforts. All the while, I felt waves of intense heat breaking against the backstop of my head. Suddenly, there was relief. The skies above my inner garden seemed to open up, and a gentle patter of cool rain descended quenching the onslaught and reducing my agony.

When I returned to my senses, I found my master hovering over me with a hand on my forehead muttering 'tenera pluviam.' Roy stood at my side supporting my weight in his gangly grip.

"You two need to get out of the line of fire as we discussed," said our master with a minuscule upward twitch of his lips at what I suspected was an unintentional pun.

Too weak to stand on my own, I clung to Roy as he made his way to the stairway. From my muddled mind emerged an odd notion. I couldn't ever remember embracing my cousin in so close a fashion. Roy wasn't much of a one for hugs. It felt nice to have his stalwart support in my time of need. Roy seemed to sense my mood as he carefully eased me down the steps, for he met my gaze and rewarded me with a brief squeeze of affection.

"Over here!" came a shout from our left.

Across the inner ward at the base of the east tower, stood the lady Megan beckoning us thither. I wondered what she wanted, for I suspected I was out of this fight. My inner garden had been scorched down to nubs, and the charred wreckage of my formerly beautiful bow hung impotent from the leather cord that attached it to my belt. Nevertheless, when 'my lady' called, could her oath sworn protector tarry? I thought the knightly answer should be: 'Nay,' or perhaps even: 'Heck Nay.' So I parted from my cousin's conjoining carry, staggering to regain my proper balance, and swayed across the courtyard. Roy fretfully paced along behind.

"Inside. Quickly," commanded my lady.

I had never been inside the dovecote before and was at first disconcerted by the spectacle which greeted my eyes. I was inside of an enormous cylinder of stone with a series of wooden stairways and broad platforms spiraling up around its outer edges. The platforms encroached ever more thoroughly upon the open central area until they merged high above. Neatly racked around the periphery were sets of cages containing a variety of birds from chickens and geese to more exotic specimens. The thick stone walls were pierced in many places by narrow crossed slits through which rays of the afternoon sun slanted. Several of the cages on this lower floor had obviously been moved about to make room for archers to stand at the lower holes. Others had been slid together to form makeshift stairways to reach holes higher up. Atop these stood a hodge-podge assortment of Meadowfork's citizenry plying crossbows through the bird holes cum arrow slits. There was the foul odor of fowl droppings and a cacophony of cackling, squawking, cooing and gobbling birds. It was a lot to take in all at once.

"Find an arrow slit and show us how tis done, Lucas," shouted Lady Megan above the clamor.

Disheartened, I mutely lifted up my ruined crossbow for display. No sooner had I marked the look of betrayal upon my lady's face than Kevin Monohan came rushing over from his place at the circle's edge.

"Here, use mine," he entreated, proffering me his instrument.

I wound it experimentally. It provided much less resistance than had my witchwood special and put me in mind of my earliest days at the practice pitch. Tempted by Kevin's selfless offer, I nonetheless thrust his gift back to him. I had a better idea.

"Listen up," I shouted above the caws and screeches, capturing the attention of most of Megan's citizen soldiers. "Kindly remove your crank handles and resume your positions. I will be winding for you. Just load, aim, and release your quarrels. When ready for a rewind, aim your weapon upward and I will get to you as soon as I may."

Some stared at me as though I were daft, but many complied at once, and soon the others followed.

"Let's make a difference!" a smiling Lady Megan proclaimed by way of inspiration.

Her enthusiasm proved to be infectious, for as soon as their raised crossbows began winding themselves to the ready, a ragged cheer went up from Megan's minions. I didn't have much time between windings to wonder where Roy had gone, but I soon glimpsed him on a platform high above rocking forward and back. I grinned like a fiend because, for once, I suspected I knew what the devil he was up to. I redoubled my efforts, winding those crossbows one by one almost as quickly as each signaled their readiness. I couldn't see what the result was upon the field of war, but I suspected that a nearly continuous rain of quarrels from our position should produce an impact.

Hollering: 'Refresh your ammunition,' I took a moment to check up on my cousin. Royland had positioned himself before Farmer Jenkins' stack of hives. Out from them poured their tiny workers in a steady stream to gather and swarm above the tower's central area. Rallied into a state of heightened agitation by my cousin's gift, they swirled about in gauzy sheets which soon came to resemble an angry tornado. With a circular arm gesture Roy guided this malevolent mass to funnel through the upper holes and out onto the field of battle beyond.

"Resume loosing," I shouted as I returned to winding with a vengeance.

The effect of the two-pronged assault was immediate. I could hear the shrill, confused and anguished cries of our enemies howling their dismay. Not since my earliest days as an apprentice had I suffered such dizziness from my winding. Nevertheless, I persevered. When I was almost at the limit of my endurance, the citizens I was supporting rather suddenly ceased to signal. Pausing to suck in a breath, the holding of which was another bad habit I thought I had purged, I awaited information.

"They're all running off," said Goodman Warrley excitedly from atop his cage.

The soft-spoken greengrocer wiped at his brow as he looked around at the others in the room.

"I think we routed the blighters, Vaughn!" declared old Maud with glee.

Ignoring my nausea, I stood up from the cage upon which I had perched and sauntered stiffly over to stand beside Megan. She was peering through an arrow slit ensconced conveniently at the height of her head. Noting my approach, she gave way marginally that I might share this somewhat limited window on the world without. They were right. From this perspective at least, not a living enemy remained in sight. There were only swirling swarms of bees and the bodies of the goblin dead littering the courtyard.

A cheer arose once more from the doughty citizens brigade, a hearty huzzah we heard echoed from the parapet above and beyond the former fray. Hugs, back-slapping, and laughter were exchanged among the denizens of the dovecote as crossbows clattered to the floor to rest unattended.

Turning toward me, her face mere inches away, Megan drew me into her wide-eyed blue gaze and said, "That was part three of my plan. What did you think of it?"

***

The days that followed were harrowing indeed. I became better acquainted with the Westarbor Citizen's Brigade. It included not only the twelve crossbow wielders, but also a great many others involved in various projects to aid in the war effort. These worthy souls were all pledged to 'make a difference,' despite their stations. Megan was their ringleader, her authority stemming straight from the baron. And I had to confess to some surprise that such a serious responsibility had been entrusted to a girl of only thirteen summers. Nearly fourteen summers, I hastily corrected myself. But any initial misgivings or doubts others may have had of her abilities had melted away after the performance of the dovecote. The knights were *still* talking about the withering assault that had issued from the east tower to turn the tide of battle just at the height of the hostilities. Add to that; her people clearly adored her. They very nearly worshiped at her feet.

At the baron's command, our enemies were permitted to retrieve their dead from that dread field without hindrance. The goblins might be barbaric, but on this point we could agree. The bones of the fallen should be treated with respect and accorded the dignity that was their proper due. If only the living were also granted such grace, what a wonder our world could become. As a more practical consideration, removal of the carrion would slow the creeping advance of disease which hunted ever at the heels of war. In this, our foes efforts were as much for our benefit as their own.

The goblins remained encamped upon the hill, bitterly licking their wounds from their first failed foray. Sir Declan had posited that their initial attack had merely been made to assess our defenses; an opening move in a long game that had yet to play out. The knights chafed at the wearisome waiting. Being men of action, they yearned for a chance to take to the field against the foe and drive them hence. There were constant whispers and suggestions among the men of sallying forth to break the intolerable siege. Sir Declan, however, urged patience. He cited relevant passages from the code and reasoned that each day we held our ground brought the enemy one step closer to another disastrous (for them) assault upon our walls. It was a battle of wills, he advised his men. If the chief failed to feed his ogres, confidence in his coalition would crumble. And in the desperate, mistaken acts that would surely follow, our conviction would be proven the stronger. It was still a tough sell.

The situation was made worse that very night when the taunting commenced. From somewhere, the goblins had obtained a farm horse which they killed, spitted through, and proceeded to roast whole. This was all done in plain view of the keep. All throughout the night while ogres turned the great spit, the goblins pranced about and pantomimed being knights jousting from their steeds.

As if this weren't bad enough, other goblins emerged with the petticoats and nightgowns of young maidens they had obviously looted from the homes of Meadowfork. With these, they cavorted all about issuing incomprehensible threats in their distinctive shrill voices with raspy overtones. A fiddler among their ranks struck up a jaunty tune as they mimed dancing with the besmirched garments, waltzing about with them as though they were alive. Their musician was uncommonly skillful; his tune was almost worth the taunts.

When this failed to elicit much response, the little fiends soon fell to emulating copulation with their erstwhile 'dance partners,' finishing up by running them through repeatedly with their sharp little swords. Despite the language barrier, the threat they implied was clear enough. Along with everyone else, I took offense at this, of course. But having no sisters to worry about, nor a mother for that matter, their antics failed to arouse my ire. Even the soldiers who were off watch were deprived of their rest, for the goblin drums would often strike up an unsettling tempo in odd hours of the night. Even through the keep's walls their deep, hollow reverberations always sounded disconcertingly close by.

It was better during the hours of daylight, but only marginally so. At first enthused by our initial victory, the people soon grew restless from enforced inactivity. Crowded together in their ill-lit, unsanitary halls and with naught to keep them occupied, many became dispirited in their squalid, incommodious existence. Tempers flared and fights broke out over the most trivial of matters - a blanket in one instance. Yet too, from among these long-time neighbors there arose heroes and exemplars whose honorable and selfless acts did much to ease their suffering.

The lady Westarbor was one such paragon. She and her ladies had chosen to remain at the keep to give succor to her people. She moved among them as a shining beacon of mercy. Many a frightened child was soothed by her hand, and long would be remembered the sacrifices made by the great lady to care for the ill and infirm.

One particular example was the babe. In one of the lower halls, there was a new mother whose infant wouldn't stop crying. This irritated and angered the others nearby. The situation worsened when the babe began to show early signs of the pox. Being deathly afraid of contracting the often fatal disease, none would help the poor mother who had already been deprived of sleep for days on end. In fact, many began demanding her removal from among them. Upon hearing of the situation, the baroness rushed down to the sweltering hall and rescued the poor child and her weeping mother. They were taken to her ladyship's own suite of rooms and given rest upon fresh linens. The mother was bidden to sleep while the baroness herself and her maid, Agatha, took charge of the infant's care. Cool baths and ointments soothed the symptoms and greatly increased the child's chances for survival.

When the baron questioned the wisdom of his wife's exposure to the dread disease, she assured him she was safe. Having learned from the milkmaids that suffering through cowpox rendered one immune to the blight of smallpox, the baroness and her ladies had all arranged to contract the lesser ailment when last there had been an outbreak. None of the ladies of *her* court wanted to chance contracting smallpox, which often left disfiguring scars upon one's complexion. Persisting in his fretting, our liege cast doubt upon the efficacy of such a treatment, disparaging  the soundness of placing one's faith in an old wives' tale. Her ladyship glibly countered with: 'And just who might know better about such matters than old wives? They didn't get old by being stupid, after all.'

Royland and I visited our parents and the others as often as we were able. Our fathers had been officially cleared of suspicion and had rejoined the town's population. We asked if there was anything we could bring them, thinking that some better food or some kind of entertainment might prove a blessing. It turned out what they were most hungry for was information. Any scrap of news about the status of the siege or even a bit of castle gossip was considered a tremendous boon to be shared among the evacuees. Many were busy employing what they had learned of fletching to replenish our supplies of quarrels and arrows. We had expended more of these than we could afford. Megan's citizen brigade fetched them the needed supplies and coordinated such endeavors.

Roy apologized to Farmer Jenkins for the hard use of his hives. Word of the deed had garnered the good farmer increased status among the other refugees, and even the nobles honored his sacrifice. The good farmer was permitted to go and check up on his tiny charges. He reported that the queens and their egg chambers remained intact. And though much depleted by Royland's feat, the hives should survive and recover by next spring. As he had told the chancellor, honeybees died when they stung someone. It was worth noting that the robust swarms that had helped to repel the goblins would not be as potent a second time.

We didn't get as much chance to visit as we would have liked because we were soon commanded to return to our old shifts as in the mygalom days. Only Master Chadwick, Roy and I were blessed with mage sight. We were to take it in turns to mount a continuous watch upon the horde, walking the walls and remaining alert for any sign of duplicity or activity by our magical counterparts among them. Our shepherd's spell of wakefulness translated well to the duties of a wartime sentry.

It could be worse, I thought. At least it had started raining.

As I slogged along through the wind and sheets of rain attentive for any hint of magic, I thought vindictively of our little foes huddled in their tents atop the hill. Of course, many had doubtless taken refuge in the abandoned buildings of Meadowfork, but enough of them had to maintain their uncomfortable post to keep us bottled up. Peels of rolling thunder crashed as the battlement I trod was alternately cast in bright relief by swift flashes of lightning or plunged into utter darkness in their sudden aftermath. Since their shaman was a user of fire, and our greatest wizard relied upon water, we reasoned we were safe from attack for at least as long as the weather remained our ally. That, and the thoroughfare they would need to traverse was a muddy mess.

I paused and peered out from the west tower whose spire provided at least some shelter from the downpour. The mill stream gushed out in a fury as the pond itself sought to overflow its banks. Some water even slopped into the race, causing the great wheel to turn in fits and starts with an occasional creaking groan that could be heard even over this distance. The many barrels lining our battlement had all been filled to capacity and were brimming over from the runoff we had caught. One day soon I hoped my master would enlighten me as to how he used magic to remain dry, but for now, I relished the rain.

****

Reports from the baron's men in the field continued to trickle in. The word had come that the goblins were bringing in some rather ominous siege equipment from all the way out at the pass, hampered heavily by the inclement conditions. I was suddenly gratified we had taken the time to demolish Bradlebury Bridge and felt this vindicated our decision. The main storms had passed, but the skies yet remained sunless, their introductory deluge having given way to a steady drencher with no signs of letting up. For nearly a full week we were granted this reprieve, but as all good things pass, so too did this blessing of the heavens. As the day dawned clear and sultry we saw the steam arising from the sopping, sodden outer courtyard to be blown before a steady westerly wind which heralded our asylum's end. And still they waited.

A message had arrived from the king. In it, he wrote of inconsequential things and asked why the baron was late with his correspondence. Nor was there any mention of the fast horse messengers Sir Declan had sent out weeks ago from the eastern fiefs. His majesty had  made reference to earlier notes which the baron had not received. We suspected that not all of his majesty's notes were getting through. The goblins had taken to hunting the blue-banded birds with a fervor, and every day fewer returned to their roost in the east tower after their daily foraging. The baron had finally ordered Peter to cloister some in an enclosed roost to be fed seed like the foreign roosts. In that manner, at least some might be preserved. It was all very frustrating.

Our foes numbers had swollen twofold as their fellows and supply wagons continued to drift in from the west. Faith in Sir Declan's waiting game had begun to falter. Many cited the goblin's patient wait of twenty years while they had tunneled and prepared. Would it not be best to sally forth and end them ere they could gather still more allies to array against us? Sir Declan, however, remained firm in his commitment to his strategy of outlasting the enemy's longanimity. And our good knight commander clearly enjoyed the utmost confidence of his liege.

Then came the day when the siege tower arrived. It was a huge framework of wood and hides. From a distance, its true proportions could not be properly appreciated. It looked for all the world as though some demented genius had taken the Cain's barn, upended it, and set it on wheels. It was pulled by a train of no fewer than three dozen ogres who appeared tiny by comparison. The tower had its own drummer to mark the time as they hauled on ropes, moving it forward step by weary step. Upon closer approach, it was briefly lost from view when it moved behind the hilltop beyond the mill. More ogres from among our besiegers rushed to join their brothers in the daunting task of conveying it up to our foe's position.

The top came into view first and the rest was slowly revealed as the giants strained to lug the massive monolith up that hill step by grueling step. Bum! ba-ba-bah-bah. Bum! ba-ba-bah-bah. When it finally came to rest atop that grim rise, its threat was made clear. Groups of goblins gleefully entered its open sides and disappeared from our sight behind its armored frontage. They reappeared at its crest in what seemed like only seconds. Clearly, the thing was riddled with stairways and ladders well suited to our foes' dimensions up which masses of them could scurry in a trice. They practiced throwing open a small drawbridge at its summit that appeared suspiciously well matched to the height of our walls. At its base, were several heavy screws. These massive, steel-headed logs, if swung or turned by ogres within, looked like they could wreck havoc upon our gates or perhaps even breach the fastness of our stone walls themselves. A nutcracker indeed. Say what you like about the goblins, but their clever engineers built far beyond their tiny size and had gained our grudging respect.

Nor was this the only intimidating surprise our tiny adversaries revealed to us this day. For in the distance, ominous drumbeats portended the arrival of yet another grim package. This turned out to be a trebuchet. Our liege had often desired a few catapults atop his keep's battlement. He had even had Javier draw up plans for such, but he had never gotten around to funding the endeavor. Priority had instead been given to his many other projects of more immediate benefit to his people. This was a preference he might now, in hindsight, not live to regret. We felt our time was running out as Sir Declan desperately sought strategies to counter the threats these new elements would pose.

That night our foes tormented us by making merry. Their campfires burned brightly, and we perceived in their feasting and singing an excited expectation. Tomorrow morning, then, they would fall upon us. Their morale was such that a good commander could easily divine their intent. And in their joyous songs, the grim but defiant defenders of Westarbor Keep heard naught but the dirge of our doom.

***

The morning dawned bright and clear, much to our dismay. Our forces stood ready to encounter the enemy once more. After an all-night strategy session, even Sir Declan looked tired and worn, and our poor master seemed downright miserable. It had been agreed that his apprentices would have to deal with the siege engines while he alone faced off against the goblins' magical might. While far from ideal, it was the best plan that could be cobbled together in the limited time allotted. So as our master took center stage on the battlement, Roy and I stood over by the east tower, ready to do our part. Megan had been disappointed that we wouldn't be joining her archers within, but as there was a trapdoor leading down into the dovecote, that remained an option for later.

This push by the enemy commenced in a much more orderly fashion and seemed more well thought out than previously. After their standard drumming introduction, the goblins failed to rush pell-mell down the thoroughfare. Instead, they presented us with a new surprise. It appeared our foes had been busy during the long hiatus that followed our prior engagement. They had used the time to construct numerous mobile wooden palisades behind which they huddled as they advanced. Borne up by an ogre on each end they advanced at a mere walk. Though far less impressive than their former reckless charge, this proved proof against our advantage in archery. To add insult to injury, their palisades had clearly been made from the shopfronts of Meadowfork. The goblins had even made it a point to leave the various, familiar business placards and shingles intact.

In the lead position, marched 'Harvey's Fine Smithing' with its painted anvil. This was followed by the boot with 'A.J. Tillerson, proprietor' engraved, and a plethora of others. It was disheartening, which I suspected was no less than their intent. As the key business district of Meadowfork paraded down the hill, goblin drums resumed their annoying marching cadence. As they neared goblin archery range, several split off, sliding to either side of the outer courtyard, but 'Harvey's Fine Smithing' continued to advance.

Sir Declan ordered a volley of flaming arrows sent at the enemy barriers, But such was the goblin shamans' command of fire that this tactic was quickly shown to be worthless. No sooner would a shopfront catch than its flames were promptly snuffed out by a brief burst of magic. At least this revealed to me where some of the shamans were positioned. The extinguishing spells were coming from behind 'Burns Dry Goods.' Who ever said goblins couldn't be ironic? This storefront sat strangely forward in the goblins' advance. I would have expected them to stay back in the rear as they previously had done.

All the while, the smithy's storefront continued its unaccompanied advance, finally swerving to the left straight toward my position. After a last sudden dash, it was finally brought to rest leaning against the base of the east tower blocking the majority of the arrow slits through which Megan's people plied their crossbows. Of course, this exposed the ogres who had been hauling it to a punishing volley of arrows loosed by our archers up on the battlement. The brutes tried to run, but lacking many other targets, our men loosed upon them until they lay still, having sprouted enough goose feathers to lay eggs had they survived.

Even so, our wily adversaries were not done with their devilment. I sensed a surge of magic emanating from the dry goods store, and the smithy began to burn. This was not a bright, destructive flame, but rather an insidious smoldering from which ominous black clouds of smoke began to billow. The smoke soon took shape as a towering wall of blackness obscuring visibility even from the dovecote's upper holes. It rippled like a thing alive and hung there unnaturally, no doubt managed by the little red-cape peering cautiously out from the dry good shop's shutters. Worse still, the smoke was funneling into the holes. This would render the bees quiescent and was even now driving Megan's people choking and retching out into the fresh air of the inner ward. It was a brilliant tactic which I might have applauded had it been to our benefit.

It was at this time that our foemen chose to employ their trebuchet up on the hill. With a resounding 'Flump!' the counterweight of the great wooden contraption dropped, causing its arm to stretch skyward and launching its grim package toward the keep. As the great stone sailed into the sky, all paused to track its dread trajectory, and all save for one awaited its inevitable descent.

"Capturam petram," cried out my cousin just as the stone slowed to the apex of its climb.

Although at this distance, even Royland lacked the strength to halt the boulder's downward plummet, he still possessed the wherewithal to nudge and guide it to a target more to our liking. Choosing 'Holcomb's Feed and Grain,' behind which a substantial group of goblin archers had amassed, he bore it down to impact with meteoric might. The erstwhile purveyor of animal fodder was obliterated, and our archers promptly set to picking off any exposed goblin beyond it who had survived.

I only hoped that when my turn came, I could be as successful. The arm of the trebuchet was being slowly ratcheted back into position. It would be quite some time ere it was poised to launch once more. That is, if the goblins even deigned to do so, for its advantage had been nullified, nay even turned against them. We had hoped that our surprise maneuver could be employed *after* the goblins' mighty siege tower had been deployed. Had this been the case, we could have eliminated two weapons from our opponent's arsenal in a single stroke. But as my uncle Robert had repeatedly told me, 'if you hope in one hand and defecate in the other, there's one hand that's always predictably heavier.' I braced myself to enact our backup strategy.

Before any of that could come about, another event transpired in the goblins' unfolding plan of attack. Their archer's had entered the fray, opening up the shutters on their shop fronts and engaging with our soldiers from behind the cover of windows and doorways. A particularly vicious exchange had erupted between our men on the wall and 'Madame Pennington's Soap Boutique.' Unmindful of the archery exchange, Shastageheggin the shaman emerged from 'Burns Dry Goods' and swaggered to the fore. The space in front of him was soon alight with flash-burning arrows the residual ashes of which he casually waived aside as he advanced.

"Don't waste your arrows," shouted Sir Declan over the din of battle. "Leave him to the mage."

As Master Chadwick stepped forward and locked gazes with the crimson-clad shaman, he suddenly cringed and seemed to shrivel and sag. With his eyes glazed over, the old man shuddered and dove to crouch and cower behind a crenelation. With a satisfied smirk, the shaman strode forth unopposedly to stand directly before our gates. This too was a part of our plan. The most difficult decision had been to withhold this information from our men, for our ruse relied on subterfuge, and soldiers were not well-known for their acting ability.

Nevertheless, I felt shame for my master at the shocked looks of betrayal he suffered from the knights and soldiery. The baron, who was in on the scheme, played his part to perfection, appearing suitably outraged and bellowing most believably for his 'sniveling sorcerer' to face our foe. Roy and I only shared in the secret to prevent us from acting rashly and confronting the shaman on our own. It had been a wise choice to include us, for even now, I felt sharp pangs of guilt driving me to do that very thing.

Shastageheggin's intent was as clear as his arrogance. He meant to destroy the keep's main gates, depriving us of their inviolate protection and leaving us ripe for harvesting by the goblins' vastly superior numbers. By this time, the goblin warriors and their teams with scaling ladders had issued forth, keeping our men on the wall fully engaged in its defense. So too had the intimidating siege tower atop the hill at last begun its steady crawl down the lane. It appeared that my own moment for action had finally been ordained.

As the shaman began spewing fire in a roaring ray at the enchanted gates, I surrendered myself deeply to the familiar mindset of 'spacium girabit.' The tower's advance down the thoroughfare proceeded far more readily than its upward journey had done. It was still a good distance off beyond the mill at the extreme edge of my reach. However, I dared not wait too long. Pushed from behind by a full team of ogres, the titanic tower was fast gathering momentum in its eager glide down the slope. I made sure to breathe as the moments slipped past, finally selecting one as the ideal compromise between distance and resistance. I wound hard on the tower's frontmost set of wheels, reversing the direction of their spin. As I engaged, I felt that jarring, ringing sensation in my ears, followed by a wave of dizziness and nausea. Winding was meant to progress smoothly up to speed, not all at once against so great a mass. Nonetheless, my training had prepared me well, and I maintained focus, fighting the lightheaded vertigo that ensued and winning through.

The tower groaned and swayed alarmingly forward. The goblins, however, had fashioned it sturdily, curse their wretched little engineering minds, and it failed to conveniently topple over. Instead, a battle of strength ensued between the ogres, who were well endowed with that attribute, and the wildly spinning wheels of their rebellious siege engine. Of course, the turning force of the earth could overcome any number of opponents, ogre strength notwithstanding. But the battle had become more a matter of traction. The ogres strained with all their considerable might, and the wheels spun madly, throwing out mud, dirt and debris from the front of the engine. It was a battle the ogres were winning by inches as the tower slid forward through the slick, damp ground as though it rested upon skids. Roy tried to help. Having liberated a few bees from the smoke-filled east tower, he harassed the brutish ogres. He quickly found that stings from the gentle honeybees could not penetrate the ogre's leathery hides and settled on confusing them by flying about their heads and into their eyes.

While this was happening, I couldn't help but notice the other epic conflict occurring over at our keep's gates. The enchanted gates were sucking in some of Shastageheggin's magical fire to power their spell, but he was exceeding their draw by orders of magnitude and had managed to scorch them thoroughly, though they were not yet aflame. Sir Declan had ordered barrels of water overturned on the parapets above the gates. My master, meanwhile, was directing the water down through the machicolation behind the crenelation where he 'cowered.' Machicolations were holes used by the battlement's defenders through which boiling oil or other unpleasant surprises could be poured out upon aggressors at the base of the wall. Master Chadwick was causing the water to flow inward and fan out in a wide waterfall spread across the gates' surface. This resulted in an enormous cloud of steam that sizzled and popped as the cool waters cascaded down to meet the overheated wood.

The shaman redoubled his efforts and his blazing cone of flame increased in intensity. It looked to be a stalemate for as long as the barrels held out. Megan already had her people in a bucket line attempting to refill some of the empty barrels from the well in the inner ward, but this was occurring far too gradually to 'make a (significant) difference.' All the while, great clouds of steam billowed up to all but obscure my sight of the wall and its defenders. I had heard tales of the 'fog of war,' but this was far too literal for my liking. I wished my old master well as I returned to my own uphill battle. Trying to stay focused, I wound the wheels, digging a furrow in the still sodden ground and playing plowshare to a group of determined ogre farmers.

"Turn the wheel, Lucas," said Royland, coming around to stare at me and making vague gestures with his hands.

I wanted to scream at him that I was turning as hard as I could. But since he could plainly see that, I ignored his words of encouragement and remained attentive to my task.

"No, the big wheel," he failed to clarify with an aggravated look of consternation and wilder gesticulations.

Unsurprisingly, my cousin seemed at a loss for words. I saw a resolute look take shape on his features the moment the idea struck. He reached out and planted his palm on my forehead muttering 'miscere cogitata.' Although unfamiliar with the spell, my command of the old tongue was now such that I was able to decipher this as something akin to 'share thoughts' or perhaps 'share mind.' In any event, I would soon be discovering its meaning as I felt the familiar grip of magic take hold of my senses.

I don't know if I can adequately describe what it felt like to be plunged into my cousin's thoughts. All the doors of my mind had been thrown open. All of their glorious, mundane or pitiful truths had been exposed, poured out and jumbled together with Roy's own secret thoughts, longings and desires. I was seeing through two sets of eyes at once: my own, and those of my cousin looking down upon me like a mirror that had been placed a few inches too low on the wall. There was also the vague impression of hundreds of ogre faces as seen through the multifaceted eyes of the insects we controlled. A gigantic hive of swarming magic specs landed square in the middle of our formerly peaceful inner garden to nestle among its vines and drone most dreadful demands upon our attention. If this was the bedlam Royland had to contend with all the time, it was a wonder we had not gone plumb crazy in our crib. It was a miracle that Lucas was able to continue his winding during the eye blink when this all happened. Or perhaps not, we thought as we silently mouthed the words that gave comfort and rocked back and forth on our feet.

Our idea was astonishing to us. Moreover, it could now be accomplished. Our timing would need to be very precise, not done in the sloppy Lucas way. Hey, we're right here, you know. The Lucas mind possessed remarkably detailed knowledge of the mill and its tolerances and we were right to be proud of it. That's more like it. This was the final missing piece, we thought as we freed our bees; they would not be needed. Slowing our winding to a halt, we reversed directions and spun the wheels forward to begin our audacious undertaking. How did we ever manage to cope with this dizziness? It'll pass, we assured ourself.

Caught off-guard, the straining ogres fell in a clumsy heap, their final shove finding no resistance and causing the tower to lurch into motion once more. With our winding, it continued to pick up speed, slewing down the slope. We ceased winding the left wheel and concentrated exclusively on the right one, causing the massive engine to veer to the left. This caused the runaway tower to leave the open avenue of the thoroughfare and begin flattening the many palisades along the left-hand side and crushing any goblin too slow or inattentive to give way before it. That was Lucas' idea, but *we* carried out the additional calculations. As the tower approached our own position, swelling in both our sets of eyes, we wound the left wheel backwards causing it to skid to a groaning stop broadside to the castle walls. Exposed goblins already packed within began scurrying headlong down its ladders. Our men on the battlement started picking them off through the open sides like terrified turtles that had lost their shells. Now came the more exciting part.

We turned our attention toward the mill and its great wheel. We had never wound anything so large even if you included the millstone. Lucas remembered to take several deep breaths and settle our thoughts before envisioning the shadowy pinwheel and gyrating our fingers before us. We both chanted 'spacium girabit,' more for luck than anything else at this point, and laid our will upon the wheel of the mill. It slowly began to spin up in a direction contrary to the typical way in which it turned. We noticed the ogres running down the hill, perhaps with some mad notion of resuming their former responsibility. We acknowledged that ogres were strong, but we might have to lower our estimate of their intellect a bit more. Faster and faster the wheel turned until smoke began to issue forth from the friction of the main shaft. That should be enough. Now it's our turn, Roy. We calmed our thoughts and began to coax out the inner hive.

'Gloriabitur securis,' we recited as we depleted almost all of Roy's power in one swift, sure stroke. We were saddened by the sudden loss of so many hive-mites, but at least the droning subsided somewhat, and our perceptions of the world without had improved. When force axe struck and severed the main shaft, the fast-spinning water wheel bounced several times in the dry bed of its race before seeming to catch all at once and come careening toward us. Aiming wasn't a factor. We had already taken care of that when we had parked the tower. The mighty wheel empowered with the turning force of the earth moved in a direct line as guided by the tail race. It was all about the force we had imparted and assumptions made about the depth at the end of the race where the channel suddenly took a sharp left turn.

When the wheel encountered this, it became airborne just as we had predicted. It soared whirling through the air and directly into the goblin tower. As the energy of the former met the mass of the latter, the resulting violent detonation rent the air with a thunderous, grinding roar and sent splinters high into the sky along with bits of the hapless ogres whose ill-timed arrival had coincided with the collision. These showered down upon the keep and upon combatants all across the field of battle. Some were later found even so far away as Farmer Green's pasture. There was a pause in the battle as the stunned goblins, at first tracking their runaway tower, now leaned out from their cover to witness this new calamity. Westarbor's defenders failed to take proper advantage of the lapse, being themselves momentarily transfixed, as people often are by the sight of something momentous.

Just then, we felt the newly familiar tug of a grand working underway. For incensed by the losses to his people and hellbent on the destruction of the defiant gates, Shastageheggin became unhinged to the point that he would risk all. The effect seemed less profound at this distance. Nevertheless, as he ingathered in whatever manner was uniquely his own, much of the magic remaining to Roy and I was burnt away and we found myself savagely uncoupled from my cousin's mind. I was a little disoriented but jubilant just to be Lucas again and overjoyed at what had been accomplished.

"Beat that old man!" I crowed from atop the east tower, thrusting my fists into the air and pumping them up and down.

Perhaps I shouldn't have behaved so boastfully before the baron and all his knights. For my old master peered up at me from behind the stone slab where he crouched with something akin to wounded pride. Sir Declan was down to the last several barrels of water, and the flames from the shaman now rivaled those of the devil himself. Succeed or fail, the shaman was now committed, for he would conclude his ritual delirious and with no strength remaining. I was certain he lacked the focus to go at my master mind to mind. The only question was whether the gates would endure. So, with a nod, Master Chadwick stood up, stepped out upon that battlement and began a grand working of his own.

Never had I been so starved of magical energy. My magic center became non-existent upon the commencement of my master's ingathering ripples. He then uttered one of the last spells I would have expected, one not even within his preferred element; he invoked a spell we used for farming.

"Terram aratro," he boomed, leaning out over the courtyard.

And to my amazement, I beheld the most violent, broadest and deepest use of earth furrow I had ever thought to witness. It began at the west tower and proceeded in a straight line flinging up clods of earth, clouds of dust, bits of ladders and even screaming goblins to the height of the battlement itself. When it intersected Shastageheggin's position, the pompous shaman was thrown on his back by the tremulous upheaval, directing his fiery holocaust harmlessly upward. The line of destruction my master carved then continued on past the dovecote and the mill wheel's wreckage, curving at last to meet the end of the tail race. He then directed the geyser of his grand working to one final task, a spell I had in the past seen my master use on a bloated tick. As the shaman's amplified fires sputtered and ceased, and he lay there covered in brown dust and debris, he descended into impotent weakness - a worm crawling amidst the mud. The scorched gates of Westarbor Keep still stood firm, having denied our adversary even his pyhrric victory.

"Praemium," my master pronounced.

No ill befell the villainous shaman from my masters spell, for he had not been its target. Beyond the mill, the sluice gates shattered asunder unleashing a cascading torrent into the race. As the mill pond swirled and drained its contents to the lowest level since the gates were first built, the brownish waters surged and roared to fill first the race and then the keep's new improvised moat. Even the ducks were drawn down that cascading surge, squawking and trumpeting in outrage. Their unwilling regata sailed the race, its members eventually taking flight to escape the thirsty maw of my master's muddy trench to alight unharmed. With a sloppy grin, Master Chadwick sunk to his knees to join the shaman in demented dysfunction. As the goblin horde beat a hasty retreat lest further misfortune and magical mayhem befall them this day, their shaman was, of course, expediently dispatched by our longbowmen.

Sir Graham was attending my master who was whispering urgently to him as I approached, a crazed look upon his disheveled features.

"What is he saying?" asked the baron.

Sir Graham was staring at me as he answered his liege, "He said, 'top *that* apprentice,' and bade me to pump my fists at you."

I was treated once again to the baron's rich laughter; we all were. It seemed to mock the goblin's fleeing forms. It rang out across the battlement, dispelling our fears and exhaustion and even some of our sorrow for our losses this day.

***

Having been served a vicious defeat and hamstrung by the loss of their powerful shaman, we hoped the goblins would give up and go home. But once again the excrement hand proved to be the heavier. Chief Ravenbald and his horrific horde remained encamped upon our doorstep with their trebuchet poised to discharge at a moment's notice. Master Chadwick was led back to our rooms by Sebastian, there to seek repose to recover from his overuse of magic.

The baron convened his council of war to discuss our next steps. Since our master was indisposed and Roy was needed to guard against any sudden rockfalls, I was to be the magical representative. We first rehashed our victory, our liege eliciting facts and impressions of all that had occurred upon that chaotic field. We then descended further into the minutia of managing our dwindling resources.

The water hadn't yet drained away from Master Chadwick's spontaneous new moat, so we had to assume the six-foot-deep water hazard would remain a feature of any battles to come. Javier Lewis remarked that such unplanned new construction was most ill-advised. According to the good artillator, it was a miracle my master hadn't undermined the soundness of our curtain wall with his heroic antics. Our liege only smiled and tasked Javier with implementing a way his knights and their steeds might cross over the muddy trench should the need arise to sally forth.

Gerrard Keaton then made a most tedious report of our assets. It included items like an exact count of arrows we had expended and the number remaining to us; but also estimates of food reserves, the time it would take to refill water barrels, and all manner of other sundries. When it came to counting human losses, however, he deferred to Sir Declan.

Casualties among our enemies had been great indeed, but when pitted against their overall numbers; the denominator still far exceeded the numerator. We hoped that we could soon drive these numbers further toward parity. Where had that creepy thought come from? Was it possible some of Royland's mad math-brain had rubbed off on me during our merging and lingered to haunt my musings? I supposed that defeating the horde needed to be accomplished how my master once told me one should eat an elephant - one bite at a time. I returned my attention to our battle marshal's report. Although our own losses had been slight in comparison to those of our foemen, a dispassionate accounting was far more difficult. *Those* numbers had names, and many had family; each of *those* losses was keenly felt. No, there was nothing casual about casualties when they were your friends and countrymen.

I emerged late in the day from that council with my head spinning nearly as fiercely as the mill wheel I had launched earlier on. I mounted the battlement to look for my cousin just as the watch fires were lit by tired guardsmen awaiting their relief. The flames were subdued, shedding enough light to illuminate the outer courtyard, yet not so much as to blind our defenders to the doings on the hilltop beyond. I found Roy leaning on the railing of the west tower, a silent sentinel keeping watch over the enemy emplacement.

"Hail the watch," I greeted him.

"Hey, Lucas," he replied with unaccustomed warmth.

"I relieve you," said I, completing the formula. "Go and get some sleep. I've got this. But before you do, I'd like to make something clear."

The lanky lad turned to me and straightened, canting his head to one side and folding his arms before him.

"I understand why you did it," I began hesitantly, "and I certainly can't argue with the results, but never invade my mind again without my express permission. There's such a thing as *oversharing*, Roy. For instance, I now know what it's like to kiss Prissy. Don't take this the wrong way, but it's just too weird."

My cousin pursed his lips and looked abashed, quickly saying, "You're right, of course. It was hard on me too. Never again."

So promising, he stalked off toward sleep, descending to the inner ward and out of sight. My watch proceeded uneventfully as I listlessly stood guard over the great goblin war machine. I sorely missed my spell of wakefulness. My bruised magic center was still recovering from the day's harrowing exploits and there was no significant greenery nearby with which I could readily refresh it. I therefore needs must marshal my paltry but recovering reserves that I might deflect any suddenly inbound boulders the night might toss my way. And so it was with heartfelt gratitude that my bleary orbs came to rest upon my *own* relief at nearly midnight. Both figuratively and in a more literal sense, the two that approached were indeed a welcome sight for sore eyes.

"Wuff," they greeted me.

"I believe the proper phrase is: 'Hail the watch,' but I'm sure you'll get it right the next time," said my master to his companion.

"Wuff," the dog repeated, wagging his tail.

"How are you faring, master?" I asked, accepting Sampson's sloppy attentions in my extended palm.

"A bit spent, but ready to resume my place," replied the old mage. "Go and get some rest, apprentice. You did well today, and we need you fresh for the fight ahead. It wouldn't do for our worker of wondrous windings to become dog tired. Our watchful friend here shall keep me company - and keep me alert, should the need arise."

So, bidding them a goodnight, I returned to our rooms eagerly anticipating a happy reunion with my soft mattress and bedspread therein. Little did I know then that when I sank into my bed that eve, it would not be as I envisioned.

***

The fates were often unkind to the wishes of the weary. As I entered our suite, the first thing I noted was the dreadful disquietude that stridently proclaimed Royland to be unconscious. In relieving me of the watch, I began to think that Sampson and my master had gotten the better end of the deal. The second was Sebastian. When I entered into my own bedroom of the suite, I found him standing in gentleman's attire holding a fully lit candelabrum aloft to meet my entrance with an obsequious bow and a fawning, toothless smile. I had told him on more than one occasion that I was perfectly capable of undressing myself, and had bidden him to find better uses for his time.

"Well met, little master," he said, shuffling nearer. "The siege progresses apace, I hear."

"It is what it is," I said, hoping to forestall any idle banter on the topic as I made my way toward my bed.

"*Hold*, young master, for I would have a word," said he, his tone shifting to one more forceful and dancing perilously close to that of a command."

I turned to regard the wizened old chandler and was taken aback by his brazen bearing and the manic gleam in his eyes.

"I deem the hour is finally upon us," he declared. "At long last my lady's heir stands ready to receive his legacy. Long have I awaited your readiness, young master. For all these years, I have guarded the lady's bequest to her progeny. In sacred trust, I held dear my final duty to the great lady of Arbordell whose name even now I remain unworthy to speak."

Confused, my tired mind began to assemble the pieces of his scattered speech.

295

"Abigail?" I asked. "How did you know *her*? And why me? Why not Royland - or his father for that matter?"

"Robert is *unworthy*! *Never* did he possess the gift, and nor had he proper respect or reverence for his forebears. I served my lady at the height of her power. I served her well and *faithfully*. I serve her still, remaining ever watchful and true in my heart, hoping for the return of her proper heir that her glory might be restored. *You* are that heir, the son of Isabel who should have received the legacy but for the falseness of treacherous Robert. As to the son of Robert: powerful though he may be, I judge him likewise unfit. *That* one lacks soundness of *mind*."

'Pot, meet kettle,' I thought as I again struggled to derive meaning from the old man's deranged ramblings.

"What is this legacy of which you speak?" I asked simply, certain I would get no rest until the maniacal old coot had enjoyed his say.

"Ah. Now we get to the *heart* of it," he said with a cackle that swiftly descended into a phlegmy cough. "Come with me, little master. Sebastian will steer you to it, and you can see for *yourself*. If you are worthy, my lady's legacy will grant you all the power you need to lift the siege and *smite* her ancient foes."

That caught my attention. If Sebastian knew of something from my grandma that would aid us against the goblins, it behooved me to at least find out about it. I cast my spell of wakefulness to sharpen my tired mind and nodded my acquiescence.

Resting his light on the table, Sebastian bent to manipulate something near the foot of my bed. When he straightened back up, to the limited extent *that* was possible, the entire mattress hinged upward to reveal a very steep wooden stairway. It was almost a ladder that led down into the floor beneath the very spot I had unwittingly lain these past several weeks. A cool draft wafted from the darkness below.

"Go ahead, little master. Your servant will bring the light just behind."

With that, Sebastian took up the candelabrum and held it above the decrepit stairwell with an expectant smile. Reluctantly,

I mounted the narrow slats, first testing my weight upon one and finding it sturdy enough. Descending, I had an unimpeded view of Sebastian's boots as he pulled the bed back down on its hinges to lock into place with a decisive click. The way beneath me was vaguely lit by the flickering candlelight, and my shadow shrank and sharpened with each step down as we approached the stone floor below. Upon reaching this landing, I stepped from the narrow stair into a small chamber with three exits, if one counted the stairway itself. Unlike the dungeons from which I had retrieved my father, the walls appeared to be carved from native stone.

"Apologies, young master," said the chandler, obsequiously brushing the fine spider silk from my surcoat. "I haven't had cause to clean this part 'till recently. Let me lead from here on. One day, I'll help ya explore all the fine features of your castle, but for now, let's just get what we came for."

And so the wizened old servant began leading the way, brandishing his candles to clear the cobwebs from our path. It could be worse, I thought as I lost count of the turnings. At least I could retrace our steps through the cleared areas if need be. Some of the spiders were rather large, but facing off against the mygaloms had banished or superseded any terrors that mere spiders might conjure up.

We soon found ourselves in better maintained surroundings, and our light had steadied now that Sebastian was no longer using it as a makeshift machete. Onward we wove through the baffling passageways, onward and ever downward. Who could have carved all this out? I had read of dwarves who delved under the earth, but even a whole clan of such would surely require centuries to accomplish all this. Having a guide who fancied himself my servant, I supposed it could do no harm to ask.

"Sebastian, who carved out all these tunnels?"

"It was my lady's doing, of course." he said as we entered yet another sloping passageway. "All that you see here was built by her blessing. I, her humble servant, know *all* of her secret ways. Never fear, little master, old Sebastian has guided you true. Behold! We are here."

We had arrived at a chamber no different from many others we had passed. Deep below the ground, it was carved from the living stone beneath the hill. A clammy chill permeated the air as subdued light from the candles played about its confines. Something pricked at my mage sight at the room's far end, and I warily stepped forward to have a better look. Sebastian followed behind and slightly to one side, his old hand atremble with excitement.

By the dancing light of the flickering flames, I made out the magic's source. It was a handprint set into the stone of the chamber's far wall. At about shoulder height and dimpled into the otherwise smooth stone was the impression of a perfectly formed human hand slightly smaller than my own. From it emanated a subtle enchantment whose nature I could not discern.

"Well go on," urged the chandler. "If my lady finds you worthy, you shall be the heir to all of her secrets and the power of the earth shall be yours to command!"

Had I been well-rested, and not merely propped up by 'manent vigilate,' I might have turned back right there and sought out my master's council on the matter. But my master stood on watch, and the need of my people was urgent. Having committed so much time already to this endeavor, I was loath to waste still more should it prove to be a wild goose. I took the plunge and placed my hand within the beckoning indentation.

At once, my inner garden blossomed from within, its vine-like tendrils twining and growing down my right arm to fasten and lap against the alien enchantment. The doorways of my mind all opened as they had when Royland had brought about our connection. Unlike then, this touch was gentle and unhurried. I felt fingers, feather-light, running through my inner-most thoughts and private memories.

The voice, when it came, was female. It came not aloud, but from within my own mind as though from a distance. And from behind its winsome tones, I sensed both a cruel confidence and an ancient wisdom. The judgment was swift and favorable.

*Enter, son of Isabel. The prize is yours for the taking.*

At that, a section of the wall slid inward with a grinding noise, opening seams in the stone I had not previously perceived.

"She favors you," declared Sebastian in a giddy voice, gleefully shuffling from one booted foot to the other and causing his flames once again to dance about.

When I hesitated, he plucked forth one of his candles from its sconce and held it out to me saying, "Enter true heir. You must collect your legacy. *Quickly*, lest she change her mind."

"Aren't you coming?" I asked as I accepted the proffered gift.

"*Sebastian* is not welcome in my lady's most private of chambers. That would be most unbecoming, and unwise as well. No. Only the heir may enter," he said in stern decree.

Still harboring reservations and with hot wax dribbling a trail down the back of my hand, I stepped within.

CHAPTER THIRTEEN

# The Witch

"I don't know who my grandfather was; I am much more concerned to know what his grandson will be."

*~ Abraham Lincoln ~*

The room was cramped and had but two features. The first was a pedestal upon which rested a glittering gemstone. The second was a dusty skeleton lying on the floor before it. From the gem I sensed enchantment. Stepping closer and careful not to disturb the remains, I examined 'the prize.' Clear and many-faceted, it sparkled there in the dim light cast by my single tongue of flame. It was roughly the size of a hen's egg but was complex in shape. Pointed at its bottom, it had two bulbous protrusions atop its central mass. It most resembled a heart from a deck of cards if such a symbol were wrought in a full three dimensions. It hung by a bob from a golden chain which was clearly meant to be worn as a necklace.

Well, this is why we came, after all, I thought as I lifted it by the thin chain. Sebastian's 'lady' was obviously long deceased. I inspected the skeleton. Upon it, no clue remained as to its former identity. Doubtless it was her, given the location. I raised my arm to peer more closely at the gem, but it swung and twirled most awkwardly, so I took up the slack in the chain and rested it instead in the palm of my hand. When I did, I had a sinking sensation and felt a presence emerge from its glittering depths.

*Greetings, my dear*, said the voice. *Let me get a proper look at you.*

And with that, I heard another grinding sound. A slab of stone slid aside to reveal a mirror; a mirror on the wall. In it, I perceived my own familiar features overlaid by those of an old woman. My reflection faded as her features sharpened and became more substantial in the obviously enchanted looking-glass. I beheld an aged crone with sagging cheeks. The lines of her face were not the kindly laugh wrinkles I had seen on many an old granny of Meadowfork, but the hard, chiseled lines of one careworn by life and who lacked grandchildren to brighten her declining years.

"I sense you are displeased by this visage," I heard myself say as the lips of the reflection moved to the sound of my voice. "Perhaps you would prefer me as I appeared in my prime."

At this, the face looking back at me from the mirror transformed. Her silvery hair became lustrous auburn locks flowing down to frame the porcelain complexion of a face that had achieved the perfection of youth. There was no denying the fair beauty of her alluring features, but something of her stern, mature countenance remained to overshadow them.

"Am I speaking to Abigail?" I asked.

"None other," I replied as the face in the reflection once again mouthed the words. "Let's see, then. I mark your mother's influence upon your aspect. A handsome boy. Well muscled if a bit short. I suppose you'll do."

"I am not short," I said with annoyance, "I am of perfectly average height for my age."

"Of course you are, my dear," I soothed "but this grows wearisome."

And with that, I promptly lifted the chain over my neck, almost burning my ear with the candle in the process. The glistening pendant slipped beneath my doublet to rest at the center of my chest.

"Hey!" I belatedly objected as a strange duality fell over my perceptions.

My inarticulate objection went unheeded as the stone slab slid back over the recessed mirror with a scraping sound.

*That's better,* said the voice. *Let us speak of the purpose that brought you hither, child, for I sense in you some urgent need and not mere curiosity or idle wanderlust.*

"The goblins," I said, shelving my grievance for a later discussion. "They are besieging the castle and I thought to find some way to defeat them."

*Well then, fortune has smiled upon you, my dear, for we can easily teach the goblins the folly of trifling with the western wood. It is a lesson they must relearn with each succeeding generation of their loathsome ilk, but one I am more than capable of teaching. Take me to them, and I shall grant you the needed power.*

That met with my liking, so I turned on my heel and exited the chamber, returning to the room where Sebastian stood awaiting my return. The old chandler was still a candle shy of a full menorah, and his expectant eyes sought mine as I emerged.

"Did you retrieve it, young master? The witch's heart?"

I felt both sympathy and contempt stir for this bent old servant eagerly awaiting my response. I recognized the contempt as a foreign feeling from the duality of mind I now shared with Grandma Abbey. From this connection, I drew some insight into the character of the man. It seemed that Sebastian had a certain vulgar . . . *preference* . . . for being dominated by forceful women.

"Of *course* I did you old fool," I barked. "And it certainly *took* you long enough. Do you think I *liked* being trapped within a crystal for years on end?

Setting his candelabrum down, the old man abased himself. "No, my lady," he whined as he grovelled there. "I have been most neglectful of my duty. I can see that clearly now."

I was uncomfortable with the display and with grandma taking liberties with my voice, but she began to shush and soothe my ruffled feathers from within. I knew that the harsh tone in which we had spoken was actually her perverse way of *rewarding* Sebastian for his efforts. I could tell by the way he quivered there trying to stifle his toothless grin that she had succeeded.

"Arise you feckless excuse for a servant," she said as I fitted the candle back in the empty sconce. "I shall exact a fee later for your tardiness. We must return above to deal with the clans. Moreover, you are *not* to refer to us as 'my lady' again until I give you leave to do so. 'Little master' will do nicely for now."

"Yes, my . . . little master," he replied lifting himself up and taking up his candles once more. "It will be just as you decree."

And so we began our sojourn back to the surface with Sebastian leading the way. At least the sharing cut both ways, for from grandma's power over earth, I found that I was not in the least baffled by the turnings of the stone maze. It was almost as if a map of the tunnels had been imprinted on my psyche. We emerged hours before the dawn at a secluded side exit which opened directly upon the inner ward. Turning left through the sculpted gardens, we made our way toward the castle's front and the light from the watch fires beyond.

*This is new*, mused the voice as we regarded the familiar yet unknown curtain wall and its battlement.

***

As we crested the steps, the watchmen looked our way, but we had eyes only for the hills beyond.

*So they finally succeeded,* said Grandma Abbey with sorrow in her inner voice. *My beautiful forest is gone. The vile work of Sir Vincent, no doubt. Where are these goblins, then? Never mind. We can see the little miscreants.*

"Lucas, what are you doing back so soon?" said Master Chadwick stepping into the light of the watch fires. "It's been only a few hours since you departed."

He looked quizzically at Sebastian as well and nodded in polite greeting. I tried to respond but found myself unable to utter a word.

"I couldn't sleep, master," she said, "Royland is snoring again."

"Ehr . . . " whined Sampson, cocking his head to one side.

"Yes, well, I suppose he had a difficult day. Perhaps it would be best to let sleeping dogs lie."

Grandma grinned.

Sampson growled.

"Speaking of sleeping dogs," said my master with a concerned look at his companion, "please take Sampson back to our suite, Sebastian. He's had enough fresh air for tonight and plenty of time to attend to his business. I think the goblins are upsetting him."

My head nodded at the old servant when he glanced in my direction. He barely had to bend any further at all to grip Sampson by the collar and begin leading him away. Just then, we were treated to another round of the goblins' war drums.

"Ehr-wuff," Sampson protested as he half-resisted the old chandler's efforts, but they soon trotted off into the night.

"Why don't you go and get some rest yourself, master," she said. "I've got this."

Master Chadwick leveled a long-suffering look at us and said, "I believe it's time to drop the pretense. Who are you and what have you done to Lucas?"

"I never could fool *you*, Elizar," replied the witch.

"Mage sight doesn't lie," he said with a pointed look at our chest.

"I'm up here, Elizar," she smirked, "though back in the day, I often tried to get you to ogle my bosom. I told you that you would rue the day you spurned my advances, sweet cheeks."

"Abigail?" said my master with sudden alarm. "How?"

"How did I survive your raid upon my castle leading the charge with Sir Vincent and his bumbling knights? I didn't. I was *old*, Elizar, a condition I am sure you are coming to appreciate yourself. My servants had abandoned me. More's the pity; in but a few more months, I'd have had them fully transformed into my loyal beast soldiers. And my hope of rebirth in a younger body had fled."

"Rebirth? How in the world did you hope to manage *that*?"

"I intended to use 'miscere cogitata,' made permanent by enchantment. The girl, Isabel, was to be the host before she was treacherously snatched away by that disloyal, adopted 'son' of mine."

*Mother? Uncle Robert? I was floundering. As the witch who was maybe not my grandmother after all spoke on, my mind was shoved ever more firmly into the background. I emerged in my inner garden which was now surrounded and hedged in by a series of rolling hills that had arisen at its periphery. I could still 'see" and 'hear' from the witch's perspective, but it was a scene played far above as though painted on the sky of my inner realm.*

"How then are you here today?" demanded my master.

"I was forced to improvise. I had a totem which I had painstakingly crafted by my gift, the witch's heart. I had intended it as a talisman to augment my magic, but ended up using it as a vessel for my consciousness."

"Poppycock, Gail" barked my master, his skepticism dripping from every word. "The power requirements of such an enchantment are far greater than any mage, much less you, could acquire even utilizing a grand working,"

"That's right. Poor wretched little underpowered Abigail," she said in sing-song mockery of my master's denial. "There are powers, Elizar, of which you are unaware - secret powers of the earth available only to one of my affinity. Below this castle runs a ley line closer to the surface than anywhere else I have perceived. Tapping it, I can control inconceivable geomantic forces that would curl your whiskers."

"But . . . "

"Hush now, sweet cheeks," interrupted the witch. "My new apprentice and I have some goblins to attend to. But first, I think I shall extract a fee from you for all your past transgressions."

Master Chadwick began drawing up water from the well within, but the witch was quicker. Before he could unleash whatever unnamed spell he had intended, she struck like a viper. Through our shared perceptions, I could see the ley line of which she had boasted. It ran like a mighty river of force deep beneath the ground. Tapping a mere fraction of its seemingly endless energies, she constrained my master's magic center. The earth surrounding his well collapsed inward and constricted, closing off the source of his power. My master fell gasping and clutching his chest while I looked on helplessly. Was he dead? The night watchmen grew concerned at this and began to approach.

"Stay at your posts," the witch admonished them from where we stood. "My master is attempting a meditation to spy upon the goblins. They're up to something. None must interfere while he is so engaged. I will attend to him until he is done."

The casual irony of that last sentence was not lost on me, and hatred for the witch burned in my heart. I hoped she could sense it.

"Be still, child, this is the boon you wanted, after all."

*The hills surrounding my inner garden grew to new heights and some now sported granite cliff faces. I felt as though I were sinking; to be entombed and smothered by the magic of my enemy. My master had said that in a battle between mages, my opponent would seek to undermine or destroy my magic center. If I understood correctly, she could do neither as I was hosting her consciousness. Her solution, then, was this third path - imprisonment.*

Abigail then shouted in a piercing, high-pitched voice barely recognizable as my own. Though her words were in gobbledygook, I could understand them; this was one of the very few benefits of having one's mind shackled to that of an evil witch. Amplified by eldritch means, her words carried clearly to the goblin camp.

"People of the seven clans, you have violated our ancient pact. Long have your fathers known the penalty for trespass in the forest of Arbordell. And though bereft of its trees, the land has not forgotten your pledge. The land itself will be riven and rise up against you, and payment for your transgression will be meted out in blood."

That was when the hill began to shake. Being sufficiently distant from the epicenter, *we* experienced merely a quivering shudder, but that hill underwent a tremulous torment of dire proportions. Chief Ravenbald soon arrived in a storming rage. He began loudly proclaiming things we couldn't quite make out, but which sounded defiant. To cries of 'the witch!' the excitable goblins shook. Some knelt and seemed to be praying for appeasement of the calamity, while others just ran about aimlessly.

When the group of acolytes appeared, the chief pointed at our battlement and exhorted them to some action. I felt their fiery eyes fall upon us, but soon they were all lying on the trembling ground with their little red capes flapping about. The witch had struck them down just as she had my master. First the ogres fled. This was shortly followed by individual desertions which the chief tried to staunch by making a few gruesome examples. I think the final straw was when the mill collapsed, churning up great clouds of dust and depositing rubble into its race and beyond. With yips and howls the goblins turned on their chief. The last we saw of him, he was running for his life before an angry pack of his erstwhile subjects.

When the trembling subsided, the silence was absolute. Even the night insects seemed to be holding their breaths.

I won't lie; it did feel good to see our haughty goblin nemesis receive his comeuppance, but I was weeping within. Our victory had come at far too great a cost, and I feared this was only the beginning. The night watchmen stared at the bell used to toll the alarm, but its clapper remained still. After all that, none of them was so dim as to think further warning a necessity. Instead, they sent a runner to bring tidings to the baron. On the hilltop beyond the former mill, not a goblin remained in sight.

Soon, others would arrive, and I felt the witch's glee. For she had plans for their welcome.

***

When the baron mounted the battlement, the witch was ready. Before he and his men could approach, we turned to him and said in mock surprise, "Sir Vincent, as I live and breathe! And believe you me, that in itself was quite a difficult feat to accomplish. Have you come to parley with me again?"

308

Accompanying the baron were Sir Declan and Sir Trenton. Both took immediate umbrage at the disrespectful and overly familiar greeting. Having half-bared their blades, they were brought up short by a hasty gesture from their liege's raised hand.

"Who are you that possesses this boy? Declare yourself. Are you a goblin shaman, then, who has overcome my mages?"

My mocking laughter burned in my ears as the baron glanced worriedly at my master's still form.

"Who am I?" she replied. "I am one who has come to reclaim that which is mine. As the 'aggressor,' I believe the first offer is mine to extend, so I will grant you this. Leave at once. If you and all of your misbegotten knights remove yourselves from my castle and my lands, I will set aside past grievances and allow you to go in peace. Defy me, and the ramparts will run thick with your blood."

Unbowed and peering at us more intently the baron said, "I prefer always to know with whom I'm dealing. If you are not a shaman, then, mayhap are you some spirit of the woodland fey come with a grievance for our woodcutting?"

*This was terrible. She was just amusing herself with this verbal fencing. She didn't intend to bargain in good faith. I could sense her planning my liege's painful demise even as she glibly spoke of parley. When Sebastian had referred to 'smiting her ancient foes,' I thought he had meant the goblins, not my master and my liege. It could be worse, I thought . . . No; it could be no worse than this.*

"Your second guess is also well wide of the mark, you vile man. Since your brain is the size of a pea, I shall speak more plainly and in small words so that you may follow. I am she from whom you captured this castle. I am she before whom all men tremble. To put it more plainly still, I am the witch of the western wood."

The baron, nodding, seemed to take her at her word.

"If you are indeed she," he said thoughtfully, ignoring the sleights, "then perhaps we have much to discuss. I propose we dine at the keep and deliberate our disagreement in more civil environs. Release the boy and you have my word that no harm will come to you by my hand or those of my men."

"I am uninterested in a dinner party with you and your swine. My castle and its amenities will serve my needs alone. Although I *do* love some of the improvements you've made. I always wanted my own stables. The walls, however, I find a bit shaky."

And with that, the witch dipped into her power once again, causing the battlement to quake and pitching the unprepared baron forward to fall prostrate before us.

I had thought Sir Trenton impressive in battle, but when the wall began to shake, Sir Declan sprang into motion like a lion to the younger knight's ox. In an instant, he was beside us striking high and low with lethal strokes from his sword that should have left me quartered and decapitated in a trice. Alas for him and good for me, I suppose, the witch was prepared for even this. Unlike Royland's shield, the witch's protective barrier was not visible until struck. When it appeared, it resembled a series of interlocked triangles that curved around our form like the hexagonal plates on a turtle's shell. More aptly, it put me in mind of the facets of a cut gem.

The good knight soon registered that his blows were failing to have the desired effect, and his brow furrowed in thought. Before he had a chance to devise or enact a more effective stratagem, the witch cried 'iactare spheara.' Tumbling end over end, the knight was forcibly hurled the length of the battlement to impact most brutally upon the stones of the west tower. There he lay twitching and unable to rise. In the meanwhile, Sir Trenton had positioned himself in front of his father, keeping his feet, despite the trembling of the stones on which he stood.

"Have at thee then!" he roared, daring the witch to respond.

"No, son!" the baron shouted a moment later.

A wicked grin twisted my suddenly upturned lips, and the witch said, "This is your *son*? How delicious. I shall exact a fee from you. For daring to raise a hand against me, I shall return the favor. 'Suspendium tenaci.'

Raising my right arm and making a gripping gesture, I was both appalled and most pleased to see Trenton lifted off his feet.

As the tremors subsided, I swung my arm and the young knight's dangling form followed the motion, kicking and grasping at his throat. He hung in mid-air out over the front of the battlement. The baron's eyes widened with alarm.

"Please," begged the recumbent ruler. "Not my son. I will give you anything within my power if you spare him."

"Do you yield then?" asked the witch, again, with no intention of relenting either way.

"Lucas, the mill . . . " croaked Master Chadwick from where he lay face down.

The witch glanced over at the ruined building, then back to my master where he sprawled.

"You really must learn to enunciate better, Elizar," observed the witch with hurtful insouciance. "Speak up. What *about* the mill?"

Rolling to his side and with saliva trailing down from the corner of his mouth to pool upon the parapet, my old master met my gaze.

"The mill cannot grind . . . with water that has passed."

Though the witch seemed confused, I knew what my master was saying. It was the same proposition I had presented to Taylor Allen. Would I act to my utmost in the present moment or live a long life of regret for inaction, a slave to this grotesque mockery of a grandmother's governance? My answer to the dilemma was the same as his - there was really no choice at all. I simply couldn't in good conscience bear what was happening. I would strive. With every fiber of my being and with each beat of my heart, I would rail against the unrighteous restraints with which the bitter old harridan sought to bind my spirit. But how?

Having twice witnessed my master perform a grand working, I had a vague notion of how one should commence. Knowing full well the risks it entailed for the uninitiated, I determined to attempt one of my own. My master had pulled in rippling energy from his aquifer. What analogue would be of equivalent service for me? Of course. Roots. I looked about my inner garden which had become my prison, surrounded as it now was by Abigail's confining canyon.

*Granny, what big hills you have*, I shouted from the brink of hysteria. The better to fuel my effort, I thought with grim satisfaction.

From beneath my verdant meadow, I surreptitiously stretched my relentless rootlets to encroach upon and undermine the very source of my opponent's strength. Daring to draw in more power than was my own, I began my unschooled grand working. I siphoned from her hills until I could stand the strain no longer, and even as they crumbled, from my garden burst forth more tangled greenery than I had ever grown. Up climbed my leafy green vines from that shaded meadow in such profusion that, had they been real, they would have surely crested the clouds. I wound them into one gargantuan stalk that snaked upward with me riding atop it.

Finally deigning to look within, Abigail was amazed by my audacity. "Cease your struggles this instant, you foolish little flea," said she. "You can never escape and should you try, I will make you pay most dearly. For such presumptuous defiance, I shall exact a fee."

What more could she take from me? She had robbed me of my free will, wounded my poor master nigh unto death, and now stood poised to bring ruin upon my kingdom. My mind danced on the edge of madness as I defied her threat.

"A fee? Fie!" said I as my foe fumbled hastily to reinforce the walls of my prison.

My vision swam as my perspective shifted once more to the world without. My eyes were my own, but my mind remained saddled with its strange duality. I stared at the struggling Sir Trenton where he hung thrashing beyond the battlement's berm both in appalled horror and with the gleeful satisfaction of the remorseless witch. I knew that my grand working could only be sustained for but a few moments at best; I was genuinely surprised it had worked at all. I knew of no spell that could break the frightful hold that the hateful harridan had upon my body. So, directing all my pent-up power into a single supreme effort, I imagined my grand vine snaking down my left arm. Abigail was gesturing with our right arm to choke the life out of Trenton. Supported by her conduit of earthen might, her command of our body was otherwise firm. Careful not to let the right hand know what my left was doing, I willed it to my bidding.

A finger twitched.

The witch shrieked incoherently and tapped ever more deeply into her loathsome ley line, reasserting her imprisoning hills and firming their foundations.

My arm bent at its elbow, and my unsteady hand sought the hated heart that hung pulsing above my own. It was by now fused to my sternum and burrowed into the surrounding puckered flesh. With my inner garden now completely defoliated and spent and while the last vestiges of my grand working withered beneath me, I heard the witch laugh in mocking triumph. Her rocky tors below surged with renewed vigor as they suckled on her near-endless stream of energy and awaited my inevitable fall back into their stony embrace.

It mattered not, for I had grasped the prize I sought. Clenched in my trembling fist but still deeply embedded in my chest, the pulsating pendant that had stolen my will now lay firmly in my grip. I clung to it as my uplifting vines crumbled to dust and my vision faded once more. Wallowing in the weakness and inebriety that was the guaranteed aftermath of a grand working, I sought my final strength. For there were strengths of which the witch was unaware.

There was that strength that granted a noble the grace to forgive. Or the heroic heart that let simple men rise in defense of their kingdom and its people, knowing full well they placed their lives in peril thereby. There was the kindness shown by outcasts when they took a chance to shelter strangers in need. Or even the strength that caused a butcher's son to surrender his innocence to save a neighbor's child. Courage. Sacrifice. All of this I had witnessed and admired.

It was this strength I called upon now. As I hung above that dread abyss, I undertook what could be the final winding of the strangest apprenticeship in all the eleven dutchies of Osten. The crystal cage that warded the witch's heart was harder than tempered steel, but the bone and flesh which lay beneath was all too subject to human frailty. Now that I had committed myself, there was no return; we would soon see what yielded first. And if

I gave my life in the effort, that too could be counted a win for Westarbor.

The witch struggled. Belatedly realizing her danger, she tried to cajole me with unspoken promises of power and sweet blandishments of compromise even as she marshaled her might to pit against the turning of my hand. I remained resolute. We would test which was mightier: the geomantic oddity she commanded, or the turning force of the very earth itself. The ground shifted and quaked beneath our feet. I felt a shattering of my consciousness and a sharp, stabbing pain in the center of my chest.

A blackness descended on my soul. Had I failed?

CHAPTER FOURTEEN

# The Gardener

"Flowers are restful to look at. They have neither emotions nor conflicts."

*~ Sigmund Freud ~*

Things have a way of working themselves out. While I lay recuperating in the hall we were using as a hospital ward for our many injured men, Meadowfork was rebuilding and recovering from the brutal beating it had received in the past month. Most of the lances were out harrying the retreating remnants of the horde, making sure that none tarried in Westarbor or had trouble finding their way back to the pass. The tunnel at the Tillersons was under heavy guard and was to be collapsed and sealed once my master could return there.

When I had first awakened, I found father at my bedside thumbing through Javier's initial drawings of the new and improved mill. He was turning through the sheaf of pages with his three-fingered hand examining each and muttering. His stern, studious face broke into an expression of delight when he noted my regard.

Stuffing the plans aside, he said, "You really gave us quite a turn son. We wondered whether you'd make it."

I fingered the scabbed-over, heart-shaped sore upon my bare chest. That was sure to leave a scar; an unhappy memento to remind me not to handle unknown enchanted objects.

"I gave *myself* quite a turn, and I wondered the same," I replied.

"Sir Trenton is most cross with you. Thankfully, his great fall was arrested by a plunge in your master's new moat. Still, that's the second time in a twelve month you've deposited him into a muddy ditch. I have it on good authority he's saving some choice words for you for later."

Nearby, Sir Nolan was regaling the wounded soldiers with his impressions of the battle.

" . . . The baron threatened them with all the kings horses and all the kings men. Then our good liege sat atop his wall with egg on his face for . . ."

"I'm sorry, father, it wasn't me. I . . . "

"Hush son, we know. Now that the danger has passed, we're just all thankful that you're going to be alright."

A few days later, Master Chadwick came to visit. He walked with a cane since his ordeal and looked rather stylish, but he was confident he could soon return to bipedal ambulation. With only a month remaining on the apprenticeships, our master declared that both Roy and I had passed and could now consider ourselves aspirant journeymen. He claimed the siege of Westarbor Keep had been more challenging than any examination he would have devised. At least now I could have some time to relax. He interlaced his fingers over the crown of his cane as he sat on the stool beside my bed, Sampson curled at his feet.

"They've finally brought the remnant flocks back from the eastern fiefs. Tilda, Sampson and I will be returning to the ranch shortly. Do you have any questions before I go?" he asked with a wry grin that said he was braced for the onslaught.

"Only about a hundred," I replied, "Foremost, though, is this; if my mother and Uncle Robert weren't Abigail's children, then whose were they?"

"Abigail Wagge was a mage of extremely limited gifts," began the old man in his indirect manner. "The best that she could do was to move a few rocks around."

"Sounds familiar, go on."

"Abigail had never been content with her lot, having been required by the kings law to serve the mage's guild since her gift was discovered. Although lacking a husband, she managed to get with child, and refused to name the father. And unhappily, her wanton ways also made the culprit's identity rather difficult to deduce. For a light duty, she was placed in charge of the créche at our conclave. That's where the children of mages are cared for when their parents are called elsewhere. The true father of Robert was a mage named Hans Brubaker. Both he and his wife, Gretta, were sent on a mission to the south of the kingdom, the details of which I am not at liberty to reveal."

"So Royland is in fact a Brubaker?" I asked.

"Yes and no, as I shall soon elucidate. It was at this time that Abigail chose to defect from the guild. Absconding with her charge, eight-year-old Robert, and despite her delicate condition, she managed to elude pursuit and lose herself here in the western wild."

"It was many years before the two children resurfaced. Master Hans and his wife had never returned from that mission. The other Brubaker heirs had long ago divided up the estate. Your mother was married to a commoner, and neither she nor Robert showed any signs of magery. The Brubakers were reluctant to claim Robert. They needn't have worried. Your mother, the only sister he had known, was very happy where she was. And Robert showed no desire for reunion with his lost kin; he was by this time twenty-eight and he'd had quite enough of magery."

I let this sink in. So, she was likely my grandma after all. I guess that made me guilty of grand-matricide of a sort.

"That was some sound advice you gave me up on the battlement. My master is wise."

"I told you I would remember it."

"You did at that . . . sweet cheeks."

"I was wondering how long it would be before you threw that saccharine sobriquet back up in my face. Rest assured I have saved many swift retorts and witty rejoinders with which to avenge myself for such cheek. But I think I shall save them for when you're feeling better. I believe I owe you about ninety-nine more answers. When you think of the questions, write them down. Your letters will always find me at Fowler Ranch. Come, Sampson, there are sheep to be collected."

And with that, my sly old master and his shaggy assistant shuffled off on their seven legs toward greener pastures.

***

The first kiss of autumn stirred the yellowing leaves. I exited the livable portion of the mill on my way to my appointment. Roy said I was acting mopey. And just who was *he* to disparage the introversion of another? The truth was, I still felt ashamed. I knew in my mind that it had all been the witch, but part of me still felt that I had done something wrong. Agatha Grimbley had told me it was much the same for young women who had been the victims of certain kinds of violence or abuse. As I meandered down the thoroughfare, Ronnie Turner overtook me and passed me by.

While Javier finished plans for the mill, father had already been engaged to build the baron's book press. Dylan Turner assured our liege that once the ranches were back in full operation, he could supply all the raw parchment that was needed. As part of the deal, and in honor of his bravery against the goblin scout, Ronnie had been made the baron's new page. He looked quite adorable dressed in the baron's livery and wearing his small goblin-made sword as he proudly ran messages all about the keep. Although he wanted to be known as Ronald now with an eye toward 'Sir' Ronald, the townsfolk had taken to calling him 'Little Boy Blue.' I was sure he'd soon outgrow the deprecating nom de guerre. Hayden was already training him at arms and teaching him signaling on Sir Fletcher's horn.

The Day of Remembrance had come and gone. It was the first one I had missed since I was too young to recall. Royland had filled me in on the particulars. He said the speeches

318

honoring our fallen soldiery had been stirring, and the tribute to Madam Elsa had been especially poignant. Her headstone was surmounted by a stone bowl wherein her family members left offerings of seed so that her dear little friends might come and visit her place of rest. Even the bones of the witch had been interred in Meadowfork Memorial Hill. The baron himself had arranged for her marker stone saying, 'It is important we remember our history, and for good or ill, Abigail certainly left her mark.' The stone cutter had been busy this summer.

I crossed the outer courtyard and approached the main gates. Most of their blackened sections had been scraped and sanded smooth. The baron wouldn't replace them as they still bore the precious enchantment that my master refused to repeat. I trod across the moat over the temporary bridge of beams and planks. There were plans underway for a full drawbridge, but the baron was still waiting on various bits and bobs for this to happen. Most of these needed to be forged in our smithy. Master Harvey claimed it was his penance for his shopfront leading the charge against our dovecote. Once across, Sergeant Gaines smiled benignly and bade me to pass within.

Across the inner ward and to one side of the baron's new trebuchet, sat a group of ladies making homespun with their spindles. Mercy Cain was among them. When the witch's heart had shattered, the Cain curse had been broken, a fact their clan only discovered a couple of weeks later at the next new moon. The ecstatic family had returned from the Danstonshire and offered to help with the rebuilding of Meadowfork. Despite some initial distrust, they now mingled happily with the townsfolk withal. Several formal courtships had already ensued for those brave enough to request such of their stern clan patriarch. As the ladies held their distaffs aloft, Prissy had them all spellbound with the harrowing tale of her escape from the mygaloms. I nodded as I passed them by heading to the side of the castle.

" . . . Father had just finished a large wheel of cheese, and mother was at her wits end as to what to do with all the leftovers. So I was happily sitting there one morning eating my curds and whey, when along came a gigantic, ferocious . . . "

I hurried along, hoping I wasn't late. When I arrived at my destination, I didn't see her. There was only Zack. Zachariah Grek was the keep's gardener. About ten years older than I and built like an ox, the man bore a set of unfortunate features as off-putting as his name. From his lazy eye down to his hare lip he was uncomfortable to look upon. When I had first met Zack and introduced myself, he had merely scowled and glared at me. Because of his misshapen lips or perhaps in addition to them, the man stuttered. Once he realized I wasn't going away, and even more so once he noted my remarkable way with plants, he came to tolerate me.

We had worked in companionable silence for several weeks now, and I had come to realize that in addition to being a genius with topiary and a maven of all things green, Zack was quite funny. His humor tended toward the physical. Pranks like tickling your ear with a long blade of grass when you were intent on something else so you'd think it was a pestering fly were his forte. It was his deep spasmodic chuckle when you finally caught on that was the clincher; it made you want to laugh back. He had even allowed me a bit of space along the back of the gardens to conduct my own secret project. I soon found out that this was the very spot below which chamber pots were emptied each morn. Of course he didn't warn me. I had since learned to time my arrivals more carefully.

Today Zack stood with pruning shears in hand refining the figure of a horse-mounted knight all done in shrubbery.

"Hey, L-L-L-ucas," he greeted.

"Hey Zack," I returned and went straight about cleansing and weeding my area.

I had purchased a set of gloves for collecting the dreck to put on the offal pile. 'Levare' also came in handy, and I had worked out a personal spell which caused a gentle mist to render my plants as fresh as the morning dew. While weeding, I sensed the arrival of my co-conspirator.

"Did you get it?" I asked.

Mollie Green crept over crouching low behind the hedges. The purloined vase rested in her fretting hands.

"Please, Lucas, no more secret missions to filch things from m'lady's chamber. My poor heart can't take it."

"This is the last time. I promise. You did great, Mollie, and I'm sure her ladyship will be most pleased with you," I assured. "If you'll just wait a moment, you can put it right back."

Several weeks ago, I had sent Molly to collect seed pods from Megan's withered oathblooms. My lady's birthday was today, and I knew of only one thing that she treasured. My only other idea had been the witch's mirror, but we still hadn't worked out how that stone had slid aside. Furthermore, I hadn't yet forgotten my pledge not to mess with unknown enchanted things. Fortunately, I knew a way to cultivate plants very quickly indeed. My row of autumn oathbloom stood knee high and in fulsome bloom; their colors were vibrant and their petals, perfection. I filled the broad vase that Mollie had brought with the rich loam of the garden. I then began to transplant seven of the most magnificent and well-matched specimens, careful not to wither them whilst uprooting.

"Hurry, Lucas," Mollie fussed. "What if she finds it missin' afore I get back? I could get sacked!"

"Don't worry," I soothed, "They're all at the feast with the king's adjudicator. That should take them all afternoon."

"I'll p-p-put in a good w-w-word miss," Zack gallantly added.

Mollie surprised me then by flashing Zack a toothsome smile of appreciation, and there seemed to be a new spring in her step as she hauled the burgeoning vase back toward the secret way. Zack followed her with his eye as she swayed out of sight. Well, why not, I thought? My large friend could do far worse than someone as kindhearted as Mollie.

***

It was late in the afternoon when I approached the door. The feast had concluded, and all the revelers had finally been rousted out. I had received word from Tomas Parker that the baron had gotten his way about the border. Although it couldn't be proven that Lord Downham was complicit in our summer from hell, there was enough evidence to raise suspicions. Nor had the 'good lord' come to Westarbor's aid, despite proximity and a preponderance of information about our plight.

I couldn't understand my hesitation. I had faced down witches and defeated ogres, after all. Why should the opinion of a fourteen-year-old girl matter so much? Nevertheless, my heart raced and my palms itched as I finally plucked up my courage and knocked.

I overheard an exchange of feminine voices beyond and it was several moments before the door eased open partway. It was Constance who greeted me with stern regard.

"Who might I say requests the lady's grace?"

I wanted to roll my eyes and say 'It's me, Lucas,' but I sensed from her stilted tone that something more formal was the order of the day.

"You may tell her ladyship that Journeyman Aspirant Lucas Harper begs the boon of her regard."

"Would this be the same Lucas Harper who declined to attend my lady's birthday feast although specially invited?"

Uh-oh. I'd better think quick.

"The very same," I replied. "Tis the black-hearted scoundrel himself come to gloat and make light of your lady's offended sensibilities. The miserable misanthrope with the discourtesy and lack of decorum to scorn an invitation offered by the benevolent and winsome mistress of Westarbor whose grace and refinement are boundless. This scurrilous knave lacks the . . . "

As my self-castigation commenced, Constance's expression descended into shock, but from beyond the door I heard a twosome tittering which grew into loud peels of laughter. By the time I'd gotten to 'scurrilous' there came a shout from within.

"Stop. We surrender. I will receive him, Constance."

Soon the door was swung wider and parted from the numb hand of a befuddled Constance. Lynette stood beyond with blotches of red marring the fair complexion of her face and neck. Beside her stood Lady Megan. I had her on the run now, I thought. Her twin pools of soul-sucking blue were at the moment obscured by tears of mirth. Advantage, Lucas.

"So, why were you not at the feast, then?" the lady asked, her tone more sober.

"I had something important to attend to?"

"The flowers, of course, are from you, but that isn't truly your reason. You'll need a better alibi than that."

Ah. And there go those eyes again. They say confession is good for the soul. Anyone desiring friendship with Megan must needs be a saint, I suppose. Or at least honest in the first place.

"The truth is: I knew there would be tales of the siege and its battles, and I'm not yet ready to rehash all that, much less share my own experiences. I'm still working through it all. When I *am* ready, you'll be among the first to know it."

Megan looked abashed.

"I see. I sometimes see too much, me thinks. You can't imagine what a burden it is to know what another is feeling," said Lady Megan in exasperation.

"I might have an inkling," I said curtly but not without sympathy as I fingered the center of my chest.

"Oh, I didn't mean, I mean, of course you do," stammered Megan. "In any event, the flowers are lovely."

"I thought it was time to renew my vow, this time in full awareness of its responsibilities and consequences."

A complex look graced Megan's face: part amusement and part hope fading to awe as she sensed my offer was genuine. I had been told that the nobles took the oath of a protector quite seriously. I had decided that Megan was *worth* protecting, and I wanted to retain our connection. Roy said I was smitten. Was I smitten? I thought not - not in the romantic sense. I just wanted the girl to have a happy birthday and knew I would always be willing to serve and protect her anyway. I also knew she didn't have many true friends. The oath had no overtly romantic component, but it happily didn't exclude such a possibility either. I could live with that.

"Kneel," she said.

When I did so, her two ladies in waiting brought forth the vase with its distinctive orange blossoms and set it before me where I knelt. Megan disappeared down the hall to beat upon Trenton's door. When he emerged, a lengthy whispered conversation ensued. Thereafter, both came to stand before my genuflecting form. Of course. It had slipped my mind that there must be a witness. When Derrick had helped me to research the proper forms, I was focused more upon the words, but he *had* said aught about having a lady's close relative on hand.

I wondered what Trenton made of the awkward affair as he glared down at me with stern and stoic mien. The young lord's reactions had grown as indefatigable as his father's of late, whether by design or in unconscious imitation thereof. I knew it would be alright, however, when his brown eyes crinkled about their edges. So I swore my oath to the young woman who had captured my heart as witnessed by the man for whose sake I had shattered the heart of another.

"I, Lucas Harper, journeyman aspirant mage, from this hour forth will be protector to Lady Megan Arenson, daughter of Westarbor. I shall not bring it about by my deed, word, or consent, that she come to harm or dwell in captivity. Any counsel which she entrusts to me, I will keep secret. I grant her the right to call upon my assistance when in need and shall come to her aid should she require it. This shall remain true for as long as I shall draw breath upon this earth, or she sees fit to dismiss me from such service."

She was looking full upon me as I said it, so she knew my vow was true, for her gaze could pierce the hearts of men.


~ The End ~

# Afterword

Dear Reader,

I have long enjoyed reading fantasy novels myself. Being retired, I thought it would be fun and interesting to write one of my own. "Mayhem at the Mill" took about five months to write and a few more to polish and refine. I found the process of researching and writing my own novel to be fascinating and would highly recommend it to anyone with a love of books. I hope you enjoyed the story.

They say you should write about what you know and draw from your own life experiences. Though definitely not a wizard, I did tend to follow that model. For instance, you may have noticed that the novel is dedicated to my father. He was a carpenter and general contractor. As a youngster, I worked for him much as Lucas was apprenticed to Elliot. When I was around Lucas' age (many years ago), I once saw him fall from atop the second floor of a house we were building. He cracked several ribs, but was mostly alright. This was the first time I had ever seen someone go into shock. Disoriented, he kept muttering and insisting that we get back to work. The forecast was for rain that evening, and he wanted to get the structure under roof by day's end. When writing of Elliot's accident at the mill, the fright I recalled from this experience served as powerful fuel.

Just as Elliot 'was a soldier back during the goblin wars,' My real father had been a CB in the South Pacific during WWII (where he also hurt his knee). Several other characters in the book were based on people I have known. The names were, of course, changed to protect the innocent. My father passed away at the end of 2014 at the ripe old age of 94. You may have also noticed that each of the fathers In this book get hugs from their children. Those are all for you, dad!

Amazon might ask you to review the book after you order or download it. I would very much appreciate your honest opinion.

But please be respectful of others who might read such comments. Try to minimize spoilers, and let us limit the trolls to those that might beleaguer the barony…

If you would like to know more about me or my writings, please visit my website at www.thormans.org. Feel free to leave a comment or ask a question. Writers *live* for feedback from their readers. While you're there, check out the songs I wrote to accompany the stories. I plan to incorporate these in the audio versions of the books.


Till Next Time Then,

~ DBT ~